CHANGING TIDES

Books by Michael Thomas Ford

LAST SUMMER

LOOKING FOR IT

TANGLED SHEETS

FULL CIRCLE

CHANGING TIDES

THE PATH OF THE GREEN MAN

MASTERS OF MIDNIGHT
(with William J. Mann, Sean Wolfe, and Jeff Mann)

MIDNIGHT THIRSTS
(with Timothy Ridge, Greg Herren, and Sean Wolfe)

Published by Kensington Publishing Corporation

CHANGING TIDES

MICHAEL THOMAS FORD

KENSINGTON BOOKS

KENSINGTON BOOKS are published by

Kensington Publishing Corp.
850 Third Avenue
New York, NY 10022

ISBN-13: 978-0-7582-1059-3

Printed in the United States of America

For Mike Lever
CAPTAIN AND FRIEND EXTRAORDINARE

If one could be, for only an evening, whatever in the world one wished, what would it be? What secret would come out?

John Steinbeck
Sweet Thursday

Author's Note

This is a work of fiction. Although it references real places and people, no actions ascribed to said people, or theories presented within the context of the story about said people, should in any way be construed as factual. They are the thoughts and suppositions of fictional characters and, except for documented historical events, have no basis in fact.

Similarly, while the National Steinbeck Center, the Monterey Bay Aquarium, and the Hopkins Marine Station are real places, they serve in this story only as backdrops for fictional characters and events. The characters depicted in the novel who are associated with these places are not based on actual people, living or dead, and my depiction of these places should not be construed as being representative of the real-life activities of either the institutions or anyone associated with them.

Finally, the manuscript referenced in the narrative as possibly being written by John Steinbeck is entirely fictional. Steinbeck wrote no such manuscript, and the creation of it is entirely my own.

CHAPTER 1

As Ben Ransome descended through the water, he had the feeling, as he always did, that he was entering a cathedral. *Float like an angel,* he told himself. The words of his Open Water instructor passed through his thoughts as if he'd been certified only yesterday, instead of the twenty-odd years ago it had actually been.

Instinctively, he pushed the valve on the front of his drysuit and felt a puff of air enter. The suit eased its restrictive grip on his body, and his speed decreased slightly. Finning lightly so that he was horizontal, he looked down at the bottom, estimating that it was about twenty-five feet away. The visibility was fantastic, especially for early summer, when algae blooms often turned the water into a cloudy soup.

Today, though, he could see clearly the topography below him. On one large rock, a group of sea stars of various colors formed a constellation. To the right, a moon snail made its slow trek across the sand, leaving behind the peculiar egg case that resembled a piece of broken pottery. Tiny crabs, orange and red and brown, skittered in and out of cracks on their endless search for the bits of detritus upon which they feasted.

And all around him was the kelp. It was the kelp that made the place so special. It rose from the bottom in thick strands, reaching for the light. The fronds swayed lazily, rocked by the gentle current, and schools of dusky orange cigar-shaped señoritas darted through it like herds of silent jungle animals, hunted or being hunted, it was impossible to tell.

Descend like an angel, Ben thought again. *An angel falling out of heaven.* He disagreed with the last part of his instructor's description of the proper way to begin a dive. It wasn't falling *out* of heaven; it was falling *into* it. No place, he thought, was more beautiful than the world beneath the water.

As he neared the bottom, he added more air to his suit, until he was hovering less than two feet above the ocean floor. He looked at the dive computer strapped to his wrist. Twenty-nine feet. The vis was even better than he'd thought. Maintaining his position in the water, he looked up. The early morning sun streamed through the kelp, turning it a golden green. Kelp greenlings hovered in the shafts of light, and the sandy bottom was alive with shadows.

Ben set a heading on his compass and began to swim. He'd visited the site so many times, he didn't even need the compass to get where he wanted to go. Even in low vis he could find it simply by following familiar landmarks. But he was a creature of habit, and so he continued to wear and use the compass, despite the fact that he rarely looked at it.

He swam slowly, unhurried. He had time. He'd cleared his schedule for the day in anticipation of the event to come later in the afternoon. That particular appointment he wasn't as relaxed about, which is why he'd come to his favorite dive site. He needed time to prepare, to try and ready himself for what was certain to be, at best, a difficult encounter and, at worst, an unqualified disaster. It could go either way.

He pushed the troubling thoughts from his mind and concentrated on the world through which he moved. Swimming parallel to the ripples in the sand, he headed northeast, across the bottom of Whaler's Cove toward the sandstone-and-granite formation known as the Middle Reef. Neatly bisecting the cove, the reef stretched out into the Pacific to a depth of more than seventy feet. Its numerous crevasses and outcroppings provided protection for a host of undersea life, and it was there that Ben sought his treasure.

Reaching the reef, he turned north and headed into deeper water, keeping the rocks on his right-hand side. He kept his eyes trained on the changing terrain, alert for signs of his intended quarry. Ever watchful, he passed disinterestedly over the rockfish and sculpins that followed him with cautious eyes, although he paused briefly to observe a rose anemone devouring an unfortunate jelly that had drifted into its stinging grip. It was a routine act of underwater survival, yet the simple act of feeding was turned, somehow, into performance. The jelly's ravaged and impotent tentacles swirled around the anemone's translucent arms, each one tipped with the deepest pink, as they danced a brutal ballet. Dulled by poison, the jelly fluttered like a failing heart as it was pulled, inexorably, into what passed for the anemone's mouth.

At thirty-seven feet he spied a flash of yellow amidst the purple and black of the rocks, and stopped. Maintaining his position in the water column, he hovered almost motionlessly as he gazed upon the tiny creature before him. Less than three inches long, it resembled nothing so much as a slice of lemon peel, a scrap perhaps tossed over the side of a boat, a bit of refuse that had drifted down to settle, randomly, on the rock below. Closer up, however, it revealed itself to be something far more interesting than a bit of rind. Its surface was covered with hundreds of tiny bumps, and a line of black spots formed a trail that originated between two cone-shaped appendages on the animal's head and ran the length of its back, where it ended in a seven-branched spray of fernlike plumes.

As Ben observed his find, he thought, not without irritation, that its common designation—sea slug—did no justice whatsoever to the marvelousness of its design. The slug, moving nearly imperceptibly over the surface of the reef, presumably cared little about its name, but Ben was offended for it. He preferred its more noble, and accurate, classification of nudibranch, and liked even more its full proper name of *Archidoris montereyenis,* the Monterey dorid. He considered it the local representative of its genus, native to their very own Monterey Bay and therefore deserving of celebrity status.

The nudibranch, with admirable focus, was feeding. Although its outward appearance suggested a complete lack of activity, Ben knew that on its underside its ribbon of cartilaginous teeth was scraping away at the encrusting marine sponges that dotted the surface of the rock. From time to time, it revealed itself to be engaged by the furling and unfurling of its delicate branchial plume, like a flower blooming over and over again.

The creature was perfect in its design, which is why he had fallen in love with it, and with all its kind, upon their first meeting. Common to all of the world's oceans, the nudibranchs nonetheless remained objects of mystery. Although they were frequently photographed due to their uncommon beauty and their habit of remaining for a long time in one spot, making them excellent subjects, their lives were largely unrecorded. It was suspected that they contained within themselves numerous compounds with medical applications, only a few of which

were even in the beginning stages of study. It was to unlocking their
mysteries that Ben had devoted his life.

He left the yellow dorid to its feasting and continued on. Having
found one nudibranch, he now saw that the rocks were speckled with
them. Some were identical to the first, but there were others as well:
the ghostly white *Discodoris,* phantom of the reefs; *Dialula sandie-
gensis,* spotted black like an undersea cow; tiny orange *Rostanga.* The
various species existed side by side, each concerned only with locating
and consuming its particular food source, few of which were shared.
Ben had once counted seventeen distinct species on the reef in a single dive. It was believed that the waters of Whaler's Cove were home
to more than thirty.

Among them, there was one with which Ben was enamored more
than the others. He looked for it now. Unlike its kin, it was seldom so
public in its appearances, preferring to remain tucked into less acces-
sible places like a camera-shy starlet. Like Garbo. He had never seen
one roaming freely on a rock; always they were discretely situated. But
over time he had developed a knack for finding them, primarily by
blocking out all other images from his mind so that only the one he
sought registered on his vision.

It took him fifteen minutes of searching, and several false starts, before he located what he was after. When he found it, it was not on the
rock but affixed to a piece of kelp that had somehow been removed
from its stalk and now lay on the sandy bottom like a discarded length
of ribbon. The nudibranch was moving across it, a bright spot of white
against the dark green background. Having found its preferred food in
the form of a scalelike sponge that barnacled the kelp leaf in dime-
sized patches, it was in no hurry to go elsewhere.

Less than an inch in length, the animal was milky in color, almost
translucent; Ben could see the green of the kelp beneath it through
the nudibranch's outer edges. The perimeter was lined in startling yellow, and a row of similarly colored spots ringed the creature's body. Its
rhinophores, the hornlike structures at its anterior end, were pure
black.

Cadlina flavomaculata—the yellow-spotted Cadlina—although in
its case he broke from his preference for accurate scientific nomencla-
ture and called it Devil Horns, a name of his own invention. It was his
favorite, for reasons he found difficult to put into words. True, it was

the first species he had found on his own, without a more experienced diver to point it out. But something about it enchanted him, its ethereal appearance and incongruous assemblage of multicolored parts. Perhaps its reticence to be observed.

Cadlina. Caddie. His joy faltered at the thought. Caddie. His daughter. Soon to arrive back in his life. He'd gone beneath the water to escape his fears over her imminent arrival. He realized now that it was a futile effort. How could he possibly forget the child named for the object of his fascination?

A shadow, larger than usual, floated slowly across the kelp leaf, eclipsing the tiny moon of the nudibranch. Turning his head, Ben looked up in time to watch as a leopard shark, its belly a pale, luminous silver, passed a dozen feet above him. Although not at all uncommon to the waters of Monterey, a sighting of the shark was not something to pass off as an everyday occurrence. The creatures were timid, easily startled, and particularly leery of the bubbles produced by divers.

For this reason, Ben slowed his breathing, wanting to prolong the shark's visit for as long as possible. Perhaps sensing this, it turned and circled back, providing him a glimpse of its slitted gold-brown eyes. He saw then that there were two others accompanying it. The three companions moved in unison, their powerful tails snaking from side to side, their gills fluttering. Smaller fish moved away as the larger predators pressed, disinterested, through their midst, coming together again in the safety of schools once the danger had passed.

As the dark-spotted sharks turned once more and headed for open ocean, Ben gave a contented sigh, releasing the air he had been holding in his lungs and sending a net of bubbles surfaceward. Perhaps, he thought, the sharks were an omen of good luck. He hoped so. He knew he would need all the luck he could get.

When he looked back to the kelp blade, he found that the nudibranch was in the process of laying eggs. It had secreted a small ribbon of them, the beginning of what would become a spiraling wreath containing thousands. Exhibiting the same lack of urgency it applied to all of its activities, the nudibranch seemed fully prepared to continue its work for as many hours as it took.

Ben left it to its endeavors and turned back toward shallower water. Although he had enough air left in his tanks to allow him another half hour, he sensed the protective magic of the cove fading. His calm had been disturbed by the thoughts of Caddie, and he knew it was futile to try and banish the memories now that they had surfaced.

He swam back in more quickly than he had gone out, following the channel that ran down the center of the cove. As he wound his way through the kelp stalks, he noted the changes in landscape, the transition from rock to sand, the thinning of the kelp forest into more open spaces. Sand dollars, martialed in rows like silent soldiers, dutifully faced the current, while elsewhere nervous shrimp peered out from beneath protective ledges.

As his depth decreased, he released air from both his suit and his buoyancy control vest to offset the change in pressure. He attempted to remain submerged for as long as possible, until, at six feet, he found it impossible to stay down. Only then did his head break the surface, returning him to the world above.

He had made it almost all the way in. The boat ramp that provided access to the water was less than ten yards away. He swam to it and floated on his back as he removed first one fin and then the other. Then, standing, he walked slowly up the mossy ramp, sometimes using the rocks to balance himself as a small wave washed over the concrete. He'd slipped on it enough times to know that it could be treacherous, and the last thing he needed was a trip to the emergency room. He could hear Carol now, accusing him of doing it on purpose for some unspecified, but implied, selfish reason. He hoped Caddie had not inherited her mother's talent for finding malice where none existed.

Only when he was safely at the top of the ramp did he remove his mask and allow the regulator to fall from his mouth. *A safe diver is a diver who comes back to dive another day,* he told himself. Another ridiculous mantra drummed into his head all those years ago by his instructor. More junk from the old attic.

His old Volvo was parked in the lot, which was quickly filling up with cars. With only fifteen teams of divers allowed into the Pt. Lobos Reserve per day, competition was fierce for reservations, especially in the summer. As Ben walked toward his aging station wagon, he saw other divers regarding him suspiciously. Park rules dictated that, for increased safety, divers dive in pairs; you couldn't even get past the ranger station unaccompanied by a buddy. As a solo diver, Ben knew he was an object of both concern and envy. Long ago he had stopped feeling the need to explain to the curious that his scientific credentials and affiliation with the nearby Hopkins Marine Station research center exempted him from the restrictions placed on recreational divers.

"Hey, Ben. Anything to see?"

Opening the back of the wagon, Ben turned and sat down, releasing the straps on his BC and slipping it from his shoulders before answering.

"Couple of fish," he said. "Lots of water."

The man speaking to him grinned. "I see you lost your buddy again," he said. "How many does that make?"

"Oh, I guess about ninety-two," said Ben thoughtfully.

He and the man laughed.

"How are you, Davis?" Ben asked.

Davis Huffinsen nodded. "Can't complain," he said.

The ranger stood to one side, watching the divers preparing to enter the water. He and Ben had been friends for a dozen years, but Davis had been a ranger at Pt. Lobos for twice that length of time. Although there was little he didn't know about the park and its history, he had never visited the underwater portion of the reserve, something Ben found unimaginable.

"When are we going to get you wet?" he asked, as he always did.

"Maybe in the fall," answered Davis, giving the answer that varied only according to whatever season followed the current one.

"One of these days you'll say yes," Ben said. "And I'll drop dead of shock."

"Well, we can't have that," replied Davis. "So maybe I'll have to stay a drylander."

After unzipping his dry suit, Ben gently pulled his hands through the latex seals that surrounded his wrists and then did the same with the seal around his neck, lifting it up and over his head to free himself. Once the suit was off, he unzipped the insulating undergarment. The sun warmed his skin, and the light breeze cooled his body, now uncomfortably warm without the cooling effects of the water.

"Got here early," Davis remarked. "Looking for something special?"

"Just wanted to beat the crowds," said Ben. He paused. "Actually, my daughter is coming today," he added, surprised at himself for revealing the information.

"Daughter?" said Davis. "Since when do you have a daughter? Don't you need a wife for that?"

Ben smiled. "Had one of those too," he said. "It was a long time ago."

"How old?" asked Davis. "The girl, not the wife."

Ben thought a moment. "Sixteen," he answered.

Davis whistled. "Good luck," he said. "I remember when mine were sixteen. Darn near killed them. What's she like?"

Ben sighed. "I don't know," he said.

Davis shot him a glance.

"It's a long story," said Ben. "And I don't have time to tell it." He put his wet gear into the large plastic tubs he carried expressly for that purpose, laid his tank alongside them, and shut the door.

"All right then," Davis said. "Guess I'll be seeing you later."

"Later," Ben said, waving briefly as he got into the car.

He backed the car out and, nodding at Davis once more, headed for the park entrance. As he went up the dirt road toward the ranger station, he wondered what had prompted him to tell the ranger about Caddie's arrival. He'd kept her a secret for so long, why reveal her existence now?

"They had to find out sometime," he said to himself.

He looked at the clock. It was half past eleven. Carol had said she'd be in Monterey sometime after one. That gave him just enough time to get home, clean up a little, and be ready for Caddie's arrival.

"Who are you kidding?" he asked aloud as he passed the ranger station and headed for the highway. "You're never going to be ready."

CHAPTER 2

"Could you please put that window up?"

Caddie looked over at her mother. "Why?"

"Because I don't need to air-condition the entire state of California," her mother answered. The lines around her mouth were beginning to show again, the buttresses of Botox crumbling. Soon, Caddie knew, she would go for another treatment and her face would once more be wrinkle free and expressionless.

"I like the wind," Caddie objected.

Her mother pressed a button to raise the window. Caddie countered by pressing her own button. The window stalled; Caddie wondered if perhaps she could start a fire by keeping the machinery inside the car door fighting against itself. Then her mother would be forced to stop, to turn around, to go back.

"Why must you be so difficult?" her mother snapped, jabbing at another button with a manicured nail.

The button beneath Caddie's finger ceased to work, its functions deadened by the override on the driver's side. The window slid up soundlessly, sealing the car off from the outside. Immediately, Caddie felt the artificial coolness of the air-conditioning slip its chilling arms around her. She shuddered and glared at her mother.

"If the Goddess wanted us to live in bubbles, she wouldn't have created the outdoors," she said.

Behind her sunglasses, Carol shut her eyes momentarily and tightened her grip on the Lexus's wheel. She felt her skin slide over the bones of her cheeks. She knew it was slipping, like snow perched on the edge of a mountain. She would have to make an appointment with Dr. Karsegian when she got back.

Caddie reached over and turned the car's radio from the classical station Carol preferred to something raucous and nerve-jangling. Carol's first instinct was to change it back, but she'd already won one battle with her daughter. If listening to terrible music meant an otherwise stress-free remainder of the trip, she could endure it. Maybe.

"I was supposed to go see them with Sam and Bree this weekend," Caddie said, turning up the volume.

"See who?" asked Carol, her head beginning to throb.

"Them," Caddie answered, nodding toward the radio. She began to sing along with the music. " 'I remember when you told me that you never dream in color,' " she warbled.

They passed a road sign—MONTEREY 25—and Carol looked at the car's clock. They were right on time. With a little luck, she could be back in L.A. in time for dinner. As long as Ben didn't cause any problems. But Ben always caused problems. No, she corrected herself, he didn't cause problems, he *was* the problem. Ben never *caused* anything; he was the most passive–aggressive man she'd ever known, like a stubborn dog who pretended not to understand when you asked it to perform something as simple as sit.

" 'Don't you see how blind you are?' " Caddie sang, loudly and badly.

For a moment, Carol thought her daughter was speaking to her. Then she saw that Caddie was looking out the window, one hand smacking forcefully against her knee. Carol noted the nails, bitten to nothing, and resisted the urge to lecture. It wasn't her problem. Caddie wasn't her problem. At least not for the summer.

Let Ben worry about her nails, she thought. Not that he would. Not Ben. He probably wouldn't even notice their daughter's nails. Carol wondered if he would even recognize Caddie if he saw her in a crowd of other teenage girls, if she wasn't presented to him and identified, like one of his specimens.

That wasn't fair, she told herself, at least not entirely. Ben hadn't been the most attentive father, it was true, but he wasn't entirely disinterested in his child. He was just, well, Ben. People as a whole didn't particularly interest him. She didn't know why. She'd tried to figure it out at first, when they were dating, when they were first married. She'd believed then that something terrible had happened to him to shut him off from humanity, some great trauma that, when addressed, would transform him into a loving partner.

But there was nothing. No horrible family. No childhood abuse or emotional cataclysm that might account for his behavior. Despite all of her searching, she found nothing. And so she had decided to shock him into caring with a baby. No man, she was sure, could stare into the face of his own child and not be moved to feelings of overwhelming love.

She'd even allowed him to name her, hesitating only a moment when he'd suggested Cadlina. She should have known then that she'd made a grave error in believing him capable of relating to another human being. Who, after all, named a child after a slug? But she'd allowed it, comforting herself with the fact that the obvious nickname—Caddie—was not so bad.

As if sensing her mother's thoughts, Caddie turned toward Carol. "We could just go home," she said. "We don't have to keep going."

For the first time in months, Carol agreed with her daughter. They could just go home. But, she reminded herself, home had not been a particularly enjoyable place of late. Without looking at Caddie she said, "I don't think so."

Reflected in the rearview mirror, she saw Caddie's eyes darken. Then the inevitable. "I hate you."

And I hate you, she wanted to reply. *You hate me and I hate you. That makes us even.* But no mother would say such a thing. Still, she felt it, and knew that countless mothers before her had felt the same thing. Perhaps one or two had even said so. But it couldn't be true. No parent hated their child; they only hated what passed between them. And that part was true. She did hate the dark chasm that had grown, seemingly overnight, between her and Caddie.

"He doesn't even want me," Caddie continued.

"He wouldn't have asked if he didn't," said Carol instantly.

They both knew that was a lie. Caddie didn't even attempt an objection. Instead, she looked out the window and remarked, "Where is this place, Iowa? It's all farms."

"They grow a lot of produce around here," Carol said. "Artichokes. Strawberries." She couldn't think of anything else, and she knew Caddie was hardly impressed anyway. "Garlic," she added quickly. "There's some kind of garlic festival every year."

"Garlic," Caddie repeated. "That's super. Neato."

She pressed her forehead against the window. Outside, the green fields rolled by, seemingly without end. *I'm being sent to the farm,* she thought grimly. *I got myself knocked up, and now I'm going to live with Aunt Bea and Uncle Henry.*

If only I were knocked up, she thought. She'd know how to take care of that. But this—thing—with her mother was unfixable. It was like she'd woken up one day a different person. *Maybe I'm a changeling,* she told herself. *Maybe the fairies will come and steal me back.*

She thought of Sam and Bree back in L.A. They'd had plans. Well, sort of plans. Ideas, anyway. The details would have worked themselves out. But then her mother had dropped the bomb. "You're going to live with your father for the summer."

Caddie remembered with some small satisfaction her comeback. "What father?"

"There's the ocean," her mother said.

"Big deal," said Caddie. "It's the same ocean we have in L.A."

"Three months isn't going to kill you," Carol said. "It might even be fun."

Caddie looked at her. "If he's so much fun, how come you didn't stay married to him?" she asked.

She didn't want an answer, and she didn't get one. Her parents' divorce was a closed subject. It just hadn't worked out.

Three months. Three long months. Three long boring months. With her father. The prospect was in no way appealing. She tried to remember the last time she'd even seen her father. It had been at least a year. He'd been in L.A. for some kind of conference. They'd had dinner. He'd talked about something she didn't understand. Squid, maybe. Or clams. He hadn't asked her about herself at all. She'd been relieved when it was over.

Suddenly, she was overcome with a kind of panic at the prospect of living for three months with a man who spoke of nothing but clams. Turning to her mother, she said softly, "Please don't make me go."

For a moment, the hardness that surrounded her mother like a shell softened. Just for a moment, Caddie thought that she would acquiesce, swing the car around, and speed back to Los Angeles, where all would be forgiven. And then it passed, just as quickly, and Caddie knew she would not beg again.

Instead, she turned once more to the window. She told herself that it was a television screen, the images passing by nothing more than some program that could be changed at will, turned to some other, more interesting show. The blank shoreline, the soundless sea, the sky so flat and blue and soulless, all of them could be made to disappear with the press of a button, replaced by laughing voices and excitement, the thrill of nighttime in Los Angeles and the joy of being with Sam and Bree, who understood her without asking and didn't make her feel somehow broken and a disappointment.

She closed her eyes tightly. She was dreaming. She would wake up, open her eyes, and find herself asleep in her own room. She would pick up her cell phone, type out a text message, make plans for later that evening. A movie, perhaps. Maybe flirting with guys whose bravado they would test with darting eyes and laughter. Anything but the endless sand and monotonous ocean. Anything.

Her jaw clenched, and roaring filled her ears. She would stop time, reverse it, travel back to fifteen when things between her and her mother were only difficult, not impossible. She would know better this time, know when to stop. She would not make the same mistakes.

I won't, she promised. *I won't I won't I won't.*

She opened her eyes. For just a moment, she'd believed herself capable of magic. Now, reminded of her inability to bend the world to her will, she succumbed to ordinary sullenness.

"Look," her mother said. "A mall."

Caddie, lured into looking out the window, saw only a faded Kmart sign rising from the expanse of a parking lot. Surrounding the store were others like it: Bed Bath & Beyond, Barnes & Noble, Jamba Juice.

"That's not a mall," she said scornfully. "That's a *shopping center*."

Her mother made no argument. Again Caddie thought of home, of the Beverly Center and its floors of shops. The withered Kmart passed from her view like one of the tired, washed-out hookers on the wrong end of Hollywood Boulevard. She imagined it filled with fat-assed women in too-tight sweatpants, dragging screaming children down the aisles as they searched for deodorants and cheap flip-flops. *I might as well be in Van Nuys,* she thought.

She wished she'd remembered to get some pot before leaving. Probably she could find some somewhere in Monterey; you could find pot anywhere, but she was almost certain it wouldn't be any good. Probably just some shit grown by an old Deadhead in his backyard between the tomato plants and zucchini.

She didn't even have her cell phone. Her mother had taken it away, fearing—rightly—that she would use it to phone Sam and Bree and hatch some sort of escape plan. Not that she couldn't use any old phone, but the absence of her cell did make her feel adrift. It just seemed too much effort to actually dial, and she couldn't remember the numbers anyway. Speed dial had reduced her memory for such things to nothing.

"Fuck," she said loudly.

"Watch your mouth," said Carol rotely.

"Whatever," Caddie said, equally without enthusiasm. They were, both of them, too tired even for the most basic of skirmishes.

Carol turned the Lexus from the highway, exiting into Monterey. The scrubby pine trees and sand dunes were replaced by actual grass, and a town materialized seemingly out of nowhere. Caddie gazed at it hostilely, daring it to welcome her.

"It's prettier than I remember," Carol remarked. "Almost quaint."

"Welcome to Mayberry," said Caddie.

"It's historic," Carol said.

"It's *tired,*" said Caddie. "Old and tired."

"Like me," Carol said before Caddie could. "You really need to get some new material, sweetie. I've heard this act before."

Caddie retreated into silence and watched the town unfold before her. Small, boring houses. Sidewalks jammed with gift shops and used book stores and restaurants indistinguishable from one another. Nothing to entertain or entice her. Nothing surprising. Like her mother, she'd seen it all before, and she wasn't impressed.

Kayak rentals. A Safeway. Signs for the famous aquarium her mother had tried to present to her as a reason for being excited about her enforced stay in Monterey. They passed in and out of her vision, forgotten in an instant, leaving behind a sour taste and mounting resentment.

"You could have just sent me to summer camp," Caddie said.

"I could have," agreed Carol. "But this way, you'll have some time with your father."

"He doesn't even want me here," Caddie said. "Does he?"

She looked at her mother, who didn't answer immediately. "Of course he does," she said after a moment.

"Now you're the one who needs new material," said Caddie. "Or at least acting lessons."

"Look in my purse and see if the directions to your father's house are in there," Carol said.

Caddie unzipped the big leather bag and peered inside. It was filled

with the odds and ends of her mother's life—an address book, business cards from her real estate office, a lipstick. Caddie pawed through
it. She found an orange prescription bottle. Valium. She tucked it into
her hand. Beneath it was a piece of paper folded into quarters. She
drew it out along with the pills.

"Here," she said, holding out the paper while she tucked the Valium into the pocket of her sweatshirt.

"Read it," said Carol. "I'm driving."

Sighing, Caddie unfolded the paper. "Where are we?" she asked.

Carol looked for a sign. "Lighthouse," she said. "It should be near
the bottom of the directions."

Caddie read. "Turn right on Clipper," she said. "Lighthouse. Clipper.
How goddamn nautical."

"Just look for Clipper," said Carol. "It should be right up here somewhere."

"There," Caddie said, pointing. "Just past that doughnut shop."

Carol turned on her blinker, made the turn. They were heading uphill.

Caddie felt as if she were being walked to the gallows. She didn't
know why the idea of staying with her father was so unsettling, but it
was. And it was more than just because she'd never spent more than a
few days with him. Something about it felt like exile. She was removed
from everything she knew, everything she enjoyed. Everything that
made her her.

She felt like Dorothy, dropped into unfamiliar territory. Only no
good witch would appear in prom drag to help her out. No clicking together of her heels would send her home. She was on her own.

She reached into the pocket of her sweatshirt and found the bottle.
After deftly unscrewing the lid, she tipped the bottle until a single pill
fell into her palm. A sip from the bottle of water she'd been nursing
since their last stop for gas, and the pill slid down her throat. *Work
fast,* she pleaded, waiting anxiously for the pharmaceutical security
blanket to enfold her.

"Here we are," Carol said, making another turn. "Look for number
eighty-seven."

Caddie didn't want to look. She didn't want to know which of the
small, ugly houses was to be her prison for the next three months. She
didn't want to see the dull faces, like boiled potatoes, she was certain
peered out at her from behind bleary windows. She felt as if she might
be sick. With trembling fingers, she reached over and locked her door.

CHAPTER 3

Charlie looked down at the sea. Because he was stand-ing on a rock not twenty feet from shore, he didn't have to look far. In fact, he had only to look down at his own feet, which were currently covered by water up to the ankles. Then the wave swept back and he was looking at his wet boots.

He didn't feel right. Something inside of him was mak-ing him sick, like he'd eaten a bad oyster or drunk too much beer. Actually, he had drunk too much beer. But that wasn't it. Neither was it an oyster churning in his belly. It was something else, something that originated in his blood and poisoned every part of him.

His head hurt. He thought he might be sick. Looking at the sea moving back and forth, he thought for sure he might be sick. But there was only beer inside of him. Beer and poisoned blood. Nothing to speak of, but enough to kill him, he was sure of that.

All you gotta do is jump in, he told himself. Just step off.

He couldn't swim. He'd tried once, when he was maybe nine or ten. But all he'd done was throw his arms around and make a lot of noise. Water had gone into his mouth and nose, and he'd started to choke. Someone—maybe Pete—had had to run in and pull him out. He remem-bered the taste of sand when he'd pressed his face into the beach, happy just to be alive.

Another wave came, covering his shoes again. This time he got wet halfway to his knees. Tide's comin' in, he told himself.

Maybe he didn't even have to jump in. Maybe he could just stand there til the ocean got high enough that it just opened its mouth and swallowed him up. Like that Jonah in the Bible. Fella'd got swallowed up by a fish. He'd liked that story when he was a kid. His mother had read it to him. He'd pictured old Jonah sittin' there in the fish's belly. How'd he breathe in there? he'd asked his mother, and she'd told him it was a sin to question the Good Book.

His mother was dead now. Heart attack. He remembered her funeral. Lots of flowers, big white ones. They sang "Amazing Grace" and he'd cried.

Thinking about it, he cried again.

Hudson set the pages on the tray in front of him and smiled. He checked his watch. Three o'clock. He'd been traveling for—he counted in his head—almost eleven hours. Thirteen, really, since he'd arrived at the airport in New Haven two hours before his seven o'clock flight. The ticket counter hadn't even been open yet.

Connections in Philadelphia and San Francisco had brought him, finally, to the last leg of the trip. He'd considered driving from San Francisco, taking Highway 1 down the coast. He'd heard it was a beautiful drive. But it would have extended his journey by several more hours, and he was anxious to get to Monterey. He'd waited long enough.

He picked up the pages again and neatened them. They were copies, of course. The originals were safely stored in the freezer compartment of the refrigerator in his apartment in New Haven. It was a trick he'd learned his first week in graduate school. Always keep whatever you're working on in the freezer. It's the one thing that doesn't burn in a fire.

He didn't know if this was, in fact, true. But everyone did it, and so did he. Even though theses and dissertations could now safely be stored on multiple electronic devices, safe from the possibility of destruction by fire, actual paper was still susceptible. He'd scanned them, of course, and did have them stored on at least four different drives, each in a separate place. But there were still the originals.

Those he had to safeguard. And so they sat in the freezer, in a plastic bag next to the ice cubes and the ever-present box of Otter Pops that Marty kept there.

He would have liked to bring the originals, but that wasn't possible. Already they were fragile. He'd been lucky to find them in readable condition at all, considering where they'd been stored. They should have been nothing but fragments. He shuddered even thinking about that. If they'd been destroyed . . .

He couldn't go there. They hadn't been destroyed; that was all that mattered. He *had* found them. And now he was going to prove that they were as important as he believed they were.

The plane lurched slightly, and he grabbed the edge of the tray. *Don't crash,* he told the plane. *If you do, this all dies with me.*

That wasn't entirely true. He wasn't the only one who knew. He'd told a few others. But he was the only one who knew the whole story, or at least as much of it as he'd pieced together. Now, as the plane jolted once more, he wondered if this was a grave error. Being the only one to know posed some problems, his death being the greatest of them.

He clutched the papers as the plane rumbled and a voice came over the speakers. "Ladies and gentlemen, as you can see, we've encountered some turbulence. The captain asks that you please fasten your seat belts."

Hudson felt for the belt at his waist, slipping the flat end of the buckle into the metal mouth and feeling it click. The absurdity of the notion that a single piece of fabric would save him in the event that the plane plummeted to the ground was not lost on him, but he brushed it away, preferring to accept that, safely strapped in, he would arrive in Monterey in one piece.

After a minute the plane settled, and a minute after that the seat belt sign flickered off. Still, he left his on. It might, he told himself, ward off further attacks by the elements.

Looking out the window, he saw nothing but bright blue sky and the softness of clouds. This did nothing to relax him. He realized that he'd been gripping the pages in his hand. They were wrinkled, creased by the anxious embrace of his fingers. He smoothed them out. Naturally, he had other copies with him. But he would no sooner harm a copy than he would imperil the original.

He tried to concentrate on Monterey. At twenty-four, he'd never been farther west than Chicago, and then for only a few days at a Faulkner conference, where he'd delivered his paper "The Myth and Mythology of Yoknapatawpha County: The Snopes Trilogy as Greek Tragedy" to a more or less positive reception. (Except, of course, for the woman from Duke who'd suggested that his reading of *The Mansion* was superficial, but she was a Lacanian, and her behavior typical of the breed. Anyway, he'd later been delighted to hear that she'd been denied tenure and been forced to take a position at a junior college somewhere in Minnesota.)

His four years at Yale had taken him far from his undistinguished rearing in Edelson, one of Maine's less-enlightened towns, where his school's guidance counselor, upon reviewing his performance on a recently administered aptitude test, had helpfully suggested a career in either the fisheries industry or perhaps the United States Navy, where she implied that Hudson might do well in the field of radio operations. Fortunately, the intervention of a teacher had steered him toward college, and a doorway had been opened for him. He'd stepped through gladly, mostly to escape the possibility of ending up like his parents, weary of life and resentful of anyone who wasn't.

At the University of Maine he'd read Flannery O'Connor's "A Good Man is Hard to Find" and developed an instant obsession for the Southern writers. For the next year he'd kept company with Truman Capote, Carson McCullers, Eudora Welty, and William Faulkner, until a professor, tired of reading papers delving into the dreamy minds of authors bred below the Mason–Dixon line, suggested that he try exploring other areas of the American literary landscape. Reluctantly, he'd traveled north, where he'd been relieved to find that the writing, while perhaps not as weirdly intoxicating, was equally invigorating. This had led to journeys west, and by the end of his four years at the university, Hudson found himself making the pilgrimage to Yale in search of advanced degrees.

Now, having obtained his master's, he was two years into the doctoral program. And if the papers in his hands turned out to be what he thought they were, he had stumbled on a major find, one that would make his career and practically guarantee him a position of his choosing.

If they are what I think they are, he reminded himself. There was no guarantee. In fact, if anything, there was nothing but questions. Questions he hoped to find the answers to in Monterey.

He forced himself to put the papers back into his briefcase. He'd been obsessing over them the whole flight. Well, for much longer than that, of course. But the flight had only heightened his anxiety about them. After all, he was soon to find out whether they were the treasure he believed them to be or simply a dream he would have to exchange for something else.

He shut his eyes and rubbed them hard, pinching the bridge of his nose between thumb and forefinger. He recognized it as one of his father's gestures and pulled his hand away. Lincoln Jones had not been a kind man, and Hudson had not mourned when, the winter of his second year at Yale, his father had been felled by a heart attack while shoveling snow in the driveway. Nor, as far as he could tell, had his mother been terribly upset by the passing of her husband. Taken care of thanks to a surprisingly good insurance policy, Martha Jones now occupied the small, red house on Spruce Lane all by herself, her only companion a fat, orange cat called, predictably, Ginger. Hudson saw her as little as possible, an arrangement that appeared as agreeable to his mother as it was to him.

The fact that he was manifesting his father's traits was unsettling. The first time he'd recognized it in himself, he'd spoken to a therapist and had been assured that it was probably just mimicked behavior, unconscious memories burned into his mind in childhood, surfacing now that he was growing older. Still, it was disquieting. His physical resemblance to his father at his age was already too much reminder of their shared genetics; he'd hoped to jettison the more internal similarities by leaving them behind in the bedroom on Spruce Lane along with the other refuse of his childhood.

"Would you like something to drink?"

The question roused him from his thoughts. He looked up into the face of the smiling steward.

"I can't make you a Cosmo, but how about coffee or a soda?" the flight attendant asked, flashing a smile that Hudson interpreted, correctly, as the recognition of one gay man of another.

"Tomato juice?" Hudson asked.

"Regular or spicy?" the steward inquired.

"Spicy," Hudson answered.

"Spicy it is," the man said, popping open the top of a can and pouring it over ice. "Here you go. One virgin Bloody Mary."

He handed Hudson the drink and moved on. Hudson sipped at the juice, enjoying the slight burn on his lips. It vaguely crossed his mind that the steward was cute, in a blond, twinky kind of way. But that had never really been his taste in men. He preferred them more—he hated the description "straight acting," but that's what always came to mind. It was, Marty teased him, just his internalized homophobia talking.

"You try growing up in rural Maine," Hudson had said once in response. "Up there you're either normal or a limp-wristed fairy who wants to wear women's clothes."

It was true. The notion of a masculine gay man had yet to penetrate Edelson's collective consciousness, despite reruns of *Will & Grace* airing nightly on the Bangor affiliate. Or maybe things had changed since he was a boy there. But probably they hadn't. Edelson seemed to pride itself on being a good thirty years behind the rest of the country.

At any rate, it had taken him long enough to admit his own gayness. Well into his third year at the university, in fact. Practically speaking, he was still a gay adolescent, figuring out what he liked and what he needed. That he was doing it at twenty-four was just another resentment to nurse in moments of self-pity.

He had to admit, too, that it bothered him a little that the flight attendant had pegged him as one of his own. He was horrible at identifying other gay men; inevitably at parties he gravitated to men whose girlfriends or wives showed up moments before he worked up the nerve to ask them out. "What do you expect," Marty had told him after one such incident. "You didn't even know *you* were gay until you woke up in some guy's bed."

This was one of Marty's favorite stories to tell, usually loudly and to people whom Hudson would rather didn't hear it, and Hudson frequently regretted ever having told it to him. But that was, more or less, the way it had happened. Because copious quantities of alcohol had been involved, the details were a matter for debate, but what everyone involved could agree on was that Hudson had gone out drinking with some friends one Saturday night and had awakened Sunday morning in an unfamiliar room with a decidedly masculine arm thrown across his torso and a soreness in his nether regions that cause him to recall, dimly and with no small amount of embarrassment, burying his face in a pillow and gritting his teeth. The presence of a condom, clearly used, on the floor beside the bed confirmed his suspicions.

The man to whom the arm—and the condom—belonged was named Jess. He was a friend of a friend. Hudson had been introduced to him after three beers had already lowered his inhibitions, and when Jess had suggested a walk back to his dorm, Hudson had gone willingly. Whether or not he had been aware of Jess's intentions when he agreed to this was uncertain, although Jess later claimed that Hudson had kissed him first.

One thing was clear—waking up in Jess's bed had forced Hudson to accept his attraction to other men. Not that it had never occurred to him before; it had, in fact, been something that had been with him since adolescence. But Jess confirmed it in the most primitive of ways. Or, as Marty liked to say, "That boy busted your be-hymen wide open, and you haven't been the same since."

He smiled to himself. He was going to miss Marty. His roommate of two years, Marty was another candidate in Yale's doctoral program. His particular field of interest was mathematics. They'd thought upon meeting that they might be lovers, but their one attempt at sex had been a disaster, and since then they'd cohabitated in chaste domestic bliss. Marty was spending his summer chasing the elusive proof that would be evidence of the potential his professors all insisted he had. The previous night, they'd toasted to their mutual success, each assuring the other that the next few months would find him scaling new heights of academic accomplishment.

Only Marty knew the extent of Hudson's hopes for the summer, and even then he didn't know everything. Hudson had been afraid to fully voice his expectations, lest he doom them to failure by openly speaking of them. Dreams, he believed firmly, were not to be shared. It only invited disappointment. His father had taught him that; it was another inheritance he'd been unable to toss away, but he wasn't yet convinced that his father wasn't right about that one thing.

Still, he did dream. He felt the weight of his hopes in the briefcase, which he continued to hold in his lap. It was as if the pages inside were made of gold, each thin leaf weighing a dozen pounds, the enormity of them threatening to crush the bones of his feet should he let them fall.

"We'll be landing in a few minutes, so you'll need to put your seat in its full and upright position."

The steward was once again at his side. He held open a plastic garbage bag. Hudson drained the last drops of his drink, letting the ice cubes slide into his mouth, then dropped the cup into the bag. He avoided looking at the attendant.

Outside, the ocean was visible. Looking at it, Hudson found himself surprised that it wasn't a brighter shade of blue. He'd always imagined that the Pacific was somehow lighter than the cold, dull Atlantic. But the water, at least from however high up they were, was as gray as the ocean he'd swum in as a boy.

He felt the plane slope downward, felt his ears pop as they descended. He tried not to let the momentary disappointment over the Pacific's blueness grow into something larger. It was, after all, just water. He could not view it as some kind of omen regarding the success of his trip. What he sought was not under the ocean; the proximity of the sea was merely incidental.

The ground rushed up at them. The landing gear was lowered. Hudson gripped the armrests as lightly as his anxiety would allow. This was it.

In the moment just before the plane touched down, his heart stopped. It resumed beating only when the plane, rattling ferociously, taxied the length of the runway and came to rest, intact, at its final destination.

CHAPTER 4

"There's your father," Carol said as Ben opened the door to the house and walked out onto the porch. She sounded to Caddie as if she were identifying for her an unfamiliar animal at the zoo, an okapi, maybe, or a bonobo. "He looks heavier than last time."

Caddie didn't move. On the porch, her father was giving a kind of half wave, his hand moving back and forth in the vicinity of his stomach. He had a strained smile on his face, as if he'd been practicing all morning but hadn't quite gotten it down yet.

"I'm going to die," Caddie said. "Really, I am. You might as well just shoot me right now."

Her mother picked up her purse. "If it's any consolation," she said, "I'm sure he feels the same way."

Carol opened the car door and stepped out. A moment later, Caddie followed her. As she emerged from the air-conditioned cocoon into the afternoon heat, she felt as if she were stepping into hell. She slung her backpack over her shoulder and trudged reluctantly toward the house.

"Hi," Ben said. His voice was overly bright. The smile had contorted into a painful expression of fake cheer. "How was the trip?"

"It was fine," Carol answered.

Ben turned to Caddie and opened his arms. Caddie looked at him, not exactly sure what he wanted. She glanced at her mother, who nodded slightly. Caddie stepped forward, and Ben's arms surrounded her. He squeezed her tightly, so that her face was pressed painfully into his shoulder.

"How's my little girl?" Ben asked.

Caddie pulled away. She was embarrassed for her father. Stepping back, in case he tried to hug her again, she glared stonily at the boards of the porch. The white paint had flaked away in places, showing the older blue paint underneath. One board had been replaced entirely and had yet to be painted at all. It reminded her of a diseased tooth.

"Why don't we all go inside," Ben suggested when Caddie didn't say anything. "We can have some lunch."

"I've got to get going," Carol said, looking at her watch. She'd yet to even remove her sunglasses. "I have an appointment."

"Oh," Ben said. His smile faltered. "Can't you even stay for lunch? It's only half an hour. Maybe less. I can—"

"I'm already late," Carol said, cutting him off. She turned to Caddie. "Go get your bags from the car, honey."

Caddie, grateful for the reprieve from the awkward moment, took the keys her mother held out to her and retreated down the steps.

"What's the matter with you?" Ben asked Carol as soon as Caddie was out of earshot.

"You're going to have to be alone with her sooner or later, Ben," said Carol.

"But you're just dropping her off like she's a load of laundry," Ben argued. "She's your daughter."

"And she's *your* daughter too," said Carol. "If you think you can do any better with her than I can, be my guest. That's why she's here, re-member?"

"Maybe if you were a little nicer to her . . ." Ben began.

Carol laughed. "Good luck, Ben," she said as Caddie came back, a bag in each hand. She turned and gave Caddie a far less effusive ver-sion of the hug Ben had bestowed upon her earlier. "Call me in a few days," she said.

She left the two of them standing together and returned to the Lexus. Backing up, she looked at the porch, seemed to shake her head, and returned the way she had come.

Caddie and Ben stood silently for a minute, as if perhaps Carol might come back and save them from one another. Finally, Ben said, "I guess it's just you and me now."

"Guess so," said Caddie.

Ben bent to pick up her bags, but Caddie grabbed them before he could. "I'll get them," she said as Ben pulled back reflexively.

Ben held the screen door open as Caddie stepped into the house.

She was surprised to discover that it was as hot inside as it was out. "Don't you have air-conditioning?" she asked.

Ben shook his head. "These houses are so old, I don't think they could take it," he answered. "Is it that hot?"

"If there's no air-conditioning, it doesn't really matter, does it?" said Caddie.

"I could get a fan," Ben said vaguely.

Caddie ignored him. She was looking around the house. Ahead of her, down a narrow hallway, she saw the kitchen. To the left was the living room, populated with a large sofa upholstered in what looked disconcertingly like faded pink velvet and a set of mismatched armchairs that stared at one another in mute hostility from either side of a fireplace.

"Where's my room?" asked Caddie.

Ben indicated a set of stairs going up from the small entry area. "Second floor," he said. "End of the hall."

Caddie marched up the stairs, her feet landing heavily on each step. The wood groaned, and she made a mental note to test them later and note the weak spots, in case she ever had occasion to sneak out of the house at night.

The room was horrible. The wallpaper, a faded blue turned gray and patterned with ghostly pink roses, was almost certainly original. Against one wall an old brass bed, looking as ancient as the wallpaper, sagged beneath the weight of its mattress. The quilt atop it, a patchwork of dozens of different fabrics, appeared hand-stitched. Caddie imagined the room's former occupant sewing it while she died, not leaving the room for a period of years, from some consumptive disease. Opposite the bed stood a five-drawer bureau with a mirror atop it. A framed print of something—mountains, was it?—hung over the bed.

"The closet is over here," Ben said, turning the handle on the only other door in the room, as if perhaps she would never have discovered it on her own.

"There's no TV," Caddie realized, speaking the thought aloud. She tried to remember if she'd seen one in the living room but was sure she hadn't. A kind of panic gripped her.

Ben stood, his hand on the doorknob, looking at her as if she'd asked where she could stable her unicorn. Finally he scratched his nose. "Um, no," he said. "I don't really watch television."

Caddie sat on the edge of the bed, listening to the springs groan plaintively beneath her. "No air-conditioning," she said. "No television. Do I have to get water from the well?"

"The bathroom is down the hall," said Ben.

"*The* bathroom," Caddie repeated. "There's just one?"

"Do you need more than one?" asked Ben.

"Apparently not," said Caddie. She closed her eyes. The Valium wasn't doing the job; she would have to take another one. Why hadn't her mother just sent her to prison? At least there they had television.

Ben had walked over to the bed and was standing at the foot. His hands were in his pockets. "Look," he said. "I know this is hard for you. It's hard for me too."

Caddie looked at him. "Thanks," she said. "It's good to be wanted."

"That's not what I meant," said Ben. "I mean, I'm not used to living with someone else, especially a child."

"I'm not a child," Caddie said sharply. "I know you haven't been around much for, oh, nine or ten years, but just to let you know, I've grown up since you walked out."

Ben nodded. "I see that," he said quietly.

Caddie unzipped her backpack and riffled through it, pretending to look for something. She hoped her father would take the hint and leave her alone. He didn't.

"Your mother thinks . . ." he began, then stopped for a moment. "Your mother and I think it will be good for the two of us to spend the summer together."

Caddie, still rummaging furiously, said, "My mother thinks I'm out of control, and she's making you take me for the summer because she doesn't know what else to do." She stopped pawing in her backpack and looked at him. "I'm not stupid," she said shortly.

"I never . . ." Ben retorted. He watched her face, her dark, flashing eyes. "No," he said. "You're not."

Caddie pushed a strand of her long, curly hair behind one ear. Her mother was right, her father had gained weight. And his hair was grayer than she remembered. He didn't look old, exactly, just kind of more worn out. Like his house.

"Do you want something to eat?" Ben asked her.

She shook her head. He nodded. "I guess I'll just leave you to get settled, then," he said. He walked to the door, then turned. "We'll have dinner together," he said. "How about eight?"

"Whatever," said Caddie, shrugging.

"Okay," said Ben, leaving. He left the door open. Caddie listened to him walk down the hall. When the footsteps stopped, she went to the door and shut it. There was no lock.

Unpacking her two bags took little time. She hung a few things in the closet, surprised to find that her father had actually remembered to put hangers in there, and threw the rest of her clothes in the dresser drawers. The half-dozen books she'd brought were piled on the shelf of the bedside table.

Going to the window, she looked outside. Her room faced the street. Not that there was anything to look at. Across the street was another house almost identical to her father's. A couple of little kids played on the small lawn, throwing a ball around and yelling at one another. She considered shutting the window, but the room was already hot enough. She hoped she'd be able to sleep with it open. Probably she'd have to take yet another Valium.

That reminded her, and she went to her backpack and took out the bottle of pills. Opening it, she poured them into her hand and counted. She had thirty. Not nearly enough. But they would have to do. Taking one, she returned the others and capped the bottle.

She put the backpack on the floor and stretched out on the bed. Lifting her hips, she brought her butt down on the mattress and heard it let out a complaining squeak. She did it again. *Imagine what it would sound like if I was having sex on it,* she mused.

That just made her even more depressed, because it made her think about Sam. He wasn't her boyfriend, exactly, but they slept together sometimes. Then again, he also slept with Bree. And there was that one time when . . .

She didn't want to think about Sam and Bree. It just made her homesick. She kicked off her shoes and let them drop to the floor, where they made a dull thud like apples falling from a tree. Christ, you could hear every sound someone made in this house. She was going to have absolutely no privacy. She hated her mother for making her stay; she hated her father for saying she could.

In the mirror on the dresser was reflected the picture over the bed. The mirror glass, like everything else in the room, was old. The reflection was distorted, almost grainy. She squinted her eyes and tried to make out the image. It wasn't mountains after all. But what was it?

She stood up, ignoring the bed's protests, and turned to look at the

picture full-on. It was a picture of a whale. More precisely, it was a picture of men hunting a whale. The men were in a small boat. They
stood, harpoons in their hands, as the whale glared at them with its
large, baleful eye. The whale's mouth was open, showing its small,
white teeth, and several harpoons stuck out from its sides. It was
spouting water.

It was a disturbing image. She felt sorry for the whale. She wished it
could bring its massive tail down and shatter the boat, pitching the
men into the ocean. Then she noticed the sharks. Around the whale,
and around the boat as well, sharks stuck their heads above the water.
Like the whale, their mouths were open, revealing dangerous-looking
teeth.

Caddie shuddered. Why had someone hung something so unpleasant in a bedroom? Why had her father kept it there? She knew the answer to that question; he probably had never even looked at the
picture. To him it might as well have been a vase filled with flowers, or
a kitten. She was sure that if she asked, he'd have no idea what she was
talking about.

She took the picture down. Behind it, in a patch exactly the size of
the picture frame, the wallpaper was much bluer, the roses much
pinker. Knowing that people had left the ugly image there for so many
years made her hate it even more. She climbed off the bed, went to
the closet, and leaned the picture against the wall inside. She would
find something else to hang in its place, she told herself. Something
she actually wanted to have hanging over her head.

Or maybe she'd just wait and see if her father noticed the picture's
absence. He'd have to come into the room for that. She wondered if
he would. Was he going to spy on her, the way her mother did? She
kind of doubted it. But someone had to come in the room sometimes
to clean it. She couldn't imagine her father cleaning. So who did?

She realized that her father's entire life was a mystery to her. Not
that she cared, really. It had just never occurred to her to wonder how
he managed. Did he cook? He'd mentioned having dinner, but he hadn't
said anything about doing the cooking. She tried to picture him doing
laundry, or vacuuming. She couldn't even form an image of it in her
mind. It was like he was someone she'd read about in a book; she knew
just enough about him to believe that he existed. Everything else was
a blank.

The second Valium was kicking in, and that, combined with the warmth of the room, made her sleepy. She yawned. For a moment, she fought against the closing of her eyes. Then she remembered that she had absolutely nothing else to do, nowhere else to be. It was as if she were marooned on an island, alone except for the strange presence that was her father.

She breathed deeply, settling into the mattress. Within moments, she slept.

CHAPTER 5

Ben shut the door to the small office, sat in the worn wooden chair at the desk, and realized that it was the first time since he'd moved into the house three years before that he hadn't left the door open. How curious, he thought, that now he should do it without even thinking. Certainly he hadn't been conscious of wanting—or needing—to hide himself away from Caddie. And it wasn't as if he was going to engage in some activity he wouldn't want his daughter to see should she come looking for him.

No, it had been an instinctual act, the reaction of muscle and tendon to electrical commands barked down his central nervous system by some alert sentry bunkered deep in the recesses of his brain. The primitive need for protection, perhaps. An ancient defense mechanism triggered by approaching danger as yet unrecognized by his conscious mind, like animals that minutes or even hours before an earthquake could be seen scurrying for safety.

But protection from what? He considered the question. Was he afraid of his own child? He had to admit that he was. Or, if not afraid, at least wary. And now he was hiding from her, shutting himself in his office, safe behind a door that, although it had no lock and could be opened easily, created the illusion of safety.

He laughed at himself. *You're like a crab hiding under a rock,* he thought reproachfully. *Hoping the octopus won't reach under and pull you out.* He didn't open the door.

Leaning back in the chair, he listened to its familiar squeak and relaxed slightly. This was his place, his refuge. Apart from beneath the water, he felt most at home here, surrounded by the artifacts of his life: the books and papers, the pile of journals (some more than two years old) he intended to read, the coffee mug emblazoned with the name of the dive boat on which he'd spent two weeks in British Columbia photographing the underwater life of the Queen Charlotte Islands. On his desk sat a photograph of his beloved *Cadlina flavomaculata,* taken himself on one of his many dives at Pt. Lobos.

His office was a museum, a repository for the things that made him who he was. It was the one room in the house to which he had devoted the most (albeit still minimal) attention. The walls were painted a shade of blue that recalled the house on Cape Cod where he'd spent summers as a boy. The sturdy wooden desk, discovered at a local antique shop, reportedly had once belonged to a sea captain whose successful involvement in the Pacific Coast lumber trade of the eighteenth century had made him a very wealthy man. While working, Ben often ran his fingers absentmindedly over the tiny lines scored in neat rows into the desk's edge, remnants, he liked to believe, of the former owner's primitive record keeping, an early ledger of trees shipped and monies received, kept before financial success allowed for a proper bookkeeper and account books bound in leather and inscribed in ink.

Everything in the office was connected in some way with the sea. Even the lamp on the desk was in the form of an Art Deco mermaid, her tail curled gracefully about the base while one bronze arm extended up to hold the bulb beneath a shade of blue and green glass. It was the one fantastical element in the otherwise practical space, and Ben sometimes felt the need to apologize when, reaching up to pull the chain to illuminate the bulb, his hand brushed against the mermaid's bare breasts.

The lamp was currently dark. The afternoon sun lit the room more than adequately, throwing its spotlight directly onto the chair Ben occupied. He basked in the halo of warmth as he considered the problem before him. That, of course, being his daughter, and what, exactly, he was going to do with her for the next three months.

It would be far easier, he noted, if she were something slightly less complicated than a human being. A sea star, for instance, or an urchin. Anything, really, that could be opened up and dissected, its internal activities studied and understood without complication. The thoughts of a barnacle were not much of a mystery; those of his own flesh and blood were completely indecipherable. Even if he could open her up, poke around inside her and reveal her smallest secrets beneath the lens of a microscope, he was certain he would fail to grasp the complexity of her.

He had occasionally doubted, never with much sincerity, whether Caddie had, in fact, been partly his doing. Not because he questioned his then wife's fidelity in any way, or at least not any more than he would ever doubt the ability of a creature whose basic impulses for survival were driven by the need to procreate as often as possible with the most genetically desirable partners to remain monogamous. No, it wasn't because of any suspicions of adultery (what a peculiar word that was, suggesting the addition of impurity to something believed to be perfect), but simply because he didn't believe himself capable of such a thing, not in any biological way, but in a larger, less easily defined sense.

When he looked at Caddie, he did not see himself in her. He was, he knew, responsible for one half of her DNA strand and that, even so, she didn't need to resemble him to be of him. Her difference, though, went deeper even than the genetic blueprint from which she'd arisen. It was something primordial from which he recoiled, as if allergic. When she was a child, he'd held her like he might an atom bomb, fearful of activating her. Carol had laughed at him, made jokes about his clumsiness and worry over causing injury to the baby. He'd been unable to explain that it was his own life for which he feared.

Eventually Carol had discovered the weakness in him. He didn't know when it had first dawned on her that he viewed their child as something altogether unknowable, but he could pinpoint the moment when she'd revealed her knowledge to him. It was on a summer evening when Caddie, three at the time and seeing him striding up the sidewalk coming home from work, ran out on unsteady legs to greet him. She'd stumbled over a crack, a toy, some obstacle, and fallen. Her knee, scraped, had begun to bleed and she, seeing it, had let out a wail of such indignant hurt that a jay, watching the tragedy unfold from its vantage point on a fence, flew up with a startled shriek and sought safety in an oak tree.

Instead of rushing to her, picking her up, and whispering words of comfort, Ben had simply stopped and observed her actions. Her response to the actual level of physical pain he knew she was experiencing seemed excessive, and he wondered at the human inclination to overreact to stress on the body. It never occurred to him that she was merely frightened.

Before he could bring himself to the point of helping Caddie, Carol had come running from the house, drawn by the child's cries. Seeing Ben standing a dozen feet from their injured baby, she'd fixed him with a look so utterly fierce, so filled with disgust and wonder, that he'd stepped back as if struck. Only then was he able to move forward, to walk briskly toward his daughter, now cradled in his wife's arms and sobbing quietly, and inquire, "Is she all right?"

Carol had pulled Caddie back from his touch, as if he were a stranger, and taken the girl back into the house. When Ben entered a minute later, Caddie was happily chasing the dog, a foolish red and white spaniel called Hartley, around the living room. A small bandage covered her knee, and she seemed to have forgotten entirely what had moments before been the greatest calamity of her life.

Carol had said nothing, but her coolness betrayed her newfound understanding of Ben's ineptitude as a father. He'd started to apologize, then stopped, unsure what he was apologizing for and unwilling to admit to a sin he couldn't even name. But the evidence had been presented, and Carol, at least, had found him guilty.

Caddie, oblivious to her father's failings, had continued to behave toward him as she always had. And he'd attempted to act in all ways as a father should toward his child. But eventually he'd accepted that something was wrong. He loved his daughter; that was never in doubt. But he didn't feel this love as he knew others did. It didn't radiate out from his heart and enfold him in golden warmth. He felt constantly in shadow.

Carol had tried to kindle the fire of emotion in him, striking at him as a person shivering from cold might dash a flint against a rock, praying for a spark. Failing at that, she'd resorted to quarreling. He remembered the last few years of their marriage as one long fight, marked only by the level of its intensity as one or the other of them tired of battle for a time.

He'd left when Caddie was seven. She'd been old enough to understand that he would no longer be a daily part of her world, and the day he'd put a suitcase and several boxes of books into the car, she'd burst into tears that too much reminded him of the day that things had begun to unravel. Once again, it had been Carol who'd tried to soothe her pain, this time without success.

In the nine years since, he'd spent less and less time trying to locate the flaw in himself that had resulted in the dissolution of his marriage.

He and Carol forgot about the things that had brought them together, and now he thought of her as someone he knew once but only through accident of time and place, like a school friend or a neighbor from a former home. Caddie he thought of in more familial terms. He'd managed to maintain involvement in her life, albeit limited mostly to phone calls and occasional visits, both of which had decreased in frequency as she'd aged.

He'd never spoken with her about the reasons for the divorce; he wondered if Carol had. If so, how had she explained it? Had she put into words what he'd seen in her eyes that day? He found it difficult to believe, particularly when she'd never done as much for him, and when he couldn't do it for himself. How did you voice a disappointment so deep that it could only begin to be glimpsed?

He hadn't thought about these things in a very long time, and now he thought of them only dully, as if watching an old, familiar film whose action and dialogue were so familiar that paying attention was unnecessary. Still, there was the matter of the door. He looked at it again. Its blank, white face stared back at him, offering no help whatsoever. Rising, he went to it and pushed it open. It swung reluctantly, unaccustomed to being asked to perform its duty.

Ben sat down again and looked through the opening. He could see the hallway, the top of the stairs. If Caddie were to walk by, to venture downstairs for a drink or simply to get out of her room, she would undoubtedly see him sitting at his desk. She could even, he told himself, stand unnoticed in the hall for quite some time while he, oblivious to her presence, thought himself alone.

He got up and pulled the door partially closed, reducing the window on the hallway to a sliver half a foot wide. That was acceptable to him. He could see—and be seen—without being completely vulnerable. Besides, he reasoned, he was almost certain to hear her footsteps. The shortcomings of an aging house could also be its advantages.

The question of the door having been settled, he looked once more at his desk, assessing the situation. There were hastily scribbled lab notes to type up, a clipped article to file, a letter from a colleague in Mexico to answer. He considered the notes first. It would be gratifying to set them in print on his old typewriter, a rattling old Underwood he preferred to the more convenient computers in the lab, despite the near impossibility of finding ribbons for the damned thing. He liked the sound the keys made when they struck the platen, imprinting ink into paper. He enjoyed the solidity of it, the warning chirp of the bell as he neared the end of a line, the satisfaction of hitting the return arm and watching the carriage slide back into place. He even delighted in the occasional dropped letter, the J that forever sat ever so slightly beneath the line.

But Caddie might be sleeping, he reminded himself, and felt his enthusiasm fade. He couldn't make noise, not even in his own office. It would carry through the thin walls, like the scratching of rats. He didn't dare risk it.

Suddenly, he was overcome with thinking about all the things he could no longer do comfortably. Type. Play music. Walk naked from his bedroom to the bathroom. Even flushing the toilet carried with it the potential for humiliation, revealing as it did his eliminatory activity. From now on, his actions were on parade.

In a minor act of rebellion, he turned to the CD player situated on the bookcase behind him and hit Play. The mournful sound of John Coltrane's saxophone slipped into the air. It wasn't loud—he never played music loud—but for a moment he felt himself tense, awaiting the sound of a protesting voice. When it didn't come, he allowed himself to settle into the music.

That was better. He felt more normal, more himself. He wasn't sure which of his selves had greeted Carol and Caddie, but he was embarrassed by him. He'd been too effusive, overeager to please, to be liked. And Caddie hadn't liked him. He knew that. Nor had she liked the house, or her room. He knew that, too, although he was not embarrassed about that. He liked his house. If Caddie didn't, it was only because she was too used to Carol's extravagances—the big house and expensive car, the designer clothes and vacations in Aspen and Hawaii. He'd heard about these things from time to time, usually while treating Caddie to dinner at some restaurant overlooked by the Zagat guide.

He was annoyed again, this time because his daughter's disapproval was causing him to defend his home. He didn't like answering to anyone other than himself, especially someone who was essentially an unwelcome guest. He shocked himself with the admission. He'd been trying hard to believe that he wanted Caddie there. But he didn't. He wanted to be alone.

This, he felt, was the irony of parenthood, the simultaneous satisfaction found in furthering your line coupled with the inevitable resentment of having time taken away from pursuing those things that made you an individual. Of course there were parents who willingly devoted their entire lives to their children, but he'd always suspected them of mental illness, of using their young as an excuse for not fulfilling their own dreams.

He related much more to those creatures that, having fertilized their eggs, left the rest to chance. True, the mother trout never experienced the moment when her fingerling, after much toil, graduated high school. But then she rarely, if at all, had to endure the misery of being thought a bad parent. Not, he thought, that most animal parents had much to do other than care for their offspring. While the she-bear might spend two years at a time raising a cub, he doubted that she much resented the reduced opportunities for escaping uninterrupted into the pages of a Jane Austen novel.

Now you're being ridiculous, he chided himself. *You can't compare trout to humans.* Which brought him, he realized wearily, back to where he'd started. Humans *weren't* animals, at least not in an equivalent sense. His skills as a father could hardly be judged alongside those of a bull elephant or a tomcat. (Particularly, he thought, when such a comparison would result unfavorably for him.) But this also meant that he could hardly excuse his uneasy relationship with fatherhood by pointing to the laissez-faire approach of most male animals that, with some notable exceptions, limited their involvement with their progeny to the act that produced them.

Maybe, he thought, he should just accept that he would never understand his daughter and she would never understand him. Having accepted the truth of that, they would both then be free to be themselves, without worry that they were in any way responsible for one another's well-being. That seemed a fair solution to the problem, and in coming to it, he ignored the fact that Caddie had been involved in none of the discussions leading to the decision.

A minute later, he changed his mind and determined to try. There was, he told himself, no reason why he couldn't come to appreciate his daughter, if not as the flesh of his flesh, then at least as an individual. She seemed interesting enough. Perhaps, with effort, he could find something in her to cling to, some thought or feeling to which he could relate. *Maybe she likes Coltrane,* he thought hopefully. It would, at least, be something.

He would start at dinner. He would ask her about herself, find out what she hoped to do with her life. He glanced at the clock. He had an hour and a half before they reconvened, enough time for him to write down some thoughts he'd been having about a paper he was scheduled to give in October at a symposium in Tokyo on the issue of promoting marine conservation in communities built on fishing. That would help him clear his mind before tackling the much-trickier issue of learning to be a friend to his child.

Taking up his pen, he began to write.

CHAPTER 6

Caddie awoke with a start. For a moment, she thought she was still dreaming. The room she was in was the same one from her nightmare, in which she'd been kidnapped by a faceless attacker and imprisoned in a run-down house. Now, to her deep disappointment, she realized that it was all real. Only her jailor had a face.

Then she remembered dinner. What time was it? She turned and looked at the clock that sat on the bedside table. Like everything else, it seemed antiquated, its face round and numbered. No red electric eyes, just hands that swept silently around and around. It took her a moment to remember how to read the damn thing.

Seven-twenty. What time had her father said they would have dinner? Eight? She stretched and yawned. It felt more like two in the morning. The Valium had really knocked her out. Still, she wished she was still asleep. Even a nightmare was better than the reality of her situation.

She thought about going back to sleep, maybe even pretending to be asleep so that her father would leave her alone. But she was a little hungry, and food didn't sound so bad. Maybe sushi. If they even had sushi in Monterey. Somehow she doubted it.

She sat up. Despite the hour, it was still light out, that soft summer evening light that made everything appear soft, sort of out of focus. She heard the kids outside, still playing at their games. She remembered how it was, that feeling of freedom, like night and bedtime would never come, like the summer would last forever. When did that time end? When had she realized that life wasn't always going to be ice-cream sweet?

Probably when I got my first period, she thought, only half-joking. It was funny how the onset of that rite of passage seemed to coincide with so many other unpleasant realizations.

She picked up a paperback and opened it. It took reading half a page before she even remembered what the story was about. She'd chosen the book almost at random from a stack her mother had set out to take to Goodwill. It was a mystery, something about a woman who was being stalked by a man who might or might not be the same man who killed her mother twenty years before. The character interested her not at all, and the author's clunky style didn't make things any more appealing. Still, she wanted to see how it ended.

When she next looked up, it was a few minutes past eight. She shut the book and sat on the edge of the bed, preparing herself mentally for the ordeal of dinner with her father. She located her shoes, slipped them on, and waited for his knock on the door.

Ten minutes later, she was still sitting. There was no sound of her father's footsteps in the hallway. In fact, there was no sound in the house at all. *Maybe he fell asleep,* Caddie thought. That would solve her dilemma nicely.

But she knew that wasn't likely. If she knew anything about her father, it was that he was practically a slave to schedules and routines. *Predictable,* she thought. He was predictable.

Her stomach rumbled. For its sake, she decided to go in search of her father. She couldn't avoid him forever, she reasoned; she might as well get it over with.

She opened the door and stepped into the hallway. Probably, she thought, he was downstairs. Perhaps he was even making dinner, although she couldn't imagine it. But that might explain his lateness. He was probably expecting her to come down on her own.

She headed for the stairs, but paused when she heard a popping sound. It was coming from her father's office. Then she heard the music. Low. Jazzy. Sad, although she couldn't say why.

The door was open a crack, and she peeked inside. Her father sat at his desk, typing. His fingers moved steadily but awkwardly over the keys, striking them like a chicken pecking at grain. His forehead was furrowed, and his lips moved silently as he worked.

He didn't see her. For a moment she thought about saying something, maybe just clearing her throat to get his attention. But clearly he was more interested in whatever he was working on than he was in having dinner with her. After watching him for another half a minute, she stepped away from the door, leaving him alone.

The stairs let out only the slightest of creaks as she descended. The lower half of the house was darker, the light thinner and the shadows creeping in around the furniture as dusk settled over everything. Caddie walked quickly to the front door and opened it, stepping out into the warm air.

Across the street, the playing children stopped momentarily to look at her. Apparently finding her of no interest, they then returned to their game. Caddie walked down the sidewalk away from them, heading toward town.

As expected, she wasn't impressed. What she assumed was the main street of town was hardly teeming with people. A handful walked up and down, but mostly the sidewalks were empty. Even the cars that drove by her seemed anxious to be on their way to somewhere else, somewhere more lively.

She walked aimlessly, hoping against hope to find something—anything—of interest. Even a distraction would be welcome. Barring that, she decided she would settle for simply finding something to eat.

Ahead of her, a red and green neon sign proclaimed the merits of Johnny's Pizza, Best in Monterey! *I wouldn't brag about that,* thought Caddie as she entered the restaurant. The place did nothing to change her opinion. A scattering of tables were covered in the ubiquitous vinyl red-and-white-checked tablecloths found in every cheap Italian joint. Harsh lights illuminated a scarred and battered counter where customers lined up to order one of the dozen or so specialties of the house spelled out in plastic letters on the menu board overhead.

Caddie scanned the list, looking for something that sounded even remotely appetizing. She was considering a sausage calzone when a male voice interrupted her thinking. "What can I get you?"

The speaker, a young man, stood behind the counter, wiping his hands on a stained white apron. He looked at Caddie wearily, as if he'd asked the same question a million times already, which she guessed he probably had.

"I don't suppose a Chinese chicken salad is an option?" Caddie said.

"Funny," the boy said.

Caddie leaned on the counter. "I didn't think so," she said. "In that case, what do you recommend?"

The boy laughed. "It's a pizza joint," he said. "How about pizza?"

Caddie looked at him. Despite the apron, he was attractive. He looked a couple of years older than she was. His brown eyes sparkled, and his face, while certainly not model handsome, was rugged. *In a blue-collar kind of way,* she qualified. And was that actually gel in his black hair? She reappraised him favorably.

"What's your specialty?" she asked, her voice taking on a lighter tone.

"The calamari and anchovy is a big hit with tourists," he answered.

"Do I look like a tourist?" asked Caddie.

The boy gave her a lopsided grin. "You don't look like you're from around here," he said.

Caddie smiled. "I'll take that as a compliment," she said. "But no squid for me. How about pepperoni and extra cheese?"

"Good call," said the boy. "Anything to drink?"

"A Corona," Caddie said.

He looked at her. "You old enough?" he asked.

"For what?" said Caddie, looking him right in the eyes.

He hesitated a moment, then said, "Coming right up."

When he returned a minute later with her pizza slice and the beer, Caddie rooted in her pocket for her money. "How much?" she asked.

"Eight even."

Caddie counted out the money and slid it across the counter to him. As he picked it up, she let her fingers touch his. "What's your name?"

"Nick," he said. "You?"

"Caddie," she replied.

"Like the car," said Nick.

Caddie laughed. "Just like," she said, as Nick grinned at his own cleverness.

"Nice to meet you, Caddie," he said.

Caddie retreated to one of the small tables. As she ate her pizza and drank her beer, she watched Nick. He was stupid, that was for sure, but he was kind of hot. No one she would ever date back home. Definitely not. But for Monterey, he was probably as good as it got. A couple of times Nick looked back at her, flashed his grin, and nodded.

She finished her dinner and stood up. As she deposited her trash in the basket near the counter, Nick came over to her. "How long you here for?" he asked her.

"Depends," she said.

Nick looked confused. "On what?"

Caddie leaned toward him. "On whether or not I find anything interesting," she said.

Nick nodded. "Got you," he said. "So, I'm just about done for the night. I thought maybe you might want to, I don't know, take a walk or something."

Caddie looked at him. She loved this moment—the guy waiting for her answer, both of them knowing that she could totally break him by saying no. That was one thing men had in common no matter where they were from.

"Why not?" she said, seeing relief relax Nick's tensed shoulders.

"Great," he said. "Let me go clean up."

She went outside to wait for him. The beer had lightened her mood. She'd forgotten all about her father. And now the promise of distraction offered by Nick made her forget how unhappy she was. When Nick emerged a minute later, she took his hand as if they'd known one another for more than half an hour.

"Where shall we go?" she said.

"How about the beach?" Nick suggested.

Caddie, not really caring where they went, nodded, and they began to walk. Nick led her down a side street, away from the lights, until they came to what seemed to be a small park. In front of them, beyond a swatch of grass, was the ocean. It gleamed blackly beneath the stars, and the waves fell softly against the sand.

"They call this the Breakwater," Nick explained as they walked along a narrow sidewalk toward a wharf that stretched out into the water. "The navy built it back in World War II or sometime around then."

A low stone wall ran along the ocean side of the Breakwater. On the other was a parking lot edged with a boat supply store, a small dive shop, and what appeared to be a little grocery store with a restaurant situated atop it. Nick walked halfway down the wharf and stopped. Climbing onto the wall, he helped Caddie stand beside him.

"I like to sit here at night," he said as he lowered himself to the wall.

Caddie joined him. The concrete was cold against her legs. The night air, still warm, blew lazily across the water. She heard a gull call out in the darkness.

Nick reached into his jeans pocket and removed a crumpled cigarette pack. Tapping it open, he removed what Caddie saw was not a standard-issue smoke. Nick held the joint up. "Do you smoke?" he asked her.

"Sometimes," she told him. "But not usually with strange guys." She bumped her shoulder against him affectionately.

Nick lit the joint from a lighter he produced out of the same pocket. He drew on it, the end sparking up in a small orange glow. Caddie waited for him to hand it to her. When he did, she inhaled the sweet, sharp smoke and closed her eyes as it filled her lungs.

"So, tell me more," Nick said.

"About what?" asked Caddie, taking another hit off the joint.

"You," said Nick. "All I know is your name."

"You know I like pizza," Caddie countered.

Nick retrieved the joint from her. "Come on," he coaxed. "Who are you? What are you doing here?"

Caddie turned and looked at him. "What's the meaning of life? Does God really exist?" she said. "What difference does it make?"

Nick blew out a cloud of smoke. "If I'm going to kiss a girl, I kind of like to know a little bit about her," he said.

Caddie felt the pot working its magic on her brain. *It's not as good as L.A. pot,* she thought, *but it's not bad.* She wondered where Nick got it and made a mental note to ask him to get her some. Then she remembered that Nick had said he was going to kiss her. Did she want him to? She hadn't thought that far ahead. She supposed it would be okay.

Apparently, he was waiting for her to say something, maybe to give her permission. That annoyed her. She liked it when guys were a little more aggressive. She decided to punish Nick for being too nice by ignoring what he'd said.

"I'm here seeing my dad," she said.

"Seeing him?" said Nick. "What, like he's in the hospital or something?"

"No," said Caddie. "I don't live with him. I live in L.A." She waited for Nick to be impressed by this piece of information, but all he did was nod while he took another toke on the joint.

"My parents divorced a long time ago," she heard herself say. "My mom thinks it's time my dad and I got to know each other better." Why was she talking so much? Suddenly, she was anxious. It was like by mentioning her father, now she couldn't stop talking about him.

To stop herself, she kissed Nick. When she first pressed her lips against his, he was taken aback, blowing some of the pot smoke into her throat. But then his mouth opened, and his tongue explored hers. Caddie felt her father's presence retreat into the darkness as Nick's hands pulled her closer. The agitated, flittering thoughts scattered like moths beneath the lights, and she relaxed.

Nick tasted like pot and pepperoni and beer. Caddie kissed him hard, encouraging him to go further. When one of his hands slid to her breast, she let it stay there. His body beneath the skin of his T-shirt was muscled and firm, and when she ran her fingers over his cheek, the feel of stubble beneath her fingertips excited her. He was something she could lose herself in, something she understood without question. He was easy, and she welcomed that.

After a time Nick pulled away. Still holding Caddie's hand, he looked down at the water. "Look," he said, pointing.

Caddie followed his gaze and saw something glowing beneath the surface of the ocean below their feet.

"Divers," Nick said before she asked. "They dive here a lot at night."

"Why?" Caddie asked as the light moved slowly along the rock wall.

"Lots of stuff comes out at night that you can't see during the day," explained Nick. "Octopus. Stuff like that."

Caddie watched the diver's light. It grew fainter as it moved out to sea.

"He's going deeper," said Nick. "Pretty soon you'll just see a little spot of light. You should see it when there are a lot of them out here. The whole place lights up. Some of them use those colored glow sticks so they can recognize each other underwater. That's the coolest." He turned to Caddie. "You ever dive?"

"No," Caddie answered. "I don't think I'd like it."

"I bet I could get you to like it," said Nick. He leaned over and kissed her again.

When he stopped, Caddie said, "I bet you could get me to like a lot of things."

"You're a strange girl," Nick told her.

Caddie's head snapped to his face. "What do you mean?" she said.

Nick shrugged. "Not strange bad," he said. "Just strange. Different. I don't know what to make of you."

Caddie laughed. "You and the rest of the world," she said as she started to stand up.

Nick reached up and grabbed her hand. "Hey," he said. "Don't get mad. I didn't say I didn't like it."

Caddie hesitated. She looked out at the water. The diver's light was barely visible through the water. How deep was he? What was he looking at? She thought about swimming through the black water, not knowing what was swimming around with her, and a chill shook her.

"Sit down," Nick said.

Caddie waited a moment, just to let him know she was doing it of her own free will. Then she sat. Nick put his arm around her and pulled her close. This time when he kissed her, she pretended he was taking her down into the water. She closed her eyes and followed his light, going deeper and deeper, until all that lay before her was a small circle of gold light that kept the sea monsters at bay.

CHAPTER 7

It didn't look like he expected it to.

Hudson stood at the southeast end of Cannery Row. He'd parked his rental car in the lot of San Carlos Beach Park behind him. What had the clerk at the hotel called it? The Breakwater. "Look for the divers," he'd said. Hudson had thought it an odd thing to say, as dark was quickly falling, but the man had been right. There were divers on the beach. Only a couple, but they'd assured him that he was in the right place.

Cannery Row. It felt strange to be standing in a place he'd imagined so clearly in his mind, stranger to find that it resembled his idea of it almost not at all. Maybe in the daylight it would seem more like the Cannery Row depicted in John Steinbeck's novel of the same name. But now, at night, it felt more like an arcade at a county fair, all bright lights and tourists.

You're just tired, he told himself. And he was. He should have just had dinner and gone to bed, venturing out after sleeping off some of his jet lag. But he'd been unable to rest, knowing that Cannery Row was only blocks away. Finally, overcome by the irrational fear that either it or he might not survive the night, he'd gone out to see it for himself.

To his left, a large brick wall was painted with a mural of a whale. Next door, a dive flag flapped over the entrance to a shop offering 10% OFF OPEN WATER TRAINING: PADI CERTIFICATION. On his right, a hotel rose up from the street, the balconies of its rooms overlooking the Pacific. *There used to be a cannery there,* he thought vaguely.

There had once been many canneries on the street named for the abundance of processing facilities that had lined every inch of it. Now there were none. They had been replaced by shops selling T-shirts, dolphin figurines, doughnuts. There was a Starbucks, a Bubba Gump's, an ATM. Hudson felt slightly ill.

What did you expect? he asked himself. He knew Cannery Row was a tourist attraction, visited by people who mostly had probably never even heard of John Steinbeck or his famous book. They came for souvenirs, postcards, earrings, and boxes of fudge that had nothing whatever to do with the Row and its history. Maybe they would pick up a replica of one of the old cannery signs, hang it in a kitchen or den, and never think about it again. "Oh, that," they would say if someone happened to ask. "We got that in Monterey. There's the nicest shop. I bought a picture frame made out of seashells."

He was being more than a little bitter, he knew. But he couldn't help it. The commodification of history angered him. "But isn't that what Steinbeck himself was doing?" Marty had once argued when Hudson was on a tear about the indignity of having a gift shop at Ellis Island. "Didn't he manufacture a Cannery Row to fit his story?"

It wasn't the same, Hudson had argued. And it wasn't. Steinbeck hadn't invented a sanitized Cannery Row for public consumption. He'd written about it as it was, merely changing a few names. This was different. This was Cannery Row as strip mall, with all of the real history stripped away to make room for snow globes and key rings.

He tried not to think about it as he walked, looking for what might remain of Steinbeck's Cannery Row. He looked for it in the windows of the stores that lined the street, seeing nothing that Steinbeck would recognize in the T-shirts (did that one really say HARRY OTTER?) and baseball caps and mountains of knickknacks presented for consumption. Even the smell was wrong, the stink of fish and oil replaced by the aroma of mocha vanilla lattes and potpourri.

He came to the Wing Chong Grocery and stopped across the street from it. The run-down building, immortalized by Steinbeck as Lee Chong's, was clearly meant to invoke the spirit of old Cannery Row. But it, too, suffered from the effects of being made over. Hudson tried to imagine Mack, the perpetually out-of-work but good-natured ne'er-do-well of Steinbeck's books, walking in to talk the suspicious proprietor into letting him have a bottle of whiskey on credit. Then a young couple wearing matching Seattle Seahawks jerseys walked out, carrying shopping bags from the nearby Kinkade National Archive store (the Master of Shitty Art for People with Shitty Taste, Marty had once called the popular painter), and Hudson couldn't muster the strength to keep trying.

Where was it all? Where was the Bear Flag Restaurant bordello and the Palace Flophouse? Where were Dora Flood, and Eddie of the La Ida Café? When had they been replaced by women in flip-flops and men talking on cell phones? When had it all disappeared?

You didn't come here to see buildings, he reminded himself. And that was true. The buildings were merely part of something larger. Still, they were connections, physical links to another time and other people, long dead, who were very important to him.

Doc's lab should have been right here, he thought suddenly, sadly. *Across from Lee Chong's. He used to walk over there to get beer.*

He turned around. A plywood fence, its surface covered in a mural that was in turn defaced by graffiti (SKINZ RULES! LUV ME DOO) hid from view what he knew was the old Pacific Biological Laboratories of Ed "Doc" Ricketts, Steinbeck's friend and cohort in adventure. He badly wanted to see it, but the fence effectively blocked his view.

He turned and walked back the way he had come. In front of an El Torrito restaurant he stopped to look at the bronze bust of John Steinbeck. Passersby casually rubbed their hands over it, as if it were some sort of good luck charm. Hudson was tempted to stop a few and ask them if they even knew who Steinbeck was and why his bust was there, surrounded by a Ghirardelli chocolate shop and an As Seen on TV store. But he knew their blank-eyed expressions would only further depress him, and he resisted.

Once he was past the stores and hotels, the street was deserted. The dive shop, closed for the night, was the last establishment before the little park. He started to walk to his car, then turned and walked instead toward the ocean. A set of stairs, half-covered by drifting sand, led down to the beach. To his left was the hotel, its lights illuminating the stretch of sand. To his right, farther on, was a jetty. Beneath the lights that lined it he saw some figures sitting on the low wall.

Several large rocks dotted the beach. He walked to one of them and climbed up on it. The tide was ebbing, the ocean retreating and leaving behind a smooth expanse of sand. Only the longest fingers of water touched the rock when the waves reached for the shore. The top was dry, and Hudson sat without worry.

The sky was clear, the moon just shy of full and the stars glinting against the blackness. The sea murmured steadily. In the darkness, if you didn't know you were next to the ocean, it would be possible to mistake the water for a vast field of grass with the wind soughing through it.

As he watched, a figure emerged from the waves and came toward shore. The heavy-footed walk reminded him of the Creature from the Black Lagoon movies he'd loved as a kid. This creature, however, carried a set of fins in one hand and a flashlight in the other. As it neared Hudson's rock, he saw moonlight reflected off a face mask and heard the dull clinking of metal against the tank strapped to the diver's back.

"Evening," the man said as he passed.

Hudson wanted to ask him what he'd seen in the water, but conversation would have broken the mood. He was content to nod silently and let the diver be on his way. Alone again, he looked out into the night and thought about why he had come there.

No, Cannery Row was not what he had hoped. And part of him had known that it wouldn't be. Places changed. Nothing as fragile as Steinbeck's Cannery Row—a world that depended for its survival on an industry that died out almost as quickly as it had sprung up—could have survived the changing American landscape of the past sixty years. Mack, Doc, and the others could not live in what Monterey had become since the days when a man could set up house inside a discarded boiler or live on the money earned from catching frogs.

He imagined what Steinbeck would think of the new Monterey. Probably he would hate it, he thought. But perhaps not. The writer was, after all, fascinated by the progress of the human spirit. But not progress that resulted in emptiness, Hudson argued with himself, in a lack of spirit and absence of fire. Shopping, he was almost certain, would not be high on Steinbeck's list of human accomplishments.

And what of Ed Ricketts, the marine biologist who had so inspired Steinbeck, both in his writing and in his own deep interest in the ocean. Could he exist in modern-day Monterey? Hudson imagined him walking down Cannery Row, a collecting bucket in each hand. He saw him coming to the edge of the ocean, scouring the rocks for the tiny creatures he spent his life observing.

Ricketts would have loved a night like this. Perhaps he would have rolled his pants to the knee and walked into the water in search of octopuses. Or maybe he would have just sat—as Hudson was—admiring the largeness of the sea and thinking that there was time enough later for work.

Steinbeck and Ricketts. The two men had haunted him like ghosts for the past year, filling his thoughts and walking through his dreams. Now, seated in their backyard, he wished they would appear before him and answer his questions. That would make what he had to do so much easier.

But it would also rob him of the thrill of the hunt. He had a scent, and he was following it. To have the chase end so soon, and so abruptly, would be something of a letdown after all the energy he'd put into it. Still, he would give anything for a chance to sit with either man for even a few minutes.

The sound of laughter startled him from his reverie. He followed it to the jetty wall, where invisible figures sat watching who knew what. Separated by darkness, they might as well have inhabited different worlds. Yet they shared the night, the beach, the moon and the stars and the ocean.

He thought, suddenly, of Charlie Tilling. Charlie of the manuscript he'd brought with him. Charlie, who had perhaps stood near this very spot considering his own death. He, too, shared the night with Hudson and the unseen sitters on the wall. He, too, was part of Monterey. But how much a part? That was the question Hudson had yet to answer.

Behind him a dog barked. He turned and saw a shadow dart across the sand and into the water. It returned a moment later, shaking the sea from its fur and carrying a stick in its mouth. It trotted past Hudson, looking at him briefly from the corner of its eye, and he heard a man's voice speaking to it in low tones. A moment later, the dog flew by again, flinging itself into the waves.

"I'm always half-afraid he won't come out," said a voice.

Hudson turned his head and saw a man standing beside the rock. Dressed in shorts and a windbreaker, he carried a leash in one hand. He looked not at Hudson, but at the waves. "He always does, though," he added.

As if to prove this point, the dog came running up, stopping in front of the man and dropping the stick onto the sand. When his owner didn't retrieve it quickly enough, he barked once and nudged it with his nose.

"One more," the man said, picking up the stick and throwing it. The dog turned, disappearing into the dim.

"It must be nice to be so happy about a stick," said Hudson.

The man laughed as the dog returned. "Want to go home?" he said, and for a second Hudson thought he might be speaking to him, and thought about saying yes. Then he heard the snap of a leash, and the man and dog walked away, saying nothing.

You really need to get laid, he told himself. He had to admit, it had been awhile. But there were more important things to think about than finding someone to share a bed with. Still, he wouldn't mind. One night stands had never been his preferred way to meet his need for male companionship, but neither was he adverse to enjoying them from time to time. Sometimes, he thought, it was easier to make love with someone who knew nothing about you. That way you could each be whatever the other wanted.

Suddenly he was very tired. But he wasn't quite ready to go back to his hotel room. The night was too beautiful to waste. Leaving it so soon seemed wasteful. He stood up and, jumping lightly to the sand, removed his shoes and socks, tucking the later into the former and setting the shoes on the rock. He rolled his pants as close to the knee as he could and then, barefoot, he walked to the water.

The first touch made him retreat a step. It was cold, much colder than he'd expected. Again he thought of his disappointment over discovering that the Pacific was no bluer than its East Coast sibling. Nor, he now found, was it any warmer.

He tried again, letting the waves flow over his feet, steeling himself for its icy touch. Then he took another step, and another, until the water, when it came in again, reached halfway to his knees. It was bitterly cold, but he stood it. *How did Ricketts stand in this for hours at a time?* he wondered, then recalled the pictures he'd seen of the biologist in tall rubber boots and felt ashamed of his romantic inclinations.

Still, he kept walking. Something skittered over his feet with feathery lightness, and he imagined crabs, tiny fish, the inquisitive tentacles of an octopus. Was there anything in the Pacific to fear? He thought vaguely of sharks, and how they attacked most often in darkness, when they couldn't discern prey from a helpless grad student.

He stopped, having gone far enough. The water was to his knees now. He felt the edges of his pants where they'd become wet, a definite sign that he should go no farther. He looked back over his shoulder. His rock was a surprising distance away. *Low tide,* he reminded himself.

As he was looking back, he heard the rushing of water and turned just in time to see a wave, larger than the previous ones, moving toward him. He tried to back away from it but could not outrun the ocean. The wave, already crashing, hit him at waist level and sent him sprawling backward. He fell, the water rushing over his body, covering his face. He inhaled saltwater and choked. In the darkness, he was lost completely, not sure if he was facing up or down as the waves pulled and tugged at him, spinning him.

He had a very clear image of his death. He saw his body washed up on the beach, perhaps being sniffed curiously by the same dog he'd met earlier in the evening. Would the authorities know who to call? Would the saltwater ruin his student ID, his only link to his real life? Worst of all, what would become of the manuscript? He would die never knowing the truth.

And then the water was gone and he was looking up at the sky, air rushing into his lungs as he gasped, fishlike; on the sand. Before another wave could hit, he scrambled to his feet and ran back to the rock and safety. He was shivering, but the fear had left him, replaced by an overwhelming sense of joy. It was as if the sea had picked him up and tossed him the way the man had thrown the stick for the dog. He felt dizzy, almost giddy with delight at nature's whimsy.

Laughing, he picked up his shoes and walked, slowly and with great happiness, back to his car.

CHAPTER 8

Ben didn't notice the smoke rising from the pan until it was too late. The eggs were already burned. Still, he grabbed the handle, dropping it instantly as pain flared through his hand. The pan clattered to the floor, the eggs spilling over the linoleum and lying in the blackened butter like the casualties of a car crash. He looked down at the mess and nursed his hand.

"Better put that under cold water."

Caddie entered the kitchen, glanced at the ruined eggs, and sat down at the table.

"I was trying to make eggs in a hat," Ben explained as he turned on the tap and ran the water over his reddened skin. "You used to love those."

"When I was four," said Caddie. "Do you have any coffee?"

Ben nodded toward the pot sitting on the counter. Caddie, rising, shuffled over to it and poured herself a mugful. She took it back to the table and sipped it, black, not looking at her father.

Ben dried his hand and pulled several paper towels from the roll above the sink. As he bent to wipe up the remains of what should have been breakfast, he said, "What happened last night? I thought we were having dinner together."

"So did I," said Caddie shortly. "I waited until eight-fifteen. When you didn't show, I figured you'd forgotten."

Ben stood up, the wad of paper towels greasy and warm in his hand. "I didn't forget," he said.

Caddie looked at him, saying nothing. *Her mother looks like that when she's angry,* Ben thought as he turned away from her and deposited the paper towels in the wastebasket under the sink. He washed his hands, smarting a little as the warm water touched his burned fingers. It wasn't bad, though. Nothing a little aloe wouldn't take care of.

"I didn't forget," he repeated. He faced Caddie again as he dried his hands. "I was working on something and lost track of time. You should have reminded me."

Caddie nodded, looking into her coffee cup. "Maybe I didn't want to disturb you," she said.

Ben sighed. "You wouldn't have disturbed me," he said. The conversation was going badly already. On top of the ruined breakfast, it was making him tense. He decided now wasn't the time to get into it with Caddie. "So, where did you go?"

"Out," Caddie replied, typical of the teenager who doesn't want to prolong a parent's exasperation. "Into town," she added, for which Ben was thankful. At least it was something.

"What do you think?" he asked.

"Of what?" said Caddie.

"Of town," Ben said patiently.

"Oh," Caddie said. "It's all right, I guess. It's there."

It's there, Ben repeated to himself. That was all she was going to say? He felt the strain of forced conversation making him edgy. To distract himself, he opened the refrigerator and removed a carton of orange juice. When he poured the juice into a glass, it emerged in an unappealing mass of congealed pulp. He looked at the expiration date, which had passed weeks before.

"You weren't home when I went to bed," he said, dumping the juice down the sink and rinsing the glass. "I waited."

"You didn't have to," said Caddie.

"Did you eat?" he tried.

"I had some pizza," Caddie said. "Then I walked around a little."

Ben started to ask her where she'd walked, then thought better of it. Already he knew she was annoyed by his questions, and he had to remind himself that he hadn't been her father for a long time. It was new for both of them. He poured himself a cup of coffee, thankful that at least one thing in the house was edible, then seated himself at the table across from his daughter.

"It's a nice town," he said. "Monterey," he added, when Caddie said nothing. "It's very historic. Lots of things to see. Gilroy, too. They have a garlic festival coming up."

Caddie pushed some hair out of her eyes and looked right through him.

"It's a big deal," said Ben. "The garlic festival." He spooned sugar into his coffee, not caring how much he put in. He didn't like sugar anyway; it was just a distraction.

"Don't you have to go to work?" Caddie asked unexpectedly.

The spoon clattered around the edges of the mug as Ben stirred the coffee. "Yes," he said. "But I more or less make my own hours. It's one of the advantages of running your own program."

"Are you going in today?" said Caddie.

Ben nodded. "Sure," he answered. "What about you? What are your plans?"

"Maybe I'll check out that garlic festival," Caddie said. "It sounds off the hook."

Ben realized he was being mocked and saved himself further embarrassment by not informing Caddie that the festival wasn't until the end of July. Now that she'd offered him the escape of work, he considered taking her up on it. He'd half planned on spending the day with her, but more and more he wanted nothing so much as to be away from his own child.

"What are your plans for the summer?" he inquired.

Caddie looked surprised. "Plans?" she said, as if the word were completely foreign to her.

"Plans," Ben repeated. "I assume you want to do something for the next three months instead of just sitting around here."

Caddie laughed. "You mean like a job," she said. "You want me to get a job."

"I assumed you would want to," said Ben. "Isn't that what you'd be doing if you were still living at ho . . . with your mother?"

No, Caddie thought bitterly. *If I were home I'd be having fun. I'd be with my friends and not with you. I wouldn't be sitting in this crappy house listening to you tell me I should get a job.*

"What kind of job do you think I should have?" she asked.

Ben shook his head. "I don't know," he said. "What are you interested in? I think there's a Gap or something not too far downtown."

"A Gap," said Caddie. "Fantastic."

Ben started to make another suggestion, thought better of it, and pushed his coffee away. It was too sweet to drink anyway. "We can worry about that later," he said. He looked at his watch, feigning concern for the time. "I really should get to the lab."

He stood up, and for the first time noticed the T-shirt Caddie was wearing. Something about it was familiar, but it took him a moment to realize what it was. "Johnny's Pizza," he said. "That's the place a few blocks away. I've ordered from them."

Caddie, still not looking at him, said, "That's where I ate last night."

"And you bought a shirt?" said Ben, puzzled. "Why would you want a T-shirt from a pizza place?"

Caddie looked at him. "It's kitschy," she said. "Retro. I like it."

"It looks awfully big," Ben remarked. "Didn't they have your size?"

Caddie said nothing. Ben let the subject go. Probably it was just the latest style, like those ridiculous baggy pants so many of the boys in town wore, walking with their legs spread and their hands in their crotches just to keep them from falling down. And, really, what Caddie wore was the least of his problems as far as he was concerned.

"Okay," he said. "Well, I guess I'm off." He reached into his back pocket, pulled out his wallet, and opened it. "I'm afraid there's not much here to eat," he said. "But there's a Safeway. You must have seen it when you were walking. You can pick something up there." He handed Caddie two twenties. When she didn't take them, he let them fall to the table. "And tonight we will have dinner together," Ben said.

He left her there, still sipping her black coffee, and went out the front door. As he got into his old Volvo, he had the simultaneously relieving and unsettling feeling that he was escaping. *Or running away,* he thought as he started the car. *You could stay and talk to her.* He put the car in gear and backed out before he could listen to his own advice.

Inside, Caddie listened to her father leave. She, too, was relieved. Simply making an appearance at breakfast had been a major concession on her part. No, not a concession, a necessity. Not being there for dinner the night before had been risky, riskier because she hadn't returned to the house until after midnight. She'd half expected her father to be waiting up for her, ready for a fight. When she'd discovered the house dark and her father asleep in his room, she'd almost been disappointed.

But the incident with the T-shirt made up for it. That, she hoped, would give her father something to worry about all day. If, that was, he even understood the truth behind her vague replies. Her mother would have, would have known instantly that no girl with an ounce of self-respect would wear something so hideous, that the T-shirt was merely a symbol for something much bigger, for an act of rebellion that demanded confrontation.

Her father, though, had said nothing. Was it possible he truly believed she would buy and wear a shirt like that? Did he not see that it was too large on her not by design but because it had once been worn on a bigger body, a male body that had shaped it into its current shape? He had to have. Surely he couldn't be that clueless.

She imagined him driving to work, thinking about what she might have been doing instead of having dinner with him. She hoped he was. She hoped, too, that his imaginings came close to the truth.

She lifted the collar of the shirt and raised it over her nose. Breathing in, she smelled the faint remnants of pot smoke. She smelled, too, the sweat-musk of Nick's body mixed with some kind of cheap cologne. She remembered the saltiness of his neck where her lips had grazed the skin, the way his hair had crackled, gel hardened, under her fingers.

Another woman would have sensed all of this in the way she wore Nick's shirt. Like a high school ring wrapped with yarn to make it fit over a slender finger, the shirt was a trophy, a skin claimed in victory after a victorious hunt. Not that she'd had to beg Nick for it; she'd simply not given it back to him. Made sleepy by the pot and his orgasm, he hadn't even noticed. She'd left him in his bed with promises to come see him again.

She would keep the promise, she decided. This realization surprised her. She'd intended Nick to be a momentary distraction, a source of irritation to her father and proof that she couldn't be controlled. But she found that she liked him, or at least liked something about having him at her disposal. If nothing else, he was a source of fairly good pot. She'd taken some of that, too, along with the shirt.

Ultimately he would be a disappointment. They always were. But at least this time she expected nothing. Not like she had with some of the others, even though she should have known better, even though she'd been warned by friends and by her own sense of self-preservation not to get too close. Those hurts had surprised her, caught her off guard and rendered her vulnerable. But this time she knew what she was doing.

She got up and poured what was left of her coffee down the drain. It had left a bitter taste in her throat, and she asked herself why she had insisted on drinking it at all. She didn't even like coffee. She'd done it hoping to annoy her father, although she couldn't remember now why she thought something so mundane would raise his ire.

She opened the refrigerator. With the orange juice gone, it contained very little: a carton of half-and-half almost certainly well beyond safe usage, a piece of cheese mummified in plastic wrap, a container of something unpleasant in both appearance and odor that she suspected belonged not in the refrigerator but in her father's lab. She wondered where he'd gotten the eggs for his failed attempts at eggs in a hat, then decided she didn't want to know the answer.

Closing the door, she returned to her room. She opened the little bag of pot she'd stolen from Nick and expertly rolled herself a joint. It was better than the one he'd made for them last night, and she lit it with a feeling of accomplishment and superiority. She allowed herself to smoke half of it before stubbing it out and putting the remainder back in the bag. She felt light, but not out of it.

Her shower was a delight. She luxuriated in the hot water, soaping her skin and removing the traces of the previous night, knowing that they could be reapplied at any time if she so chose. Then she washed her hair, twice, deciding that she would let it dry naturally so that the curl was tighter.

By the time she was dressed in shorts and a tank top, she was ravenous. Returning to the kitchen, she picked up the money from the table, tucked it into her pocket, and walked out into the morning sunshine. Already the children, by now familiar to her, were playing at some silly game, one of them wearing a towel as a cape and, on her head, a plastic tiara. They stared at Caddie as she walked past them, and she rewarded them with a little wave.

In the bright light of day, the town held no more appeal for her than it had in the more flattering illumination of evening. If anything, it was uglier, the sun revealing the faded, worn faces of the buildings and making her squint unattractively. She wished she'd brought her sunglasses, and made a mental note to pick some up as quickly as possible.

At ten in the morning, Johnny's Pizza was already a hive of activity, which at first surprised Caddie until she realized that in addition to pizza, the shop also sold doughnuts. Judging from the steady stream of customers entering and leaving, they did a brisk business. As she passed the shop's front window she glanced inside, looking for Nick.

He was behind the counter, wearing the same apron as the day before over a new T-shirt. She thought about going in, then decided against it. She didn't want him to get his hopes up. Better to let him wonder if he would really ever see her again. Walking quickly past the restaurant, she kept going.

She got breakfast at Denny's, wolfing down an order of pancakes and bacon, surprised at her hunger. When finally she felt full, and not a little sick, she paid using one of the twenties and then walked half a block to a drugstore, where she purchased a pair of cheap sunglasses and a bottle of Diet Coke.

Back outside, she had no idea what to do next, and so found herself wandering along with the crowd of tourists that seemed to grow thicker as she followed signs pointing toward Cannery Row. What, she wondered, drew so many people there? What could possibly be so exciting?

She elected not to find out. Whatever it was, it interested her not at all. History wasn't her thing. It was, well, old. Old and boring. She didn't care about the past, only the future, even though, at the moment, she had no idea what hers held. She was free to do as she pleased.

Without purpose or direction, she simply walked. This was something of a novelty for her as, per the song by that new-wave band they played on KISS FM but whose name she never remembered, nobody walked in L.A. Not that she found the experience particularly enjoyable. If anything, it merely reminded her that she was without a car. Her father, apparently, didn't consider this a handicap, as he hadn't offered her the use of his or suggested any alternative.

When she grew tired of walking by the same stores (or at least they all looked the same to her), she turned around. Glancing at her watch, she saw that barely an hour had gone by. This seemed to her impossible, as her journey felt interminable, especially as it had resulted in the discovery of nothing of interest. But it was true. It was just after eleven, too early for lunch, and yet her day already felt as if it were over.

She sat on a nearby bench and considered her situation. Was this to be the routine of the rest of the summer? If so, she would be forced to kill herself. There was no way she was going to survive. She opened the Diet Coke, now warm and unsatisfying, and drank as much as she could stand. Then, turning her head, she looked back the way she had come. It was all uphill. She'd neglected to notice that. Now, faced with the thought of the climb back to her father's house, she was exhausted. Even the potential distraction provided by Nick didn't cheer her. She needed something more than that. But what that might be—and where she would find it—she couldn't even begin to imagine.

CHAPTER 9

"Where are the fish count reports I asked you to print out from that Channel Islands trip in March?" Ben looked into the bewildered face of the young grad student.

She shook her head. "You never asked me to print those out," she said.

"I did!" Ben thundered. "Christ, am I the only one who gets anything done around here?"

He went into his office and slammed the door. Immediately, he was sorry. He hadn't meant to yell at Angela like that. He hadn't meant to yell at all. And the fish count reports weren't important anyway, at least not at the moment. The sheephead population of San Clemente Island was going to be the same whether he had the report or not; all that mattered was that they were declining.

He leaned back in his chair and sighed deeply. What was he going to do with Caddie? Why should he have to do *anything* with her? It was like Carol had just dumped her on him with no instruction manual. How was he supposed to know how to be a father when he had no real experience at it, at least not with a child Caddie's age.

He looked at the telephone. He wanted to call Carol, to tell her to come back and take Caddie home with her. Barring that, he wanted her to tell him what to do. She was good at that; why couldn't she do it now? Maybe if he asked, he thought, she would give him some advice.

He reached for the phone, but drew his hand back as if, like the pan that morning, it would burn him. He couldn't call Carol. That would just prove to her that he was incompetent, which he knew full well she already believed anyway. And right now he couldn't say he didn't agree with her.

He looked at the framed print hanging on the wall across from his desk. It was an antique image—torn from some outdated scientific journal published who knew when—of a sea cucumber. The artist's rendering, although not entirely accurate, was nonetheless beautiful. The animal was shown in cross section, its innards painted in completely unrealistic reds and purples, the intestine that composed most of the body looping around on itself in graceful coils, while the feather-like respiratory organs were done in blue, presumably due to their association with breathing. The cucumber's skin was depicted in mottled browns, the most authentic aspect of the painting. Ben had always assumed that was because the outside of the creature was the only part actually seen firsthand by the artist.

Carol had given him the picture upon his graduation with his doctorate from UC Santa Barbara. It had cost her more than she could then afford, and he had been touched by the gesture. The print had hung in every office he'd since inhabited, a reminder to him of what had attracted him to marine biology in the first place, the deceptive simplicity of the ocean's creatures.

How easy it was to understand how a sea cucumber worked. Essentially a bag containing digestive, respiratory, and reproductive organs, it ingested food, processed it, and shat it out. The cucumber had no worries save eating and not being eaten. It didn't question its place in the order of things or have to negotiate the land mines of interpersonal relationships. Even its mating was offhand, involving the releasing of ova or spermatozoa into the surrounding water and letting someone else worry about it.

He longed for a diagram of Caddie, some neatly labeled chart that would point out the salient details and make understanding her a matter of memorization. He didn't mind study, or even research, but understanding something as complex as a sixteen-year-old girl apparently seemed to be beyond his capabilities.

A knock at the door interrupted his thinking. "Come in," he called out, and Angela entered, holding something out.

"The reports," she said.

"Thank you," Ben said kindly, hoping his tone would pass for an apology.

Angela nodded and turned to go. Ben stopped her. "Angela, can I ask you something?"

The young woman turned. How old was she? Ben wondered. Probably twenty-two or twenty-three. Still young. "Sure," she said.

Ben motioned to the chair in front of his desk. "Sit down," he said.

"Is something wrong, Dr. Ransome?" the girl asked as she took a seat in the chair.

"No," Ben reassured her. "I just want to ask you something." He hesitated while he thought about how to frame his question. "What do girls want?" he said finally.

"Sorry?" asked Angela, looking taken aback.

Ben, replaying in his mind what he thought was a clearly posed question, realized his mistake. "No," he said. "I didn't mean it that way. It's just that my daughter—"

"You have a daughter?" interrupted Angela.

Ben paused, seeing the look of surprise on the young woman's face. How long had he known her? A year now? Well, yes, he supposed the news that he had a child might come as a surprise. "Yes," he said. "She's staying with me for the summer."

Angela nodded, although astonishment remained in her eyes.

"She's sixteen," Ben continued. "And I don't understand her."

He stopped speaking. Angela continued to stare at him. When he didn't say anything further, she said, "Is that all?"

"Yes," said Ben. "I think so."

Angela laughed. "If she's sixteen, that pretty much explains it," she said. "No one understands you when you're sixteen. Did your parents understand you at that age?"

Ben thought back. At sixteen, he had been a shy, awkward boy, given to spending long hours alone in his room. His parents had seldom asked him anything about himself, and it had never occurred to him that they might want to know anything. "I don't know," he said.

"Well, I bet they didn't," said Angela. "I know mine didn't. At sixteen I was going through this phase where I wanted to be a militant animal rights activist. I put a big MEAT IS MURDER sign on the refrigerator. I told my mother that her eyeliner was responsible for the painful deaths of millions of innocent bunnies, and I wouldn't wear anything that was made out of leather. In short, I was a pain in the ass."

"How long did it last?" Ben asked hopefully.

Angela shrugged. "About six months," she said. "Then I fell in love with a guy who wore a motorcycle jacket and lived on hamburgers, and I reevaluated my stance."

Ben didn't know whether he was supposed to find that funny or not, so he just said, "Thank you."

Angela stood to go. "I know I didn't really answer your question," she said. "You know, about what girls want. If it helps any, she probably doesn't know what she wants either."

With Angela gone, Ben began to worry the question of Caddie again, like a determined dog struggling with a rope. Despite Angela's reassurance, he still believed there must be some way to understand his daughter. After all, weren't they composed of the same DNA? Weren't the genetic codes that programmed her responses at least partially the same as his?

He decided to go out. The air in the office was too close. He couldn't breathe. He'd never liked being inside; now he found it completely unbearable.

He felt better once he was breathing open air. The sun was warm, and walking gave him purpose, even if he was going nowhere in particular. He headed, by both habit and the position of the lab, toward the Monterey Bay Aquarium. It was a trip he made often, and his feet carried him there the way a horse's always returned him to his own feed trough.

The tourists annoyed him, even though he recognized their importance to the local economy, and particularly to the continued financial health of the aquarium. Still, their aimless waddling and tendency to walk four abreast, their baby strollers and the maps clutched in their hands as they looked for local landmarks, made him despise them. If one, sensing that he lived there, asked him for directions, he always politely answered, all the while wishing they would just go home and leave him in peace.

Ahead of him, a clutch of Japanese tourists stood in a confused knot, half pointing in one direction and half in the other. One of them caught his eye, and he quickly crossed the street, leaving her to get directions from someone else.

He passed the aquarium, knowing that going in at this, the busiest time, would make him wish for the destruction of all mankind. Instead, he walked swiftly down Cannery Row until the crowds thinned and the air felt less suffused with the intolerable stupidity of people on summer vacation.

He walked until he came to San Carlos Beach, where he paused to watch the divers entering and leaving the water. He had more tolerance for them because he was one of them. Even so, he found himself wishing there were fewer of them, or at least fewer of the ones for whom the ocean was nothing more than a playground.

On the beach, a dive instructor was leading a group of six wet-suited bodies into the surf, demonstrating the proper way to enter the ocean in the presence of moderate surf. The students followed, stiff-armed and awkward, their backs to the ocean and their fins slapping the wet sand. How many of those fins, he wondered, would soon be kicking up the sea floor, disturbing the homes of untold numbers of small animals?

He wondered, too, how many of the divers who used the beach knew of its other name, the Edward F. Ricketts Marine Reserve, or, if they did, knew who Ricketts was. Then again, how many of them knew that San Carlos Beach got its name from the San Carlos Canning Company, one of the area's largest and most profitable operations at the height of the sardine-packing industry? Mysteriously burned to the ground (as were many of the canneries when the boom ended due to overfishing) in 1956, all that remained of the San Carlos Canning Company were the beach that bore its name and several intake pipes that still stretched out into the sea.

The establishment of the Ricketts Marine Reserve was the work of several dedicated local divers who wanted to save the area both from overfishing and the planned erection of a gold museum. Surprisingly, it had been a difficult battle, with even the aquarium and Ben's own Hopkins Marine Station fearing that imposing restrictions on usage would limit their access to the area. Ultimately, though, the measure passed.

And Ben approved of it. There were enough places along the coast where divers interested in hunting could spear game; it was good to have one place that was off-limits. Even the clumsy feet of beginning divers were preferable to fishhooks and those who were interested only in how many pounds of fish they could remove from the water.

He walked the length of the beach, ending at the Coast Guard pier. The sound of sea lions barking greeted his ears, followed quickly by the ripe scent of their excretions. It had been a particularly fertile year for sea lion pups, and the water was full of them, splashing and jockeying for position within their established society. He stood and watched as two whiskered young males spun in the water, playing some game known only to them, chasing one another between the pilings while an older bull, feigning disinterest, sat on the deck of an unused fishing boat sunning himself.

"Damn sea lions. Eat all the fish."

Ben turned around to see who had spoken. On the other side of the pier, the side facing the beach, a man stood with a young boy. Both held fishing rods, and the man was helping the boy bait his hook. The man looked once more at the sea lions and scowled.

"Like this," he told the boy, who couldn't have been more than eight years old. The man took the boy's rod and, hanging it over the edge of the wall, dropped the baited hook into the water. He handed the boy the rod and began baiting his own hook.

"If you feel something pull, then you tug," he instructed the boy.

Ben walked over, pretending to look out at the water. "What are you fishing for?" he asked casually.

"Rockfish, mostly," the man answered, flinging his hook into the water, where it sank directly over a group of divers who were making their way along the edge of the Breakwater.

"You know, the rockfish here are pretty small," Ben said, trying to keep the anger out of his voice.

"They're big enough," said the man. "I've been fishing here since I was a kid. I don't see 'em getting any smaller."

"Look," Ben said. "This is a marine reserve. You're not supposed to fish here."

The man groaned. "Oh Christ," he said. "Here we go again. Look, Mack, why don't you mind your own business. You and I both know that no-fishing bullshit isn't enforceable. It's just something the city passed to keep you hippies happy."

"Hippies," Ben repeated. "Right. Maybe forty years ago those of us intelligent enough to know that conservation is a necessity would be hippies. Today, though, we're scientists. I happen to be a marine biologist."

"A hippie with a degree," the man said, and laughed. Beside him, his son laughed too, although nervously. "Like a fish or two makes a difference."

"Multiply a fish or two by five thousand assholes like yourself, and that's a lot of fish," said Ben.

The man snapped around. "Who you calling an asshole, buddy?"

"Do you know why there are no more canneries here?" Ben asked him, ignoring the question. "Because people assumed the fish would last forever. Well, they didn't. In something around thirty years, they took pretty much every last sardine out of these waters. It's taken the last fifty to get the levels back up to where they were."

"Maybe," the man said. "But they're back, right?"

"You're missing the point," said Ben.

"No, you're missing the point," the man argued. "I've been fishing here for forty years. My father fished here for seventy-three years. And my son is going to fish here whether you like it or not. Got it?"

Ben stared him down, debating what to do next. He knew he could call the local police. He'd done it before after catching two men spearfishing for lingcod off the beach. But the man was right; there wasn't much the local authorities could do. If he really wanted action, he would have to call in Fish & Game, and those boys more often than not sided with the local fishermen, most of whom were their friends.

"Fuck you," he said finally.

The little boy looked at him, his mouth hanging open in shock. Ben doubted it was the first time the kid had heard the word used, but he bet he'd never heard it directed at his father and, indirectly, at himself. He looked genuinely hurt. Ben kept his eyes on the father. "Fuck you," he said again. "Asshole."

He walked away as the man called after him, "No. Fuck *you!*"

He almost wished the man would attack him, use his fists instead of his mouth. Then Ben could fight back and, maybe, not feel completely helpless. Part of him wanted to hit the ignorant son of a bitch, maybe even push him off the pier in front of his kid.

He knew he was being childish, but he couldn't stop himself. Anger raged in him like a fire looking for a way out of a sealed building. He hated the man—all men like him—every man who thought it was his right to do as he pleased simply because he'd always done so. Thoughtless men, every last one of them, who honestly believed that their desire to live a certain way was more important than protecting the world's resources. Who told the forefathers of these men, when they first decided to become fishermen or crabbers or whatever, that their sons and grandsons and great-grandsons were owed some debt payable by the sea? Who told them that they had a right to take, even when they took too much? And how dare they be offended when the ocean refused to give them any more.

He had no sympathy. Turning, he once again faced the fisherman and his son. "I hope you get anisakiasis!" he shouted. The two of them stared at him, uncomprehending, and he gave them the finger before moving on.

As he reached the end of the pier, he encountered the dive instructor coming back with his students. The man, seeing Ben, held out his hand. In it were two hooks, still baited, several inches of line trailing from them. "Score one for the rockfish," he said, winking at Ben.

Ben began to chuckle. He imagined the expression on the man's face when he pulled his empty line up. He would just get another hook, some more bait. Still, it made Ben happy. Sometimes life surprised you in a good way, he thought, trying to remember why he'd needed to get out of his office in the first place.

CHAPTER 10

"So I says to her, I says, 'Since when did the county go and make you alcohol commissioner?' And she stands there gawkin' at me like I just told her she could go to Hell." Tom laughed. "You shoulda seen it, Charlie."

Charlie, grunting beneath the weight of the hundred-pound bag he was carrying, said nothing. But Tom didn't notice.

"If a man wants to have two or three beers after a day's work, who's a woman to say he can't?" he asked as he walked beside Charlie through the crossover between the Pacific Coast Cannery's processing house on the bay side of the Row and the warehouse on the other. Below them the street was filled with traffic, both human and motorized, and all around them was the stink of fish.

Adjusting the sack of sardines on his shoulder, Charlie listened as Tom laid out, in rehearsed detail, the sins committed by his wife. Charlie had never met Alice, but he had a definite picture of her. She was tall, thin as a pike, with light brown hair and a pinched face that looked like she always had the smell of vinegar in her nose. They were going on eleven years as husband and wife, and by now, Charlie assumed, they were so used to one another that there was no reason to stop.

They came to the warehouse and dropped their sacks, adding them to the pile that would be loaded onto the *southbound train that afternoon, headed for Los Angeles. It was a great stinking pyramid of fish, a monument to the industry of man, and Charlie wished more than anything that he had never been conscripted to help build it. Someone had told him once that the pyramids in Egypt had been built by thousands of slaves working for a hundred years. He knew how those men must have felt, and he guessed they probably hated those blocks of sandstone pretty much as well as he hated sardines.*

"When you boys get done admiring your work, maybe you can git yourselves back across that bridge and bring back a couple a more bags."

Even if he didn't know the voice, Charlie would have known by the smell of cigar smoke who was speaking to him. Even when he didn't have one in his mouth, Shiny Tickson smelled like burning tobacco. People said it was because his mother smoked so much when she was pregnant with him, it got into his blood and stayed there, and Charlie didn't doubt it. Shiny stank of the stuff to the point where it competed with the smell from the canneries, which was saying something.

"Ease up, Shiny," Tom said. "Train won't be here for another three hours."

"That ain't the point," said Shiny. "Point is, I ain't paying you two to stand around admiring your handiwork. Now git back there."

Shiny turned and waddled off, taking his cigar smell with him. Watching him go, Tom said, "One of these days I'm going to sock him right in the mouth. Bet you a dollar it will be before the end of the week."

Charlie started back toward the crossover. Tom waited a second, then walked fast to catch up with him.

"What's eatin' you today?" he asked Charlie. "You been quiet all morning. You sick?"

"No," Charlie said. "Just tired."

Tom put his hand on Charlie's back. Charlie tensed. Then he walked faster, so that Tom's hand fell off of its own accord. "Got to get them sacks moved," Charlie said.

"You sound like Shiny," said Tom. "Better watch out. Next thing you know, you'll be a supervisor and I'll have to start hating you instead a him."

Charlie said nothing. He just walked faster, toward the mouth of the cannery that belched its fish breath in his face.

Hudson looked up. The crossovers that had once connected the canneries with their warehouses were still there, at least a few of them. He imagined what it must have been like when the canneries were operating at full force; the billowing clouds of steam, the whistles—each with its own distinct pitch—calling the workers in whenever a new shipload of sardines arrived, every single thing suffused with the odor of fish being processed. It must have been like walking through hell, but it must also have been beautiful. He wished he could see it for himself.

He closed his eyes and pictured Charlie and Tom. He saw them clearly. Tom, short and thin, dark haired and dark eyed, alert as a terrier and always dreaming. And Charlie, taller and more solid, his coloring lighter and his mood quieter. Charlie, who washed his overalls nightly despite knowing that he would never rid them of the smell of his work but who tried anyway.

Over the past year, the two men had come to be very real to Hudson. He heard their voices when he read. He knew the cadence of their speech, the peculiar dropping of letters or drawing out of words that distinguished them from one another. He heard their footsteps as they walked overhead, traversing the crossover day after day.

In some ways, the two of them were more real to him than the people with whom he interacted in his own life. He'd invested so much time in them, so much wishing and hoping, that they had taken on nearly supernatural importance. Like most faithful, he longed for the objects of his adoration to be real, or at least for what he believed to be true to prove itself indisputably.

Marty, trying to rile him into argument, had once said, "Isn't the whole point of faith that you can never actually prove it to be true?" Perhaps what he felt for Charlie and Tom wasn't faith, then, but merely hope. Either way, he wanted to be right about them. He *needed* to be right about them, not just for what it would mean to him professionally, but because after so much time with them, he wanted them to be who he thought them to be.

He looked at his watch. It was twelve-fifteen. If he didn't hurry, he was going to be late. Returning to his car, he read the directions he'd scribbled down earlier and set off. Ten minutes later, he pulled into the driveway of a small house where a woman stood in the open doorway holding a fawn-colored pug.

She set the dog down, and as Hudson got out of the car, the dog raced up to him, snuffling. It stopped in front of him, cocked its head, and barked once, its little spring of a tail shaking happily. Hudson knelt and held out his hand, and the dog sniffed it briefly before putting his front paws on Hudson's leg and looking up into his face.

"You must be Boswell," Hudson said. The dog snorted and turned, scampering back to the porch. Hudson followed him. "And you must be Janice," he said, addressing the woman, who held out her hand.

"Hi," she said. "Come on in."

They entered the house, where several suitcases were stacked near the door. A woman appeared carrying two more. "Is there anything you're not taking?" she remarked.

"Renata, this is Hudson," said Janice.

"We're so relieved you're staying here," Renata said. "Usually one of my TAs does it, but for some reason this year they all actually have lives and are gone for the summer."

"I'm the one who should thank you," said Hudson. "I could never have come if I had to pay for a hotel."

"Marty said you're here working on something to do with Steinbeck," said Janice.

"Yes," Hudson answered. "At least I think it has something to do with him. I'm not sure yet." He knew Janice was hoping he'd say more about his project, but he'd already told her more than most people knew about it.

"Don't grill him, honey," Renata said. She turned to Hudson. "You'll have to forgive her. She's not an academic."

Janice rolled her eyes. "More ivory tower intrigue, I suppose," she said.

Renata put her arms around Janice and kissed her on the cheek. "You have no idea how lucky you are to have a real job," she said.

"Well, one of us has to," replied Janice, feigning irritation. "How else could we afford this lavish adventure?"

Renata laughed. "She means how else could we afford to spend four weeks in Ohio fixing up my dead grandmother's house?" she said to Hudson. She gave Janice a squeeze. "You'll be happy when we sell it and make a killing," she told her.

"This is what I get for letting her watch too much Learning Channel," she quipped.

"Why don't you show Hudson around while I load up the car," Renata suggested.

Janice, with Boswell at her heels, gave Hudson a quick tour of the house. "There's not much to tell you," she said. "The washer and dryer are in the basement. Use whatever you want. Don't burn the place down. That's pretty much it. You have all our numbers if you need anything. Any questions?"

Hudson shook his head. "I don't think so," he said.

"I'm sorry we can't leave the car," said Janice. "Renata doesn't want to fly with Boswell, so we're driving. To Ohio," she added, as if she'd just realized where they were going. She closed her eyes and sighed. "And both of them get carsick."

Hudson stifled a laugh.

"I'd better leave before I think better of it," said Janice, walking back into the living room. She picked up Boswell and walked outside. Hudson followed, standing on the porch. Renata, closing the trunk, waved and got in. Janice gave one last look at the house.

"It will be fine," Hudson reassured her.

After they left he waited twenty minutes in case they came back for something they forgot, then brought his bags inside. Taking them upstairs, he considered staying in the master bedroom, as Janice had told him he could, then opted for the smaller guest bedroom. He unpacked quickly, not having brought all that many clothes, then returned to the downstairs.

The house had a sunporch, a small screened-in room off the kitchen. It contained a comfortably sagging couch, which from the amount of dog hair on it looked as if it doubled as Boswell's bed. Sitting on it, Hudson opened his briefcase and removed the manuscript and several books, which he set on the table in front of him. In addition to a biography of John Steinbeck, he'd also brought his well-read and battered copies of *Cannery Row* and its sequel, *Sweet Thursday*.

These he stacked on top of each other, so that the books formed a little tower beside the manuscript.

He looked around the room. He still couldn't quite believe that
he'd lucked into the house-sitting opportunity. Renata and Janice were
friends of Marty's, their relationship stretching back to when all three
were undergrads. The phone call from Renata bemoaning their lack of
trustworthy sitters had come in the midst of Hudson's deep depres-
sion over not having the finances to fund a trip to California. Marty had
solved both of their problems within seconds.

And now here he was. He still couldn't quite believe it, and part of
him kept expecting something to bring it all crashing down. He'd
found out about the opportunity only three weeks ago, and he'd spent
the intervening time worrying that Renata and Janice would break up,
or that the dead grandmother would miraculously be resurrected, or
even that Ohio would for some reason secede from the United States
and refuse entry to outsiders. But none of these things had happened
(although he supposed they still could), and he had the house to himself.

With nothing now impeding his progress, he was surprisingly unsure of how to proceed. He had ideas, of course, leads and starting
points and possible connections. But suddenly he found himself reluctant to take advantage of any of them. *What if I'm wrong?* he thought,
voicing the question that had lurked from the beginning beneath the
surface of his theory.

There was always the possibility. And when he was honest about it,
he knew that it was more than a possibility; it was a likelihood. The
chances of his being right about the manuscript, its author, its possible
origins, were small. Yet he'd never given up believing, despite having
no concrete evidence to support his claim. Now that he had a chance
to establish proof, he found his resolve wavering, and it all came down
to one simple truth: he didn't want to be wrong.

As he always did when he found himself uneasy about his work, he
took up the manuscript. Just holding it, he felt himself calming, his
doubts ebbing away. It was the manuscript that gave him hope. He
took strength from it the way he might take heat from a fire to drive
away a chill. It was the source of everything, at least everything that
mattered to him at that moment. He opened it and let the story
soothe him.

"Come on," Tom said. "Let's get us some beer."

Charlie opened his mouth to decline the invitation, but found himself saying, "All right."

Tom clapped him on the shoulder and steered him up the street to the bar, which was full of men exactly like themselves. Their shift over, they'd gathered to talk, as if all day their minds had been under the control of the canneries and only now were their thoughts and words their own.

Tom drank one whole beer before he spoke again. When he did it was to say, "Give me another." Charlie, still nursing his first, wrapped his hand around the cold bottle and wished he'd said no to Tom.

"I think I'll just head home," he said.

Tom shook his head. "Nope," he said. "It's not right to let a friend get drunk by himself. Next thing you know, I'll be making a visit to the cathouse and spending all my money on one of them girls. It's your duty to stop me, Charlie."

"Those girls'd take one smell of you and send you packing," said a man to their right. "Not enough silver in your pocket to make a girl put up with that."

"Say!" cried Tom. "Who are you to talk? You stink just as high as I do!"

"Didn't say I didn't," said the man. "Just said."

"Well, you best unsay it fore I pop you one," Tom said. "No man tells me I stink too much for some cathouse girl."

The man was bigger than Tom by at least a head and a half, an Irishman by the look of him. He fixed Tom with one dark eye and grinned, showing the gaps in his teeth. "You want to fight me, Tiny?" he said.

"Damn right I do!" Tom said.

The man stood up. "All right then," he said. "Why don't we just step—"

Before he could finish, Tom hit him on the chin. The man fell back, caught by the man behind him. He hung there in the fellow's arms for a second, looking surprised, then let out a roar like a bull when the brand touches his flank.

It all happened faster than Charlie could take it in. The big man stepped forward. Tom tried to hit him again, but this time the Irishman got to him first. Charlie saw him raise his fist, and then Tom was flying backwards. He hit the floor hard and just lay there, staring up at the ceiling as if maybe he was dead. A couple of people crowded around him, looking down at him and waiting for him to move.

Charlie went over to his friend. Tom's eyes were open, and there was blood coming out of his nose, but he was stunned. Then all of a sudden it was like the breath came back to him. He took a big gulp of air, sat up straight as a board, and said, "Jesus Christ! Where's that damn son-of-a-bitch?"

He tried to stand up, but Charlie stopped him. Tom beat against him with his fists, hollering about how he was going to kill the Mick, but the man had already forgotten about him. Before Tom could get himself killed, Charlie wrestled him out the door and into the street.

"Why'd you do that?" Tom said. "Why didn't you let me at him?"

Charlie looked at him. He looked wounded, both in body and spirit. Charlie knew that Tom believed he could take the Irishman. He believed it with all of his heart. And that made Charlie want to keep him out of the fight even more. He didn't want to see him learn he couldn't.

"Come on," he said. "You showed him well enough."

He started walking. After a moment, Tom came too. He walked quietly, his hands stuffed in the pockets of his overalls. After a few minutes he started laughing.

"I guess I did at that," he said. "I guess I did show him. How about that?"

Charlie didn't look at him. "Sure," he said. "How about that?"

CHAPTER 11

Faced with the long walk home, Caddie decided instead to visit Nick at the pizza parlor, her plan to leave him hanging for a day or two outweighed by her aversion to getting any hotter and sweatier. Besides, she reasoned, it would give her a chance to rest before the final push back to the house.

Still, she was overheated when she reached Johnny's. Her hair felt frizzy instead of curly, although a quick glance in a store window reassured her that she still looked presentable. Besides, guys rarely noticed the things that to girls were a matter of social life and death. Nick, she knew, would be thrilled just to see her.

She entered the restaurant and paused, letting her eyes adjust to the change in light. When she removed her sunglasses, she saw that Nick was at the counter talking to a customer, a girl about her own age. Caddie walked up to them.

"Hey, Nick," she said.

Nick glanced up, and Caddie saw an unexpected expression on his face, a momentary lack of emotion, as if he was trying to place where he had seen her. Then he smiled. "Caddie. Hey."

The girl turned to look at Caddie. She was pretty, with short dark hair and skin that, early in the summer, still looked as if she'd spent months in the sun. Caddie envied her.

"Caddie," Nick said. "This is Nicole. My girlfriend."

Caddie, who had started to smile at the girl, found her mouth freezing in what she was sure was a grimace. Had she heard Nick correctly? Had he said Nicole was his girlfriend?

"Hi," Nicole said, apparently oblivious to the emotional upheaval taking place in Caddie's mind.

"Caddie's visiting her dad for the summer," Nick said, talking quickly and shooting glances at Caddie.

"Cool," said Nicole. "Are you having fun?"

Caddie, for whom time had slowed immeasurably, stared at her for a moment while she processed the question. Then she nodded. "Yeah," she said. She looked at Nick. "I've met some really great people."

Nick's eyes widened, as if he was begging Caddie not to say anything. Caddie turned away from him and faced Nicole, who said, "People here are really friendly."

"Caddie came in last night," Nick said, although Nicole had asked for no explanation of their acquaintance. "You know, while you were visiting your sister in Salinas," he added, as if maybe she'd forgotten.

That's why he was able to have me over, Caddie thought. "Nick was nice enough to show me around town," she added.

"Isn't it pretty?" said Nicole. "Where are you from?"

"L.A.," Caddie answered.

"Then this probably seems like practically the country to you," Nicole remarked. "I grew up here, so I don't know anywhere else, really."

Nick said nothing, wiping the counter needlessly with a towel while Caddie tried to decide in which direction to take the conversation. Before she could make up her mind, Nicole said, "Are you getting anything? I was just about to have some lunch."

Caddie didn't even have to look at Nick to feel him begging her to say no. "That would be great," she said.

A few minutes later, seated at a table while Nick watched them anxiously from the kitchen, Caddie continued her conversation with his girlfriend. She found herself fascinated by Nicole's apparent inability to sense the tension in the room. *Or maybe she just doesn't want to know,* she thought. She could understand that.

"How long have you and Nick been together?" she asked between bites of pizza.

"God," replied Nicole. "Forever. Since seventh or eighth grade."

"You're kidding," Caddie said.

Nicole shook her head. "We broke up a few times. You know, like you do when you're a kid. But we've pretty much been together for seven years now."

"Unbelievable," said Caddie. "I didn't think anybody still did that." She thought about it. Seven years. That was about how long her parents had been married. Nick and Nicole (how way too cute was that?) had already bested them.

"Want to know something else?" said Nicole, smiling. She leaned closer to Caddie. "We're the only ones each other have done it with."

Caddie found herself embarrassed for the other girl, not just because she knew that in Nick's case this was a lie, but because Nicole seemed to think this was something to be proud of. "You've never slept with another guy?" she said.

Nicole shook her head. "Just Nick," she said. "What about you?"

For a moment Caddie thought Nicole was asking her if she'd slept with Nick. Then she realized she was just asking about the presence of any kind of boyfriend in her life. "No," she said. "I don't have a boyfriend. Not right now, anyway."

"Nick has a brother," Nicole said. "Joey. Really sweet. Maybe we could all go out sometime."

Caddie was having a hard time hating this girl, although she badly wanted to. She was stupid, or at least way too naive for her own good. Nick, Caddie thought, was probably sleeping with every girl in town. Meanwhile, Nicole was undoubtedly planning their wedding. She deserved to know what her boyfriend was really like.

"Nicole," Caddie said. "Don't you ever wonder what it would be like to date different guys?"

"Why?" said Nicole. "Nick's perfect for me. He understands me."

But do you understand him? Caddie thought. Clearly, she didn't. Which was kind of surprising, given that guys were pretty simple. They wanted to sleep with everyone and they didn't want you to care that they did it.

"Yeah, but do you ever think about what else is out there?" Caddie couldn't help pushing the issue a little more.

"I'm happy," Nicole said. "That's really all that matters, right?"

"Maybe it is," said Caddie. "I wouldn't know. I guess I've never been happy."

"That's sad," Nicole said, and when Caddie looked at her, she saw pity in the girl's eyes. Seeing it made her feel queasy. She didn't want pity from anyone, least of all a girl who thought Monterey was Wonderland and that her cheating boyfriend was Prince Charming.

"That came out wrong," Caddie said quickly. "I mean, I've been happy. Just not with any one guy."

"You're still young," Nicole said sagely. "It will happen."

Caddie almost laughed at her. She sounded so old. But what was she, maybe nineteen? She talked as if her whole life were already set in stone. Which, Caddie guessed, it more or less was. She would probably marry Nick, have a couple of kids, and live in Monterey until she died. *But she'll be happy,* she told herself. And she probably would be. Even if she did realize that Nick was an asshole, she'd probably continue to love him just the same. She was that kind of girl, the kind who made her life what she wanted it to be, no matter how much pretending it took.

"I'm so glad we met," Nicole was saying, bringing Caddie's attention back to the conversation. "I don't know why, but I feel like we're going to be friends. Besides, if Nick likes you, I like you. He has good taste."

She laughed at her own joke. Caddie wiped her lips with her napkin, pretending she had too much food in her mouth to respond. She didn't want to be Nicole's friend. In fact, she hoped she never had to see the girl again, although she doubted she'd be able to avoid her forever. Johnny's was pretty much on her way no matter where she walked in Monterey. She was bound to run into Nicole—and Nick—one of these days.

To her dismay, Nicole was waving Nick over to the table. He came and sat down, noticeably moving his chair away from Caddie and closer to his girlfriend. He put his arm around the back of Nicole's chair. "So, what are you two talking about?" he asked.

"You," said Nicole, laying her hand on his knee. "Caddie was telling me how gorgeous she thinks you are, and I was telling her she better keep her hands off you." She looked at Caddie and winked, while Nick paled and scratched his ear nervously.

"Nicole says I should meet your brother," Caddie said.

"Right," Nicole agreed. "Don't you think Joey would like her?"

Nick nodded. "Sure," he said. "I guess."

Nicole slapped his knee. "What's the matter with you?" she asked. "You're acting all weird."

Nick shrugged. "Dad's on my ass," he said. "You know how it is."

"I don't think she does," Caddie remarked under her breath, watching his eyes shift away from her.

Nicole, not hearing her, continued talking. "Well, I think Joey would love her. What are you doing tonight?" she asked Caddie.

"Tonight?" Caddie thought quickly. "Tonight my dad is making dinner for me. Sorry."

Nicole frowned. "Okay, but we're definitely going out sometime this week. Give me your number."

"Actually, I don't even know what it is," Caddie said truthfully. "I didn't bring my cell with me, and I always use speed dial if I have to call my father."

"Well, here's mine," Nicole said, producing a pen from her bag and scribbling on a napkin. She handed it to Caddie. "Now you promise you'll call me."

"Sure," Caddie said, folding the napkin and tucking it into her pocket.

"Excuse me," Nicole said, getting up. "I need to visit the little girls' room."

She left Caddie alone with Nick. As soon as she was out of earshot Caddie said, "You're an asshole."

Nick put his hands up. "I know," he said. "I know."

Caddie waited for him to continue, but he didn't. "That's it?" she said. "You know? How about 'I'm sorry'?"

"I'm sorry," Nick said obediently.

"No, you're not!" Caddie snapped. "You're just horny. And stupid. She's a nice girl. She thinks you love her."

"I do love her," said Nick defensively.

Caddie snorted. "She thinks she's the only girl you've been with."

Nick leaned back in his chair. "What do you want me to say?" he asked her. "We've been together six years."

"Seven," said Caddie.

"Seven years," said Nick. "That's a long time with one girl."

"So break up with her," Caddie suggested. "Don't lie to her."

Nick shook his head. "I can't," he said. "It would break her heart."

Caddie stared at him. "You're something else," she said. "You think you're so wonderful that she wouldn't be able to live without you? Here's a news flash—she's in love with being in love, not with you. And you'd better pray she never figures that out, because then you really will be sorry."

"Thank you, Dr. Phil," Nick cracked. "I was good enough for you, wasn't I?"

"That's the sad thing," Caddie said.

Nick smiled. "Come on," he said. "You liked it as much as I did." He put his elbows on the table and leaned toward her. "And I bet you wouldn't mind doing it again either."

No, I wouldn't, Caddie thought to herself. *And that's even sadder.* But to Nick she said, "You weren't that good. Maybe I should give your brother a try, like Nicole said."

"Hey, I can set it up," said Nick. "Maybe you'd like a Pirelli brothers sandwich."

Nicole, returning from the bathroom, took her seat. "You two planning what we're going to do this week?" she asked.

"I suggested a couple of things," Nick said.

"Anything sound good?" Nicole asked Caddie.

Caddie looked at Nick. "Not so far," she said.

"Well, we'll come up with something," said Nicole. She looked at her watch. "But I've got to get back to work. I'm five minutes late."

She gave Nick a kiss. "Bye, honey," she said. "I'll see you tonight. And I'll see you later," she added to Caddie. "Don't forget—call me."

After Nicole left, Caddie started to get up and leave as well. But Nick stopped her by grabbing her wrist. "I'm not a bad guy," he said. "I may be an asshole, but I'm not a bad guy."

"Why should I care?" Caddie asked him.

"I guess you shouldn't," said Nick, letting go of her arm. "But please, don't tell Nicole."

Caddie let him sweat it out for a long moment. "I won't," she said. "But only because I like her. I still think you're a piece of shit."

She dropped her trash in the garbage and left. Outside, she looked left up the hill toward her father's house and found that she didn't want to go there. She wanted to do something. Finding out that Nick had lied to her was annoying, not because she cared about him but because she'd wanted to be the one who used him. Somehow that hadn't seemed wrong. Now, though, she wondered if it was. Was she any better than he was? She'd had no intention of falling in love with him; she'd just wanted some sex and some more pot. But now she couldn't do it, not because she had any respect for Nick, but because she wanted Nicole to be able to keep living in her fantasy world. *Someone might as well be happy,* she thought.

She found herself walking back toward downtown. The early afternoon sun seemed to have intensified, and she wished she'd applied sunscreen. She was going to burn, and she hated peeling. It made her feel like a leper, and she could never resist picking at the stray pieces of skin. *But maybe that's what I need,* she told herself. *Maybe I need to get out of this skin. Maybe there's a better me underneath this one.*

She crossed the street, moving out of what little shade there was and stepping into the full sun. It caressed her bare shoulders greedily. *Go ahead,* she thought. *Get it over with.*

CHAPTER 12

As Ben walked back toward Hopkins, the rush he'd gotten from cursing at the fisherman faded into mild embarrassment. Yes, it had felt good to vent his frustration, but ultimately it was an adolescent response to the situation. Still, he had to admit that he'd enjoyed himself. After all, he reasoned stubbornly, stupid people required stupid measures. They seldom understood reason.

Oh, who are you kidding, he argued with himself. *You're just making excuses.*

Along with the decrease in satisfaction came the return of the thoughts that had driven him from the office in the first place. He still had no better idea of how to deal with Caddie than he'd had an hour ago. She wasn't stupid; if she were, he would just give up and tolerate her until it was time for her to leave. But she was smart. Too smart, he suspected. That made it all the more difficult. He couldn't fool her with platitudes, or even bribery. He had to try to actually understand her.

He was so deep into his thoughts that he didn't even notice the man standing on the sidewalk until he'd bumped into him. The collision of their bodies, slight as it was, came as a shock. Instinctively, he froze for a moment while his brain ran through the list of possible responses. Perhaps atoning for his earlier rudeness, he opted to apologize. "Pardon me," he said.

"It's okay," the man said. "No harm done. And I shouldn't just be standing here. I was just trying to get a better look."

Ben, not understanding, followed the man's gaze to a plywood wall. "Ricketts's lab," he said, recognizing the place instantly.

"Yes," said the man, sounding pleased. "You know it?"

"Doesn't everybody in Monterey?" Ben replied.

The man laughed. "Not if my experience is typical," he said. "And if they do know what it is, that's all they know. No one can tell me anything about it."

"I guess there's not much to tell," said Ben. "The official name was Pacific Biological Laboratories. Ricketts started it in Pacific Grove in 1923. Moved it here in, I think it was 1928. This was Ocean Avenue then; didn't become Cannery Row until 1958, although everyone called it that anyway. The place burned down in '36 from a fire that started next door at the Del Mar Cannery. He rebuilt and worked here 'til 1948."

"When he died," the man said.

Ben nodded. "Three days before his fifty-first birthday."

"You know a lot about the guy," the man said. "You should give tours."

"You live here long enough, you pick things up," said Ben.

They stood in silence, looking at the wall. Then the man sighed. "I wish I could get inside and take a look," he said. "Do you know why it's boarded up?"

"To keep people out," Ben answered. "It's privately owned now. They only give tours a couple of times a year, usually as part of the Steinbeck hoopla. Actually, the wall isn't usually here. I think they're doing some repair work."

"It's too bad," said the man. "About it being hard to get into, I mean," he clarified. "It seems like all the places from that time are gone."

Ben turned and nodded across the street. "That coffeehouse there, Kalisa's, that's where La Ida Café was," he said. "And the Lone Star brothel, what Steinbeck called the Bear Flag, that was where Mackerel Jack's is now."

The man contemplated the two sites. "Not quite the same, is it?" he remarked.

"Well, Kalisa tries," said Ben. "But I think old Flora Woods would turn over in her grave if she saw her fun house selling T-shirts and plastic otters."

The man laughed. "You're a Steinbeck fan," he said.

"In a roundabout way," said Ben. "I was an Ed Ricketts fan first. Ever since I read *Between Pacific Tides* in school. That led me to the Sea of

Cortez stuff, and then I thought I better check out Steinbeck and see what all the fuss was about."

"Usually it's the other way around," said the man. "People want to know about Ricketts because they read about Doc in the novels."

"Well," said Ben, "I guess writers are more appealing than marine biologists. So what's your interest in the lab?"

"It's not so much the lab as it is the man," the man answered. He looked at Ben. "I'm one of those people who finds himself curious about the real Doc. He was quite an influence on Steinbeck."

"Best friends," Ben said. He looked at the run-down building sitting behind the fence. "Those two needed one another."

"Why do you say that?" asked the man.

"I don't know," Ben answered, finding himself surprised at having made the comment. "That just popped out. But now that I've said it, it's true. I don't think either one would have been the man he was without the other one coming into his life."

The man looked at him. "You're an interesting fellow," he said. "It's been good talking to you, Mister . . ."

"Ransome," Ben said. "Ben Ransome."

"Hudson Jones," the man said, offering his hand. "I appreciate the information. I guess I'm lucky that I bumped into you."

"If I recall," Ben said, "I was the one who did the bumping."

"Well, you've more than made up for it," Hudson told him. "How can I repay you? Maybe a cup of coffee?"

Ben started to protest. Then he thought about returning to his office. He knew he would just sit there and brood. Maybe, he thought, it would do him some good to sit and talk to a complete stranger about something they had in common. If nothing else, it would allow him to put off thinking about Caddie for a little while.

"All right," he said. "I wouldn't mind some coffee. Shall we go to Kalisa's in honor of old Flora?"

"By all means," Hudson agreed.

A minute later they were seated at a small table, their coffee in front of them. Ben took a sip, then methodically added two and a half packets of sugar to it, followed by two-thirds of one small container of creamer.

"Is that the magic formula?" Hudson asked him, watching the procedure.

Ben, stirring the coffee, wasn't sure how to respond. Was the man teasing him? Normally he would think so. But nothing he'd seen about Hudson so far led him to believe the man was one to make fun. Rather than retreat into silence, as he might otherwise do, he found himself making a joke. "I discovered it right after I figured out how to turn lead into gold," he said dryly.

Hudson grinned. "I hope you don't think I was making fun," he said. "It's just that it's so exact."

"Occupational hazard, I guess," Ben said. He noticed that Hudson was waiting for further explanation. "I'm a scientist," he said.

"Oh," said Hudson. "That explains the Ed Ricketts thing too, then. I was wondering about that."

Why didn't you just ask? Ben thought, bemused. "I'm a marine biologist," he told Hudson, saving the man from having to ask any more questions about the subject. "At Hopkins Marine Station."

Hudson nodded, and Ben understood that the man had no idea what Hopkins was. It didn't matter. They weren't there to talk about him anyway.

"I was never good at science," Hudson said. "Once, in chemistry class, I got the beakers mixed up and managed to create some sort of toxic fumes. Well, toxicish. Anyway, they had to evacuate the whole floor. Oh, and I almost failed biology because I wouldn't dissect a frog. My father had to threaten the school with a lawsuit so that they'd let me write a paper instead. I still got a D."

Ben didn't know how to respond to this information. His conversations were generally limited to discussions of field reports and lab findings. It had been a long time since he'd been asked to comment on someone's personal stories. He found himself looking into his coffee cup, unable to think of anything to say.

Hudson saved him by continuing to talk. "English was my thing," he said. "Books. Words. I couldn't for the life of me understand how elements formed compounds or whatever it is they do, but words made sense."

"Which explains the Steinbeck thing," said Ben, referencing Hudson's earlier comment.

"Which explains the Steinbeck thing," Hudson agreed, nodding. "Although I didn't get interested in him until later. When I was a kid it was all Paul Zindel and Madeleine L'Engle. And, of course, Jackie Collins when no one was looking."

"Of course," said Ben, trying to remember if he knew who Jackie Collins was and failing.

"It's funny, isn't it?" Hudson said. "You're Mr. Science and I'm Mr. Words, but we both love Steinbeck."

Ben raised his eyebrows. "I never really thought about it," he said. Then he asked, "Are you here researching something about Steinbeck?"

Hudson looked up at him with an expression that surprised Ben. There was a look in his eyes that was almost feral, on guard, as if Ben had done something to make him suspicious. Then it was gone, as quickly as it had appeared, and Hudson was once again regarding pleasantly.

"Yes," he said simply. "I'm working on a paper for grad school."

That explained it. Ben understood all about grad school, about the endless writing and research, the quest for something to study that was unique, something not already claimed by someone else. He recalled his own horror at discovering, while working on his master's, that he'd elected to pursue the same subject as an archrival, a situation that added even more pressure to an already-difficult situation but which ultimately had forced him to work harder and, as a result, produce the more original thesis. He knew now why Hudson had seemed wary. He knew, too, that further questions about the subject would make the other man uneasy.

"People often assume Doc and Ricketts are the same person," he said, going back to the subject that had originally brought them together. "But they weren't. Not really. I think Doc was an idealized version of Ricketts, maybe the man Steinbeck knew he wanted to be. Or maybe the man Steinbeck wanted him to be."

"I've always thought that myself," said Hudson. "I was hoping that being here would help me figure it out."

"Maybe," Ben said. "As you've already seen, though, even Monterey has turned into what it thinks people want it to be. It's a sort of Disneyized Cannery Row. People don't want to know about how they wiped out all the sardines, or how the original Japanese fishermen were pushed out by the white ones when they realized there was money to be made. The place has almost become a myth, filled with happy bums and heart-of-gold whores."

"And Doc," said Hudson.

"And Doc," Ben echoed.

"All writing is a lie in some way," Hudson said thoughtfully. "Like you said, maybe Steinbeck wrote about it the way he wanted to see it. Did you know he wrote his ex-wife out of the Sea of Cortez account?"

"No," said Ben. "I've never heard that."

"Took her right out," Hudson said. "They fought the whole time she was there, and he didn't want to write about her. He thought the story would read better if it was just him and the boys going on an adventure."

"He's probably right about that," Ben said. "I can think of a few trips I'd rather remember without my wife in them."

"Well, Carol Steinbeck probably felt the same way about John," Hudson said. "It would be interesting to hear her side of the story."

Ben had forgotten that Steinbeck had been married to a Carol, too. He thought of his Carol. His ex-Carol. She also had her side of the story. Their story. He wondered how she told it, how he came across to people who knew him only from her description of their marriage. *I wonder if I would recognize myself?* he thought.

"I've taken up a lot of your time," Hudson said, checking his watch. "I didn't mean to. But I appreciate it."

Ben drained the last of his coffee. "It's all right," he said. "I wasn't in any hurry to get back to the lab."

"I know that feeling," said Hudson. "I'm kind of putting things off as well. I was hoping that walking around would help me focus a little better."

Ben stood up. He could tell that, despite his comments, Hudson was hoping he wouldn't leave. He recognized the pull of procrastination. After all, he was deep in its thrall himself. The temptation to suggest a second cup of coffee was strong. But he fought it off, telling himself that it was for Hudson's sake that he was leaving.

"You know," he said. "I might be able to arrange for you to get inside Ricketts's place," he said, surprising himself.

Hudson's head snapped up. "You're kidding," he said.

"I might," Ben repeated. "I'll ask around. Monterey is a pretty small place."

"That would be amazing," Hudson said, fumbling in his backpack. "Here's my number."

Ben accepted the piece of paper. Hudson's obvious excitement was refreshing. It wasn't often he saw someone so happy over the prospect of seeing the inside of a marine biologist's office. He couldn't even stand to be inside his own at the moment. He lifted the paper. "I'll see what I can do," he said.

He left Kalisa's followed by Hudson's repeated thanks. What a peculiar day it had been, he mused. First his run-in with the fisherman, and then an entirely different kind of run-in with Hudson Jones. And all of it completely accidental, occurring only because he'd decided to take a walk. Had he sat in his office, stewing over his problem with Caddie, he would still be there, undoubtedly no closer to finding a solution. This, he thought, was infinitely better.

As he walked, he thought about Steinbeck some more. How long had it been since he'd read *Cannery Row*? He thought back, realizing that it had been at least ten years. He'd read it first in grad school, simply because, as he'd told Hudson, reading Ricketts's classic *Between Pacific Tides* had led him to the Sea of Cortez material coauthored by Ricketts and Steinbeck, and then to Steinbeck himself. But his interest in Cannery Row, both the place and the book, had at that time been only tangential to his interest in Ricketts's scholarly work. It wasn't until he'd moved there that he'd thought to read the book with a different perspective.

Maybe it was time to look at it again. After ten years, surely his perspective on Monterey had changed enough that his reading of the book would be more nuanced. And he hadn't read anything for pleasure in, well, in too long.

He was passing the aquarium. Stopping, he turned and walked toward the members' entrance at the rear of the building. Flashing his card, he walked up the stairs past the jellyfish exhibit, crossing into the main building via the walkway, and descended past the life-size orca models that were suspended from the ceiling as if they were flying. Then he entered the teeming gift shop, moving through the mobs of tourists looking at stuffed seal pups and dolphin calendars. The book section was at the rear of the shop, inconveniently nestled between the posters and a storeroom door. Fortunately, it was sparsely populated, and he had no trouble finding the well-marked display of Steinbeck-related material.

Picking up a copy of *Cannery Row,* a pile of which sat on the shelf, he made his way to the lesser-used checkout stand in the shop's far corner. There he had to wait while an elderly woman, apparently doing her Christmas shopping, paid for half a dozen ocean-themed items. He briefly reprimanded himself for not simply going to a bookstore, and weighed the value of his member discount against the frustration of having to listen to the woman prattle on about how darling Victoria was just going to love her harp seal barrettes.

Then it was his turn. He paid, declined the offered bag, and exited the museum through the closer main entrance. He was so relieved to be leaving the tourists behind that he didn't notice as he passed not ten feet away from his daughter as she made her way through the doors and into the main rotunda.

CHAPTER 13

For twenty-three bucks, this place better be amazing, Caddie thought. She couldn't believe it cost so much to get into a freaking aquarium. And that was with the student discount. She'd almost turned right around and left, but the thought of sitting in the house with nothing to do made her stay.

She looked around. Admittedly, the place was beautiful. She could do without the whales and dolphins hanging from the ceiling, but other than that it was a pretty amazing place. She walked over to an information stand and picked up a map, then put it back again. She didn't really care what she saw; she was just killing time.

Her attention was drawn by a sudden collective shriek that came from a knot of people standing before a display ahead of her. Curious, she went to see what all the fuss was about and discovered that two sea otters were putting on a show for the assembled visitors. The animals frisked about the tank, batting at one another and doing barrel rolls, swimming up to the glass and bringing their little whiskered faces close to the children standing in front. The kids reached out, squealing, and the otters retreated, chasing each other to the surface somewhere out of sight above the onlookers.

They were cute, but Caddie wasn't in the mood for waiting around for their return. She moved on, retracing the path her father had walked not fifteen minutes before. Entering the smaller Outer Bay Wing of the aquarium, she entered a dimly lit hallway that promised to take her to the mysterious world of the jellies.

Looking through the round windows set in the walls, she watched the jellyfish float, their long tentacles hanging beneath them. At first they seemed nothing more than amorphous blobs, bits of gelatin dropped into the water and left to hang there. But the longer she watched them, the more alive they became. Within the bowl-shaped bodies she noticed specks of color. She started to notice the delicate ripples of movement, the fluttering of flowerlike central cores, the almost-imperceptible exhibitions of decisive motion, easily missed by those who, glancing at the jellies and seeing nothing, moved past them to more interesting specimens.

The jellyfish changed as she moved through the gallery, becoming larger and more fantastic. Some, reminiscent of eggs, featured yellow centers suspended in cloudy white bodies. Others, with tentacles yards long, swam in never-ending circles, their arms entwined, living knotwork with no end and no beginning.

She was reluctantly impressed. The jellies were undeniably beautiful. She liked, too, that their beauty was inextricably tied to their deadliness. What made them so awesome to behold also made them efficient killers, their spectacular colorations and variety of designs being not merely decorative but entirely functional.

Still, she grew tired of them after twenty minutes and moved on after being jostled once too often by other visitors who, disoriented by the lack of lighting that made the jellyfish appear in such startling relief, neglected to notice her presence and stepped on her feet or ran into her with baby buggies. Coming full circle, she exited the exhibit very near to where she had entered.

Dismissing a display devoted to vanishing ocean wildlife as needlessly depressing, her next stop was devoted to the Outer Bays. This, she quickly saw, was essentially an enormous fish tank, stretching floor to ceiling and extending from one side of the cavernous room to the other. Behind the glass, a variety of sea life swam past: huge yellowfin tuna, sleek and sharp-eyed barracuda, a pair of sea turtles.

The star of the attraction, however, proved to be a juvenile great white shark, which she learned by reading a sign placed nearby had been successfully kept at the aquarium for some months after being accidentally caught in a fisherman's net. Because the tank and its inhabitants were so large, it was difficult to tell where the shark was. However, the unmistakable gasps of the crowd alerted Caddie to its presence.

The shark, seemingly unaffected by its celebrity, passed by several feet above the heads of its audience. It was perhaps four feet long, a perfect miniature of what Caddie imagined a great white to be. Its black eye revealed nothing of its thoughts as it moved, its tail curving in a gentle S and its mouth open wide enough to show the teeth of nightmares. The other fish, when it approached, either swam away or formed tight clusters with their like kind.

"Apparently it took a bite out of one of the tuna last week," a woman said to her companion.

"I think he's cute," said a child beside her, and the woman laughed.

"Sharks aren't cute, honey. They eat people."

Caddie, seeing the look of consternation on the child's face, said, "I think he's cute too."

The child grinned as her mother, glancing quickly at Caddie, tried to push her way closer to the tank. *Keep fighting, kid,* Caddie thought.

The shark having gone, she lost interest in trying to differentiate one type of tuna from another. To her they were all big silver fish, more interesting as sushi than as living things. She hoped the little great white ate a few more of them, wished even more that she could see it do so. *That would be something,* she thought, imagining the carnage.

She decided to explore the other wing of the aquarium, reached by crossing a narrow walkway that passed over the heads of entering visitors. Reaching the far end, she saw below her another huge tank. Unlike the other one, however, this one was filled with rocks and plants in addition to fish. Also, there was color. Instead of the monotonous variations of silver, these fish were alive with yellows and reds. The rocks, too, were pretty in purple and brown, much more interesting than the endless blue of the open ocean.

She followed a set of stairs down and approached the tank. The various signs affixed around the bottom identified the habitat as one of California's famous kelp forests. And indeed, kelp was central to the design. It filled the tank, reaching forty or more feet to the top of the room. Some unseen magic created movement, causing the kelp to sway back and forth slowly, the myriad stalks moving in unison first in one direction and then the other. Fish darted in and out of the thick fronds.

Sensing movement of another kind, Caddie looked toward a group of rocks in time to see something slither out. A yard or more long, its body was mottled gray and black, looking much like the rocks from which it had emerged. The snakelike body culminated in a huge, monstrous head that resembled nothing so much as the face of a very old man. Large eyes sat above a huge, thick-lipped mouth as the creature rested on the sandy bottom.

Caddie searched the various signs until she found the animal's picture and identified it as a wolf eel. The eel's description assured her that its ferocious appearance belied a gentle nature, a claim she found hard to believe. From the look of the thing, it could take her whole hand off if it wanted to.

Behind her a set of bleacher-like benches were arranged auditorium style. A handful of people sat on them, watching the kelp forest tableau. Caddie decided to join them. Her feet hurt anyway, and sitting down allowed her to view the tank without having to fight for real estate near the glass. Choosing the least occupied of the benches, she sat down.

Seconds later, her solitude was taken away as a family of five moved past her and, predictably, chose to sit right beside her. The mother, holding one child on her lap and trying to get a second to settle down, asked her husband how much longer it was going to be. "The show starts in a couple of minutes," he replied tiredly before instructing the remaining child to stop kicking his feet against the bench.

As if the man were cuing a scene, a voice erupted from invisible speakers to announce, "The afternoon feeding is about to begin at the kelp forest exhibit." This was followed by a sudden influx of bodies as people streamed in from all sides, quickly filling up the benches and the surrounding standing areas. Caddie, looking for a means of escape, found her way blocked and the crowd impenetrable without drawing unwanted attention to herself. And so she sat, annoyed at herself for having fallen into a trap and thus appearing to be yet one more tourist slavering for entertainment.

The calm within the tank was broken as a body descended from the ceiling. It was a diver. His head was encased fully in a mask that allowed him to look out at the audience and, as Caddie discovered, speak to them through a microphone. He hovered amidst the kelp as the fish, clearly well used to the routine, swarmed about him with great interest.

"Good afternoon." The voice, although slightly tinny, was warm. "Welcome to the kelp forest exhibit of the Monterey Bay Aquarium. My name is Brian, and I'll be your tour guide today."

Reaching into a bag at his side, he removed from it a handful of something and released it into the water. The fish, frenzied, darted around him, eating. "As you can see," Brian said, "they know when it's lunchtime."

He then launched into a description of the kelp forest ecosystem, presenting facts about the fish that Caddie heard and then immediately forgot. She was more interested in the way in which the diver hung so effortlessly in the water. He moved his legs only occasionally, and yet he neither fell nor rose. She found herself looking at his face through the mask and realizing that he was cute.

How does he know all this stuff? she wondered. She tried to picture herself giving a talk to so many people. There was no way, not only because she knew nothing about the ocean, but because she couldn't stand the idea of all those faces looking at her.

"This little fellow is a garibaldi," Brian said, pointing to a bright orange fish that seemed to be attacking his mask. "He's the state fish of California. Right now he thinks I'm trying to get at the eggs he's guarding in his nest over there; that's why he's getting all up in my face."

A ripple of laughter ran through the audience. Brian went on to tell them about the sheephead, a large pink and black striped fish that kept itself near the bottom of the tank. "Do you think that sheephead is a boy or a girl?" he asked.

"A boy!" one of Caddie's younger neighbors called out, while elsewhere the opposing view was presented by someone else.

"Well, you're both right," Brian said. "The female sheephead can actually change from a girl to a boy when there aren't enough males around to reproduce."

"Dude," a teenage boy behind Caddy said to his friend, "it's a transvestite fish."

"Actually, it's a transsexual fish," Caddie said, turning around. "Transvestites just wear the clothing of the opposite sex."

The boy laughed as she turned back around. She noticed the mother next to her give her a questioning glance and resisted the urge to lean over and say, "I know because I'm wearing men's underwear right now."

"I bet you guys have a lot of questions," Brian said, and a dozen hands shot up.

"Why doesn't the eel eat the other fish?" was followed by "Do fish sleep?" "Can you eat kelp?" and other questions, all of which Brian answered with, Caddie thought, enormous patience considering the stupidity of most of them.

"Anyone else?" asked Brian when the raised hands had all been lowered. "How about the pretty girl in the third row. You look like you have a question."

Caddie looked around, surprised that he would call on someone specifically. She was even more surprised a moment later when she realized that people had turned and were looking at her. She looked at Brian, floating behind the glass, and held a finger to her chest.

"Yes, you," he said. "What would you like to know about the kelp forest?"

Knowing she was turning red, Caddie was thankful for the low lighting. However, the realization that a hundred people were waiting to hear what came out of her mouth made it impossible for her to think. She just sat there, shaking her head.

"Come on," said the boy behind her. "Ask him something else about those queer fish, like do they take turns being the man."

He and his buddy erupted in horsey laughter. Thankfully, the anger she felt at his remark helped Caddie focus her thoughts. "If you could be any animal that lives in the kelp forest, what would you be?" she said loudly.

There was some tittering from the crowd, but she saw Brian smile behind his mask. "That's a good one," he said. "I guess I would want to be a sea lion."

"Why?" Caddie found herself saying.

"Because they don't worry about anything," said Brian. "They just play all the time. And when they're not playing, they're sleeping. I think that's a pretty good life."

The audience applauded as Brian thanked them for coming and waved good-bye. As they filed out, he rose out of view, until only the tips of his fins were visible. Then they too disappeared as, Caddie assumed, he got out of the tank.

She stood up, stretched, and left the animals of the kelp forest to do whatever it was they did when no one was around. Having already seen most of the aquarium, she returned to the second floor and checked out the remaining sights. It was as she was watching the bizarre-looking cuttlefish that she sensed someone standing too close to her and turned to see Brian there. The wet suit was gone, replaced by shorts and a T-shirt bearing the aquarium's logo. His blond hair, cut short, stuck up in unruly spikes.

"Hi," he said.

"You look different without your work clothes on," Caddie said.

"I hope I didn't embarrass you," he said. "You just looked like you wanted to murder someone."

"So you thought you'd poke me and see if I exploded?" she asked. "Nice."

"Hey, it works with the puffer fish," said Brian, smiling. His eyes, a greenish brown, asked her to forgive him.

"Is this how you always pick up girls?" Caddie said.

"Usually the uniform is all it takes," answered Brian. "Who can resist a guy in neoprene?"

Caddie turned back to the cuttlefish, which hovered, alien-like, an inch above the sand. The edges of its blue-tinged mantle rippled incessantly while one weird gold eye, the iris a black W, stared back at Caddie. A cluster of fingerlike tentacles dangled from its head, twitching idly at the water.

"That is one seriously weird fish," she remarked.

"Actually, it's not a fish," said Brian. "It's a mollusc. It's related to snails, squid, and octopuses."

"Look at you, getting all Jacques Cousteau," said Caddie.

Brian ran his hand through his hair. "I like marine biology," he said.

"You should meet my father," Caddie told him. "He works over at that Hopkins Marine whatever."

"And you don't know the difference between a fish and a cuttlefish?"

Caddie faced him. "I didn't inherit the fish-loving gene, I guess," she said. "Besides, if it's not a fish, then they shouldn't put *fish* in its name. It should be the cuttlepus or something."

"I liked your question," Brian said.

"Sorry it wasn't all scientific," said Caddie.

"No," Brian said. "I really liked it. It was different. You heard what everyone else asked. It's almost always like that. It's nice to have someone ask something interesting."

"Well, I try," said Caddie.

Brian, pointing at the cuttlefish, said, "Did you know they can change color? Like chameleons, only way more sophisticated. They have these receptors on their skin that can reflect light in a bunch of different colors, so they can blend in with their surroundings."

"That would be a neat trick," Caddie said.

Brian looked at her. "I don't think you could blend in anywhere," he said. "You're too pretty."

Caddie snorted. "Next you'll tell me that my tentacles are the longest ones you've ever seen."

"I've seen longer," said Brian. "But I'm not really a tentacle man anyway, so it's all good."

Caddie was enjoying the flirtation, even if it was a little too reminiscent of her first meeting with Nick, which she'd actually managed to forget about until then. But Brian was no Nick. He seemed to actually have a brain. *But he might also have a girlfriend,* she reminded herself.

"So I didn't just track you down to apologize," Brian said, hesitating enough that Caddie knew what was coming. "I was wondering if you might like to hang out."

"Hang out?" said Caddie. "You mean like play video games and read comic books?"

"I mean like maybe dinner or a movie, smart-ass," Brian replied.

"Now you're calling me names?" said Caddie. "I have to tell you, neoprene suit or not, you're not doing so well here."

"Okay," Brian said. "Let me start over. Would you be interested in getting something to eat and seeing a movie?"

"With you?" asked Caddie.

"With me," Brian said.

Caddie bit her lip, thinking. Brian watched her, obviously nervous. It was sweet, she thought. And he was cute.

"Okay," she said. "But you'd better take me somewhere nice."

CHAPTER 14

"Have you found the Holy Grail yet?"

Hearing Marty's voice on the phone, Hudson laughed. "Give me a few more days," he replied. "Those Knights Templar were clever boys, you know. They hid it pretty well."

Marty chuckled. "So, how's Monterey?"

"Interesting," Hudson told his friend. "It feels strange being here. I've just sort of been walking around, taking it all in."

"Talking to ghosts," Marty remarked.

"Something like that," said Hudson. He appreciated that Marty understood. It was difficult to explain his feelings to people who weren't from the academic world, who had never lived through the singularly lonely and paranoiac experience that was chasing a theory. He liked that he could shorthand his feelings and that Marty would know what he meant.

"How long do you think it will take?" Marty continued.

Hudson sighed. "About ten minutes if I find out I'm wrong," he said. "But if I'm right, it could be awhile."

"Well, take your time," said Marty. "It's nice having the place to myself."

Hudson knew he was teasing. Marty hated living alone; whenever Hudson went away for any length of time, he almost immediately reverted to a state of near squalor. Laundry went undone, piling up on the floor around Marty's bed. Dishes, when he didn't simply eat straight out of cans, sat unwashed in precarious piles. Showering became a biweekly event.

"Have you turned into Mr. Severin yet?" asked Hudson, a reference to a professor of Marty's who, failing to turn up for class following one three-week winter break, had been discovered dead in his office at home, surrounded by years-old stacks of mathematics journals and drifts of accumulated filth, his toes half eaten by his three starving cats.

"Not so far," Marty answered. "But it will be your fault if I do. You shouldn't have left me."

"You poor thing," Hudson teased. "I'm sure you can find some comely undergraduate who needs help with his calculus to take care of you."

"Speaking of which," said Marty, "how's the man action there?"

"One gay bar," Hudson informed him. "And I understand it's mainly filled with pool-playing dykes. My sexual drought seems destined to continue unabated."

Marty feigned a sigh of sympathy, to which Hudson said, "I know you feel my pain." This was followed by the sound of beeping.

"I've got to go," said Marty. "That's my dinner."

"Please tell me you didn't use the microwave," Hudson said.

"Relax," said Marty. "It's just a can of soup."

"Can!" Hudson exclaimed. "As in metal? Are you—"

"I'll call you in a few days," said Marty, and hung up.

Hudson started to call back, then put the phone down. Visions of the house going up in flames filled his thoughts. He couldn't believe Marty would do something so stupid. *Yes I can,* he corrected himself. *The man doesn't even know you're supposed to add water.* But he didn't call back.

Instead, he looked at his own dinner. He'd picked up Chinese from a restaurant nearby. Now the cartons sat open before him on the table on the sunporch. It was a warm night, still very much light, and the room retained a feeling of summer, as if it had soaked into the very fabric of the couch. Hudson took up a fork, plunged it into the Schezuan pork, and took a bite.

It had been a good day, he thought. His initial disappointment in the state of Cannery Row had dissipated somewhat, mostly due to his meeting with Ben Ransome. Knowing that someone else lamented the effects wrought by time and progress made him feel that he at least had company in his desire to experience life as it was. And if Ben could get him into Ed Ricketts's lab, that would be a real thrill.

He would try not to get his hopes up. In his experience, people often made promises but seldom came through. He'd given Ben his number, and that was really all he could do. Still, he hoped he would call, if only because it would be nice to talk to him again.

Switching from the pork to the tangy slickness of sweet and sour chicken, he turned over the pages of the manuscript that he'd spread out on the table. He'd been making notes—again—and wanted to compare a later section to the one concerning Tom's near-battle at the bar.

> *It seemed to Charlie, walking home, that the Row was something of a dream. Whenever he thought he understood it, it changed itself, becoming a new mystery. Some days he woke up thinking that he knew who he was, and where he was going. But as soon as he stepped outside, he would find himself once again in an unfamiliar landscape. It made his head hurt, trying to figure it out. So he'd mostly stopped trying.*
>
> *He'd once accused the place of deliberately trying to make him crazy. Its treachery, he'd announced to the man next to him at the bar where he'd been drinking steadily for some time, was now clear to him. Cannery Row wanted his soul. Well, he'd said, he'd be damned if he'd let any building built of fish stink and oil have him. He'd leave, by God, and leave that night.*
>
> *Of course, he hadn't. He'd meant to. He'd even gone so far as to pack a suitcase. But somewhere between trying to choose what undershirts to take and which to leave behind, he'd fallen tiredly onto his bed and fallen asleep. In the morning he'd woken up, eyed the suitcase suspiciously as if it had crept into the room during the night and meant to rob him, and tried to remember why he'd gone to sleep with his boots on.*
>
> *He'd since come to accept the Row as a reality. Still, he resented it, insulted it in his thoughts, if not to its person, lest it hear him and exact some kind of revenge. He regarded it the way he regarded immunizations, or the United States Congress. It wasn't for him to understand, but he respected it as something capable of both great harm and great good.*
>
> *Now, having left Tom at his own doorstep, he wondered*

if maybe he wasn't wrong about taking such a stance. For it seemed to him that the Row was becoming a harder and harder master. It was asking too much of its people. They were tired. He saw it in their faces. He felt it in his bones.

Look at Tom. Something was making him unhappy. While the obvious source of misery was usually a wife, Charlie suspected that Alice was no worse nor no better than any other woman. It was something else that was eating at Tom and making him act the way he did. And Charlie had felt it too. It was like something had bit him, and now the itch was starting to get too bad to ignore.

He reached his boarding house and went up to his room. He was too late for supper, and he didn't want to ask Mrs. Ring to make him up a plate, even though he knew she'd do it.

She'd cleaned his room. The floor was swept, and the window was open. He'd left it closed. Now the air came in. It smelled like sardines. He closed the window, then took his boots off. He didn't sit on the bed. Instead, he removed his overalls and carried them into the bathroom. He'd taken the room because of the bathroom. He didn't like to share, didn't like people knowing the secrets of his body.

He filled the sink and, taking up the small box of De-Luxe Laundry Powder he kept on the shelf beside it, sprinkled some into the water. It foamed up nicely, making drifts of white bubbles he thought probably looked like snow, which he'd never seen.

He washed the overalls, taking care to work the soap into the stains. Then he removed his shirt and washed that too, particularly the collar and the cuffs, where his body left its marks.

He drained the sink and ran fresh water over the clothes until no more soap came out. Then he wrung out as much of the water as he could and hung the clothes over the line he'd nailed up between the walls over the tub. The tub faucet had not worked for some time, but he bathed in the sink anyway and didn't miss it.

He returned to the bedroom. This time he did sit on the bed, his bare feet on the floor and his hands in his lap. He got up again and turned on the radio. A girl's voice filled his room, singing something about a robin and its nest. Charlie sat down again and listened to her for a minute, but then the song ended and a commercial for Ford automobiles came on. He had no use for a Ford, so he ignored it.

He wondered what Tom was doing. Probably he was asleep already. Maybe Alice had helped him off with his clothes. Or maybe she'd just let him fall into bed with them on. He doubted that. Women didn't like things dirty. She'd probably made him take off his overalls and shirt, even if she hadn't made him wash.

What would it be like to take care of someone like Tom? he wondered. Did Alice worry, or was she used to his behavior? She must be, he thought. After all, they'd been married a long time.

Tom was twenty-eight. Charlie knew this because Tom had mentioned once when his birthday was. It was August the seventeenth. He'd remembered it, and when that date had come around, Charlie had bought Tom a beer. Tom had been surprised that Charlie remembered. He'd clapped his hand on Charlie's back and told him what a friend he was. But he hadn't asked Charlie his own birth date, which was February the ninth.

On Charlie's last birthday he was twenty-six. He'd received a nice letter from his brother, Pete, who was living in Oklahoma and working on his wife's father's farm. Pete had wished him many happy returns and told him that he was welcome anytime he wanted to come visit, and was he thinking about getting married yet, because it was a good thing to be married. Charlie still had the letter, in a box in his closet. One of these days, he would write Pete back and tell him he was just fine.

He thought about being married. Pete made it sound like the best thing that could ever happen to a man. But Tom told him he was lucky he wasn't hampered by any woman. He told Charlie he wished they could trade places sometime, because he was starting to forget what it was like to be a free man.

Maybe he should get married. Maybe it would settle him

and make him stop feeling so itchy. If he was married, maybe he wouldn't feel like he was getting eaten up a little bit at a time with every passing day. If he had a wife, he'd mean something to somebody. That, he thought, would be a good feeling. Maybe the most wonderful feeling in the world.

Tom had married Alice when he was just seventeen and she was sixteen. He'd once told Charlie that they'd had to get married because Alice thought she might be having a baby. She hadn't, but by then they were already living in an apartment over a pharmacy and it was too late to do anything about it. Tom had told Charlie that since Alice hadn't produced any baby in all the time they'd been married that he sometimes thought maybe she'd made the whole thing up about that first baby on purpose, but he couldn't prove it and she wouldn't say.

Pete and his wife had two babies. Charlie had never met them, but he knew all about them from Pete's letters. They were five and three, two boys, Pete Jr. and Amos, named after his and Charlie's grandfather. Pete said he'd saved Otis, which was their dead father's name, for Charlie to give to his own son. Charlie had thanked him for his kindness, although he thought he maybe preferred the name Luke.

Before Luke, though, there was the matter of a wife. He hadn't found one yet, although he admitted he hadn't looked too hard. There had been one girl, the sister of a friend, who he'd visited a few times. But after three conversations he'd run out of things to talk about, and had not returned.

He thought again about leaving. Maybe there was nothing for him on Cannery Row anymore. Maybe, like the girl, he'd run out of things to say to it. And then he thought that maybe that was what was making Tom and so many of the other men so itchy. Maybe they couldn't be married to the canneries and their wives too. That's why they were restless, because they were in love with Cannery Row like they would be with a girl, loving her even though she made them miserable.

Pleased with himself at having arrived at such a pro-found conclusion, Charlie lay down on the bed. He told himself that the next time he wrote to Pete he would tell them that he was married, married to an ugly, snarling girl with breath like the hold of a boat. He imagined Pete scratching his head and reading Charlie's letter to his wife, and he laughed.

Hudson, having finished the chicken, set the carton down. He scrawled a note on the margin of the manuscript, reminding himself to look into something he recalled reading in a Steinbeck biography but couldn't quite place. Then he gathered up the remnants of his dinner and carried them to the kitchen.

I should cook, he told himself. After all, he had the time, and the kitchen was well stocked. But it seemed like a lot of effort to cook for just himself. At least at home he had Marty. Alone, he found it hard to muster the enthusiasm to settle on a recipe, shop for the ingredients, and then actually put it all together. It was so much easier to just look at a menu and wait.

The cleaning up accomplished in under a minute, he thought about his next step. Tomorrow he would make a visit to the Steinbeck Center in nearby Salinas. He had no idea what he would find there, or whether it would bring his journey to a screeching halt, but he was excited. Whatever happened, he was getting closer to an answer.

As he was throwing away the bag his food had come in, he noticed that he'd failed to open his fortune cookie. After snapping it in half, he removed the slip of paper and looked at it. " 'What you look for is not always what you find,' " he read aloud. "Great. Just what I needed to hear. Nothing like a cookie to make you neurotic."

He crumpled it up and tossed the fortune into the trash along with the uneaten pieces.

CHAPTER 15

Hearing the hiss of water turning to steam, Ben turned from where he was slicing a tomato at the sink just in time to see the pot on the stove boil over. Dropping the knife in his hand, he went to the stove, cursing his lapse in concentration, and turned the flame down. The foaming water in the pot quieted, and he repositioned the pot on the burner.

He returned to the tomato, half of which was already cut and stacked in a neat, if uneven, pile. He finished the remaining half, then started on an avocado. Glancing at the clock, he wondered when Caddie was coming home. Already past six, he'd expected her some time ago.

He checked the table. Two places were set, the plates flanked by napkins and silverware. He'd even picked up some flowers on the way home, thinking that the big pink and orange gerbera daisies would liven up the dining room. Now, looking at them standing in an empty coffee can—the only thing he could find in the house that resembled a vase—he worried that they were silly.

A timer went off, and he returned to the kitchen. Beside the big pot of water, a smaller pot held spaghetti sauce. It had come from a jar, but he didn't think Caddie would mind. At least he hoped not. He thought, a little unkindly, that Carol had never been a particularly good cook when they were together. He hoped she hadn't improved much over the years. He wanted Caddie to see that, if not chef-worthy, his food was at least as good as her mother's.

He opened the door and checked the garlic bread. He'd found the recipe online and followed it exactly. He was pleased to see that it appeared to have worked successfully. He turned the oven down to warm and shut the door. Pausing, he went over the list of dinner items: pasta with sauce, garlic bread, salad. Everything was done except the pasta. Opening the box of spaghetti, he dumped it into the boiling water. All that was missing was Caddie.

It's going to be fine, he reassured himself as he waited, not certain if he meant the pasta or dinner with his daughter. He was surprisingly nervous. Dinner out would have been easier. But he was pleased that he had elected to cook. Stressful as it was he'd managed it, he thought, quite well.

He read the back of the spaghetti box for at least the fifth time since purchasing it. Six minutes, it said. He looked at his watch. How long had it been? He hadn't noted the time the pasta had gone into its bath. He grew anxious, afraid that he might now overcook it, and poked at the strands in the pot with a wood spoon. Several of them seemed to be stuck to the bottom, which further upset him. *I should have bought a backup box,* he thought darkly.

He thought he heard a door shut, and looked up. But nobody came into the kitchen, and when he called out "Caddie?" in a hopeful voice, there was no response. Across the street the neighbor children were singing some nonsensical song as they jumped rope. He heard the slapping of the rope against the sidewalk.

He waited two minutes, then turned the flame off and carried the pasta pot to the sink. He had no strainer, so he drained the water by holding the lid on with his thumbs and leaving only the narrowest opening between it and the far side of the pot. As he tipped the pot forward, steam erupted and the pasta slid forward, hitting the lid. Startled, Ben let his grip falter, and the lid fell with a crash into the sink. The pasta tumbled after it, landing with a wet plop and slithering, along with the water, toward the drain.

He managed to stop it, creating a dam with the lid and preventing the majority of the pasta from escaping. What was left he scooped up using the salad tongs and returned to the pot. Then, rattled by the near disaster, he stood and sipped at a glass of merlot, eyeing the pasta suspiciously lest it make another attempt at escape.

It was now a quarter to seven, and Caddie was officially late. He tried to recall if he'd given her an exact time, and suspected he hadn't. Still, she should have been there by now. He wondered if he should have waited for her to get there before cooking the pasta, but it couldn't be helped now.

He began putting things in bowls, the salads in individual ones and the pasta and sauce into larger communal serving dishes. He withdrew from the refrigerator the bottle of Italian dressing and the Parmesan cheese he'd picked up along with the other groceries and removed the protective plastic wrappers from each. He considered putting the dressing on, then decided that it would be better to let Caddie do it herself.

After carrying each dish to the table, he had nothing to do but wait. He drank a full glass of wine and poured himself another. As he emptied that one, he found himself growing hypersensitive to noises. He jumped when a car door opened, and any sound that resembled footsteps on the stairs caused him to go to the front door. But each time the steps belonged to someone else, and the cars stopped in front of other houses.

At seven-thirty, he sat down at the table and poked listlessly at the pasta. It had formed an unappetizing ball, now grown cold, and the strands left gummy paste on the fork. The garlic bread, too, had not been made more appealing by the loss of heat. Only the salad retained some of its freshness. He picked at it listlessly, putting a piece of avocado in his mouth. It was mushy, and he was forced to wash it down with more wine.

At eight o'clock he accepted that he had been stood up. Leaving the food on the table, he took the bottle of wine and retreated to his study. He was a little surprised to find that his feelings were hurt, that he was actually thinking thoughts along the lines of, *Doesn't she know how much work I put into that dinner?* When he thought these things, it was his mother's voice he heard saying them. Had she ever really done so, he wondered, or was it only natural to think of her because he associated cooking with motherhood?

Then he recalled a night when he was perhaps ten. Caught up in a game of kickball, he'd forgotten to be home at his usual time. Arriving almost an hour late, he'd found his mother scraping his untouched plate into the garbage. Despite his apologies, she'd refused to let go of her anger, telling Ben that such ungratefulness wasn't to be tolerated. He'd appealed to his father, who in a rare instance of deference to his wife, had agreed that Ben should be sent to his room without his supper. It had seemed grossly unfair to Ben, and he'd spent the night planning in great detail how, as soon as his parents were asleep, he would run away and take up residence in the fort he and some friends had built from cardboard boxes in the nearby woods. Ultimately his anger had fallen prey to his weariness, and he'd fallen asleep. In the morning there had been breakfast as usual, and no one mentioned his crime of the previous evening.

Caddie isn't a little boy, he reminded himself. *She's sixteen. She should be able to get home for dinner.* Part of him wanted to invent excuses for her, mostly because he didn't want to think that her absence had anything to do with how she felt about him. He preferred to think that she'd become engrossed in some local attraction, even that she'd forgotten the address, than that she was deliberately snubbing his attempt to thaw the divide between them.

Maybe she left, he considered. Thinking of his own aborted escape attempt, he got up and went to her room to see if she'd packed up and gone elsewhere, to whatever fort of her own she preferred to living with him. But her clothes were still in the closet, her books and CDs stacked on the bedside table. She was still there.

He sat down on her bed. Who is this girl? he asked himself. Where had she come from? He tried to remember her birth, thought for the first time in many years of the room where Carol, panting and chewing on bits of ice he fed to her from a paper cup, efficiently and without incident brought Caddie into the world. Then she had been in his arms, looking up at him with indignation and surprise as he counted her fingers and toes.

Sixteen years had changed her into something he didn't recognize. Gone was the infant who had trusted him implicitly, also the five-year-old girl who had asked him whether Santa Claus was real and had believed him when he said that he was as real as air. Somewhere she had been replaced by this changeling, this shadow daughter who assumed that every word of his was a lie, every affection for her artificial.

When he'd announced his separation from Carol, his mother had begged him to reconsider for Caddie's sake, brushing aside his argument that a child's happiness didn't necessarily outweigh that of her parents. She'd disagreed with such desperate fervor that he came to suspect that she spoke out of experience, and for the first time he questioned whether his parents' marriage had been a happy one, although he couldn't bring himself to ask either of them. Now he wondered if perhaps she hadn't been right. Maybe, if he'd stayed, Caddie wouldn't be unhappy now.

That theory, he told himself from some part of his brain still operat-

ing with scientific detachment, was flawed. There was no way of knowing what might have happened. The uncontrollable variables were too
many, the number of possible outcomes immeasurable. Any conclusion reached through such an equation was unreliable and would have
to be discarded.

He had never been a religious person. Even as a child he had found
the notion of an omnipotent creator who punished his creations in-
consistently for minor infractions of a vaguely defined moral code to
be unthinkable to anyone with an ounce of sense. Later he had added
such concepts as karma and the inevitability of fate to the list of beliefs
unsupported by rational thought.

Now, however, he saw how a person might believe such things.
Surely his actions had had an effect on Caddie. She had told him as
much herself. And believing that maybe her current behavior could be
explained away merely by pointing to something he'd done nine years
earlier was easier than trying to unravel the complicated workings of a
teenage girl's mind.

But at some point didn't his responsibility for her personal happiness end? Was it really his due that he should now suffer for something
he'd done not out of selfishness but to preserve his own sanity? He
heard his ten-year-old self assert angrily that it was not.

It occurred to him that Caddie's failure to come home could be the
result of some accident, and for a moment he was actually relieved to
think this might be true. Then fatherly concern overrode this temporary reprieve, and for a time he truly did consider the various possible
emergencies that might be keeping her from returning. His thoughts
flashed upon scenes of auto accident, sickness, even murder, all of
them with Caddie playing the central figure. He tried to remember,
was she diabetic or allergic to bees?

Again, it was some fatherly instinct, long dormant but not dead,
that told him that none of these things were anything more than random thoughts. Caddie simply hadn't come home because she didn't
want to. Wherever she was, she was there because she preferred it to
being with him. The real question was whether this was simple thought-
lessness or deliberate cruelty.

He thought suddenly of the T-shirt that Caddie had been wearing at
breakfast that morning. She'd said that she'd bought it, but he was almost certain she was lying. Remembering the size of it, Ben realized

that he'd overlooked the obvious. And she had sat there, teasing him, maybe even hoping he would realize that she'd been with some boy.

He wasn't angry, not about the boy. He wasn't naive enough to think that a sixteen-year-old, especially an attractive one hell-bent on expressing her independence, was still a virgin. That it was his daughter who was the girl in question made it slightly more unsettling than if it had been someone else's daughter, and he fully intended to ask Carol if she'd had a talk with Caddie about the subject. But it wasn't the possibility of sex that bothered him; it was the knowledge that Caddie had wanted him to be upset, that she might have slept with someone just to spite him.

Maybe that's where she was, out with the same boy, hoping that her father would come looking for her or, more likely, wait up for her to return so that he could tell her that under no circumstances was she to behave like some backstreet whore while living under his roof. Was that what she wanted—a scene? Something to justify her loathing for him?

Well, she wasn't going to get it. Ben stood up, took a final glance around the room, and returned to his office. He'd moved from hurt to fear to guilt, and now had arrived at indignation. If Caddie wanted to play games with him, she would have to do better than this. Not only wouldn't he wait up for her, he wouldn't even gratify her by being angry. It would be a hollow victory for her, and he hoped she would be wise enough to, if not end her war against him, at least call a stalemate.

The bottle on his desk was empty, and the glass beside it less than a third full. Had he really drunk so much? His head felt light, but he wasn't at all sick, merely pleasantly unfocused. The idea of working on his paper came to him, but he dismissed it as too much effort. He wanted to do something he didn't have to think about.

The copy of *Cannery Row* that he'd purchased earlier in the day was sitting near the typewriter. He picked it up. On the cover a man with the wide, soft-eyed face of a manual laborer sat on a step before a wooden door, smiling for the camera as a cigarette burned in his hand. He wore a sailor's peacoat and a cap that rested far back on his head. Ben imagined that somebody had chosen the photograph because he or she felt it perfectly captured the spirit of the old cannery workers. And maybe it did, but he found the look of unenlightened bliss on the man's face faintly disturbing, as if he had no idea that one day the photograph for which he'd been paid perhaps fifty cents, or maybe just a

bottle of beer, to pose for would one day be looked upon with senti-
mental affection by readers who thought they knew who he was because they had just read a story about men who resembled him. *Sort
of like people who insist they know who God is because they've heard
a couple of stories,* Ben thought acidly.

Opening the book, he began to read. He'd forgotten how decep-
tively simple Steinbeck's prose was, how reading him felt like listening
to someone talk. He'd forgotten, too, how easy it was to get caught up
in the various interconnected stories that made up the novel. He
found himself turning page after page, often chuckling at a particularly
wry turn of phrase, occasionally nodding in agreement with something the author said.

He read for perhaps an hour. Then, closing the book, he leaned
back in his chair and thought about Steinbeck's world. It would be
nice, he thought, to live in a time and a place where his biggest problem was how he was going to afford a jug of wine. This was a simplifi-
cation of that world, he knew that, but it was pleasant to think about.

That caused him to remember the young man. What had his name
been? He found the scrap of paper he'd put on his desk earlier in the
day and looked at it. Hudson. That was it. Hudson Jones. It sounded
like a clothing store, or a law firm. At any rate, it had been enjoyable
talking to him. He hadn't had a conversation about anything other
than work in some time.

He remembered then, too, his promise to see about getting Hudson a look inside Ed Ricketts's lab. He would give Al Blackmore a call
in the morning, see what he could do. He'd given Al some abalone last
year, so he owed him a favor. If anyone could get them behind that plywood fence, it was Al. He knew everyone in Monterey.

Glancing at his calendar, Ben saw that he had a dive scheduled for
the next morning. Suddenly he regretted the empty wine bottle. While
the more potentially troublesome aspects of having alcohol in his system would more than have worn off by the time he got into the water,
he was going to have a whale of a headache. He tried not to think
about it as he got up and went to the bathroom in search of aspirin. If
he got to bed now, he hoped, it wouldn't be so bad.

He took the aspirin and brushed his teeth. On his way to the bedroom, he saw the light in the stairway and remembered that he hadn't
cleaned up. *It can wait,* he told himself as he flipped the switch on the
wall, plunging the downstairs into darkness.

CHAPTER 16

"I bet you've never had a squid burrito," Brian said as he backed his car into a spot and turned the engine off.

"And I bet I never will," said Caddie, making a face.

"Come on," Brian teased. "Where's your sense of adventure? If I'd known you were one of those girly-girls, I never would have asked you out."

Caddie fixed him with a fierce look. "Who are you calling a girly-girl, buddy?" she said.

Brian grinned. "Prove it, then," he said. "Try the squid burrito."

The idea of such a thing sickened Caddie. She imagined a tortilla filled with slimy tentacles. But she wasn't about to give Brian the satisfaction of thinking she was some kind of prissy ditz. "You're on," she said as she opened the car door.

Taqueria Del Mar didn't look like anything special. A faded mural of a fishing boat covered one wall, and the fluorescent lights cast a harsh glare over the beat-up tables and old linoleum floor. As they walked in, Caddie wondered why any guy who wanted to impress her would bring her to such a place, and her opinion of Brian dropped a few notches.

"*Hola, amiga,*" Brian said to the woman standing behind the counter. When she saw him, her tired face took on a renewed glow, and she smiled warmly. "*Hola, amigo,*" she said cheerfully.

Brian leaned against the counter. "*Dos burritos de calamar,*" he said. "*Y dos horchatas,*" he added.

The woman nodded and went to prepare the food. Caddie sat on one of the tall stools that lined the counter. "Look at you, speaking Spanish," she said.

Brian shrugged. "I spent last summer working with Iemanya Ocean-ica, tagging sharks in the Sea of Cortez," he told her. "I picked up a lit-tle bit."

"Sharks, huh?" Caddie said. "You weren't kidding when you said you were into this marine biology suff."

"I'd be back there this year, but I have to earn some money for school," said Brian. "I made a deal with my parents, last summer doing volunteer work and this summer getting paid. So twice a day I get in the kelp tank and feed the fish. The rest of the time I help maintain the habitats."

"So you're a fish maid," Caddie joked.

Brian pretended to be offended. "I prefer to think of myself as a ma-rine sanitation engineer," he said. "Maid sounds so cheap."

The woman returned with their food and placed it on the counter. "*Gracias,*" Brian said as he picked up the tray and carried it to a table.

Sitting down, Caddie looked skeptically at the burrito. It looked normal, but she knew that inside lurked the dreaded squid. She watched as Brian picked up his burrito and took a big bite. Hesitantly, she poked at hers with a plastic fork.

"What are you waiting for?" Brian asked, watching her. "Dig in."

Here goes nothing, Caddie told herself, stabbing the burrito and cutting off a chunk. She tried not to look at what was inside as she raised the fork and stuck it in her mouth. She chewed slowly, and was surprised to find that the burrito was delicious.

"Well?" Brian asked.

Caddie nodded and swallowed. "It's fantastic," she said, taking a second bite.

"I don't want to say I told you so," said Brian. "But I told you so."

Caddie ate for a minute, then tried the drink Brian had ordered for her. The horchata was a milky white, flecked with brown and smelling of fruit and spices. She took a sip and found that she liked it.

"Don't tell me you've never had horchata either," Brian said, watch-ing her taste the beverage. "What, do you live in a cave?"

"We can't all be world travelers," Caddie said, responding to his taunt with a sarcastic look.

"I just thought someone who grew up in Monterey would have al-ready had her horizons broadened," said Brian.

"I didn't grow up here," Caddie told him. "In fact, I'd never even been here until this week."

"But I thought you said your father—"

"My parents are divorced," said Caddie before Brian finished his sentence. "I'm just here—"

She hesitated. She'd been about to explain that she was only there because her mother had made her. Then she remembered, Brian was a college student. That meant he was at least nineteen, maybe even twenty. If he knew she was sixteen, he probably wouldn't want to go out with her. She did some quick thinking.

"I'm here for the summer," she said. "But I go to school in L.A."

"What are you studying?" Brian, busy adding pico de gallo to his burrito, wasn't looking at her, and so missed the look of momentary panic that flashed across Caddie's face as she tried to choose from one of a multitude of possible lies.

"History," she said, grasping at the first thing that came to mind.

"History," Brian repeated, sounding impressed. "What's your favorite period?"

Caddie, who at that moment couldn't think of a single historical era besides the 70s, bought herself some time by saying, "No girl has a favorite period. They all suck."

Brian snorted. "I guess I asked for that," he said.

Caddie, relieved, suddenly found that her brain had begun working again. "I guess I'm most interested in the Renaissance," she said casually. "You know, when everything was changing and there was all of that great art and music and . . . stuff," she finished, wishing she'd stopped when she was ahead.

But if he noticed her fumble, Brian didn't show it. He was working on the second half of his burrito. "I didn't much get into history in school," he said. "To me it was just a bunch of dead guys. No offense," he added. "I'm sure it's actually really fascinating."

Caddie shook her head. "Not really," she agreed, relieved he hadn't started asking her about her favorite king of France or something. "I'm considering switching to film or something next year."

"Now that's something interesting," said Brian. "I love movies. What's your favorite?"

"What's with you and favorites?" countered Caddie.

"I don't know," Brian said. "I guess it's a fun way to get to know someone."

Caddie drank more of the horchata before replying. "I guess my favorite movie would have to be *Pan's Labyrinth,*" she said, thinking about the last movie she had seen with Sam Bree. "What about you?"

"*Pirates of the Caribbean,*" Brian said. When he saw Caddie looking surprised he continued. "What? I didn't say I was deep. Actually, it was one of only two movies we had on the boat last summer. The guy who was supposed to bring them forgot them, so we had to watch that and *Steel Magnolias* for two weeks straight, until we got back to La Paz and could get some different ones."

"I'd think you would hate it, then," said Caddie.

"I think it's a case of that, what do they call it—Stockholm Syndrome. You know, where you spend so much time with the person torturing you that you kind of fall in love."

"So you're in love with Johnny Depp," said Caddie.

Brian paused, as if considering her statement. "No," he said eventually. "I don't like guys with facial hair."

"Tell me more about the sharks," Caddie prodded, trying to keep the conversation away from herself and what she was or was not studying at her fictitious college.

"Sharks are amazing," said Brian, instantly enthused. "What we're doing to them is absolutely fucking insane. We should be worshiping these things as gods. I mean, they're one of the last things left around from the dinosaurs. So what do we do, we kill them off by the millions."

He looked over at Caddie. "Sorry," he said. "I get carried away. But you're probably used to that, what with your dad being a marine biologist."

Caddie nodded vaguely. She'd actually never heard her father talk about anything to do with his work, at least nothing she'd listened to very carefully. She didn't know if he had an opinion about sharks or not.

"Anyway, they're beautiful," Brian continued. "Just amazing. You know how they always say that they have dead eyes? It's not true. A shark's eyes are absolutely perfect."

He continued to talk about sharks—their eyes and every other part of them—for a good ten minutes, while Caddie ate her burrito and listened. She enjoyed hearing Brian talk. He was completely different from her father, who couldn't tell an interesting story to save his life. If he ever got as excited as Brian did, she might actually have cared about what he did. As it was, she didn't even really know what it was he worked on.

"One time we were down there and Juan—he's one of the scientists—pointed behind me," said Brian, still talking about his experiences the summer before. "There was this big school of hammerheads. There must have been fifteen or twenty of them. They swam right by us, like they saw divers every day of their lives. They couldn't have cared less."

"Wow," Caddie remarked, not sure how else to respond. To her the idea of being near a bunch of sharks sounded more like a suicide attempt than something to get excited about.

She drained the last of the horchata from her glass and wiped her fingers on a napkin. Brian, who had finished several minutes before, piled everything on the tray, then picked up a paper from a pile that was sitting on the floor near their table. "Let's see what's playing," he said, opening the paper and leafing through. He found the movie listings and folded the paper over, laying it on the table and smoothing it with his hand.

"Anything good?" Caddie asked.

"You're the movie expert," Brian replied. "I'll let you pick."

"What are my choices?"

"I'll narrow it down to three for you," said Brian. "A Hugh Grant comedy, some horror flick that I think is about a bunch of ghosts who are pissed off at Lindsay Lohan, or George Clooney playing George Clooney." He looked at Caddie with his eyebrows raised. "Well?"

"Gee, I don't know," Caddie said, folding her hands and looking serious. "That's a tough one. I guess I'll have to go with A. Hugh Grant."

"Then Hugh Grant it is," Brian said. "It starts in twenty minutes, so let's go."

They returned to his car and drove to the theater, walking in just in time for the previews. Brian followed Caddie to a seat in one of the rear rows, where they were far removed from the handful of other people in the sparsely filled room. When, halfway through the movie, Brian found Caddie's hand and held it, she made no attempt to take it back.

Afterward, once more seated in Brian's car, Caddie wondered if her night with him might end as her date with Nick had. Instead, Brian looked at the clock and said, "I've got to be at the aquarium by six. Do you mind if I take you home?"

"Sure," said Caddie, not sure if she was disappointed or relieved that he hadn't attempted to get her into bed.

Luckily, she remembered the name of the street her father lived on, although the exact number escaped her. It didn't matter, as she would know it by sight, and Brian knew how to get there. He drove slowly, the windows down and the warm summer night all around them.

"I hope you had fun," he said after they'd ridden in silence for a few minutes. "Because I did."

Caddie, who had been looking out the window, turned to him. "I did," she said. "Nothing says romance like squid burritos and a Hugh Grant movie."

"True," said Brian. "I don't know what I can do to top that. Maybe we should just call it quits right now and save ourselves the disappointment."

Caddie's heart lurched as a sick feeling filled her stomach. Was he saying he didn't want to see her again? He'd held her hand, but that was nothing. Guys did all kinds of things with girls they didn't really like. Hell, *she* did things with guys she didn't really like. Why should Brian be any different?

They reached Clipper Street. Seeing her father's house, Caddie told Brian where to stop. She noticed that he left the engine running. "I guess I'll see you," she said, reaching for the door handle.

"Don't I get a good-night kiss?" Brian asked, stopping her.

Caddie looked at him.

"Unless you don't kiss on the first date," said Brian, apparently sensing her hesitation. "I'm sorry. I didn't mean to be a jerk."

Caddie answered him by leaning over and kissing him. After a moment, his arms went around her and he kissed her back. But only for a minute, and without aggression. Then he pulled back.

"Can I call you tomorrow?" he asked her.

"I'd like that," she answered.

Brian opened the glove compartment and rooted through the contents. He pulled out a pen and a piece of paper, which he handed to Caddie.

"What is this?" Caddie asked, looking at the paper. "A speeding ticket?"

Brian grinned. "Fifty-five in a forty-five zone," he said. "Sorry, officer."

Caddie laughed, writing her number on the ticket and handing it back to Brian.

This time, when she opened the door, he let her go. She stood and watched him as he turned the car around. He blew her a kiss as he drove away.

She walked to the front door not quite sure how she felt. She liked Brian. But she wasn't sure how he felt about her. His kiss had been nice, but she was used to guys wanting more than nice. Maybe, she thought, Brian had sensed that she was younger than she was pretending to be. Maybe he knew she was a phony. Before she'd reached the front steps, she'd already decided that she wouldn't hear from him again.

Inside, the house was dark. She fumbled for the light switch, found it, and flicked the hall light on. Then she looked at her watch. It was almost eleven. Her father was probably in bed.

She went to the kitchen and saw that the sink was piled with dirty pots. Open jars and half a stick of butter—now softened and ever so slowly forming a thick puddle—littered the countertop. She smelled the sharp tang of pasta sauce.

Then she remembered her dinner date with her father. She'd forgotten all about it. Surveying the mess he'd made of the kitchen, it occurred to her that he'd gone to a lot of trouble. When she saw the dining room table, still set as if any moment someone would sit down at it and enjoy the dinner that was waiting, she felt a pang of remorse.

Almost instantly, she banished it. So she'd forgotten about dinner. Her father had forgotten all about *her* the night before. Why should she be any different? *Besides,* she told herself, examining the contents of the serving bowls, *it was only pasta.* Anyone could make pasta. It wasn't as if her father had done that much. Her mind flashed on the number of dishes in the kitchen, but that, too, she elected to ignore. It was only pasta. *And the sauce came out of a jar,* she told herself.

She switched off the lights and went upstairs, half expecting her father to appear and confront her about missing dinner. When he didn't, she told herself that he must not be very upset at her. *If he was,* she thought, *he would have waited up. It's not that late.*

She glanced at his bedroom door, saw that the narrow slit at the bottom was dark, and moved on to his office. The door was open, and inside the room was still. Moonlight coated the empty chair, and the polished surfaces of the typewriter keys winked like tiny eyes in the darkness.

She hurried past and went to her room. Shutting the door, she sank with relief onto her bed, ignoring its muffled protestations. No, she wasn't sorry. She didn't owe her father anything. Besides, it was just one stupid spaghetti dinner. He probably didn't even care that she hadn't been there. *Why should he start now?* she asked herself.

She undressed quickly and, after a quick trip down the hall to the bathroom, climbed into bed. She considered taking a Valium, but a quick count of them decided her against it. There was enough pot, though, for a small joint. She deftly rolled it and took a hit, blowing the smoke toward the open window.

Turning off her light, she sat in the half dark, letting the pot relax her. Maybe Brian would call her, she thought. She would like that. And maybe, next time, he'd try a little harder. She would like that, too. Thinking about it, the dirty dishes downstairs faded from memory, replaced by fantasies about what the summer might hold for her. By the time she'd smoked the joint down to its end, she had forgotten all about them.

CHAPTER 17

The young woman behind the desk looked up at Hudson and smiled faintly. "Can I help you?" she asked.

"Yes," Hudson said. "You can." Her attitude annoyed him, and he assumed a tone of sarcastic politeness. Then, realizing that he was merely nervous, he stopped himself. He cleared his throat and began again. "My name is Hudson Jones," he said. "I have an appointment with Helen Guerneyser."

"One moment," the young woman said, picking up the phone and pressing a button. A moment later she said, in a much more lively voice, "A Mr. Jones is here."

She hung up and was opening her mouth to tell Hudson that he could sit and wait when a woman came striding out from the reaches behind the receptionist's desk. Perhaps sixty, she wore a red suit that fitted her slim frame flawlessly. A cream-colored blouse beneath the jacket was open at the throat, revealing a neat string of pearls. Her hair, auburn and artfully cut in a flattering short style, complemented her fair skin. Hudson observed all of this during the ten seconds it took for Helen Guerneyser to round the desk and hold out her hand.

"It's a pleasure to meet you," she said, grasping his fingers in hers. "I feel like we've known one another for some time, what with all of the e-mails."

Hudson nodded. "I know," he agreed. "But I have to tell you, you're not what I expected."

Helen Guerneyser peered at him over small, gold-framed spectacles. "Is that so?" she said.

Hudson, alarmed, fell all over himself trying to apologize. "I didn't mean . . . It's just that . . ."

The woman put a hand on his arm. "Please," she said. "I know what you're saying. I don't exactly fit your idea of an archivist, right?"

Relieved, Hudson ran a hand through his hair. "Yes," he said. "I was imagining someone dowdier, more . . ." He stopped again, realizing he'd made things worse for himself. "Not that archivists are dowdy or—"

Helen laughed. "It's all right," she told him. "I couldn't agree more. We're often a stuffy bunch. But as it happens, I came to archiving by way of the business world."

Hudson sighed. "I'm so sorry," he said. "Can we start over?"

The woman led him past the desk and down a short hallway, where they entered an office that was as far removed from Hudson's idea of an archivist's den as Helen Guerneyser was from his idea of an archivist. She motioned to a chair in front of her desk, and he sat down.

"For many years I worked in banking," Helen told him, picking up their conversation. "My involvement with the Steinbeck Center began when my husband was asked to be on the board. He was something of a community fixture in those days. Unfortunately, he was also something of an intellectual wasteland."

Hudson, surprised to hear her say something like that about her husband, started to speak.

"I can say that now because the old fool is dead," Helen said, saving him from the awkward moment. "And I didn't say he was stupid. He had a great head for money. He just wasn't a man of letters, only numbers." She paused, smiling quietly at some private joke. "Anyway," she continued, "fortunately for Wallace, I *do* have an interest in the arts. I was able to converse with the more literate members of the board, while he helped them to amass quite a substantial fortune. Gradually, I became more involved. One thing led to another, and when Wallace died, I saw no reason to cease my association with the Center. Instead, I bought myself some training and here I am."

Hudson leaned back in his chair and crossed one leg over the other, his ankle resting on the opposite knee. "That's quite a story," he said.

"I've discovered that Steinbeck has a way of bringing people together in curious ways," Helen announced. "It was part of his magic, I think. I've seen a fisherman who barely made it past the sixth grade discuss *The Moon Is Down* with a college professor, and quite vigorously, I might add. There's something about the man that seduces you in the best sense of that word."

A change had come over her voice, a kind of dreamy quality that suggested a longing for far-off places, or the remembrance of a first love. In another setting, Hudson might have mistaken it for the voice of a woman recalling a favorite suitor. But he knew what Helen meant; he'd felt it himself. It was, after all, why he was sitting in a chair in her office.

"Did your husband know about this affair you were having with Mr. Steinbeck?" Hudson asked.

Helen laughed briskly. "I like you, Mr. Jones," she said. "I liked you well enough from our e-mail conversations, but now I know that I truly like you. And to answer your question, my husband no more understood my affair with John Steinbeck than I understood his love of golf. Some things are simply mysteries to outsiders. Now, are you finally going to tell me what brings you all the way to Salinas from Yale University? Surely you haven't come just to get a look at me."

"No," Hudson answered. "Although that's an added benefit." He hesitated, choosing his words carefully. He'd told Helen Guerneyser sort of a half truth about his project. Partly this had been pure professional paranoia, but also he'd wanted to wait until he was at the National Steinbeck Center before he revealed too much. The truth was, he was afraid that if he told anyone the full story, they might prevent him from getting his answer.

"Well, as I said in my e-mails," he began again, "I'm doing my thesis on Steinbeck's journals. I'm interested in looking at the materials that haven't been given widespread study." He glanced at the archivist's face, trying to read her reception to his story, but found there only polite attention.

"Everybody has looked at the *Grapes of Wrath* material," he continued. "Also the *East of Eden* notes. Even the Sea of Cortez stuff has been done to death. I'm more interested in the lesser known books— *The Moon Is Down*, *The Wayward Bus*—things like that. What I really want to do is compare what Steinbeck was living, what he was feeling, to what ended up in those books."

He stopped, hoping he'd said enough to convince Helen Guerneyser that he was sincere. He'd had a great deal of time to come up with a plausible explanation for his research. Waiting for her response, though, he wondered with no small amount of worry whether he had done enough. Even to him the story sounded weak.

The archivist sat back in her chair. "As I'm sure you know, Steinbeck's papers are scattered all across the country. Stanford, of course, has the largest collection. But Steinbeck himself didn't seem to care too much about preserving such things, and certainly he never made provisions for his papers to be gathered in one place." A manicured hand fluttered in the air as she talked, the light sparkling off a diamond ring that Hudson found himself staring at to keep from looking at her face.

"We, however, have the majority of his journals," Helen continued. "As well as a great number of files of articles he found of interest. Steinbeck clipped and saved everything that he thought might be useful to his writing, which for a man with such a broad range of interests amounted to a considerable pile of paper." She shook her head. "No wonder his wives were always complaining about his being absent; they probably just couldn't find him beneath all the junk."

Hudson realized that he was shaking his leg nervously. He clapped a hand over his ankle and pinned it to his knee, forcing himself to remain quiet. He wasn't sure what the archivist was getting at, but he expected her at any moment to tell him that it was time for him to leave and never come back.

"It's always puzzled me why more people aren't interested in Steinbeck's journals," she said. "I myself have only looked through maybe a dozen of them. There's simply too much there to absorb easily. Every page, it seems, could yield a book."

Hudson held his breath, sensing that they were arriving at the moment he'd been waiting for—and dreading—since his first e-mail to Helen Guerneyser.

"I think it's an excellent idea," she said. "Although I think you might have bitten off more than you can chew. You might want to focus on one or two books or, even better, a specific period of Steinbeck's life."

Hudson nodded enthusiastically, agreeing with everything, resisting the urge to cheer or throw himself at the archivist's feet. He felt as if the gates of heaven itself had been opened to him. "Thank you," he managed.

"There are rules, of course," said Helen. "We aren't the public library. You may have access to whatever you wish, but you may not take anything out. Nor may you make photocopies of anything; the paper isn't getting any younger. If you want copies, ask me and I'll see to that for you." She eyed Hudson, fixing him with a keen stare. "Are you a coffee drinker, Mr. Jones?"

Hudson, bewildered, said, "I like the odd Starbucks now and again."

"Well, finish it before you come in here," Helen said. "That goes for water, juices, tea, what have you. No liquids of any kind around the materials. As far as the National Steinbeck Center is concerned, the blue laws are in effect. The man himself would call us all a bunch of tight prohibitionists, but we can't run the risk of some clumsy academic knocking over a Diet Pepsi and ruining things for everyone."

"No coffee," said Hudson. "Anything else?"

"Just one," Helen said. "If you find anything really scandalous, you let me know. There's nothing I like better than good dirt."

"Absolutely," said Hudson. "So, when can I start?"

"Right now," Helen said, standing up. "Follow me."

She left the office, Hudson right behind. Walking through the lobby of the building, she stopped at an elevator and pressed a button. The doors slid open and they stepped into the cool confines of the metal box.

"Like most people, we keep our old stuff in the basement," Helen joked as they descended. "Fortunately, ours is a little less damp than most."

The doors opened and they emerged into another hallway. Helen led the way to yet another door, and they stepped into a small, sparsely furnished room that looked very much like just about every library research room Hudson had ever spent time in. Two large wooden tables were situated side by side, each with two chairs tucked neatly underneath. Reading lamps provided assistance to those overhead. Otherwise, the room was bare.

"Do you have any idea at all what you'd like to see first?" Helen asked him.

Hudson placed his briefcase on one of the tables. "Not entirely," he said. "I was thinking perhaps the journals from 1948."

"All of them? There are at least seven, if I recall."

"How about the last half," Hudson suggested. "Maybe from summer on. I think that's when he first started thinking about the story that turned into *East of Eden*."

"Not exactly one of his lesser known works," remarked the archivist, and Hudson knew she was thinking about his claim to be interested mostly in Steinbeck's more minor creations.

"No," he agreed. "But it's well documented, and I want to see how directly he comments about his creative process in his journals. I think it will help me understand the level of honesty, if you will, about his ideas that he was willing to commit to paper."

"I'll be right back," said Helen. She exited through the sole door, leaving him alone.

Hudson paced. Afraid he'd revealed himself to be lying, or at least unsure of himself, he worried that Helen Guerneyser would see through him. *So what?* he asked himself. *So what if she knows what you're after? She might even be able to help.*

He was tempted. Surely if anyone knew anything about the manuscript, it would be someone like the archivist. He might be able to solve the mystery with one question. But he knew it couldn't be that easy. If what he had was what he thought it was, there would have been some mention of it somewhere. Something so important wouldn't just appear out of nowhere.

Then maybe you're wrong about it, said the voice of his doubt. *Maybe no one knows about it because there's nothing to know.*

It was an old argument, one he'd had with himself time and again. But he didn't believe it. He couldn't believe it. There was something too real about the manuscript, something that urged him on, told him to keep digging until he found the truth.

The door opened and Helen entered carrying a large box, which she set on the table. "Here you are," she said. "I'll leave you to it. When you're done, just leave everything here and come upstairs. If you find anything you want copied, leave it here and I'll see to it later." She walked to the door, pausing and looking back at Hudson. "Good luck," she said, and left him alone with the box.

Hudson sat down. He pulled the box toward him, lifted the lid, and looked inside. A stack of notebooks rested inside, no two of them alike. It was as if Steinbeck had written in whatever was at hand, with no thought to uniformity. Hudson reflected, with only the slightest hint of annoyance, that writers were selfish creatures, seldom considering the needs of future researchers when amassing the bits and pieces that would one day represent their creative processes. How much easier it would be, he thought, if they would have the courtesy to compile indexes to their own lives, like those people who worked for the *New York Times* writing obituaries for the not-yet-dead.

He removed the first notebook. The cover, a grubby brown marred by splotches of grease, was the cover of any of a million identical notebooks. But when he turned to the first page, the book revealed its true beauty. There, in a compact, tidy script that filled line after line, were the inner thoughts of John Steinbeck.

He couldn't believe he was holding a book that Steinbeck himself had held in his hands. His eyes ran over the words, making sense of none of them as his thoughts ran wild. What was in here? What would he find?

He shut his eyes and forced his mind to calm. Only when he felt the surge of excitement simmer to low boil did he open them again. This time, the neatly penned words flowed smoothly and, beginning with an entry for June the first, he began to read.

CHAPTER 18

The sound of a car door slamming woke Caddie up. Immediately the dream she'd been having—something about being at a concert with Sam and Bree but being unable to find them in the crowd—faded away, but the feelings of disorientation and frustration remained. She glanced wearily at the clock. It was only seven.

She tried to go back to sleep, realized she had to pee badly, and reluctantly threw back the covers. The temperature had dropped during the night, and the room was chilly. Caddie rubbed her bare arms as she walked down the hallway, wishing she'd shut her bedroom window.

Having peed, she decided that she wanted a drink. Her mouth tasted like pot, her tongue thick and pasty and altogether unpleasant. She brushed her teeth quickly and, feeling slightly more alive, went downstairs. As she passed through the dining room, she saw that the table had been cleared. In the kitchen, the dish drainer was stacked neatly with freshly washed dishes. The scrubber in the sink was still wet. *He must have gotten up practically at dawn,* she thought as she filled a glass from the tap.

She finished her drink, rinsed the glass, and placed it in the drainer. While heading back to the stairs, she noticed that the front door was open and went to close it. Through the screen door, she saw her father standing in the driveway. The rear of his Volvo was open, and the ground around him was littered with what Caddie recognized as dive gear.

She was about to turn away and escape to the safety of her room when her father, looking up, saw her. "Good morning," he said.

"Morning," Caddie replied. She waited for the accusations she was sure were coming, but her father went back to sorting the gear into piles.

I should probably make nice, Caddie thought, dreading the prospect. Her defiance of the night before was reduced in the light of day to a feeling of vague regret, a transformation brought about not only by sleep but also by her father's apparent refusal to be angry with her. Goaded on by a stubborn refusal to let him be morally superior to her, she opened the door and stepped out onto the porch. Perhaps if she gave him the opportunity, she thought, she might yet get a satisfying argument out of him.

"How'd you sleep?" her father asked her, picking up a tank and sliding it into the car.

"Fine," Caddie said. She hoped her carefully adopted attitude of disinterest would spark him into action. When, to her frustration, her father said nothing for some time, merely adding more things to the car, she said, "Going diving?"

Her father nodded. "Pt. Lobos," he said. The name meant nothing to her, and she didn't ask for more information. She didn't care where he was going, only that he was going and that she might once again have the day to herself.

"You could come," her father said, not looking at her as he put a plastic box filled with gloves, a mask, and other items she didn't recognize on top of the tanks already in the car.

Caddie forced a yawn. "I don't dive," she said.

Her father shut the Volvo's rear door. He was wearing a baseball cap with the name of a dive operator—PNG Muck Divers—embroidered on it. As he talked, he took it off and held it in his hands, running his fingers back and forth along the brim. "You don't?" he asked.

Caddie shook her head. "No," she said.

Her father seemed genuinely surprised. She didn't know why. It wasn't like she or her mother was the one all into marine biology. And it wasn't like he'd ever offered to teach her.

"I could teach you," he said, as if hearing her thoughts. "If you want to. I'm a certified instructor. You know, so I can teach the research assistants if they need it. I don't actually teach classes or anything. But I could—"

"That's okay," said Caddie, interrupting. His earnestness was bothering her. It made it difficult to pick a fight. "I don't really want to."

Her father stopped fondling his hat. "Okay," he said. "Well, I guess I'll get going. Have a nice day."

He got into the car and started it. Caddie, half expecting him to get out and finally start the fight she still felt herself longing for, waited a minute. Then, not wanting him to think she had anything else to say, she went inside and shut the door.

It had been an unsatisfying encounter. Her father's refusal to even broach the subject of her behavior of the night before erased any feelings of sympathy for him she might have had five minutes before. *Obviously,* she told herself, *he doesn't care.*

By the time she got back to her room, she had managed to convince herself that she was the one who should be angry. Even her father's invitation to accompany him, his offer to teach her to dive, seemed an affront. She saw him as weak, afraid of his own daughter. *Why else would he let me get away with something like that?* she asked herself. His lack of backbone disgusted her.

"I would have been pissed," she said aloud, laughing roughly at her father's meekness.

She got into bed and picked up her book. What, she thought as she found the page where she'd left off, was she going to do today? It was nice to have her father out of her hair, but suddenly she saw herself sitting in the same room, in the same bed, reading the same book (or slight variations on it) day after day, week after week, until her mother came and returned her to civilization.

"Fuck!" she said, slamming the book closed.

She couldn't live with him. She just couldn't do it. How was she supposed to deal with someone who didn't even get angry? *It's like he's goddamn Gandhi or something,* she thought. He hadn't questioned her about Nick's shirt. He'd said nothing about her obvious dis of last night, hadn't even seemed to expect an apology. What was she supposed to do with someone like that?

Part of her argued that she should be thrilled to be living with a father who, apparently, didn't care what she did. She could stay out whenever she wanted to. She could get high. She could lie around all day. *I could fuck any guy I want to,* she added. *He probably wouldn't care if I did it right there in his bed.*

The problem, she saw, wasn't that her father didn't care what she did, it was that his disinterest took all the fun out of doing any of it. A number of sessions with her mother's therapist—plus thousands of hours of watching *The O.C.* and VH1's *Behind the Music*—had helped her realize that she frequently did what she did not because she really enjoyed it (although it did provide a temporary thrill that was undeniable) but because she liked getting a rise out of people. As she'd remarked to Sam and Bree following one of her meetings with the therapist, "It was way more fun to be a problem child before therapy and antidepressants."

Clearly, she hadn't abandoned the whole bad girl thing entirely, and she didn't intend to. Even though she knew it was a temporary diversion from figuring out who she wanted to be when she grew up, she enjoyed herself, at least usually. Bree called it psychological masturbation. And the way she felt when she shocked or angered people really wasn't all that different from the way she felt when she came. It took her out of her body for a while, made her feel in control.

Her father made her feel out of control. And she didn't like it. She'd feel better if he agreed to fight her; at least then she could tell if she was winning. With an opponent who kept letting you hit him, who never got up after being knocked down the first time, there was no joy in the fight. She needed someone to hit back.

At least her mother had tried. Their arguments were spectacular, the verbal equivalent of the most gorgeously fucked-up Jackson Pollock canvas, with splatters of blame and accusations streaked across the surface like ugly scars. In the midst of them, caught up in the wonder and the glory, Caddie felt alive. Inspiration sparked from her, and her soul was poured out in vivid color. It was only later, when she stepped back and saw the finished product displayed like art on a museum wall, that she found she hadn't quite captured what she'd wanted to after all.

Still, incomplete work was better than none at all. She'd succeeded in pushing her mother to the brink, hadn't she? She'd managed to get herself sent away. And while she now dearly wished she'd never gone so far, there was some satisfaction in having accomplished it so neatly. She saw her success as a measure of her own powers, rather than the result of her mother's failings, and from this she took strength.

But her father, he was something altogether different. She didn't understand him. She'd thought she knew where to begin picking him apart, where the edges of the scab were, but she'd been wrong. She couldn't get to him by simply hammering away at his heart, as she'd hoped. He didn't seem to have one to break.

She needed to know more about him if she was going to get him to understand the depths of her loathing. She once again got out of bed, this time pulling on a sweatshirt against the coolness of the air and putting on a pair of socks. Then she headed down the hall to her father's bedroom.

The door was open, depriving her of the joy of physically invading his private space. She walked in and stood there, looking around. Like her own room, his was sparsely furnished. The bed, she noted with some interest, was not centered, as she would have expected, but pushed against one wall, so that the right side was unusable. Apparently, he didn't expect anyone other than himself to be sleeping there. *That explains a lot,* she thought.

She investigated the bedside table. On top were several books, all of them scientific in nature: a history of the oyster, the something about great white sharks, a guide to the seaweeds of the Pacific coast. *No wonder you sleep alone,* Caddie thought, overcome by the dreariness of her father's nighttime reading. Only one novel—John Steinbeck's *Cannery Row*, a bookmark (really just a scrap of paper) stuck perhaps twenty pages in—provided any hint that her father might be interested in something other than his work. *And even that's about Monterey,* thought Caddie, dismissing the book as nonrevelatory.

The table had one drawer, which she opened hopefully. She'd often found interesting things in bedside table drawers. Her mother, for example, kept in hers a vibrator shaped like a dolphin and a bottle of Vicodin, and she'd once found, while snooping through the bedroom of a couple for whom she sometimes babysat, a stack of Polaroids featuring the husband of the pair dressed in women's underpants while being spanked by a woman in a Mardi Gras mask.

Her father's drawer contained a number of objects, each of which she examined in turn. First was a pair of eyeglasses, utile and dull. Then there were a number of pairs of shoelaces, all of them meant for black dress shoes, and an assortment of plastic collar stays of the sort that came preinserted in department store dress shirts. A wristwatch, the hands stopped at 7:20, lay in an impotent heap of gold links. Beside it, an expired membership card to a local gym remained affixed to the paper on which it had been mailed.

Caddie shut the drawer with a groan. There was absolutely nothing of interest. No condoms. No phone numbers on scraps of paper. No drugs, not even aspirin or sleeping pills. It was the drawer of an old man. *An old man who died fifty years ago,* she thought. Her father, she concluded, was completely devoid of personality.

Across from the bed, a dresser leaned against the wall as if it were trying hard not to be noticed. She went to it and pulled open the uppermost of its four drawers. It was filled with underwear—boxer shorts—all of them white and each one folded into a neat rectangle. They were stacked like firewood, alternating directions so that the waistband of one aligned with the leg openings of the next. Beside the undershorts were rows of socks, equally neat and equally predictable.

The second drawer contained T-shirts. These, at least, came in a variety of colors. Many featured the logos of dive shops, dive boats, or other diving-oriented businesses. Still, the sameness of them rendered them interchangeable in Caddie's mind. She closed the drawer as if sealing a coffin.

The third drawer held shorts and sweatshirts, and was rewarded with only the briefest of inspections. The fourth contained everything that didn't, for one reason or another, fit into the categories represented by the other drawers. She gave the contents a cursory look, then abandoned her investigation of the bureau, which seemed to settle with relief back into its state of weary resignation.

Her possibilities nearly exhausted, she opened the door of the closet. She was unsurprised to find it filled with shirts, all hung facing the same direction and with the buttons tidily done up, as well as a row of pants, all of them khaki in color and neatly pressed. On the floor several pairs of shoes sat obediently, like well-trained dogs.

Above the hanging rod was a shelf. On this there were sweaters, and beside these was a box made of cardboard, about a foot long and half as much tall. Caddie grabbed it and lifted it down, carrying it without hope to the bed, where she sat. She lifted the lid, expecting to find inside further proof of her father's dullness. Instead, she found it filled with papers and photographs.

The first item she withdrew was a diploma, folded into thirds, from the University of Washington, awarding Ben Ransome a bachelor of science degree in marine biology. It was dated June 17, 1985, and there was a round brown ring, as if from the bottom of a coffee cup, on one corner of it. Caddie laid it aside and kept digging. There were other papers—certificates of commendation from various marine-oriented groups, the title to the Volvo, a stack of California Department of Fish & Game abalone catch report cards dating back half a dozen years.

She was beginning to think that she'd hit another dead end when she came across the first envelope. It was red, faded to a dusty pink, and on the front was scrawled, in a child's first attempt at writing, DAD. She lifted the flap and drew out a card. It was a Valentine, handmade and embarrassing, for she recognized the work as her own. On the outside was a drawing of what she guessed was a whale swimming in a sea of blue squiggles. A fountain of hearts spouted from its blowhole, and it smiled joyfully. Inside she had written a message: HAPY VALUNTINE DAY DADDY. I LOVE U. CADDIE.

How old had she been? She tried to remember and couldn't. Probably four or five. Had she made the card in school, or had her mother helped her? She stared at the card, but nothing came to her. It was as if the Valentine had been made by some other child who had signed her name to it.

She quickly put it back into the envelope. Beneath it was another card, also from her. This one was store-bought, a birthday card featuring Snoopy, inside her signature and another declaration of love. This time she'd dotted the "I" in her name with a heart. *Ugh,* she thought, looking at it. When had she been such a freak?

There were more envelopes, but she left them alone, having no interest in seeing further proof of her childhood sweetness. Instead, she leafed through the remaining items, only glancing at them, lest she come upon something else she didn't want to see. In this way, she almost missed the photograph. It had been stuck between two envelopes, and she would have missed it had not the sudden flash of a face caught her attention amidst the sea of paper.

It was a picture of her. Actually, a picture of her and her father. He was standing beside a Christmas tree, holding her in his arms. She was reaching out toward the tree, an ornament dangling from her fingers as she tried to hang it on a branch. She recognized the ornament. It was a glass mushroom. If you looked carefully, though, you saw that it was actually a short, fat girl with a mushroom hat. She had always loved that ornament, and her father had always helped her hang it in a special place on the tree.

In the photo, her father was looking at her with a strange expression. It was a look somewhere between awe and fear, as if he'd just seen her for the very first time and half expected her to turn and bite him. *Or like he's afraid he might drop me,* she thought.

She spent another moment looking at the photo, then put it back.

She'd suddenly lost interest in excavating her father's past. She felt tired, and somewhat nauseated, as if by unsealing the box she'd released some kind of poisonous gas into the room. Wasn't that how the archaeologists who'd discovered King Tut's tomb had died? *I've unleashed the curse of Ben Ransome,* Caddie thought, without humor, as she returned the box to the closet and shut the door.

She left her father's bedroom. As soon as she was past the door, she breathed more easily.

CHAPTER 19

The inflatable boat rocked on the surface of the ocean. Ben, trying to put on his BC, nearly fell over the side as a swell passed beneath them. He was saved when Angela, reacting quickly, reached out and grabbed his arm.

"Thanks," Ben said.

Angela, her BC already on and fastened securely, sat on the side of the boat, waiting for Ben to finish. "You seem a little distracted today," she remarked. "Is everything all right?"

Ben, cinching his waist strap, checked to make sure that the air hose was connected to his dry suit. "I'm okay," he said. "I just wish we could have used the real boat instead of this bathtub toy."

Angela bit her lip, hiding her amusement by spitting into her mask, then turning and rinsing it in the water. She knew Ben preferred the other boat and that he was mad at himself for not requisitioning it as he was supposed to. Instead, one of the other teams had gotten to it first, leaving them with the Zodiac. She didn't mind it so much. She seldom, if ever, got seasick. But Ben was cursed with a sensitive stomach. Already he'd thrown up once during the ride over. And sitting on a rocking boat was the worst thing for someone who was prone to motion sickness.

"I'm just about ready," Ben said, attaching the clip on his underwater light to one of the D-rings on his BC. He picked up the camera resting on the boat's bottom and handed it to Angela. She took it and held it on her lap as Ben, placing his regulator in his mouth and adjusting his mask, rolled backward into the water. When he bobbed back up, he placed one fist on top of his head, the universal sign that everything was okay.

Leaning over, Angela handed him his camera. When Ben had it securely in hand, she handed him a second one, hers, and then repeated his roll into the water. She came up beside him, and he handed her camera over.

"We'll go down and circle the pinnacle coming back up," Ben said. "Nice and easy. Photograph whatever you see. It's good practice."

Angela nodded. Ben gave her the thumbs-down sign indicating that he was ready to descend. She mirrored him, and they both released air from their BCs, gently submerging. As the water closed over their heads and the weight in their BC pockets helped them sink, they leveled out and floated horizontally.

Ben fidgeted with his camera. It was a temperamental thing, and every time he used it he swore he was going to replace it. There was even a newer one sitting in a box on his office floor back at the station. But he knew how to use this one, and the thought of having to start all over again was unappealing. So he put up with its quirks and hoped each time that it would reward him with a good picture or two.

The water was murky, a cloudy greenish-brown that provided only a few feet of visibility. Even Angela, only perhaps five feet from him, was nothing more than a shadow against the curtain of particulate matter that had turned the ocean into what one of his fellow biologists quaintly termed "a big bowl of ick." It was one of the trade-offs they endured for being able to dive so close to the mysterious Monterey Canyon. The cold waters allowed for a greater diversity of marine life, but it came with a price, namely, the food that fed so much of that diverse life. Every upwelling from the canyon brought with it great sweeping drifts of microorganisms that covered everything in a living veil, much like, Ben always imagined, the dust storms that tormented the prairie states. Divers unaccustomed to it, and even some who were, often convinced themselves that sea monsters, both real and imagined, lurked behind this scrim and refused to dive when the visibility was low.

Ben himself had experienced several times the unsettling sensation of being bumped by something unseen while passing through the shadowed water. While the likely culprits were the seals and sea lions abundant in the local waters, it was easy to see how a more active mind might go immediately to far more gruesome possibilities. He was pleased, therefore, to see that Angela seemed to be at ease in the conditions. She had been a diver for less than a year, and her experience prior to arriving at the station had been limited to the warm, clear waters of Hawaii. But she had learned quickly and was now Ben's most able assistant.

At about twenty feet they suddenly dropped into near-perfect visibility. It was momentarily startling, as if someone had thrown open a window shade. The pinnacle, which had heretofore been obscured, sprang into view, a massive tower of rock not a dozen feet from where Ben and Angela floated. Had he not been expecting it, Ben might have found himself chilled by the realization that the sea could hide such a monstrous secret from him. As it was, he greeted the pinnacle like an old friend, which is what it was.

They continued their descent, stopping at eighty feet. The protocols of diving required them to begin their dive deep and move gradually to shallower water, where the air in their tanks would last longer and where the nitrogen that built up in their blood at depth could be off-gassed safely. Because they could stay at that depth for only a short time, Ben immediately began to search for documentable subjects. A quarter way around the pinnacle, he saw a flash of light from Angela's strobe and silently congratulated her on her efficiency.

The dive was primarily for Angela's benefit, to give her more practical experience photographing undersea life. For Ben it was almost purely recreational, although he was shooting as well. He began with a *Hermissenda crassicornis* nudibranch he discovered feeding along the edge of a sponge. Looking through the view screen on the back of his camera, he zoomed in on the creature until he could see the distinctive yellow stripe, edged in orange, that bisected its body. On either side of this line, the gorgeous brown cerata, tipped in yellow and white, formed a dense forest covering the nudibranch's back.

He was trying to get a good shot of its rhinophores, the rings that circled them like bracelets on the slimmest of wrists so different from those of most nudibranchs. But he was having trouble with the zoom, and the *Hermissenda*'s head kept going in and out of focus as he fumbled with the controls through his thick gloves. It, of course, was the perfect model, holding its pose beautifully while he ineptly attempted to capture its beauty.

Finally he got a shot that looked halfway decent. He pressed the button, was rewarded with a burst of light, and moved on. The pinnacle was, quite literally, crawling with life, and mostly he chose his subjects not by any scientific criteria but by how lovely they were to look at. When he framed a sea star within his window, it wasn't because it was at all unusual (it was a common *Dermasterias imbricata,* he remembered, testing his knowledge) but because the blue-ring top snail crawling along across one leathery arm (Was it *Caliostoma annulatum* or *ligatum*? He could never remember.) made it appear that the sea star was wearing a beautiful brooch.

He snapped a number of pictures—a tiny kelp crab that waved its half-inch-long pincers menacingly; a corraline sculpin perched on a small outcropping, where it blended seamlessly with the purple and gray rock; a colony of translucent thumblike tunicates. These were the familiar occupants of the pinnacle, often seen yet still, to Ben, awe-inspiring. He looked upon them as he might a UFO, filled with wonder that things so alien and so beautiful could coexist with him, a great clumsy animal who had to strap a tank of air to his back to enter their world.

They were working their way up, first to seventy feet, then to sixty. As they circled the pinnacle, moving clockwise up the spire, Ben looked at Angela, her fins fluttering as she attempted to stay still long enough to photograph a tiny pincushion-like Cockerell's Dorid (*Limacia cockerelli* he recited automatically) and thought suddenly of Caddie. They weren't that far apart in years. The girl swimming beside him could easily have been his daughter. But she wasn't, and his actual daughter was on dry land some sixty feet above him.

He'd offered to bring her, he reminded himself. He'd made the effort. It was Caddie who had said no, who had rejected his extended hand just as she'd rejected his dinner the night before. But he'd decided to let that go. There was no point in having an argument. Obviously, she had been trying to upset him (he found it impossible to believe she could simply have forgotten), and if he let her believe that she had, she would just do it again. It was better, he thought, to ignore her, as Carol had forced him to do when Caddie was an infant and she cried for long periods of time, seemingly for no reason. "Just let her work it out," Carol had said, while Ben, his nerves tight from hearing his daughter wail in the next room, had wanted to run and snatch her up. He'd secretly accused Carol of heartlessness, even when, after an hour or less, a quick check on Caddie proved that she was indeed sleeping peacefully.

He would leave her alone now, too, he'd decided. Let her work it out on her own. Whatever "it" was. Apart from a wholesale hatred of him, he couldn't think of anything specific that would make her so determined to upset him. Then again, he'd never been very good at understanding the unspoken needs of other people. He always assumed that they would tell him what they wanted and was repeatedly surprised when, more often than not, they left it to him to guess.

A sudden tugging on his fin made him turn his head. Angela was looking into his face, her eyes wide with excitement. She motioned to him to follow her, then turned and swam off. When she stopped, pointing into a crack in the rock, Ben followed her finger to see what she'd been so anxious to show him.

A tiny red face looked back at him. It was attached to a thin body perhaps a foot long. The creature's tail was curled, and it peered up at Ben with an expression of utter surprise. The gills on either side of its neck fluttered as it breathed.

Angela held up her hands, asking him what the animal was. Ben held his hand out, the fingers flat together and turned vertically, and made the sinuous motion that represented an eel. Angela responded with a look of disdain that clearly indicated that she knew full well that it was an eel. Ben then held his hands together, the palms a short distance apart. *It's a baby,* he telegraphed at her.

It was, specifically, a juvenile Wolf Eel. And it was a good find. While adult eels were a not-uncommon sight in Monterey, sightings of their young were rare. They most often stayed well hidden, coming out only when they were large enough to protect themselves. This one, apparently, had decided he was tough enough to handle any potential predators.

Ben tried to think of a good sign for wolf eel, as Angela was waiting for more clarification. Finally, he lifted his head and pretended to bay. A stream of bubbles flew from his regulator, and when they cleared he saw Angela nodding enthusiastically and clapping her hands together, the childish but completely appropriate sign for having discovered something thrilling.

Ben motioned for Angela to take pictures of the eel. He hovered vertically in the water column as she did, silently appreciating her patience with what was a difficult undertaking. Not only did she have to juggle the mechanical intricacies of the underwater camera, she had to do it while not making any moves that would frighten her skittish subject. Again, Ben found himself thinking about Caddie. Surely by now she would not only have scared off the little wolf eel, but she would probably somehow be blaming him for it.

Maybe that's what fathers are for, he thought. Someone had to be the scapegoat. After all, it wasn't that far back in human history when the king of a land might be killed as an offering to the gods when something went wrong. The prevailing philosophy—that the king was in charge and therefore should be held responsible for the failings of his kingdom—could with little trouble be applied to fatherhood. Particularly, he thought, by an angry child.

If Caddie wanted to use him as a whipping boy, he saw little he could do to change her mind. Still, he wished things could be different. He'd had an ambivalent relationship with his own father, a kind of mutual disinterest that, while not hostile, was uncomfortable for both of them. They remained strangers to one another until the day of his father's death, at which point Frank Ransome had become a silent and seldom-seen ghost who haunted the halls of his son's memory.

Is that how Caddie would remember him when he was dead? Would she, should she come across a photograph of him, need a minute to remember exactly who he was, as Ben once had when a picture of his father had fallen from a box of old papers he was carrying from his garage to the garbage can? Looking at the unsmiling face staring up at him from the ground, Ben's first thought had been that it was a photograph of one of the more humorless American presidents, perhaps Hoover or Johnson. Only after recognizing the dog sitting beside the man, a surly shepherd that went by the name of Prince and that had once bitten Ben, requiring seven stitches to his hand, did Ben remember his father. Even then, the memory was more about the dog, which his father had refused to get rid of following the attack and which Ben had feared until its death nine years later. He recalled, too, that a framed photo of Prince had hung beside his own school portrait in the hallway between the bathroom and his bedroom, where he passed it several times a day.

Although warm enough during the dive, Ben realized that he was now quite cold. He got Angela's attention and indicated that they should begin their ascent to the surface. She nodded, looked back at the wolf eel, which had retreated into its den, and the two of them resumed their circling of the pinnacle.

They moved more quickly now, decreasing their depth at a steady but unhurried pace. When they arrived at the layer of algae, they rose to fifteen feet and stopped there, pausing three minutes as an added precaution against complications from decompression. Unable to see, the minutes passed slowly as Ben checked his computer repeatedly, waiting for the counter on his display to reach zero and free him to surface. Finally it did, and he kicked up through the last dozen feet, breaking the surface not far from the Zodiac. Angela followed shortly after.

"I think your computer cheats," she said as they made the short swim to the boat. "You always seem to have a shorter safety stop than I do."

"But you always have more air left than I do," Ben joked. "So that makes us even."

Still in the water, he removed his BC, inflating it to keep it afloat while he gripped the rope running along the Zodiac's side and heaved himself into the boat, propelling himself up with his fins. Then he turned and retrieved from Angela the two cameras and her BC. A moment later she slid gracefully over the side.

"How come I look like a walrus when I do that and you look like a mermaid?" Ben joked as Angela deftly removed her fins and stowed them in her mesh dive bag.

Angela started to speak, but Ben cut her off. "Don't answer that," he said.

"I can't believe that juvenile wolf eel," said Angela, pulling off her hood and shaking her hair. "He was absolutely gorgeous."

She continued to talk about the wolf eel as Ben stowed his gear and started up the boat's motor. Even during the bumpy, loud ride back to Hopkins she rhapsodized about the dive. Listening to her, Ben tried to imagine Caddie being so excited about, well, anything. He wasn't sure she was capable of an emotion more exuberant than boredom.

He was tempted to ask Angela about her relationship with her father, then remembered that they'd already had that discussion, at least in an abbreviated fashion. She'd suggested that Caddie was simply going through a phase. He hoped she was right. *But even if she is,* he thought as they neared the dock, *I doubt she'll be out of it before the summer's over.*

CHAPTER 20

When Brian called at two in the afternoon, Caddie was taking her second nap of the day. Actually, this second rest was accidental, occurring when she fell asleep in the middle of the last chapter of the book she was reading. Having gotten that far, she'd found that she didn't care who had committed the murders that were central to the novel's story, and despite her best efforts to remain with the characters to the end, she found it impossible to remain awake. She had been asleep for approximately thirty-five minutes when the phone rang, waking her up.

Her father, she discovered while racing through the house in an attempt to locate the source of the ringing, had only one phone. This was installed in the kitchen, requiring her to run down the stairs, in the process slipping and hitting her knee on the newel post. Cursing and limping, she made it to the phone on the seventh ring, for once happy that her father's apparent disinterest in entering the twenty-first century meant either that his ancient (to her) phone had no answering mechanism or that he had failed to turn it on.

"Hello," she said, rubbing her smarting knee.

"Caddie?" replied a male voice.

For a moment she thought it was Sam, and her heart swelled with relief and joy. Finally, a voice from home. She started to express her pleasure at hearing from a friend when the voice continued. "It's Brian."

"Oh," she said, momentarily disappointed. "Hi."

"Is this a bad time?" Brian asked.

Caddie rallied herself. "No," she answered, trying to sound more enthusiastic. "I just fell on the stairs and whacked my knee. How are you?"

"I'm fine," said Brian. "You're sure you're all right? I don't want to be responsible for crippling you or anything."

Caddie laughed. Now over both the pain of her fall and the dashing of her hopes for news from Sam, she was actually pleased to be talking to Brian. "I'll send you the emergency room bill," she teased.

"I just wanted to say I had a good time last night," Brian continued. "I know you're supposed to wait two days—or maybe it's three, whatever—before you call, but I was thinking about you this morning while I was cutting up fish."

"You really know how to make a girl feel special," said Caddie. "I've never been compared to fish parts before."

Brian groaned. "That's not what I meant," he said. "See, this is why men can't talk to women. You never know when we're complimenting you. Me, I'd be thrilled if you compared me to chum."

Caddie took the phone (it was at least cordless, which she thought was something of a miracle) into the living room and sat on the couch, pulling her legs up and nestling into the pillows. "I'm not sure if you're up to chum," she teased. "Maybe bait."

"I'm hanging up now," said Brian, and when there was dead silence, Caddie thought maybe he had.

"Hello?" she said.

It was Brian's turn to laugh. "Ha!" he said. "You missed me."

"Listen, chum," said Caddie.

"No," Brian interrupted. "You listen. How about meeting me at the aquarium this afternoon? Say around four? Then we can hang out for a while."

"I don't know," said Caddie, pretending to be hesitant. "Oprah's supposed to have a really great show today. I'm not sure if I can tear myself away."

"Well, I hope you and Oprah have a good time," Brian replied. "I'll just sit here with my fish parts and think about you."

"Don't even go there," said Caddie. "Where should I meet you?"

"Come in the front entrance," Brian told her. "Tell them you're meeting me, and they'll tell you where to go."

"You carry that much weight around there, huh?" said Caddie.

"Hey, in the land of the fish, the guy with the chum is king," Brian said proudly.

Caddie said good-bye and hung up. She still wasn't sure exactly what she thought of Brian. He was cute, and funny, and nice. *Pretty much everything that would usually send you screaming,* she told herself. *Especially the nice part.* Nice guys generally weren't that interesting, mostly because there was no challenge there. Perversely, she tended to go for guys who either didn't show enough interest in her or showed enough but showed just as much in a couple of others girls as well. Nice was hard for her.

Still, he made her laugh, and that was something. Besides, she reasoned, there was nothing else going on in her life. Brian might not be the most exciting guy, but he was a guy, and in a place like Monterey, that was enough, at least for the moment.

She looked at her watch. She had about ninety minutes before she was meeting Brian. That gave her enough time for a shower and maybe a quick lunch before she headed out. She went upstairs, spent her time in the bathroom, and came down again forty minutes later ready for something to eat.

In the kitchen she opened the refrigerator and looked inside, expecting to find it as bare as she had the day before. Instead she found it filled with plastic containers. She opened one, revealing spaghetti. Another held pasta sauce. She realized that she was staring at the remains of the dinner she'd failed to show up for.

She took the food to the table and got a bowl from the cupboard. After spooning pasta into it, she poured some of the sauce on top. Two minutes later, while she waited impatiently by the sink, the microwave on the counter dinged and she took the bowl out. The spaghetti had relaxed, and the sauce coated it in a thick blanket of tomatoes. Caddie located the salt and pepper shakers and sprinkled a little of each onto her food.

She ate quickly. When she was done, she washed the bowl and fork in the sink, dried them, and put them away again. The containers she shook so that the contents appeared untouched, then returned them to the refrigerator. If her father opened them, she thought, he wouldn't be able to tell if she'd eaten anything or not.

She went upstairs and brushed her teeth, checking them for stray pieces of basil. Her skin looked good, as did her hair. All in all, she was pretty pleased with her appearance. She was wearing jeans and a blue T-shirt. Blue, everyone told her, was her color. She'd read somewhere that wearing blue relaxed people and made them feel they could trust you. *That's probably why Valium is blue,* she thought.

That reminded her. She returned to her bedroom and took the bottle of pills from her backpack. Tipping one into her hand, she popped it into her mouth and swallowed, chasing it with some water from the glass on the bedside table. She didn't feel anxious, but as Sam always said, you could never feel too relaxed.

Grabbing her sunglasses, she left the house and headed for the aquarium. She walked slowly, not wanting to arrive all hot and sweaty. Passing Johnny's, she didn't even look to see if Nick was working. She thought vaguely about maybe calling Nicole one of these days, just to see what happened if the three of them really did hang out. But if she knew guys, Nick had probably already made up some bullshit story to tell Nicole. Probably he'd told her that Caddie had come on to him and that it wasn't a good idea to get too friendly. *And I'm sure she believed every word,* Caddie thought disdainfully.

When she reached the aquarium, she approached the ticket window. "I'm here to meet one of the volunteers," she told the woman behind the glass. "His name is Brian—" She stopped, realizing she didn't know Brian's last name. "He does the show in the kelp tank," she said.

"Brian Foster," the woman said. "Are you here for volunteer training?"

From the woman's tone, Caddie got the impression that saying no would result in her being asked to pay the admission fee, so she nodded. "Yeah, I'm thinking about it."

"Go in and head to the left," the woman instructed her. "All the way back. You'll see a door that says STAFF ONLY. Go in and ask for Brian. They'll know where he is."

"Thanks," Caddie said as the woman turned her attention to the next person in line. She pushed open one of the big doors and went inside. Following instructions, she walked toward the kelp tank area and found the door. She half expected an alarm to sound when she pushed on the handle, but the door swung open without incident, admitting her into a room filled with tanks and machinery.

"Can I help you?" asked a young man wearing an aquarium T-shirt like the one Brian had.

"I'm looking for Brian Foster," Caddie said.

The guy pointed. "Over there," he said. "He just finished his show."

Caddie walked in the indicated direction. Turning a corner, she found Brian standing in his wet suit. Seeing her, he smiled. "You're just in time to watch me strip," he said.

"Do I have to put a dollar in your wet suit?" Caddie asked.

Brian pulled a cord at the rear of his suit, drawing a zipper down. He tugged the front of the wet suit down, sliding first one arm and then the other out. His chest was bare, and Caddie admired his lean, well-defined physique.

"You're checking me out," Brian said as he bent over and tugged the suit down past his waist.

"Right," Caddie said. "I'm overcome with desire. Please, fish boy."

Brian pulled one leg out of the wet suit, turning it inside out in the process. He did have on a bathing suit, but Caddie still got a look at his legs. She pretended not to notice.

Brian hung the suit on a nearby rack, which already held half a dozen other wet suits. An assortment of other gear was piled on the floor nearby. Caddie recognized some of it as stuff her father had, although what it was used for was a mystery.

"Do you dive?" Brian asked, noticing her looking at the equipment.

"No," Caddie said. "I never learned."

"I'm surprised your dad never taught you," Brian remarked, drying himself with a towel. "You know, with him being a marine biologist and all."

Caddie shrugged. "I guess he never had time," she said.

Brian toweled his hair. "Want to learn?" he asked her. "I could teach you."

Caddie looked doubtfully at the dive gear. "I don't know," she said. "It looks kind of complicated."

"It's not," said Brian, pulling on a T-shirt. He knelt beside the equipment. "Not once you know what it is and how to use it."

Caddie joined him on the floor as Brian picked up a short cylindrical object from which three hoses hung down, each one attached to another piece of equipment. "This is your regulator," Brian said. He placed a mouthpiece between his teeth and talked around it. "You breathe through this," he said, demonstrating before removing the regulator from his mouth.

He went piece by piece, showing her the computer; the low-pressure hose that, he explained, attached to her buoyancy control device and allowed her to inflate or deflate it as necessary; and then BC itself. "There's not a lot more too it," he told her. "You just need to learn how to use it all."

"How long would it take?" Caddie asked him.

"A couple of hours," said Brian. "It's not rocket science."

Caddie looked again at the gear. "Okay," she said. "It might be fun."

"It *will* be fun," Brian said, taking her hand and helping her stand up. "After all, you're going to learn from the best."

"I thought Jacques Cousteau was dead," Caddie said, trying to look confused.

To her surprise, Brian kissed her. When he pulled back he said, "Still want to go with Jacques?"

Caddie shook her head. "I'll stick with you," she said.

"Good answer," Brian said. "Now let's get out of here."

"Where are we going?" asked Caddie as he led her toward the door.

"My house," Brian said. He stopped. "Is that okay?" he asked her.

"Sure," said Caddie. "That's great."

As they walked through the aquarium and out to Brian's car, she wondered exactly what he had in mind for the rest of the afternoon. He'd been so hesitant the night before that she didn't know what to think.

When they arrived at his place—a small, shabby house not all that much different from her father's, but in worse shape—Brian pushed open the unlocked front door and Caddie walked in. The house was decorated in what Caddie thought of as Trash Night Eclectic, a phrase she'd coined to describe furnishings gleaned from the unwanted things set out on sidewalks the world over on the night before garbage pickup. Not that anything was dirty or broken, just mismatched and on the far side of being new, or even middle-aged.

"I know, it looks like a frat house," Brian said. "It all came with the place. The house is owned by some old guy who supports the aquarium. He lets summer workers live here free. I figured I'd rather stay here and pocket the money than spend a couple hundred bucks a month for someplace with better chairs."

Caddie couldn't argue with that. "Besides," she told him, "it's not that bad."

"You hungry?" Brian called from the other room, where he'd disappeared a moment earlier.

"A little," Caddie answered. The pasta she'd downed before meeting him had been good, but now she found she wanted something more.

Brian was gone another minute or two. When he came back he said, "I called for takeout. It should be here in twenty minutes."

"What'll we do until then?" Caddie asked him.

Brian put his arms around her waist. "Have I shown you the bedroom?" he asked.

Caddie let him take her upstairs and into the bedroom that, in another house, was her father's bedroom. She approached the bed— this one centered on the wall and unmade—and sat on it. Brian, putting his hand on her shoulders, pushed her gently back and straddled her. Then he leaned down and kissed her.

This time his kiss was anything but tentative. His tongue explored Caddie's mouth, probing and insistent. She kissed him back, her hands on his lower back, pulling him into her. She felt his hardness through his shorts and slid her hand down to meet him.

The kiss went on without pause. Brian, grabbing her wrist, put her arm behind her head, then brought her other arm up. Pinning her, he rubbed himself against her in short thrusts, all the while looking into her eyes and holding his mouth just out of reach as she tried to kiss him. Then he sat up, releasing her wrists. His shirt came off, and Caddie ran her fingers down the tight planes of his torso. His skin was warm to the touch, the hair on his stomach soft as she followed it down to the waistband of his shorts.

As she was reaching for the button holding him closed, the doorbell rang. Brian looked down at her. "Do you mind getting that?" he said. He glanced meaningfully at his crotch, which was tenting out significantly.

He got up and fished in a pocket. "This should do it," he said, handing her some crumpled bills. As she straightened her clothes he kissed her and cupped a breast. "Hurry back," he said.

The doorbell rang again as Caddie went down the stairs. "Coming!" she called out.

She opened the door. Nick, gazing at her in surprise, stood there holding a pizza box.

"Hey," he said after a moment.

Caddie leaned against the door frame. "Hey," she said.

"I didn't know you lived here," said Nick. "I've only ever seen that aquarium guy here."

"I don't live here," Caddie answered, letting him fill in the rest for himself. She wondered if he was smart enough to know what she was implying, and found herself hoping he was.

Nick nodded. "Oh," he said, his voice telling Caddie that he knew exactly what she meant.

"How much is it?" she asked.

Nick looked down and moved his lips, as if trying to calculate the cost of the pizza. "Fourteen seventy-five," he said.

Caddie looked at the bills in her hand. Brian had given her a five and a ten. She handed them to Nick, not even bothering to smooth them out. "Here," she said, taking the box from his hands and going back in the house. She gave him one last look as she shut the door. "Keep the change."

CHAPTER 21

"Have you found it yet?"

Hudson opened his eyes. By the window, a shadowy figure stood looking out at the moon. As Hudson tried to get his sleep-heavy mind to begin working, the figure turned toward him. "Have you found it yet?" it asked again. It was a man's voice, soft yet firm.

Hudson shook himself awake, the realization that he was not alone in the room turning quickly from confusion to fear. He rubbed his face with his hands, as if trying to wipe the grime away from a dirty window.

The man, still in shadow, took a seat in the armchair beside the window. He placed his hands on the arms, tapping his fingers restlessly as he crossed one leg over the other. There was something familiar in the gesture; a picture flashed across Hudson's vision, disappeared almost as quickly. He smelled tobacco, rich and earthy. Then, as if the lid had been throw open on some inner trove of memories, he saw the glint of moonlight off the ring on the left hand, recognized without question the anxious shaking of the crossed foot.

"Paul," he whispered.

"You haven't answered my question," the man replied. "Have you found it?"

Hudson peered into the dim, trying to see the face hidden within it, but darkness swarmed like bees, obscuring everything. Only the hands, endlessly tapping, were illuminated.

"No," Hudson said, "I haven't. But I think I'm close."

"You think, or you are?" asked the voice.

"I am," answered Hudson.

Laughter, short and wistful, greeted his words. "Still doubting your-self, I see," the man's voice reproached him.

The shadow rose and stepped forward, into the light. Hudson looked up into the handsome face of a man perhaps fifteen years his senior. His hair, short and neatly trimmed, reflected the silver of the moon. His eyes were dark, and his mouth curled in a smile both sweet and sad.

"Paul." Hudson repeated the name. "Why?"

Paul reached out and touched Hudson's face. His fingers moved gently down the younger man's neck, tracing the gentle curve of his collarbone and coming to rest on his chest. Hudson felt his blood beat harder. He reached up with his own hand to touch Paul's where it covered his heart.

He awoke with a start. Panicked, he sat up and looked around the room. It was empty. No one stood at the window. No figure watched him from the chair. The air smelled only of the sea and the lemon trees. There was no odor of tobacco, no gentle scratching of fingers, no voice from the dark. He was alone.

The sheet covering his body was damp with sweat. It clung to him in places with clammy fingers. Hudson pulled it down, letting the warm summer night stroke him with calming fingers. His heart, he re-alized, was indeed beating too quickly. That part had been no dream.

He reached for the glass of water he'd placed on his nightstand. Warm now, it nonetheless slaked his thirst. The simple process of holding the glass, feeling the water go down his throat, proved to him that he was awake. The dream was gone.

He drained the glass and sat it down again. Without it, he felt sud-denly vulnerable, as if without it to anchor him to the real world he might slip back into the darkness. Quickly he reached over and turned on the light. A soft yellow circle surrounded him as the shadows re-treated.

Paul. He could say the name now without fear. No, he thought, it wasn't fear he'd felt at Paul's touch. It was longing. Still, longing was its own kind of haunting, worse perhaps because it went on forever un-fulfilled. And no matter how much he might want it, Paul's touch was gone from him forever.

Don't, he told himself. *Don't let yourself go there. He's gone.*

He needed a distraction. Instinctively, he reached for a book, then remembered that he'd left it downstairs. Disinclined to leave the island of his bed to descend into the shadow world of the house, he looked again and saw the stack of papers. He took them up with relief, noticing as he did that the clock said half past three.

The papers were copies, made for him by Helen Guerneyser from the materials he'd looked at the previous afternoon. Hudson had feared at first that the number of pages would be excessive, but the archivist had made no objection, sending him away from his first day of research with a thick stack of paper and an open invitation to come back whenever he liked.

He pulled his knees up and leaned the papers against them. Mostly he had requested copies of Steinbeck's journals. Seated in the reading room, he had been afraid to really look at them, as if he were being watched by some invisible monitor ready to revoke his privileges for any breach of scholarly protocol. Alone in his room, however, he read them with the same excitement with which he'd once read his sister's diary, purloined from its not-so-secret hiding place beneath the sweaters in her dresser drawer and spirited to his own room for leisurely perusal.

While his sister's journal had been filled with adolescent despair over parents who didn't understand her and boys who didn't love her, Steinbeck's were most notable for his observations of those around him. It was easy to get lost in the descriptions of characters who entered and exited his life like players in film. At some point, though, Hudson had begun to wonder how much of the writing—fine as it was—was meant as distraction. Almost as if Steinbeck had fully expected that one day his words would be pored over by those looking for insight into his work, the entries were engaging yet almost uniformly without reference to his personal feelings, at least apart from those having to do with his writing.

However, there were moments of seemingly dull revelation hidden among the glittering stones, tiny chunks of unpolished ore that were easily overlooked. They were tucked into a paragraph here and there, almost as if they were afterthoughts to something more important and not worth the effort of elaboration. Noticing one, Hudson had begun to find others, in the same way that the sandy expanse of a beach could hide a multitude of beautiful shells, if only one could train the eye to see the bits of purple, or blue, or green beneath.

Small, neat starbursts penned in red in the margins indicated potential lines of interest. Many pages—sometimes five, six, seven, or more in succession—bore no such indicators; most had only one or two. It was these that Hudson looked at now, recalling why he had found them worthy of notice.

The first group of pages came from entries written in the weeks following the death of Ed Ricketts. Here Steinbeck had written with unusual candor about the loss of his friend. But even within such emotion Hudson detected a note of deception, not of fact, but of something deeper. Steinbeck's grief seemed, if anything, too commonplace. It was the grief of someone unable to see the true extent of his loss, uncharacteristic of Steinbeck's usually unflinching exploration of human feeling, whether his own or that of another.

One line, though, buried amidst many others, had glimmered with a peculiar fluorescence of meaning. "With Ed's death," Steinbeck wrote, "the tides have changed. I feel myself retreating, becoming smaller, like a patch of beach that is swallowed up by the rising water."

He read the line again. "The tides have changed," he said aloud. It was an unremarkable analogy, perfectly apt in its description of grief. But for Hudson it had another connection. He fumbled with the papers in his hands, looking for the copies he had brought with him from home.

He found what he was looking for on page seventy-two of the typescript.

> *The tide was retreating, pulling away from the shore like the cover being lifted from a bed and revealing the naked sleeping forms beneath it. Charlie thought again of that morning, of the still air of the room and the motes of dust floating in the sun like insects trapped forever in amber. He thought, too, of his hand on the quilt, his fingers tracing the lines of the squares and diamonds pieced together by unknown hands. And then of the other hand, the one beneath, the one tracing the same patterns on his naked flesh. Thinking of this, he grew smaller, his body shrinking even as the memory loomed larger and larger, until its great black mouth opened and he was swallowed up.*

"It's a common metaphor," Hudson said, speaking as if to someone else. "It doesn't *prove* anything."

No, he thought, it didn't. At least not on its own. But with *more,* with something definite, he could argue a strong case. Even then, he supposed, there would be those who disbelieved. Probably someone would even accuse him of manufacturing the manuscript himself. It had been done before, he remembered. That woman at Wellesley had claimed to have found a poem by Christina Rossetti, supposedly a long-sought-after companion to "Goblin Market." She had even gone so far as to write the fraudulent poem on paper from the correct era, although where she got it was anyone's guess.

It was the ink that was her undoing. She'd used a kind of German black that, although certainly employed by writers of Rossetti's time, was known to break down over time in a very particular way that the more common cuttlefish ink did not. Although the woman had made a valiant attempt to make the manuscript appear aged, a simple laboratory test revealed the ink to be less than a year old, and the hoax was revealed to the not-insignificant satisfaction of skeptics, most of whom had spent their own lives in search of the same prize and were now free to believe that it still waited somewhere to be found.

Hudson's manuscript, while not nearly as old, was still nonetheless a matter for great debate. Typed instead of handwritten, it could have come out of one of a million different machines. The type was perfectly ordinary, no dropped "e" or off-center "r" to provide even a small physical clue to the pages' origins. The paper, too, was common and undistinguished by either texture or watermark. It could, he knew, have been nearly anywhere by anyone.

But it wasn't. He was certain of it. Paul, the only other one to know the full story, had been certain of it. The thought stopped him. Once again, Paul's ghost had entered the room. Hudson felt him, hovering in the corner, watching. He heard again the question—Have you found it yet?—and he pulled the sheet up against the chill that seemed now to seep under the closed door.

Go away, he thought, closing his eyes. *Please. Just go away. This is hard enough.*

He shook, fighting back fear and sorrow. Something in the room, something beyond his tight-closed eyelids, moved almost imperceptibly. He felt it as a breath of air, just for a moment across his cheek. Then it was gone. When he opened his eyes, he saw that the sky outside the window was touched with the first light of coming morning.

He returned to the manuscript. Reading to make the dawn come faster, and not in search of clues, he turned to a random page and began.

> The dog, a mix of retriever and terrier with the less
> agreeable physical characteristics of both breeds, was sniff-
> ing, with great interest, the bottom two feet of the wall be-
> longing to the Kingfisher Cannery's loading platform.
> Several hundred pounds of sardines had recently occu-
> pied the dock above, and the bricks were stained with the
> proof of their temporary residency. The dog was licking the
> streaks of fish-scented water with the satisfaction of one
> whose last meal was far enough behind him so as to be for-
> gotten, and consequently did not see the man behind him
> or hear the rock that was thrown by the man's hand. Only
> when the missile struck him in the side did the dog turn
> from his dinner, giving a sharp cry and flattening his ears
> alongside his head.
>
> "Go on!" shouted the man. "Git!"
>
> The dog, not knowing what sin he had committed but
> sensing that it was a great one, nonetheless could not leave
> behind such a temptation as was presented to him by the
> fishy water. He attempted to get in one more lick. In hesi-
> tating, he doomed himself. The man, irritated beyond rea-
> son at being disobeyed by a dog, rushed forward. Swinging
> his leg back, he delivered a ferocious kick to the dog's un-
> derside.
>
> "I said git!" he repeated, as if perhaps the dog had sim-
> ply not heard him the first time.
>
> The dog, who had fallen to the ground, looked up at his
> attacker with uncomprehending eyes. He wagged his tail
> limply and gave a little whine, for which he was rewarded
> with another blow. Stunned, he tried to stand and run, but
> could only sway slightly from side to side. His tail contin-
> ued its back-and-forth motion, as if he still believed he
> could save himself.
>
> As the man prepared to strike again Charlie, who had
> been watching the encounter from across the street, found
> himself running at great speed toward him. As he ran, he
> raised his fist, so that when it connected with the side of the

man's head, it did so with enormous force. The man, caught not only by surprise but off balance, flew into the wall, where his head met the brick with a dull thud. Like the dog, he attempted to stand, but without the benefit of a wagging tail he found the effort too great, and collapsed to the ground.

Charlie, kneeling before the dog, caught the trembling creature up in his arms. As he walked away, the dog looked into his face. Charlie could feel its heart beating through the bony cage of its chest. When its warm tongue licked his hand, he screwed up his eyes against the brightness of the sun and breathed deeply.

"Why'd you do that for?" Tom appeared at Charlie's side. His breath smelled of beer.

"It wasn't right," Charlie said.

Tom scratched his head. "It's jus' an old dog," he informed Charlie, as if perhaps this was knowledge his friend did not possess. "An old dog," he repeated.

"He shouldn't of thrown a rock at it," said Charlie. He shifted the dog in his arms, cradling its hind legs as he might a baby. "It's just hungry is all. It wasn't bothering nobody."

Tom whistled. "You know who that was you knocked down back there?" he asked. He didn't wait for an answer. "That was Poker Greenwood. You don't want to mess with Poker." He shook his head wearily at the tragedy of the situation.

"Too late for that," said Charlie. "I already done it. Besides, he shouldn't of hurt this dog."

"That there dog should of gone and done what Poker told it to," Tom said. He looked at the dog accusingly, and it growled low in its throat. "Well, you should of," Tom told it.

They walked far enough that they were at the door to Charlie's rooming house. "What now?" Tom asked him. "You gonna put that old dog down now and come have a beer with me?"

Charlie shook his head. "Guess I'll take him inside," he said. "He's still hungry. Guess I can give him somethin'."

Tom looked at the dog, then at Charlie. He put his hand

on Charlie's shoulder. *"You are one crazy son-of-a-bitch,"* he said. *"Knockin' down Poker Greenwood cause he took after this here old dog."*

He petted the dog roughly on the head, ignoring the growl and the narrowed eyes. "You are one lucky dog," he told it. "You got yourself a good man here. A good man."

He patted Charlie once more on the back, then walked away, singing the words to a song he appeared to be making up as he went along. Charlie watched him for a moment, then went inside. He carried the dog up the stairs to his room. Mrs. Ring, hearing him, looked out her door. When she saw the dog, she came out to have a look at it.

"Man was beating it," Charlie said before she could object. "Hurt him pretty good."

Mrs. Ring opened her mouth, then shut it again with a snap. She eyed the dog for a moment, then reached out to stroke it. The dog shrank back against Charlie. Then, understanding that Mrs. Ring meant him no harm, he allowed himself to be petted.

"You got some food for it?" Mrs. Ring asked Charlie.

Charlie nodded. "Got some hamburger," he said.

Mrs. Ring sighed. "Take him on up," she said. "Poor thing."

Charlie nodded his thanks and climbed the rest of the stairs. Once in his room, he sat down on the bed with the dog in his lap. It had stopped shaking and was panting softly. Charlie rubbed its ears. "Good boy," he said. "You're a good boy."

Not knowing why, he buried his head in the dog's fur. It smelled of oil and fish and salt. "You're a good boy," Charlie said as tears began to form in his eyes. "A good boy."

Hudson put the pages down. He had read the passage before, many times in fact. But still it moved him. *He just wants something to love,* he thought. *Someone to love and to love him back.*

He yawned. Although it was nearing five—a perfectly reasonable time to get up—he wasn't quite ready. He put the manuscript and the copied pages to one side. *Five minutes,* he told himself.

It was much later than that when he awoke to the sound of his cell phone ringing. He fumbled for it on the bedside table, knocking over the empty water glass, which hit the floor and shattered.

"Shit!" he said, looking at the pieces.

"Pardon?" said a voice, and Hudson realized that he'd managed to answer the call.

"No," he said quickly. "I mean, hello. Who is this?"

"It's Ben Ransome."

Hudson had to think hard to recall where he'd heard the name before. Then, in a rush, it all came back to him: Monterey, Ricketts, coffee. "Ben," he said, relieved. "It's good to hear from you."

"I hope I didn't wake you," Ben said.

Hudson glanced at the clock. It was after nine. "No," he said. "I've been up for hours."

"Well," said Ben, "I was calling to see if you might be free for dinner tonight. At my house. I thought we could continue our conversation about Steinbeck and Ricketts."

"Dinner," Hudson repeated. "Sure. That sounds great. What time?"

"How about seven?" Ben suggested.

"Seven is fine," said Hudson.

"Great," said Ben. "Here's the address." Hudson searched for a pen and scribbled down the address Ben gave him. "I'll see you tonight," Ben said when he was done.

Hudson barely had time to respond in kind before the call was ended. He set the phone on the table and stared at it. He was filled with a vague sense of unease. But why? He knew it had nothing to do with Ben Ransome or his call. It was something left over from the night. He'd been dreaming about something, but now he couldn't remember what it was. An image lurked in the recesses of his thoughts, just out of sight. He tried to call it forth, but it retreated swiftly.

He noticed the papers strewn over the bed, and remembered. The dog. He saw it emerge from the darkness, its tail wagging hopefully. *That's what it was,* he told himself. *It was just the dog.*

CHAPTER 22

"Can anyone tell me how deep the Monterey Canyon is?"

A young man, his face bearing the harsh red eruptions of new acne, raised his hand. "Two thousand feet?" he said hesitantly.

"Try again," Ben said as the boy looked down at the floor and rubbed self-consciously at a spot on his chin.

He waited for someone else to speak but was met with a sea of blank faces. After a full minute had passed, he sighed and gave them the answer. "The canyon bottom reaches a depth of around eleven thousand eight hundred feet," he announced.

He paused, expecting at least one or two of them to be impressed. When they clearly weren't, he continued. "That makes it roughly the same size as the Grand Canyon," he told them. This time there were a few appreciative nods. *At least some of them have been on family vacations,* Ben thought, trying not to be annoyed. But it was too late; he was already annoyed. He hated addressing the summer interns, the dozen or so high school students selected to spend a month at the station learning about marine biology. Most of them were the spawn of generous donors, accepted into the program in return for their parents' continued financial support. Two or three had a genuine interest in the ocean; the rest just took up space and got in the way.

It was a condition of Ben's funding that he oversee the intern program. He resented the time it took away from his own work, and each year it was more and more difficult to feign enthusiasm for what he considered enforced babysitting. This year, however, Angela had offered to help him shepherd the would-be biologists, for which he was more than grateful. He looked at her, standing beside him, and shook his head. She stifled a laugh.

"Because the Canyon comes so close to the shore here, we have a wonderful opportunity to study deep-sea life that we otherwise would probably never get to see," Angela said, picking up the spiel she and Ben had rehearsed earlier that morning. "Numerous new species have been discovered by researchers utilizing our submarine program."

Ben listened as Angela described some of the research projects carried out at Hopkins. *She sounds so enthusiastic,* he thought. *I remember when I sounded like that.* But that had been quite a few years earlier. Now he was just weary of trying to make other people excited. His own work still interested him, but he wished he didn't have to bother with all of the other stuff, the administrative duties and asskissing that seemed to be necessary to keep going. He hated that so much research was dependent on the beneficence of people with money, people who were usually more interested in the glory of patronage than in the actual discoveries their largesse made possible. He was always amazed by how much people were willing to give just to have their name attached to a newly discovered species of octopus. *One of these days I'll probably have to name a nudibranch Archidoris Paris Hilton,* he thought, unamused by the thought.

"So we hope all of you enjoy your time here at the Hopkins Marine Station. If you have any questions, feel free to ask me or Dr. Ransome."

Ben, sensing the weight of two dozen eyes suddenly falling upon him, was jolted back to the moment. He smiled stiffly. "Yes," he said. "Ask me anything." *Now go away and leave me alone,* he added silently.

The interns obeyed, scattering to their assigned areas of the facilities, becoming somebody else's problem, at least for the moment. Ben, sighing, retreated to his office with Angela. She shut the door as Ben dropped with relief into his chair.

"That wasn't so bad," Angela said.

Ben rubbed his temples. "I'm too old for this," he said.

"You're not old," said Angela. "They're too young."

Ben smiled. "They get younger every year," he remarked.

"Well, I made sure none of them was assigned to your project," said Angela. "That should help."

"Thank you," Ben said, genuinely grateful. "I don't think I could stand another year with some stupid girl who insists on calling nudi-branchs 'snails.' "

"Hey," Angela admonished him, "I was one of those girls once."

Ben looked at her with surprise. "You were an intern here?"

"Seven years ago," Angela answered. "But you wouldn't remember. I worked with Dr. Rashid."

"Seaweed," Ben said. "I remember her. She was researching cancer treatments."

Angela nodded. "Well, she decided there was more money in cosmetics," she said. "Now she and her seaweed are coming up with ways to erase fine lines and wrinkles."

"Why didn't you tell me before?" asked Ben. "About being an intern, I mean."

Angela shrugged. "I knew you wouldn't remember," she said. "Besides, it's not important."

Ben looked at her. "So you fell in love with seaweed and decided to make it a career," he said. "Interesting."

"Actually, it wasn't seaweed," said Angela. "It was a basket star."

"Really?" Ben said.

Angela nodded. "They brought one up from one of the Canyon trips," she said. "It was the weirdest thing I'd ever seen. I really wanted to know more about it, but of course I was too cool for that sort of thing." She laughed and shook her head. "If it wasn't about music or boys, it wasn't cool enough for me," she added. "But I never forgot that basket star, and eventually I figured out that it was way cooler than music and boys. That's when I decided to study marine biology."

Ben leaned back in his chair and regarded the grad student from a new perspective. "So what you're saying is that there's hope for these little morons," he said.

"Well, for some of them," said Angela. "Probably most of them will go right on being little morons. But you never know. One of them might fall in love with a squid or a decorator crab."

"I guess I should give them a little more credit," Ben said.

"Just a little," agreed Angela.

"How come you're so much smarter than I am?" Ben asked her.

"Not smarter," Angela corrected him, "just younger."

"Hey!" Ben objected.

Angela held up her hands. "All I'm saying is that maybe you've forgotten what it was like to be their age. I'm starting to, but I still remember it well enough to know that they haven't figured out who they are yet."

"You're right," Ben admitted. "I don't think it's so much forgetting, though, as it is not wanting to remember. As I recall, it wasn't all that much fun. At least, not for me."

"It's fun for some of them," said Angela. "But mostly it's not. You're old enough to know you want to be somebody, but you're not old enough to be it. That's frustrating."

Ben nodded. He understood that. *That's where Caddie is right now,* he thought suddenly. *She's trying to be somebody she's not ready to be.* He'd been so consumed with figuring out who they were in each other's lives that he'd neglected to realize that she couldn't know that until she knew who she was.

"The boy," Ben said suddenly, and Angela looked up. "The one with the face," Ben added, waving his hand in front of his chin to indicate the acne he recalled as the young man's most distinguishing feature.

"What about him?" Angela asked.

"What's he assigned to?" said Ben.

Angela looked down at a list attached to the clipboard she carried. "Rhodes Latrell," she read, running her finger along the page. "He's working with Dr. Patcher."

"Salps," Ben said dismissively. "Nobody cares about salps. Take him off that and put him with us."

"With us?" Angela repeated.

"With us," Ben confirmed. He saw that Angela was looking at him with an expression that combined wonder and amusement. "Nobody cares about salps," he said again.

"I'll take care of it," Angela said. "Anything else?"

Ben shook his head. "No," he said. "Send him in when you get a chance."

"Great," said Angela. "I'll get back to analyzing the extraction data from those dorids we brought in the other day. That is if they're still in the refrigerator. I blended a dozen of them and Jenkins almost drank them. He thought they were a smoothie."

"That's not a bad idea," Ben said. "Nudibranch smoothies. I bet Jamba Juice would go for it. We can say they're full of antioxidants."

"Okay, Dr. Rashid," said Angela, standing up. "I'll get right on that."

"It was just a suggestion," Ben called out to her retreating back. "We can even name it after you. We'll call it 'Angela's Archidoris Antioxidant.' "

Angela shut the door without responding. Ben, grinning, beat a tattoo on his desktop. He felt immensely better. Angela was a great girl. *Woman,* he corrected himself. *She's a great woman.* Suddenly, he wished he knew someone he could set her up with. There was no one at Hopkins, at least no one he would want to see her with. And he had no idea what kind of guy she might be interested in anyway.

Then he thought of Hudson Jones. He and Angela were probably close in age. Hudson was a good-looking guy, and he seemed intelligent. Yes, he thought, they might be good together. And since Hudson was coming to dinner that night, he had the perfect opportunity to introduce them.

He was now in a much-improved mood. He would invite Angela to dinner, but he wouldn't tell her about Hudson. Nor would he tell Hudson about Angela. It was perfectly natural that he would have the two of them over. *Except that you've never had anyone over before,* he reminded himself. He brushed the thought aside. It didn't matter. Angela would come, and Hudson had no idea that he was Ben's first dinner guest in recent memory.

Having come up with a plan, he realized that he had given almost no thought to dinner itself. Pasta had been in the back of his mind, but now that seemed inadequate. The problem was, he didn't know how to make anything else. It was his one culinary accomplishment. *And you saw how well it went over with Caddie,* he thought.

Caddie. He'd been avoiding thinking about her. They'd had dinner together the night before, a strained half hour during which they'd downed Chinese food that Ben had picked up on his way home. He'd asked Caddie about her day and gotten vague answers in response. He hadn't pressed her. She'd at least deigned to eat with him, which was an improvement over the previous two nights.

After dinner she'd retreated to her room, claiming exhaustion. Ben had let her go, happy to spend the evening alone in his office. Peaceful disinterest was preferable to outright hostility, and if Caddie didn't want to talk about her life with him, he would let her have her secrets. *How much trouble can she get into in Monterey anyway?* he'd thought. It wasn't like L.A., with its endless temptations for a young woman.

Part of him hoped Caddie wouldn't make an appearance at dinner that night. Immediately he felt guilty for thinking such a thing. Of course he wanted Caddie there. *But only if she behaves herself,* he admitted. Suddenly his mind flashed back to when Caddie was three or four. Carol had wanted to take Caddie to dinner with them at a restaurant that, while hardly gourmet dining, was several notches above fast food. Ben had protested. "What if she acts up?" he'd said. "She'll bother the other diners."

"She's a child," Carol had argued. "Of course she's going to act up. And we'll deal with it."

There had been a big argument, and ultimately Ben had lost. They'd taken Caddie, and she had acted up, refusing to eat what they ordered for her and throwing a tantrum. Ben, mindful of the annoyed glances from other patrons, had begged Carol to leave. "She'll never learn if we give in to her," Carol had said. And so they'd stayed, Ben trying to eat his steak while Carol, with great patience, calmed Caddie down and got her to at least try her spaghetti.

Spaghetti, he thought. *She wouldn't eat it for me then, and she won't now.* It was ironic, in the most obvious yet painful of ways. He had been unable to understand his child then, and he was unable to understand her now. Then again, he reasoned, Carol couldn't handle her now either. The problem of Caddie had grown too big for both of them. Or perhaps Carol had just run out of patience. *Or maybe now she cares what other people think,* thought Ben. What was acceptable at three was, at sixteen, more difficult to defend against the reproachful looks of strangers.

As quickly as it had brightened, his mood soured. He hated that thinking about his daughter had this effect on him. Yet it did, and he couldn't help it. She was like the equation he couldn't solve, the missing piece of a puzzle that eluded finding.

A soft knock on the door interrupted his thoughts. "Come in," he called gruffly, his irritation tinting his tone.

The door opened and a pimpled face looked in. "Dr. Ransome?" the boy said.

Ben tried to remember the young man's name. Already it had escaped his memory. *Crete?* he thought. *It was a city.* Then it came to him. "Rhodes," he said, trying to sound welcoming. "Come in."

Rhodes entered the office and walked timidly to a chair. He looked at it for a moment, like a dog unsure of whether it was allowed on the furniture. Then he sat. He rested his hands in his lap, worrying them together. "Angela said you wanted to see me," he said.

"Are you interested in salps?" Ben asked him.

Rhodes's eyes looked down in the expression of shameful worry that Ben had noted earlier. *He's not sure what the right answer is,* Ben thought. *He thinks I'll be mad if he picks the wrong one.* The parent in him badly wanted to tell the young man that it was all right; the scientist in him wanted to wait for the boy to decide. In the end, science won out. He waited, watching Rhodes work through the possible results of the available responses.

"Not really," he said finally, not looking at Ben.

"Me neither," Ben said. Rhodes looked up at him, surprise and relief in his face. "But don't tell Dr. Patcher I said that," said Ben. "She thinks they're endlessly fascinating."

Rhodes rewarded him with a smile that flashed briefly and vanished again beneath the mask of uncertainty. *He's still not sure he's not in trouble,* thought Ben. "What do you know about nudibranchs?" he asked.

Rhodes shrugged in the ubiquitous teenage response. "They're snails, right?" he said.

"They're slugs," Ben corrected him. "Would you like to help us study them?"

Again came the shrug. "I guess so," said Rhodes. "What would I be doing?"

"Can you dive?" asked Ben.

This time Rhodes nodded. "I was certified two years ago," he said.

"Excellent," said Ben. "Then you can come on dives with us. Also, you'll help Angela and me in the lab. Does that sound all right with you?"

"Sure," Rhodes said, his voice devoid of excitement.

"Or you can stay with Dr. Patcher and her salps," said Ben, determined to get more from the boy than simple agreement.

"I'll take the nudibranchs," said Rhodes quickly.

"Good," Ben said. "Why don't you go see what Angela is doing. Tell her you need to fill out the research diving forms."

Rhodes stood up. As he walked to the door, Ben stopped him with a question. "Rhodes, why are you here?"

Rhodes turned. "Honestly?" he said.

Ben nodded, and Rhodes bit his lip. "It was either this or baseball camp," he said. "And I suck at baseball."

Ben made a mental note to find out who Rhodes's father was and how much he'd donated to the program. But he appreciated the boy's honesty. "We're happy to have you," he said.

Alone again, his thoughts returned to Caddie. Like Rhodes, she was with him because the alternative was worse. So why couldn't he talk to her the way he'd just talked to Rhodes? Why had he been able to understand what the young man needed when he couldn't even begin to understand what his daughter needed?

Answering that question, if it even could be answered, would have to wait. At the moment he had more pressing concerns. *Like what to serve for dinner,* he thought, and wondered how hard it would be to roast a chicken.

CHAPTER 23

"I feel like a lobster." Caddie pulled at the neck of her wet suit. "I'm boiling in this thing."

"Here," said Brian. He tugged at the zipper on the back of the suit, pulling it halfway down. "Is that better?"

"A little," answered Caddie. "I can't believe how hot these things are."

"You won't think it's too hot once we're in the water," said Brian. "The water's probably fifty-three, fifty-four degrees."

"Why aren't we wearing that kind of suit?" asked Caddie, nodding at two divers walking toward the beach.

"Dry suits?" said Brian. "You don't really need one. Besides, they're more complicated. You have enough to worry about. Now let's go over the reg again."

Caddie knelt beside him on the grass where they'd laid out their gear. Brian had borrowed some for her from a friend, and he'd showed her how to put it together. The regulator was attached to the tank, which in turn was strapped to the BC. Brian picked up the reg and handed it to her. Caddie put it in her mouth and dutifully breathed in and out a few times before removing it.

"That's pretty much it," Brian told her. "Oh, except for buoyancy. You're going to have to learn how to put air into your BC so that you float under the water. That's what you use this for." He picked up a thick corrugated hose attached to the front of the BC at the shoulder. It ended in what looked like a regulator.

"How's it work?" Caddie asked.

Brian pressed a small button on the regulator end and the BC puffed with air. "You use this bigger button to let it out again," he explained, showing her.

"That looks easy enough," said Caddie.

Brian laughed. "You think so?" he said. "Wait 'til you try it underwater."

"What else?" asked Caddie, ignoring him.

"Now we get you in the water," said Brian. "That's how you learn. Just do what I show you and you'll be fine."

Caddie, anxious to get going, allowed Brian to help her on with a neoprene hood, which he tucked beneath the neck of her wet suit before zipping her up again. Caddie puffed her cheeks in and out, getting used to the tight feel of the hood.

Next Brian lifted her BC, holding the bottom of the air cylinder on the back as she slipped her arms through the straps. When he let go, the weight of the tank caused her to almost tumble over. But Brian steadied her, and she recentered herself, bending forward as Brian secured the velcro waist belt. Then he picked up two narrow pouches.

"What are those?" asked Caddie as Brian slipped the first pouch into an opening on the side of her BC.

"Your weights," he informed her. "How else do you think you get under the water?"

"More weight?" Caddie complained as Brian snapped the weight pouch into place. "This crap already weighs half a ton."

"Don't worry," Brian said. "You won't feel it in the water."

Caddie was beginning to think that learning to dive was a big mistake. She was hot and sweaty. The hood seemed to surround her like a giant hand, and she suddenly felt like she couldn't breathe. As Brian slid the second pouch into the other side of her BC, she closed her eyes and tried to breathe. Brian, oblivious to her rising discomfort, began to put on his own gear.

I don't want to do this, Caddie thought as she waited for Brian. *I want to take it all off.* She was just about to tell Brian as much when, snapping the last of his weight pouches in place, he said, "Ready?"

Caddie nodded. Brian handed her a mask, some gloves, and a pair of fins, which she held in her hand as they walked across the grassy area to the beach. With each step Caddie grew more and more miserable, and when they finally reached the beach after traversing a short flight of stairs, she sat down on the nearest rock to catch her breath.

"Put your mask and fins on here," Brian instructed her as he slipped his gloves on and got ready. "I'll help you in."

Caddie pulled on the first glove. Her fingers felt thick and useless, which they indeed proved to be when she tried to pull the second glove on. Determined not to ask Brian for help, she grabbed the end with her teeth and pulled, inching the material over her hand until it was on. *I feel like I have paws,* she thought, looking at her hands, now twice their normal size.

"Coming?" Brian asked her. He was standing a dozen feet from her. His mask was on his face, and he was holding his fins.

Caddie, annoyed at the impatient tone of his question, ignored him as she pulled the mask strap over her head and adjusted the mask on her face. With the mask over her nose, the suffocating feeling intensified, but she fought it down, breathing through her mouth. "Ready," she said, standing up and joining Brian.

They walked together to the edge of the water. The ocean was calm and flat, and only the smallest of waves lapped at the sand. When the first one washed over her foot, Caddie tensed for the cold. When none came, she realized that what Brian had said about the wet suit was true. It wasn't at all cold.

"Lean on me and put your fins on," Brian told her.

Caddie did what he said, balancing herself with a hand on his shoulder while she pulled a fin onto one foot. It went on more easily than she expected, and she tightened the strap around her ankle with a satisfied tug. *This is going to be a piece of cake,* she told herself as she put the second fin on.

"Now we'll walk in," said Brian. "But you'll have to walk backward because you have fins on, so you'll have to trust me."

Her arm through Brian's, Caddie shuffled awkwardly toward the ocean. Unable to see anything, she had to rely on him, which she didn't like. It made her feel helpless. *It's just until we're in the water,* she told herself.

She felt the water hit her legs. As they proceeded, it rose to her waist, and then a wave crashed lightly against her lower back. At the same time, she felt water begin to seep into her wet suit. Now she was cold, but only momentarily.

"Okay, you can turn around," said Brian.

Caddie turned, moving her finned feet carefully. She was in the ocean. Although the beach was less than fifteen feet behind her, she had the sensation of being in another world. Water was all around her.

She looked down through her mask and saw the sandy bottom. A crab scrabbled away from her fin on tiny legs.

"We can swim the rest of the way," said Brian. "Just put some air in your BC so you don't sink."

Caddie, remembering what he'd shown her, pressed the smaller of the two buttons on the inflator and felt her BC swell around her. When it felt full enough, she stopped. Brian had put his snorkel in his mouth, and she aped him, finding it where it was attached to her mask strap and slipping the end in her mouth. Then, falling forward, she swam.

She'd snorkeled before, but only in warm water. This was different. As they moved to deeper water, the landscape beneath them changed dramatically. The sand gave way to rocks, and then to areas thick with kelp. *It really does look like the exhibit at the museum,* Caddie thought. *It's beautiful.*

After a minute she felt something tug on her arm and looked over to see Brian floating vertically in the water. She lifted her head, bobbing, to see why he'd stopped.

"We'll go down here," Brian told her.

"How do I do that?" Caddie asked.

"Just let the air out of your BC," said Brian. "Like this." He put his regulator in his mouth, held his inflator hose up, and pressed a button. Air hissed out, and a moment later Brian began to sink out of sight. Caddie watched his head sink beneath the surface.

Here goes nothing, she thought as she did as he had. She breathed air in through the regulator as her BC deflated. Then the sky was gone and she saw nothing but water, brown and green. A moment of terror seized her as she realized that she was underwater, but a gasp on her regulator assured her that she could still breathe, and she calmed down. She fell quickly. She saw kelp rushing by her and wondered if she was going too quickly. Brian hadn't said anything about how to stop the fall, and she seemed to be moving both too quickly and in slow motion through the water. *Like Alice down the rabbit hole,* she thought as she waited to see what would happen.

Her feet hit the bottom with a jolt and she stood there, not knowing what to do. She looked around for Brian and saw him hovering horizontally beside her. Behind his mask, his eyes were laughing at her. She started to tell him off, then remembered that she couldn't talk. Instead, she glared at him and waited for him to show her what to do.

Pointing to her inflator hose, Brian mimed pushing the button to put air into it. At first Caddie didn't understand. Then Brian indicated that she should float like he was, and she began to figure out what he wanted her to do. She pressed the button gently, letting a little air in. As her BC inflated, she attempted to hover like Brian was. Instead, she crashed to the bottom, landing heavily in the sand.

She added some more air, and this time she began to rise up. It was a strange feeling, and she felt out of control. She added too much air and felt herself rising quickly. But Brian grabbed her and, holding onto her, showed her how to let air out of her BC so that she was once again going down. Finally, she was more or less hovering in the water next to him, although she still wasn't entirely comfortable. *There's too much to remember,* she thought as Brian, holding her hand, began to swim.

She kicked, propelling herself forward. She'd thought that diving would make her feel like a fish. Instead, she felt like a hippo. *A completely ungraceful hippo,* she thought moodily. And Brian was wrong; she *was* cold. Also, her ears hurt. She moved her jaw from side to side, as she did when her ears hurt during airplane takeoffs, and the pain subsided.

Brian was swimming toward what looked like a big pipe. When they reached it, Caddie saw that it was exactly that, an old pipe, rusted and covered with all kinds of sea life. Following it, they continued to swim, Brian on one side and Caddie on the other. He'd let go of her hand, and she now found it a little easier to maneuver herself.

Despite the novelty, she found herself kind of bored. Apart from a lot of kelp and some fish, there wasn't much to look at. A starfish, orange against the dark rust of the pipe, momentarily distracted her. But she'd seen lots of starfish (although admittedly they had mostly been dried and decorating the walls of beachside restaurants), and this one was unremarkable apart from the fact that it was alive.

She looked down, to the side of the pipe, and saw what appeared to be white and black flowers growing in a small patch in the sand. Intrigued, she tried to get closer to them. As she neared, however, the flowers retreated into themselves, disappearing and leaving behind only short, naked stumps like dead fingers. Amazed, Caddie waited to see if they returned. A moment later, one of the fingers expanded and tiny filaments emerged, blooming into a white flower. Caddie reached out a gloved finger and touched it, sending it back into hiding.

What the hell is that? she wondered. She looked for Brian, wanting to show him the remarkable find. He was a few feet away, waiting. She pointed to the flower-things, and he swam over to look. When he saw what she was pointing at, he shook his head as if to say, "I know what those are." Then he turned and swam off.

Caddie wanted to stay and wait for the flower-things to come back. She was surprised that Brian was treating them so casually. She wanted to know more about them. Brian, however, seemed to want to keep going.

Now as they swam she looked at the ocean with new eyes. It was as if the flower-things had granted her some magic powers. *Like those girls in the stories who get grease in their eyes and can see the fairy world,* she thought. And she did feel now that she was in some other world, one filled with things she'd never even imagined.

A crab, its back decorated with bits of shells and strands of kelp, crawled across the pipe. Meeting another crab, it raised its pincers, and the two danced around one another until the second crab, smaller and with a bright orange carapace, seemed to fall down the side of the pipe like a skier caught in an avalanche. It caught itself and sat, motionless, on the skin of the pipe, its tiny mouth working busily.

It was, Caddie saw, a world of conflicts and intrigues. Its citizens, most of them weirdly beautiful, carried on oblivious to the world above. And she, Caddie thought, was equally oblivious to their world. It had never occurred to her that so much life not only lived beneath the water but went on beneath the water. She felt she'd discovered an entirely new civilization where before she'd seen only darkness and wet.

She left the little crab behind, seeing something in the sand that she wanted to investigate. What appeared to be a scrap of purple material was waving gently in the current, as if someone had dropped a handkerchief or thrown away the wrapper from a candy bar. Caddie, finding herself annoyed at the idea that someone would do such a thing, intended to pick it up, although it occurred to her as she reached that paper that she had nowhere to put it.

But it wasn't waste. It was an animal. At least she thought it was an animal. It didn't look like anything she'd ever seen. Perhaps half a foot in length, it had a soft purplish body from which extended what she could only think to describe as feathers, although really they were more like flags, flaps of pale pink that covered the creature's back and fluttered as if a breeze were blowing them. It was unlike anything she'd ever seen, and she hadn't the faintest clue what it was. *It looks like something Stevie Nicks would wear as a shawl,* she thought with amusement.

The creature moved slowly over the sand, doing what Caddie had no idea. She watched as it approached one of the flowerlike things she had seen earlier. With excruciating slowness it touched the thing's stalk, sending it into retreat. Undeterred, the creature seemed to climb the stalk, its body sliding upward in a series of undulations. Then it stopped. When, a few moments later, the stalk opened and its owner emerged, the creature pounced, its head surrounding the head of its victim.

Caddie was enthralled. Clearly, the creature was eating. But what was it eating, and what was it itself? She had absolutely no frame of reference for understanding these things, and the complete mystery of them delighted her. When she saw Brian swim up beside her and point in the direction from which they'd come, she left the scene only with much reluctance.

The swim back was quicker, as if Brian was in a hurry to return to land. Caddie kept up with him until suddenly she felt herself rising quickly toward the surface. She fumbled with her inflator hose, trying to let some air out of her BC, but before she could even find the button she was at the surface. A moment later, Brian appeared beside her.

"What happened?" Caddie asked, finally finding the right button and releasing some air.

"You were too shallow to stay down," said Brian. "You need to let air out as you get shallower."

"How do I know I'm getting shallower?" asked Caddie.

Brian reached over and held up another of Caddie's hoses, this one attached to a large gauge. "Look at your dive computer," he said. "How much air do you have left?"

"I don't know," Caddie said. "Is that on there too?"

"I guess I skipped a few things," said Brian. "We turned around because I was getting low on air." He looked at Caddie's computer. "You have a ton left," he said. "Not bad for your first dive. Did you have a good time?"

"What were those things we saw?" asked Caddie.

"The thing that looked like a flower is a kind of tube anemone," Brian answered. "And that purple thing is a nudibranch."

"Nudibranch," Caddie repeated. She recognized the word from one of her father's boring dinner conversations. "That's what they are?"

"There are a lot of different kinds," said Brian. "That one is *Dendronotus iris.* We call it the rainbow nudibranch because it comes in a couple of different colors. Little-known fact—it's the only nudibranch that swims," he added. "Although it's not very good at it."

"It was eating that anemone, right?" said Caddie.

"That's it's favorite food," Brian explained. "It also lays its eggs around the anemone's tube. I always imagine the anemone sit there looking at those eggs like the ones in *Alien,* just waiting for the babies to pop out and eat them."

"Yeah," Caddie said vaguely as they swam on their backs toward the beach. She couldn't get the nudibranch out of her head. It was so beautiful. And that's what her father studied. His work had never seemed interesting to her, but now that she'd seen one for herself, she thought she understood, at least a little bit, why he was into nudibranchs.

But he probably doesn't even notice how pretty they are, she told herself. *He's just interested in what's inside them.*

She wasn't like him, though. Where her father saw cold, hard science, she saw something more. Beauty. Magic. Wonder. Things he could never understand.

I'm not like him, she repeated to herself, and kicked for shore.

CHAPTER 24

"The lasagna is just about done," Angela said, shutting the oven door. "How's that salad coming?"

"You know, when I invited you to dinner, I didn't intend for you to *make* it," Ben said as he chopped a carrot into thin rings.

"It's lasagna," said Angela, washing her hands at the sink. "You throw some stuff into a pan and let it cook. It's no biggie."

"Not for you," said Ben. "I was just going to pick something up at Tilly Gort's."

Angela made a face. "The all-natural place?" she said.

"What?" said Ben, seeing her expression.

"Nothing," Angela said quickly. "It's just that it's so . . . all-natural."

"I like their curried couscous," Ben countered. "Besides, aren't all of you hip young things supposed to be into health food?"

"Hip young things?" Angela said. "And what are you, withered and old?"

Ben set the knife down and swept the pile of carrots into the salad bowl. "You know what I mean," he said.

Angela, leaning back against the counter, pushed her hair behind an ear. "You're pretty hip yourself, you know," she said.

The front door opened, and Ben was pleased to see Caddie come into the kitchen. When she saw Angela, she stopped and looked from her to her father. "Hi," she said.

"Caddie, this is Angela," Ben said. "Angela is one of the grad students working with us."

"Oh," Caddie said, as if some unspoken question had been answered. "Hi."

"Your father's told me a lot about you," said Angela.

Caddie looked at her father but said nothing. Ben, too, was quiet, busying himself with a tomato. "Angela is having dinner with us," he said.

Caddie nodded. "I'm going to go take a shower," she said, leaving quickly with a nod at Angela.

"She doesn't seem so hostile," Angela remarked quietly, coming to stand beside Ben.

"I think we caught her off guard," said Ben. "She probably thought you were a date or something." He laughed shortly.

"What's so funny about that?" Angela said, hitting him lightly on the arm.

"Me having a date," said Ben. "Especially with someone like you."

"You don't think very highly of yourself, do you?" Angela remarked, going once more to the oven and opening the door.

Ben started to answer but stopped. He didn't know how to answer the question. Even if he did, he wasn't sure he wanted to. He was used to Angela being his assistant. Although their relationship had become more casual of late, he still saw her as something of a daughter, not a psychiatrist. He cleared his throat. "I hope you don't mind, but I invited another friend to dinner," he said.

Angela pulled the lasagna out of the oven and set it on the stovetop. "And here I thought I had you all to myself," she said.

"His name is Hudson," Ben said. "He's a grad student. Like you."

"Biology?" Angela asked, tearing off some tinfoil and covering the lasagna pan.

"English," said Ben.

"My last boyfriend was an English major," Angela said. "He was completely obsessed with Eudora Welty. It was way too much for me. I mean, how do you compete with a dead woman?"

"I guess you can't," Ben answered, feeling a little lost. He was rescued by a knock on the door. "Come in!" he called.

Hudson, carrying a bottle of wine, came into the kitchen. "I hope I'm not too early," he said.

"You have perfect timing," said Angela. "I just took the lasagna out." She held out her hand. "Angela Rossiter," she said.

"Hudson Jones. It's good to meet you."

"Tell me, how do you feel about Eudora Welty?" Angela asked him.

Hudson hesitated a moment. "I guess my favorite of her stories is 'The Wide Net,' " he said. "The novels I'm not so fond of."

Angela turned to Ben. "See?" she said. "They all have a thing for Eudora Welty."

"Did I miss something?" Hudson said, looking confused.

Ben took the bottle from him and fished a wine opener from one of the drawers. "Angela had a bad experience with an English major," he explained.

"Oh," said Hudson. "Well, if it helps any, she looked way too much like my grandmother for me to have a thing for her."

Angela laughed. "I like this one," she said to Ben, who was pouring the wine into glasses.

"Is it just the three of us?" asked Hudson, accepting a glass from Ben.

"Four," Ben told him. "Caddie will be down in a minute."

Hudson sipped his wine. "Dinner smells great," he remarked.

"You have Angela to thank for that," said Ben. He was pleased that Hudson and Angela seemed to be getting on. *I had a feeling they would,* he congratulated himself.

"Here's our fourth now," Angela said, and Hudson turned to look at Caddie. Freshly showered, she was wearing a white T-shirt underneath a yellow long-sleeved shirt. Her hair, freed from its ponytail, fell loosely around her face. Seeing Hudson, she smiled brightly.

"You must be Caddie," said Hudson. "Your father—"

"Has told you so much about me," Caddie interrupted. "I'm hearing that a lot."

Ben, listening while he put the salad into four bowls, heard the sarcasm in her voice. But it was mixed with a playfulness he'd never heard in her tone before. It took him a moment to realize what it was. *She's flirting with him,* he thought with surprise.

He turned and looked at his daughter. She was leaning against the doorway, nodding at something Hudson was saying. Then she laughed, a glittery run of girlish enthusiasm. Ben, confused, searched for Angela and found her cutting the lasagna into squares. If she noticed Caddie's flirtation with Hudson, she didn't show it in her expression.

"All right," Angela announced. "Dinner's on. Everyone into the dining room."

The four of them went into the other room. Ben took his usual seat, while Angela took the one opposite. Caddie and Hudson occupied the other chairs, facing one another across the table. Angela picked up Caddie's plate and spooned a piece of lasagna onto it. Caddie nodded as it was set before her, but her eyes were on Hudson.

"Hudson is interested in John Steinbeck," Ben announced to no one in particular. Watching Caddie's behavior, he was filled with a sudden unease, as if his plan were about to be undone and he needed to shore it up before it was too late.

"Steinbeck," said Angela. "We had to read *Of Mice and Men* in high school. I hated it."

Ben felt his stomach sink. But as he passed Ben a plate of lasagna, Hudson said, "It's not one of my favorites either. I think they assign it because it's so short."

Ben poked at the lasagna, waiting for everyone to be served. He glanced nervously from Angela to Hudson.

"We had to read *The Pearl*," said Caddie, startling her father into looking at her. She was spooning green beans from a bowl onto her plate.

"What did you think of it?" Hudson asked her.

"I thought it was interesting," said Caddie. "You know, the whole thing about getting what you think you want but it not being enough. Isn't that what happens to all of these rock stars and movie stars? But in the novel it happens to people who don't have anything. It's like he was trying to show that people are all the same."

"I think Steinbeck was saying that sometimes you don't know what you already have until someone takes it away from you," said Hudson. "They have each other, and their baby. Then, because of the pearl, they almost lose it all."

"All I know is that I got a C-minus on the paper I wrote," Angela commented. "I haven't read anything else by Steinbeck since then."

"Hudson is also interested in Ed Ricketts," Ben said quickly.

Angela's face brightened. "Now *he* was an interesting man," she said.

She began to talk about Ricketts with Hudson. Ben, pleased that he had turned the conversation around, sat and ate quietly, watching the two of them converse. It was a few minutes before he realized that Caddie hadn't said a word in some time. He looked at her and discovered her picking at her food. From time to time she cast dark looks at Angela.

Ben groaned internally. In averting one disaster, he had created another. Caddie was clearly jealous of the attention Hudson was paying to Angela. *Can't she see that he wouldn't be interested in her?* Ben wondered. He marveled at the inability, or reluctance, of young women to see that someone wasn't at all right for them. He supposed men did it too, but not nearly so often or so spectacularly.

"How was your day?" he asked his daughter, hoping to coax her into conversation.

"Fine," Caddie said shortly.

"What did you do?" Ben pushed.

"Nothing much," said Caddie. "Walked around town a little."

"That sounds fun," Ben said brightly, receiving nothing in reply.

"So, Caddie, what are you doing this summer?" Hudson asked, taking a break from discussing Ed Ricketts.

Ben watched the transformation come over Caddie. The look of petulance disappeared, replaced by bright-eyed enthusiasm. "I haven't really decided," she said. "Do you have any ideas?"

Hudson tipped his glass and looked thoughtful. "No," he said finally. "I'm afraid my summers when I was your age usually involved working in my father's hardware store and visiting my grandparents in Florida for two weeks. And not in the Disney World part of Florida either, I might add. The buggy, humid part where everyone eats dinner at three o'clock and goes to bed by seven."

"What do you like to do?" Angela asked Caddie.

Ben waited for her answer. He was curious to find out what his daughter was interested in, as so far she'd shown a fondness only for avoiding him in as many ways as possible.

Caddie shrugged. "The usual stuff, I guess," she said. "Mostly I hang out with my friends."

"Let me guess," Angela said. "At the mall?" She laughed gently.

"No, not at the mall," snapped Caddie.

"I'm sorry," Angela apologized. "I just meant that when I was your age, that's what we did."

Caddie set her fork down. "I like to write songs," she said. "The words, anyway. I can't write music very well."

Ben, surprised, said, "What kind of songs?"

"Just songs," Caddie said. She seemed uncomfortable, and Ben decided against asking her if she would share one with them.

"There you are," Hudson said, putting his hands up.

"What?" said Caddie.

"You can be a roaming troubadour," he said. "Charge people ten bucks to have you sing for them."

Ben waited for Caddie to get up and leave the table. Instead, she looked at Hudson and smiled. "That's not a bad idea," she said. "I could start with the people in line at the aquarium. It takes forever to get in there. I bet they'd love to have some entertainment."

"You've been to the aquarium?" Ben asked her.

Caddie looked at him, then down at her plate, where she focused her concentration on her lasagna. "I ran in the other day," she said. "There was nothing else to do."

"You should have told me you were going," said Ben. "You could have gotten in free with my member card."

"It was a last-minute thing," said Caddie. "Anyway, they gave me the student rate."

"Well, what did you think of it?" Angela asked.

"It has a lot of fish," answered Caddie without enthusiasm.

"It's the best aquarium in the country," said Angela. "You know your father helped them set up the kelp forest exhibit."

Caddie said nothing, so Ben stepped in. "It really is a pretty amazing place," he said. "You know they were the first aquarium to keep a great white alive in captivity."

"Yeah, so they could get people to pay to look at it," Caddie muttered.

Ben looked across the table at Angela. She gave him a sympathetic nod. He was grateful for her presence at the table. Even if she raised Caddie's ire, she made him feel less alone.

"Do you dive, Caddie?" Hudson asked.

Caddie shook her head. "No," she said.

"Me neither," said Hudson. "I've always thought it would be fun, though."

"You should have Ben teach you," Angela suggested. "He's a great instructor."

"Really?" Hudson said, looking at Ben. "I'd love that. I mean, if it isn't too much trouble. I don't know how long it takes or anything."

"Not long," Ben told him. "A couple of sessions in the pool to teach you the skills, then the certification dives in the ocean. We could do it in a couple of days."

"It would be fun," said Angela. "Then we could all go diving together."

Hudson looked at Caddie. "What about you?" he said. "Are you up for it?"

Caddie looked first at Angela, then at Ben. Ben could see her wrestling with something, coming to some kind of decision. For a moment he thought she was going to accept from Hudson the gift that she had refused from him. Then she shook her head. "I don't think so," she said. "I'm not really a water person."

CHAPTER 25

By his fourth visit to the Steinbeck Center, Hudson felt he was close to an answer. He'd combed through the journals, and while nothing in them could be called proof of his assertions, he felt certain that he was right. He just needed one concrete piece of proof, one solid connection that would stand against the protests he knew would confront his claim once he revealed it publicly.

The problem, of course, was that he wasn't at all sure this evidence existed. Without it, he was left with unsupportable suppositions. While he believed himself correct, he was familiar enough with the world of academia to know that believing in yourself meant nothing if you didn't have substantiating materials to back you up.

He pushed the journal he was looking at away and rested his head in his hands, rubbing his eyes. He was so close, yet he might as well be standing on the wrong side of an uncrossable chasm. What he wanted—what he needed—was just out of reach, hidden behind pages and pages of seemingly unrelated entries about one man's life.

He brought the journal back in front of him and read.

> *Went with Ed to the tide pools last night to collect octopus. Wonderful little creatures, smart like dogs. In the bucket they reach out to one another with their arms. Asking or telling, I can't say. Maybe they just want to know that they aren't alone.*

It was a beautiful observation, as so much of Steinbeck's thoughts were. But beauty wasn't proof, and insinuation wasn't enough to back up such an explosive claim as the one Hudson was contemplating. He sighed, closing the journal and thinking that maybe it was time to leave for the day. He was frustrated, and frustration made research a misery, as it generally resulted in grasping at straws. He couldn't afford to be careless. Not with this.

He was pulling his papers together, deciding what he did and did not want copies of, when the door to the research room opened and Helen Guerneyser walked in. She had with her a gentleman easily in his eighties. He was dressed in the costume of the quintessential college professor—khaki pants and a white shirt beneath a blue-gray wool jacket. His hair, surprisingly intact, was thick and white.

"Hudson, I have someone I'd like you to meet," Helen said. "This is Edgar Macready."

"How do you do?" the man said, clasping Hudson's hand in a warm, soft grip.

"I'm well, thank you," Hudson replied. He wasn't sure what else to say, as Macready's name didn't mean anything to him. He hoped he wasn't supposed to know who he was.

"Edgar was a friend of John's," Helen said, helping him out.

"Knew him in the forties," Macready said. "He and Ricketts both. Course, I was a bit younger than they were," he added, his blue eyes twinkling.

"How did you know them?" asked Hudson, thrilled to be talking to someone who knew the men personally.

"Oh, we all did," said Macready, waving his hand. "Couldn't live in Monterey and not know John and Ed."

"Edgar is being modest," Helen said. "He was Ed's assistant for a time."

Macready laughed. "Errand boy, more like it," he said. "But thank you for the promotion, Helen."

Helen smiled. "I'll leave you two to talk," she said.

"Please, sit down," Hudson said as the archivist left. He pulled out a chair for Macready, who settled into it with a sigh.

"I'm not sure I can be much help to you," he said. "Helen didn't say exactly what it is you're after."

Hudson chose his words carefully. "I'm researching some of the influences on Steinbeck's work," he said vaguely, hoping the man wouldn't press him too much.

He didn't. Rather, he nodded as if Hudson's explanation made complete sense. "Well, ask away," he said. "I'll tell you what I know. As Helen said, I did some work for Ricketts. Mostly cleaning up and mailing packages for pocket money. But of course Steinbeck came around a lot. I was there for a couple of the famous parties." He laughed. "Boy, did they know how to have parties."

"Were they as wild as people say?" Hudson asked him. "You know, all the drinking and the . . . women." He threw out the last word cautiously.

Macready was nodding. "Sure," he said. "They drank a lot. Course, everyone did then. Men, anyway. Girls, too, but they didn't make such a show of it. Didn't want to be considered loose."

"Did Ricketts have a lot of women around?" Hudson inquired. "They say he was quite a ladies' man."

"Depends what you mean by that," Macready said thoughtfully. "Women certainly liked *him*. There was something about him made them comfortable with him. He helped a lot of them out."

"The girls at Flora's," suggested Hudson.

"Them and others," Macready answered. "Never turned away a woman who needed help."

"What about his own girlfriends?" said Hudson. "He had quite a few."

"Sure, sure," agreed Macready. "But not so many as people think. Not so many as Doc in the Steinbeck books did either. I think maybe that's how they—he and Steinbeck—wanted people to think of him."

"But it wasn't true?" Hudson pressed.

"It was a long time ago," said Macready uncertainly. "You know how it is, you remember some things, forget a lot of others."

Hudson, sensing that the man was becoming uncomfortable, considered where to take the conversation next. Macready, he thought, knew more than he was saying. It was almost as if he was protecting the image of someone he admired.

"What did he and Steinbeck talk about?" he asked, changing tack.

Macready visibly relaxed. "Anything and everything," he said. "I didn't understand the half of it most of the time. They'd get going on about philosophy or religion and I'd just stand at the sink washing bottles and feeling like an ignorant cuss. Sometimes they'd try to explain it to me, and I was always afraid to tell them I had no idea what they were saying. If they weren't half drunk and needed me to go get them more beer, they probably would have kicked me out of there for being so damn stupid."

"Did Ricketts ever talk about Steinbeck with you when John wasn't around?" said Hudson.

Macready didn't answer right away. He seemed to be thinking. Then he nodded. "Now that you bring it up, he did," he said. "Only once. It was one afternoon when I was helping him prepare those frogs of his for shipping. Steinbeck had been gone awhile. I don't know where, but he hadn't been around in probably two, three weeks. Ed was in a black mood, and I think it was because he missed his drinking buddy. Anyway, we were packing up frogs, and all of a sudden he asks me if I have a best friend. I told him I did. His name was Charlie Proctor. Then Ed asks me if I love him. 'Who?' I asked him, and he said, 'Charlie. Do you love him?' "

Macready paused. The expression on his face was thoughtful, almost sad, as if something about the memory disturbed him. Hudson waited patiently for him to continue. *Charlie,* he thought while he waited. Then he warned himself. *Don't grasp at straws. It's only a name.*

"I didn't understand what he meant," Macready continued. "I said, 'I guess I do, sure.' He was looking at me with those dark eyes of his, and when I said that he sort of smiled at me. 'That's good, Eddie,' he said. He always called me Eddie, like I was his son or something. 'That's good,' he said. 'A man should love his best friend. Because someday that might be all you have.' Then he got real quiet, and after a while he said, 'I love John like that. I love him so much I'd die for him if I had to.' Only he didn't say it like he was saying it to me. And it wasn't like he was saying it to himself either. It sounded like he was saying it to someone I couldn't see."

Macready stopped speaking and looked through Hudson. After a long moment he shook his head. "I haven't thought of that in years," he said. "Probably not since the day it happened. Not until you asked me about it." He gave a short laugh. "Funny the things that stick in your head."

Hudson, his heart racing, was making notes on a piece of paper. "What do you think he meant by what he said?" he asked.

Macready cocked his head. "That he loved John?" he said. "I guess just that they were each other's best friend. I don't think anyone understood either of them the way they did each other. That was mighty important to Ricketts. Especially that it was someone like Steinbeck. Of course, Steinbeck admired Ed like crazy too. They were like two halves of the same person."

Hudson, busy writing, looked up. "Two halves of the same person," he repeated.

"You like that?" asked Macready. "It just came to me. But that's what it was like. Ricketts inspired Steinbeck, and Steinbeck immortalized Ed in his books. They gave each other what they each wanted most in the world."

Hudson set down his pen. It was time to ask the question that was foremost on his mind, and there was no way to do it gently. "Do you think their relationship was ever . . ." He hesitated. "More than just a friendship?" he finished.

Macready regarded him with a puzzled look. "You mean were they queer?" he asked, his voice harsh. "They weren't queer."

"No," Hudson said quickly. "Of course not. But maybe there was an . . . affection . . . between them."

"They both liked women," said Macready. "There was nothing pansy about either of them. Christ, can't men be friends without being queer?"

"I'm sorry," said Hudson. "I didn't mean to imply that. I'm just trying to figure out what Ricketts meant when he said he loved Steinbeck."

"He meant that he loved him!" Macready said forcefully. "A man can love another man. That doesn't mean they're . . ." His voice trailed off as he stood up. "I should go," he said. "My wife is expecting me, and you know how women are when you keep them waiting."

Hudson stood, wishing he could find some way to get the man to stay. "Perhaps we can talk again," he suggested.

Macready nodded but didn't respond. As he walked toward the door, Hudson said, "Thank you for sharing your stories with me."

Macready, his hand on the doorknob, turned and fixed him with a look both wary and, Hudson thought, sad. "I shouldn't have spoken like I did," he said. "I don't want you to misunderstand."

"It's all right," said Hudson. "I think I understand what you meant."

Macready nodded. "They were good men," he said. "Both of them."

Hudson said nothing, as he could think of no appropriate response. Macready gave another short nod and left. Hudson watched him walk slowly toward the elevator, then sat down and looked at the notes he'd scribbled down.

"I still don't have anything I can use," he said out loud to himself. "Even if I printed this, Macready would deny he'd said it, or at least claim he was quoted out of context."

And maybe he was, he thought with disappointment. After all, he was relying on memories that were probably seventy years old. Who knew what Ricketts had really said to him, or how much of it was completely fictional. Memory was a wonderful thing, capable of both great revelation and great trickery. Although he wanted everything Macready had told him to be true—and true in the way he hoped it was true—Hudson knew he couldn't rely on it.

He'd come closer to solving the mystery than he'd ever been, but in some ways he was even further from the truth. So what if Ricketts had told an adolescent boy that he loved Steinbeck? Macready was right, it was completely normal for one friend to express his love for another. But, Hudson argued, it wasn't so much the words that were used but how they were used. *We're back to the whole context problem,* he thought. *Isn't that what it always comes down to?*

He was interrupted in his disappointment and frustration by the arrival of Helen Guerneyser. She breezed into the room with her usual efficiency. "Well," she said, "was Edgar any help?"

Hudson didn't want her to think he was ungrateful. "He had some great stories," he said.

Helen regarded him with narrowed eyes. "I sense a but," she said.

Hudson couldn't help but smile. "You're good," he said. "It's not so much a 'but' as it is more questions. And between you and me, I don't think I'll ever find the answers I want."

"You're not researching Steinbeck's influences, are you?" said Helen.

Hudson shook his head. "I am and I'm not," he admitted. "I'm trying to pinpoint one particular influence."

"And you don't want to tell me what it is," Helen stated matter-of-factly.

"Not yet," said Hudson. "Is that all right?"

Helen waved his question away. "Of course it is," she said. "But I admit that I'm intrigued. When someone keeps something as close as you have, it's usually big."

Hudson knew she was hoping he would confide in her. But he

wasn't ready to. Not yet. Macready's reaction to his question had reminded him of what shaky terrain he was traversing. And he needed
the access Helen Guerneyser afforded him.

"Maybe it's not so big," he said finally. "But it's important to me."

"Say no more," Helen said. "Just promise me you'll tell me when
you have your answer."

"That I can promise," said Hudson. "That is if I *do* get it," he added.

Helen pointed at him with one well-manicured finger. "That's
enough out of you, young man," she said. "Now get back to work. I'm
an impatient woman, and now you've piqued my curiosity."

"Yes, ma'am," said Hudson, sitting up straight in his chair and assuming a studious look.

Helen waved good-bye and left. Hudson was glad she had come to
see him. He felt that they'd developed a kind of friendship in the short
time he'd been coming to the center, and it was nice to think she was
on his side. *Just like John and Ed were on each other's side,* he
thought.

No, not like that. But the thought made him realize that there were
indeed many different ways to define friendship. *And love,* he added.
"And love," he said, as if someone else had made the comment.

Maybe he was totally wrong. Maybe there was nothing to the whole
thing—the manuscript, his theory, any of it. Maybe he was just chasing
a dream that didn't exist, chasing it because he so badly wanted it to
be true.

Worst of all, he wondered if maybe he was only doing it because it
kept Paul alive. *No,* he told himself. *It's more than that.* It was what
Paul had wanted more than anything, and what Hudson wanted now
was to help him achieve his dream. *Our dream,* he corrected himself.
It's mine too.

He gathered up his materials and stuffed them into his briefcase.
He'd been living with this mystery too long to let it go now. He had to
see it through. But sitting in that room all alone, the whispers of doubt
telling him there was nothing left to look for, he wasn't sure he could.

He left the room quickly, glancing over his shoulder as if someone
might be watching. Edgar Macready's voice echoed in his head as he
ran for the elevator. *They weren't queer. They were good men.*

CHAPTER 26

"It's like something out of a pirate story."

Hudson and Ben were standing at the top of the cliff overlooking Whaler's Cove. A hundred feet below them the ocean crashed over the tops of the reefs. Gulls circled overhead and the wind, hot like the breath of a giant, rippled the tall rye grass, leaving a track like the passing of a great brown snake.

"Funny you should say that," Ben remarked. "This is where Stevenson got his inspiration for *Treasure Island.*"

"Stevenson?" said Hudson. "What was he doing in Monterey?"

"Ah," Ben replied. "That's an interesting story. He came here for a woman, Fanny Osbourne, who, unfortunately for everyone concerned, was already married."

"So he came here to leap to his death," Hudson suggested.

"I never thought of that," said Ben. "Maybe. It would certainly be a good place to die. I don't think you'll find many more beautiful spots."

"Get back to the story," Hudson said. "Did he get the girl or not?"

"He did," Ben said. "But only after a messy divorce during which Fanny lost custody of her son for being a wanton woman. Then the happy couple returned to Britain."

"The perils of love," Hudson remarked.

"The Spanish called this place Punta de los Lobos Marinos," said Ben. "The Point of the Sea Wolves. Much more dramatic than Pt. Lobos, but it doesn't fit on a map as easily." He looked out to sea. "They said the winds howling through here reminded them of the wolves from home."

"It's all terribly romantic," Hudson commented. "Fated lovers. Howling wolves. Spanish sailors. A pirate story. All it needs is a ghost."

Ben turned and walked away from the edge of the cliff, along the path that led to the forest of cypress and scrub pine. Hudson followed him. As they walked, monarch butterflies fluttered up from the grass like tiny explosions of fireworks.

"The trouble with romance is that it becomes something else," Ben said as they walked. "Sea wolves become ordinary wolves. A pirate story becomes required reading. The fated lovers turn into a bickering couple who blame each other for everything they've given up to be together."

"Sounds like you've been burned," Hudson remarked, then regretted having said it. "Sorry," he apologized.

"Don't be," said Ben. "It's a natural assumption. But really it's just a scientific observation. Romance is an impermanence. It can't be measured."

"But you know when you feel it," Hudson objected. "And you know when it's gone."

"Or maybe you just think it's there in the first place," said Ben. "By the way, what did you think of Angela?"

"Angela?" said Hudson, taken aback for a moment. "She was nice. Why?"

"She hasn't stopped talking about you since we had dinner the other night," Ben told him. "I think she might be interested in seeing you again."

Hudson walked a few paces, trying to decide how to respond to this news. "I thought you didn't believe in romance," he said finally.

"I don't believe in God either," said Ben. "But that doesn't stop millions of other people from believing in him."

They stepped into the forest, and immediately the air was cooler, as if the cypress trees caught the wind in their arms and held it there, the branches twisting into their strange shapes from the force of the battle. Hudson picked at a beard of gray-green moss that hung down. It crumbled in his hands, and he let the pieces fall to the ground.

"I don't think Angela would be very happy with me," he told Ben.

"Why's that?" Ben asked.

"Because I like boys," said Hudson. When Ben stopped and looked at him he corrected himself. "Not boys as in boys," he said. "Boys as in men. It's just that most men act like boys, so . . ." His voice trailed off as he realized he was babbling.

"You mean you're gay," Ben said.

"That's what I'm trying to say, yes," said Hudson.

Ben seemed to think for a moment. "In that case, I think you're probably right about Angela," he said, as if he'd come to a conclusion about some problem that had been troubling him. "It wouldn't be very convenient, her having a gay boyfriend. Well, not in the romance department anyway."

"No," Hudson said. "Probably not."

Ben resumed walking. They were passing through the last of the cypress trees and emerging once again into the sunlight. The path had joined the makeshift road leading back toward the park entrance. They walked a few yards and then Ben stopped. He lifted his arm in front of Hudson's chest, stopping him. "Look," he said softly, and pointed.

Twenty feet away, in the shadows of the scrub pine, two deer stood in the grass. Their ears twitched idly as they turned their heads from side to side. Hudson watched them, holding his breath, afraid that any noise might startle them and send them running. It was such a perfect picture that he wanted it to go on forever.

The quiet was interrupted by the sound of a car coming toward them. Ben and Hudson stepped off the road to let it pass, and when Hudson looked back, the deer were gone. The place where they'd been looked untouched, as if they'd simply vanished or never existed at all.

"Another romance—poof," Ben said, snapping his fingers as a magician might.

"But they were there," said Hudson. "And we saw them. That doesn't just disappear."

"But what did we really see?" Ben asked him. "Let me guess, you saw nature in all of its perfect glory. The sun on the trees. The deer in the grass. It was beautiful, right?"

"Right," said Hudson. "Didn't you think so?"

"It was beautiful," Ben agreed. "But the reality is that we were looking at two animals whose fur is more than likely crawling with fleas, who harbor half a dozen parasites in their digestive tracts, and who breed so much that they're straining the ecosystem."

"If you're trying to turn me into a cynic, it won't work," said Hudson. "I'm incurable."

"Then there's no hope for you," Ben informed him with mock gravity.

They had taken a fork in the road and now were walking toward the water rather than away from it. The grass gave way to gravel, and then to the sand and asphalt of the parking area where they'd left Ben's Volvo. Ben walked to the car, opened the door, and removed two plastic grocery bags, which he carried to one of the two picnic tables situated on the lot's outer edge by the cinder block bathrooms. Hudson sat down opposite him as Ben handed him one of the bags, the lunches they'd picked up at a Safeway in town before making the trip to Pt. Lobos.

Ben unwrapped his sandwich and twisted the top from a bottle of water. "Can I ask you something?" he said as Hudson tore open a bag of chips and put one in his mouth. Hudson nodded in response to Ben's question, crunching the chip between his teeth.

"If you're such a hopeless romantic, how come you don't have a partner. Boyfriend. Whatever."

"I did," Hudson answered. "Once."

"He wasn't as romantic, eh?" Ben remarked, removing the bread from the top of his roast beef sandwich and squeezing mustard from a plastic pack onto the meat.

"He died," said Hudson.

Ben looked up. "I guess it's my turn to say I'm sorry," he said.

"It's okay," Hudson told him. "To answer your question, no, he wasn't exactly the romantic type. He was more like you. Methodical. Logical. Reliable."

"You sound like you're describing a car," said Ben.

Hudson took a bite of his sandwich. The turkey was dry, he noticed. He wished he'd taken more mustard packets. But the tomato was good, and the lettuce wasn't at all soggy. He chewed slowly, thinking about Ben's comment.

"Paul was the kid at school you always wanted to be like," he said. "Smart, handsome, totally charming. He could get people to do just about anything he wanted." He took a sip of 7UP and set the bottle on the edge of the sandwich wrapper to keep it from blowing away. "I take that back," he said. "Paul never had to get people to do anything. They wanted to. He had this thing about him where people wanted to take care of him, almost as if he were a child. I don't think he even realized it."

"Did you?" asked Ben. "Want to take care of him, I mean."

Hudson wiped a bit of mustard from his lip. "Yes," he said. "And I did. At least until the end."

Ben was breaking up a piece of bread, which he tossed to the small group of tiny birds that had been watching them from a few feet away. They descended on the crumbs, snatching them up and looking at him expectantly. "How did he die?" Ben asked, wiping his hands together to get rid of the last bits of bread.

"Cancer," Hudson said quickly. "It happened really quickly. He was diagnosed in June and died in September."

"How long ago?" asked Ben.

"Two years," Hudson answered. "Almost, anyway. That's how long we were together, too. He's been dead almost as long as I knew him. I hadn't thought of that until now."

"I'm sorry to have brought it up," said Ben.

Hudson picked up the second half of his sandwich. Although Ben was already finished with his, Hudson ate slowly. "No," he said between bites. "It's good to think about him. I tried not to at first. I thought it would help me move on. I was wrong."

"There's been nobody since him?" Ben asked.

Hudson shook his head. "Nobody that stuck around longer than a night," he said. "Sorry if that was too much information."

Ben laughed. "I don't shock that easily," he replied. "Besides, I think Caddie's doing a bit of that herself at the moment. Like you said, it doesn't help to pretend it isn't happening."

"She's a little young for that, isn't she?" said Hudson.

"I think so," Ben said. "But I'm her father, so I'm hardly objective."

"What about that scientific remove you were talking about?" Hudson teased.

Ben crumpled his bag and tossed it into the nearby garbage can. "I'm finding it a little difficult to maintain that when it comes to Caddie," he said.

"You sound surprised," said Hudson.

"Frankly, I am," Ben admitted. "I thought—hoped—I'd be able to approach this whole situation with at least a reasonable hope of understanding how it's supposed to work. I'm afraid to say that I seem to be failing miserably."

"She's a girl," said Hudson. "A person."

"I'm finding that out," Ben said. "It was easier when she was just my daughter, especially when she was her mother's problem. Then she was more or less an abstraction. Now she's . . ." His voice faded away as he searched for the right words.

"Reality," Hudson suggested.

Ben nodded. "It's like the difference between theoretical physics and engineering," he said. "Those theoretical guys can sit around for days talking about how ants building a colony in Africa can result in floods in New Orleans, but try to get them to make a levee out of sandbags and they don't have a clue what to do."

Hudson, like Ben minutes before, threw some bread to the birds. He watched as one, a small junco, grabbed a piece that barely fit in its mouth and stood, puffed up and menacing, as larger birds attempted to take its prize. If it dropped the bread in order to break it into smaller pieces, it risked losing it altogether. But unless it did, it wouldn't get to eat, as the piece was too large to swallow whole.

"Good luck, fellah," Hudson said sympathetically.

Ben grunted, and Hudson looked up. "Not you," he said. "Mr. Bird here."

Ben looked under the table, where the junco was hopping away from three determined chickadees. "Looks like he's outnumbered," he commented.

"Caddie seemed okay at dinner the other night," Hudson said, getting back to the topic at hand.

"That's because she had an audience," said Ben. "Every night since then we've had the usual one-word-answer conversations."

"Give her some time," Hudson said. "She'll come around."

Ben didn't say anything. He was looking over Hudson's shoulder at something behind them. Hudson turned and saw two divers slowly walking up the ramp from the ocean. They were talking and laughing with one another.

"Anything down there, boys?" Ben called out.

The men walked toward them, stopping just short of the picnic area so that the water from their suits dripped into the sand. The first, a stout man with very red hair and a matching beard, greeted them with, "Ben Ransome, you dirty son of a bitch. What's this favor you wanted to ask me about?" He turned to his companion, a short, thin man with salt-and-pepper hair and a scar that crossed diagonally through both upper and lower lips in a thin white line. "Ben here left a message for me saying he needs something from me," he told him. "This after he's skipped out on poker night for three months straight."

"Bastard," the second man said jovially to Ben, shaking his head.

"Now, Al," Ben said to the red-haired man. "I think I've left enough of my money on your table that you can do me one little favor."

"Well, what is it?" Al demanded. "Might as well ask so I can say no."

Ben indicated Hudson. "Al, meet Hudson Jones. Hudson, these dive rats are Al Blackmore and Ollie Kipperling. No bigger thieves and liars in Monterey than these two."

"Then I definitely want to know you," said Hudson, nodding at the men as they erupted in laughter.

"Hudson here is doing some research on Ed Ricketts," Ben explained.

"And you're wondering if I can get you into the lab," said Al before Ben could continue. He glowered at Ben. "What do I look like, the goddamn Visitors' Bureau?"

"I'd say you're just about the same color as their hut on the Row," said Ben calmly, and Al and Ollie laughed some more.

"I'll see what I can do," said Al. "No promises," he added, looking at Hudson.

"I won't hold you to any," Hudson assured him.

Al smiled. "I like this one," he said to Ben. "Bring him to poker night. We're getting together next Tuesday." He looked at Hudson. "You play poker?"

"Badly," Hudson told him.

"That's the best way," said Al. "Bring cash. We'll be gentle."

The two men said their good-byes and retreated to a beat-up pick-up at the lot's far end. "They seem nice," Hudson said to Ben when they were gone.

"Al's a good guy," Ben said. "Ollie too. Al's the one who first took me diving here. He's been coming since he was a kid."

"What's his connection to the Ricketts lab?" Hudson asked.

"That's not entirely clear," said Ben with a lopsided grin. "Technically, the lab is owned by the city. Unofficially, it's controlled by a group of old-timers who don't want to see it turned into a tourist trap like the rest of Cannery Row. Al's the ringleader, if you will. He lets the city run tours a couple of times a year during the Steinbeck celebration, and he and his buddies maintain the place. In exchange, the city doesn't interfere."

"Don't people ever ask why the lab isn't open to the public?" asked Hudson.

"Sure they do," said Ben. "And the Steinbeck folks would love for it to be on permanent display. But Al knows the right people, or at least knows the right people's secrets." He laughed. "He's quite a character."

Hudson wondered what Helen Guerneyser thought about Al Blackwood. He might just have to ask her the next time he saw her. Then again, he didn't want her thinking he was friends with someone who was apparently her enemy.

They walked to the Volvo, waved good-bye to Al and Ollie after once again promising to show up for poker night, and drove toward the park entrance. Hudson, looking out the window, searched for the deer but saw nothing. Beside him, Ben drove with one arm on the edge of the open window. He liked Ben and was pleased they had been brought together.

Then why did you lie to him about Paul? asked a voice in his head.

He leaned out the window so that the wind blew his hair into a tangle and the roaring drowned out the question, which echoed through his head like the howling of the sea wolves.

CHAPTER 27

Caddie, watching the nudibranch laying its endless coil of eggs around the base of the tube anemone, turned and looked with irritation at Brian. He was tugging on her fin and motioning for her to follow him. She looked once more at the nudibranch and reluctantly left it.

They were once again following the pipe. This time, following a lesson from Brian, Caddie knew how to use the dive computer that hung on her left side. She looked at it now. They were at forty-five feet. The temperature was fifty-two. And, she saw, she had more than half a tank of air left after almost thirty minutes underwater.

She liked knowing all of this. Besides providing a measure of safety, it made her more confident. She'd realized after their first dive that Brian wasn't the best teacher. Since then, she'd deliberately asked questions and made him answer them. He seemed amused by her desire to understand how the equipment worked, but she didn't care.

Ahead of her, Brian was swimming quickly. *How does he see anything?* Caddie wondered. *Where's he in such a hurry to get to?*

She kicked harder to catch up with him. A glance at her gauge showed that they were at fifty feet. It was the deepest she'd been. When she looked up, she couldn't see the surface, although shafts of sunlight penetrated the water and she could see quite a distance ahead of her.

She was surprised when the pipe suddenly came to an end. They paused, and while Brian fiddled with something on his computer, Caddie peered into the open mouth of the pipe. A large fish, long and thin, looked back at her. It was resting on its stomach, the fins on either side moving slowly, as if it was fanning its brown mottled skin. Its mouth was open, and she saw that it was filled with a row of tiny, sharp teeth. Large dark eyes watched her warily. *What are you?* Caddie thought at it, but the fish only blinked its eyes and fanned more rapidly.

Brian tapped her on the shoulder and pointed, indicating their new direction. Caddie followed him across a barren stretch of sand, the landscape dotted with the occasional sea star but nothing else. Already the sea stars had become overly familiar to her, and she let her eyes pass over them in search of more interesting sights.

A few more kicks brought them to something that took her breath away. A cluster of rocks rose from the sand, and all over them huge white flowers bloomed on stalks thicker than her arm. *They look like something out of a Dr. Seuss book,* she thought. The flowers, some of them at least three feet tall, swayed like palm trees. The top of each was capped in cauliflower-shaped petals (she could think of no other word for them) seemingly spun from cotton.

Brian swam up and over the rocks, hovering just above the strange things. Caddie followed, trying her best to maintain her buoyancy and not crash into the flowers. When she was over them, she looked down. *They're anemones,* she thought. *Not like the tube anemones, or the short round ones, but they're anemones.*

The anemones' petals were moving in and out. At first she thought they were just being moved around by the water, but then she saw that the movements were deliberate. The anemones, like dozens of ghostly conductors, were making music only they could hear, drawing water into their open mouths. *They're eating,* Caddie realized, and the idea thrilled her.

Brian led her over the field of anemones. It felt to Caddie as if they were soaring over snow-capped mountains. Below them the anemones floated like clouds. She was disappointed when they reached the other side of the rocks and returned to the plain old sand. But Brian swam around the far edge of the outcropping, and Caddie saw that in addition to the anemones, the rocks were covered with nudibranchs, crabs, and many other things that roamed the anemone forest like jungle animals.

All too soon it was over. Apparently recognizing some landmark Caddie couldn't identify, Brian headed away from the rocks. Caddie, with a last look at the anemones, went with him. She didn't know how Brian knew where to go, but she had no choice but to trust him. She made a mental note to ask him about getting around with more than just a vague idea of where the shore was. And now that she thought about it, with the pipe for reference, she didn't even know where that was. For all she knew, they could be swimming out to sea.

Then the pipe appeared, and she relaxed. The fish was still there, and she winked at it as they passed by. *See you later,* she thought. Brian, as she'd discovered was his habit, was swimming quickly back to shore. She wished he would slow down, but a glance at her computer showed that she was running low on air, so she increased her pace and swam beside him until, at about fifteen feet, they both ascended.

"How'd you like the metridiums?" Brian asked as they floated on the surface, not far from shore.

"Metridiums," said Caddie. She tried the odd-sounding word again. "Metridiums. They're anemones, right?"

Brian nodded. "Good call. We'll make a marine biologist out of you yet."

Caddie snorted and started toward shore. This time it was Brian who had to catch up with her.

An hour later they were in Brian's bedroom. Brian, naked, was stretched on his back. Caddie, wearing one of Brian's T-shirts, was sitting on the side of the bed, trying not to look at his penis. Soft, it reminded her of a baby rat, all pink and helpless looking. Even Brian's balls were hairless. She wondered if he shaved them, considered asking, then decided she didn't want to know.

"Wow," Brian said, putting his hand on her thigh and petting her like a puppy. "That was something, wasn't it?"

Caddie grunted. "Mmm," she said vaguely. She stood up, Brian's hand sliding from her leg, and walked into the bathroom that adjoined the bedroom. She shut the door behind her and turned on the water in the sink. Then she sat on the toilet, her elbows cradled in the T-shirt and her fists pressed together.

She hadn't come. Not even gotten close. Brian had pumped away at her, and she'd tried, but she couldn't. Instead, she'd thought about the metridiums. She'd closed her eyes, imagining she was swimming above them, naked, her skin caressed by their gentle petals. But Brian's breath on her neck, his sweaty skin sticking to hers, had ruined everything. Finally he had come, shuddering and gritting his teeth in an absurd grimace of release before falling beside her.

"You okay in there?" Brian's voice penetrated through the door and the sound of the water.

"Yeah," Caddie called back. She stood and flushed the toilet. Then, turning off the water, she returned to the bedroom and picked up her underwear from the floor, slipping it on.

"Want to grab some dinner?" Brian asked. He was still naked, absent-mindedly playing with himself while he talked, as if his dick were some kind of toy.

Caddie shook her head. "I've got some stuff to do at home," she said.

"How about diving tomorrow afternoon?" Brian suggested.

Caddie removed his T-shirt and tossed it on the bed. She put her own on, tucking it into her jeans. "I'll call you in the morning," she said. "But probably."

"Great," Brian said as he slipped his T-shirt over his head and stood up. He grabbed Caddie and kissed her. She felt his dick against her hand and recoiled at the stickiness of it.

"I'll talk to you later," she said, breaking off the kiss and wishing she could wash her hand before she left.

She had to wait until she got home. Even then, she had to endure a conversation with her father first. He was waiting for her, and when she walked in he said, "Do you have a minute to talk?"

She was tempted to say, "Do you mind if I wash this dick juice off my hand first?" Instead, she flopped down on the musty sofa and waited for him to say what he had to say.

Her father, though, said nothing. He sat in a chair across from her, opening and closing his mouth. It reminded her of the fish that lived in the end of the pipe, and she almost laughed. Then he spoke. "I'd like to get to know you better," he said.

"Better than what?" Caddie said automatically.

"You're my daughter," Ben said. "I'm your father. Even if we haven't really acted like it for the past few years."

"Ten years," Caddie corrected him.

"Actually, it's only nine," said Ben.

Caddie crossed her arms over her chest. Her father sucked one cheek in, and she knew that he was biting it. It was something she did too. It drove her mother crazy. Now she knew where she'd gotten it from, and the realization annoyed her.

"I want to start over," her father said. "Now. Can we do that?"

Caddie regarded him cooly. "Why?" she said.

"Because I want to," her father told her. "And I think—despite what you've been doing—you want to too."

"What I've been doing?" Caddie said. "What's that supposed to mean?"

Her father waved a hand at her. "You know," he said. "Not coming home for dinner. Not talking. Doing whatever it is you . . . do."

Caddie shook her head. "You think you know everything about me, don't you?" she said. "You don't know anything."

"Well, now I'm trying to find out who you are," said Ben.

Caddie stood up. "You'll never know who I am," she said harshly. "Because I'm *not* you. And you're the only thing you care about. Oh, except maybe for your stupid nudibranchs. Why don't you just stick with them?"

She rushed from the room, stomping up the stairs, deliberately hitting each step with a forceful "clop" of her clogs. Then she was in the bathroom with the water streaming into the sink. It was too hot, but she didn't temper it with cold. She scrubbed her hands until they were raw and red. Only then did she turn the cold tap on and try to soothe the burning on her skin.

As she let the water run she looked into the mirror. Her face was red from the sun; she'd forgotten to apply sunscreen before going diving, and now she had an angry-looking burn. It was going to peel, she could tell.

She touched her nose gingerly with one finger, testing it for pain. The skin was hot, as if the sun were trapped beneath it. She ran her finger down the length of her nose, then pulled it away and looked at herself.

She didn't resemble her mother. Her nose was wider, her lips fuller, and her cheekbones higher. Her eyes, too, were dissimilar. When she was younger it had bothered her a little. She used to look in the mirror, searching for some proof that she had come from the woman who claimed to be her mother. For a time—her fantasies fueled by watching one too many made-for-Lifetime movies—she had thought she might be adopted, even stolen from some other family.

Looking at herself now, she knew why she didn't have her mother's features. She had her father's. When she looked at her nose, she saw his nose. Her mouth, her cheekbones, even her eye color—they all belonged to him. Only her hair was her own. She grabbed it in her fists, pulled it across her face so that her features were hidden behind it. She peered out through the thicket of curls, and her eye stared back at her.

You can't hide who you are, she thought.

She let go of her hair, and it fell back. Revealed, her face looked back at her accusingly. She scrunched up her nose, pushing the tip up with her finger so that she appeared to have a snout. *Even your teeth look like his,* she thought, noting the slightly crooked eye teeth on either side of her mouth. They were longer than the others, and pointed. She hated them, but her orthodontist wouldn't file them down, citing the potential for damage to the nerves. It was something else to blame her father for, she realized, adding it to the list of grievances she carried in her head.

She turned the tap off and looked at her reflection again. *That's me,* she thought, examining the girl in the mirror. *That's what people see when they look at me.* She pushed her face closer to the mirror. *But who am I?*

Her father had said he wanted to know who she was. *I don't even know who I am,* she thought. *How can he ever know?*

For the second time that day she sat down on the toilet to think. It was appropriate, she thought. Wasn't a toilet where you dumped everything you didn't want inside of you? It was too bad she couldn't flush her feelings down it as well. *Maybe then I'd feel better,* she thought.

She fished in her pocket and found the Valium she'd put there that morning. She hadn't taken one in a day or two. Now she popped it in her mouth and worked up enough spit to swallow it down. Still, it burned her throat. Not that it would probably help anyway. She had to take two, sometimes three, now to get the mellow feeling she used to get from one. But it was a habit, and she figured it couldn't hurt.

She wished she'd gotten some pot from Brian. It had been a relief to find out he smoked. His stuff wasn't as good as the stuff Nick had, but it did the trick. She could use some now to take her away from herself.

You'd just have to come back again, she told herself.

"Why don't you shut the fuck up?" she said, hitting her thighs with her fists. "Just shut up."

She was crying. The tears slipped from her eyes and ran down her cheeks. They were hot, and their touch tormented her burned skin. When she wiped them away, her face was left feeling raw. She stood and looked at herself. Ugly red smears scarred her cheeks. She was looking at the face of a monster, someone she wanted to run from.

She opened the bathroom door and, before she could change her mind, ran down the stairs. Her father was still sitting where she'd left him. His hands hung limply between his knees, and he looked tired.

"All right," Caddie said, sitting on the couch and taking a deep breath. "What do you want to know?"

CHAPTER 28

Ben looked at his daughter. Caddie, sitting across from him, had her arms across her chest in a defensive posture. It wasn't, he thought, a great way to begin. But he feared that if he didn't take her up on her unexpected offer to talk, he might never get another chance.

The only problem was, he couldn't think of a single thing to ask her. All the questions that had passed through his mind over the past few days suddenly ran together as one, their voices drowning one another out until he couldn't hear a single one. Who? What? When? Where? How? Before he could complete one thought, another shoved it aside, clamoring for attention.

"What's your favorite color?" He heard himself ask the question, but couldn't believe he'd actually done so.

"My favorite color?" Caddie repeated. "That's what you want to know?"

Ben scratched his forehead distractedly. "Yes," he said, trying to sound confident. "Yes. What's your favorite color?"

Caddie sighed deeply and shook her head. "Blue," she said, raising her hands and returning them to their protective position. "I guess it would be blue."

"Blue," Ben repeated, nodding his head as if this information were terribly important. "Blue," he said again. "Blue is good. I like blue too. I wouldn't say it's my favorite, but I like it. I prefer green."

Caddie said nothing. Ben cleared his throat. "How about food?" he said.

"Yeah," Caddie said. "I like food."

"What kind?" asked Ben, grasping for something—anything—to say. He could almost physically feel the conversation turning cold, and anxiously rubbed his hands on his thighs to warm them.

Caddie studied him. "What is this?" she asked. "A first date? Can't you come up with some actual questions instead of this small-talk shit?"

"Why do you swear so much?" Ben asked. "It makes you sound like a whore."

Caddie stared, her mouth open. Ben, realizing that he'd said the wrong thing, tried to minimize the damage. "I didn't mean it like that," he said quickly. "I just meant that that kind of language—"

"Is the kind of language whores use," Caddie finished. "Well, maybe that's what I am then. A whore." She spat the last word. Ben, hearing it, felt himself blush.

"It just makes you sound low-class," he said.

"I'm sorry I'm not living up to your high expectations," said Caddie. "I guess I shouldn't have skipped all of those charm school classes."

"Let's back up," Ben suggested. "Okay?" He looked at Caddie, watching her face. Her mouth was a tight line, and her fingers dug into her sides as she hugged herself. Finally, she shrugged.

"Whatever," she said.

Ben sighed, trying to relax. He paused, clearing his mind so that he could, hopefully, get the conversation back on track. "What kind of things do you like to do?" he tried.

Caddie considered the question. Ben couldn't tell whether she was really thinking about it or if she was trying to come up with the answer that would most successfully express her disdain for it.

"I like to write," Caddie said finally.

"Write," said Ben.

"Nothing big," Caddie said quickly. "It's not like I have the Great American Novel hiding under my bed or anything. Mostly I write poems."

Ben started to reply, but Caddie cut him off. "I'm not reading you any of them, so don't ask," she said. "Anyway, I didn't bring any with me."

Ben was trying to imagine this sullen, angry girl writing poems. He wondered what they were about. *Probably about how much she hates me,* he thought. He doubted very much that Caddie went in for rhymes about kittens and love.

"I was never very good at writing," he told Caddie. "I could never quite figure out how to say what was in my head."

To his surprise, Caddie made a sound that was almost like a laugh. She was nodding her head as if she understood what he meant. It was an encouraging sign, and Ben decided to keep going with the line of conversation.

"Science is a lot easier for me," he said. "*That* I can write about, because mostly it's all about facts and numbers. You don't have to tell anyone *why* you think octopi are interesting."

"I'm not good at science," said Caddie. "I barely passed biology last year."

"I could have helped you with that," Ben said.

"You could have," said Caddie, "if you'd been around."

Her tone had cooled again. Ben, desperately wanting to avoid slipping back into frosty silence, began to speak rapidly. "Have you thought about college?" he asked. "What you might want to study?"

"Not really," Caddie answered.

He could tell he was losing her interest, and racked his brain for something more lively to discuss. "Do you have a boyfriend?" he blurted out.

The question indeed got Caddie's attention. "Are we back to the whore thing?" she asked. "That's what you want to know, right? You want to know if I'm *fucking* anyone?"

Ben blushed at her emphasis of the word. For a moment he considered telling Caddie that he just assumed she was sleeping with someone. But he knew that was what she wanted him to do. He'd never seen someone so ready for a fight.

"No," he said. "I was just asking if you have a boyfriend."

"Maybe I have a girlfriend," Caddie answered. "Did you ever think about that? Maybe I'm a big muff diver."

"Are you?" Ben asked.

"Would you care if I were?" Caddie countered.

"No," Ben said without hesitation. "I wouldn't care. I just want you to be happy."

"Happy," Caddie repeated. "Everybody wants me to be happy. But no one seems to know what that is."

"Even you?" Ben asked.

"Especially me," said Caddie.

Her honesty surprised him. Even more, it confused him. He felt that he should have some kind of answer for her, but he didn't. If anything, he knew just what she meant. But if he said that, would she understand that he wasn't just trying to show her that they had something in common? He was supposed to be the adult. She probably expected him to know what life was all about. If he told her that he had as many doubts as she did, how would that help?

"What do you think would make you happy?" he tried.

Caddie was looking away, staring at a spot on the wall. She shook her head. "I don't know," she said. "Maybe nothing."

"Well, let's look at it another way," said Ben. "What's making you *unhappy*?"

Caddie swung her face toward him. "Being here," she said.

Ben tried to ignore the stab of pain her answer sent through him. "Do you really think you would be happier back with your mother?" he asked.

"I wouldn't be any less happy," said Caddie.

Ben looked into her eyes. "Do you hate me that much?" he asked quietly.

He saw something change in Caddie's face, a softening of the muscles, a shifting of the eyes away from him. "It's not you," she said. "Not all you, anyway."

"But I'm a big part of it," Ben said. "Right?"

Caddie didn't say anything. In a strange way, this made Ben feel better. He'd expected her to agree with his assessment; her not doing so gave him hope that perhaps she was ready to admit that she didn't blame him for everything.

"Right," she said.

He felt as if he'd been punched in the stomach. The breath left him, and all he could do was sit and nod stupidly, as if he were admitting his guilt. Caddie stared at the floor. Neither spoke for a long time.

It was Caddie who broke the silence. "I don't hate you," she said. "I'm angry. There's a difference."

Ben nodded. He understood what she meant. Still, it hurt to know that he was the cause of her unhappiness, even if only partially. He'd known before, of course. But this was different. Caddie's voice was that of a little girl, not an irate teenager. It was easier to take when she was yelling. Then he could dodge her words as he would rocks, seeing them only as missiles designed to inflict pain. Now, though, he felt the full impact of her admission. He had hurt her.

"I'm sorry," he said.

"About what?" said Caddie.

Ben shrugged. "About everything, I guess," he said. "Mostly I'm sorry that you're unhappy. I wish I could change that."

What he really wanted to say was, *Tell me how to make it better!* But he knew Caddie had no more idea of how he could do that than he did. That, he told himself, was something else they had in common.

"Maybe we should go back to talking about favorite colors," Caddie suggested.

Ben laughed. To his surprise, Caddie did too. She drew one leg up, placing her foot on the couch and wrapping her arms around her knee. He recognized the gesture; it was one of Carol's. So, Caddie had inherited more than just her eyes from her mother. He was oddly jealous to see so much of his ex-wife coming through in Caddie, as though his absence, and not genetics, were responsible for his inability to find himself in his own child.

"Thai," Caddie said.

"What?" Ben asked, confused.

"Thai food," Caddie elaborated. "I like Thai food. And Japanese. I pretty much like everything, actually."

"Me too," Ben told her. "Except for broccoli. I've always hated broccoli."

Caddie made a face. "Broccoli sucks," she said firmly. "Mom eats broccoli all the time."

"I remember," said Ben.

"It makes her fart something fierce," Caddie remarked.

Ben smiled. *Broccoli,* he thought. *Is that what we have in common—not liking broccoli?* It wasn't much to go on, but he would take it. At least it was something to start with.

"How about roller coasters?" asked Caddie unexpectedly. "Are you pro or con?"

"Well, I haven't been on one since before you were born," Ben answered. "But as I recall, I liked them. In fact, I remember having one of my first fights with your mother about her not wanting to go on one."

"I figured I got it from you," said Caddie, sounding almost pleased. "I love them, and Mom would never take me on them when I was a kid. She always had to talk some other adult in line into letting me go with them."

Ben imagined Caddie seated beside some unknown man, her face filled with joy as she rode the crest of a roller coaster. "I would have taken you," he told her. "We would have sat in the first car."

"That's the best one," Caddie agreed. "You can't see anyone else, and it makes you feel like you're flying."

Again Ben remarked on the small connections that existed, unseen, between them. Broccoli. Roller coasters. There was nothing unique whatsoever about these things. Suddenly, however, they were immeasurably important to him. They were ties, however insubstantial, to the young woman sitting across from him. If he could just find a few more, perhaps they would not feel like such strangers to one another.

"I guess there isn't that much to know after all."

Ben, startled by Caddie's voice, looked at her. "What do you mean?" he asked.

"Just that there's not a lot to talk about," said Caddie. "I guess I'm not that interesting."

"No," said Ben. His heart was beating more quickly, and he realized that he was afraid that Caddie would stop talking now. "You are interesting. To me."

"But not to anyone else?" Caddie said.

"To anyone, probably," said Ben. "But right now to me especially."

"I'm guessing this is why you don't date much," said Caddie.

At first Ben thought that she was angry again, but she was smiling a little, and he realized that she was merely teasing him.

"So, what else?" Caddie asked.

There were so many things that Ben wanted to talk to her about now that they'd started—what she wanted from him, where they could go from here, what she was doing when she didn't come home. This last question was the most pressing, and also the last one he wanted to raise. He feared that Caddie would just pull back into her shell, and although he worried about what she was doing, he knew that, at least for the moment, he had to let her keep that part of herself a secret.

"How about dinner?" he suggested. "All of this talking is making me hungry."

"I could do that," Caddie said. "I've even been known to eat *and* talk."

Ben stood up. He was feeling good. Caddie stood as well, and suddenly they were facing one another. *This is the part where we hug,* thought Ben. He started to reach out.

"I'm going to put a sweatshirt on," said Caddie, moving quickly past him. "It was getting kind of cold out there."

Ben let her go. *Don't push her,* he told himself as he listened to her walk up the stairs. This time, there was no pounding of feet, just the soft groan of wood. It was, Ben thought, the loveliest sound he had ever heard.

CHAPTER 29

Hudson stood up and pulled the mask from his head. He was hyperventilating and looked around for a way out of the pool. A second later, Ben was standing beside him, his hand on Hudson's shoulder. "What happened?" he asked.

"I couldn't breathe," Hudson said. "It felt like I was drowning."

"Put your regulator in," Ben ordered. When Hudson didn't respond, he took the regulator and helped it to Hudson's lips. Reluctantly, Hudson opened his mouth and closed it around the rubber mouthpiece.

"Now breathe," said Ben.

Hudson breathed. Air rushed into his lungs. He exhaled, then did it again, in case the first time was a fluke. Again the air flowed into his lungs. He let the regulator drop from his mouth and looked at Ben. "It really did feel like I was drowning," he said sheepishly.

"That's because your body knows it's not supposed to be in an all-water environment," said Ben. "It's a natural response. What you have to do is trick it into believing it's okay. Which it is," he added emphatically. "Nothing bad is going to happen to you. Especially not in four feet of water. Now, shall we give it another go?"

Hudson nodded and put the regulator back in his mouth. With Ben in front of him, watching closely, he knelt down until the water was halfway up his mask. Then he stretched out flat on the bottom of the pool. Immediately he felt the urge to bolt for the surface. Ben, perhaps sensing this, grabbed both of his hands and held them. Hudson looked into his eyes, focusing on them as he breathed.

Everything's fine, he told himself. *Everything's fine.*

After a minute of just breathing, he realized that everything was indeed fine. The air was flowing through the regulator just as Ben had promised it would. He was breathing normally, and no water was streaming into his throat. He was so elated by the realization that he gave a little giggle and squeezed Ben's hands.

Ben let go and indicated that Hudson should watch him. Then he took the regulator from his mouth and let it hang down. He pointed at his lips, from which issued a small but steady stream of bubbles. *Right,* Hudson thought. *He said never to hold your breath.*

With slow and deliberate movements, Ben retrieved the regulator by sweeping his hand down along his thigh and up toward his shoulder. The regulator hose, hooked on his arm, came with it. Ben placed it back in his mouth, blew out an exaggerated blast of air, and held his hands up to indicate that the entire process was nothing at all.

For you maybe, Hudson thought. Now it was his turn to try. He hesitated, starting to breathe more quickly. *Calm down,* he ordered himself, and waited until he felt his pulse slow. Then, just as Ben had instructed him to do, he took a breath and removed the regulator. Fighting the fear that the air in his lungs would never last long enough for him to complete the task, he imitated Ben's arm movement. When the regulator appeared, as if by magic, in his hand, he placed it with great relief in his mouth and blew out to clear it of water. When the bubbles cleared, he saw Ben flashing him a big OK sign. Then he pointed with his thumb to the surface, and they both rose through the few feet of water.

"That was perfect," Ben said.

"I had a good teacher," said Hudson. "Thanks for walking me through that whole drowning thing."

"You just need more practice," Ben told him. "The problems come when instructors don't give students enough pool time. They throw them in the ocean after a couple of hours of pool work, and it's a disaster. Especially in water like we have here."

"What do you mean?" asked Hudson.

"It's cold, there's current, and the visibility is low," Ben explained. "I've seen divers with twenty years' experience in warm water diving come here and completely freak out."

"That makes me feel so much better," Hudson told him.

"You'll be fine," Ben reassured him. "I always say that divers who are trained in Monterey are the best divers in the world. Now, you ready for the deep end?"

Hudson glanced toward the far end of the pool.

"It's only nine feet," said Ben.

Hudson looked at him. "Yeah, but that's *twice* as deep as I've been," he said.

Ben laughed. "Put your reg in," he said. "It's sink or swim time."

For the next hour Ben put Hudson through his paces. They'd gone over everything beforehand on the pool deck, but it was different performing the skills in the pool. Several times Hudson thought he wouldn't be able to get through everything, but with Ben's patient help he eventually got to the point where he felt, if not completely competent, at least comfortable. When Ben signaled for him to go up, he did so with a twinge of disappointment that their time was over.

"That's enough for tonight," Ben said, removing his mask and rubbing his face. "I think another pool session and you'll be ready for the ocean."

"Just one?" Hudson said as he swam to the shallow end.

"Trust me, I won't let you drown," said Ben, removing his BC and lifting it onto the pool deck. "It would be bad for my reputation."

"Do people really drown?" asked Hudson as he got out.

Ben nodded. "Every year we have a couple of deaths around here," he said. "Usually some overweight middle-aged guy who has a heart attack. Something happens underwater, he panics, and boom."

Hudson turned the valve on his tank, shutting off the air. Then he removed the regulator. "I can't even imagine that," he said.

"What's the number one rule of diving?" Ben asked him.

"Never hold your breath," Hudson said without thinking.

"So you do pay attention," said Ben, grinning.

"You only said it about eighteen thousand times," Hudson teased.

"What's the number two rule, then?" said Ben, putting his tank in the rack that ran the length of the room.

Hudson had to think for a moment. "There's nothing that can happen to you underwater that you can't take care of underwater."

"You get a gold star," Ben said. "That's what those overweight middle-aged guys forget. Did you know that they find the majority of dead scuba divers on the bottom with their weights still in their BCs and their tanks full of air?" He shook his head. "If they'd just stop for a minute and not panic, they wouldn't be dead scuba divers," he concluded.

Hudson set his tank next to Ben's. "Well, I can assure you that at the first sign of trouble, I will be happy to drop my weights and head for the surface," he said. "But right now I'm heading for those showers. I'm freezing."

"Sissy," Ben called after him as Hudson trotted toward the locker room.

Hudson was standing beneath the hot spray of the shower when Ben came into the room. He was naked, and for a moment Hudson was shocked to see his body so openly displayed. He himself still had on his bathing suit, which clung to him in an unpleasantly cool way.

"Do you always shower with your clothes on?" Ben asked him, turning on a showerhead and waiting for it to heat up.

Hudson kept his eyes on Ben's face. "It's a holdover from gym class," he said. "I hated showering in front of everyone."

Ben nodded and stepped under the water, his back to Hudson. Hudson took the opportunity to examine Ben's physique. It was what Marty referred to as "comfy chair" in shape, not fat but definitely twenty pounds on the far side of slim. Still, it wasn't at all bad.

"I think it's a generational thing," said Ben, turning around so that Hudson had to pretend to be looking at something on the floor. "They made us shower whether we liked it or not. I guess I got used to it. Besides, it's just a body, right? There's nothing exactly exciting about it."

That's because you're straight, Hudson wanted to say. *If I were a naked woman, you might feel differently.* Instead, he turned the water off and reached for his towel. Only when it was safely around his waist and he was in front of the locker holding his clothes did he remove his swimsuit.

"By the way," Ben said, walking in as he dried himself, "I meant to tell you, you were right about Caddie."

"How so?" Hudson asked as Ben, who had the locker beside his, stood close enough that Hudson could feel the heat coming off his bare skin.

"She finally talked to me," said Ben, turning so that Hudson's arm brushed against the hair on his chest.

"That's great," Hudson said, shutting the locker door and retreating to the sink. "What did you talk about?"

"Nothing too deep," Ben replied. He was pulling on his boxer shorts, and Hudson saw his reflection in the mirror as he reached inside and adjusted himself. "We basically played catch-up. I didn't want to push her too hard. But it's a start."

"Congratulations," Hudson said. "It must feel good."

"It feels scary," said Ben. "I don't think I'm very good at the whole father thing."

"You're a great teacher," Hudson said. "You'll be a great father too." He turned around. Ben was buttoning up his shirt. "Remember," Hudson told him, "there's nothing that can happen with a daughter that you can't handle with a . . . That didn't go as well as I'd hoped," he said. "But you get the idea."

Ben was looking down at his shirt with a puzzled expression.

"The buttons aren't lined up right," said Hudson. He walked over and undid the top two, so that the shirt hung correctly. He was about to rebutton them but stepped back. *What are you doing?* he asked himself.

"Thanks," Ben said, buttoning the shirt himself. "And for the vote of confidence. I'm still not convinced I can pull it off. Teenage girls aren't exactly my specialty." He finished buttoning his shirt and tucked it into his jeans. "*People* aren't exactly my specialty," he added.

"She just wants you to listen to her," said Hudson, picking up the bag with his towel and wet swimsuit in it. "That's all anyone wants, really."

Ben ran his hand over his short-cropped hair, leaving it exactly the way it was before he touched it. "I think Caddie wants more than that," he said. "I think she wants the last nine years back, and I can't give her that."

"Then give her the next nine years," said Hudson. "And the nine after that, until you run out of years."

Ben put his arm around Hudson's shoulder and steered him toward the door. "Come on," he said. "You can buy your teacher a beer."

They went to a little English pub on one of the wharfs. Seated at a rough wooden table, Ben waved to the waitress, a tall, thin woman easily sixty if she was a day. She walked toward them with a jaunty aloofness, peering at them over eyeglasses studded with rhinestones.

"What'll it be, professor?" she asked when she got there.

Ben laughed. "A Boddingtons and a pickled egg," he announced, and the waitress lifted one pencil-thin eyebrow. "Just one?" she asked, glancing at Hudson.

"A pickled egg?" he said, making a face.

"Come on," said Ben. "You only live once. And they're fantastic with beer."

Hudson shut his menu. "Okay," he said. "Make it two of everything."

The waitress retreated to the bar, returning a minute later with two tall cans and two small glasses, each containing a hard-boiled egg. She set one of each before Hudson and Ben. Ben picked his egg up and popped it, whole, into his mouth. He squinted his eyes as he chewed, shaking his head when he was through and taking a long swallow of beer.

Hudson eyed his egg warily. He lifted the glass and sniffed. The aroma of vinegar penetrated his nose, and he quickly set the glass down. "I'm not eating that," he said firmly.

"Come on," said Ben. "You can do it."

"It's disgusting," Hudson asserted. "You eat it."

"I had mine," said Ben. "Now it's your turn. Where's your spirit of adventure?"

"It's been overwhelmed by my sense of smell," Hudson replied.

"Steinbeck loved them," Ben informed him. "He ate two a day. At least."

"He did not," Hudson countered.

"Stella!" Ben shouted. The old waitress turned around. "Bring the picture."

She nodded and went behind the bar. When she returned she was carrying a frame in her hand. She brought it to the table and set it down.

"See," Ben said, picking it up. He held it up for Hudson to see. It was a faded black-and-white print. The bar looked much the same as it currently did. A group of men were seated at a table. They were each holding up an egg. In the middle, his big ears and long face unmistakable, was John Steinbeck. Behind him stood a younger version of Stella; her hair was darker but the bored expression was the same. She regarded the men balefully, as if she couldn't wait for them to leave.

"I told you," Ben crowed. "Stella's eggs are part of literary history. Isn't that right, Stella?"

"Sure," she said. "I'm practically one of the muses." She took the picture back from Ben and left.

"Now will you eat it?" asked Ben.

"Just because Steinbeck did?" Hudson answered. "No way. If I was interested in Hemingway, would you try to get me to stick a rifle in my mouth?"

Ben shook his head. "All right," he said. He let out a long sigh. "I guess I'll just have to eat it myself." He reached for Hudson's glass, but Hudson stopped him.

"Fine," he said. "I'll eat the damn thing."

Ben, grinning, watched as he picked the egg up from the glass and held it between his thumb and forefinger. "I can't believe I'm doing this," Hudson said, and put the egg in his mouth. He chewed quickly, his eyes shut. The egg was both salty and sour, not altogether unpleasant. When he felt he'd chewed it enough, he swallowed it down. "Happy?" he asked Ben as he gulped his beer to wash away the taste of the egg.

"Nope," Ben said, and Hudson looked at him, not understanding. "You just lost me a dollar," said Ben.

Stella walked over as Ben fished a buck from his wallet and held it up. The waitress took it and stuffed it into her shirt pocket. As she walked away, Hudson looked at Ben, bewildered.

"It's amazing what you can do with Photoshop," said Ben.

Hudson's mouth fell open. "You set me up!" he cried.

"Stella's been running that racket for forty years," said Ben. "I fell for it myself when I first came here. I figured I could earn my dollar back."

Hudson shook his head. "And I thought you were a good guy," he said. "Bastard."

Ben chuckled and drank some more of his beer. He looked at Hudson and chuckled some more. Hudson held out for about a minute, and then he too started to laugh. When they both had wrung as much as they could from the moment, Hudson said, "I'm really glad I ran into you that day."

Ben looked at his beer, then up at Hudson. He nodded. "I am too," he said.

CHAPTER 30

"Hey," said the voice on the phone. "What's up?"

"Bree," Caddie said happily. "It's me. How—"

"I'm not here, so leave a message," interrupted Bree's voice.

Fuck, Caddie thought as she hung up the phone. She'd forgotten about Bree's message. She thought it was funny when people assumed they were talking to her and started to talk. Caddie thought it was funny too. At least, she had. Now it just annoyed her. She picked up the phone and dialed again.

"Yeah?" said a sleepy voice.

"Sam," said Caddie. "It's me."

"Me who?" Sam sounded groggy and confused.

He's high, Caddie thought, irritated.

"It's Caddie, Sam," she said. "Caddie. Remember? It hasn't been that long, dude."

"Caddie," Sam said. He sounded pleased, but she knew it was mostly the pot. He'd be pleased if she'd said she was calling to conduct a poll on his opinions on applesauce. "Where are you?" he asked.

"Still in Monterey," Caddie answered.

"Monterey," Sam repeated. "Cool."

Caddie rolled her eyes, although no one was there to see her. "What have you guys been up to?" she asked.

Sam was quiet for a minute. She heard rustling, as if he were trying to extricate himself from a big sheet of plastic wrap. He was still in bed, she realized, probably sleeping off his first high of the day. She heard a mumble of voices, and then a female voice came on. "Cad?" said Bree.

"So that's where you are," Caddie said. "I tried your cell."

"I turned it off," Bree said. "Sorry. I didn't know you were going to call. Are you okay?"

"I'm fine, Mom," Caddie joked. "So what's the deal, are you and Sam a thing now?"

"You know," Bree said, and Caddie could see her hunching one shoulder up, as she always did when she was answering a question with no definite answer. "It fills a void," she added.

Caddie laughed. "Well, I hope you and your void are satisfied," she teased.

Bree snorted. "You've seen it," she said. "It does the job."

"I'm sure," Caddie replied. She had a mental image of Sam, naked. *He does have a nice one,* she thought. This made her think of Brian. She would call him later. If she felt like it.

"How's your dad?" Bree asked her.

Caddie hesitated, unsure of how to answer the question. The truth was, they'd actually started talking a little bit. But she'd bitched so much about being forced to come live with him that she feared she'd sound like an idiot if she admitted as much. "Not filling any void," she said.

"That's not an image I need in my head," Bree cracked.

"Don't be a cunt," said Caddie. "I meant my *emotional* void. Don't forget, I'm an abandoned child."

She slipped easily into the familiar pattern, talking to Bree without actually saying anything. But now she was painfully aware of the superficiality of their banter. *We just talk around stuff,* she thought. And it was true. They were, both of them, masters of the comeback and the offhand comment, proficient at cutting situations—and people—down to a manageable size. There was something enjoyable in it, a feeling of control that was satisfying and comforting, but ultimately it left her feeling hollow.

"I miss you," she said, trying for some genuine emotion.

"Yeah," said Bree.

Caddie waited for more but didn't get it. "This place really sucks," she tried, reverting to form.

"Not as much as this place sucks," said Bree. "It's totally boring."

"I know something you can suck." Sam's voice floated through the phone. Caddie heard him laugh his goofy, stoned laugh. She knew just what he was doing, pushing his long hair behind his ears and grinning stupidly, probably grabbing his crotch.

"Suck this," Bree told him. "Christ," she said to Caddie, "you'd think he never got any."

Caddie wanted to hang up. She'd thought talking to her friends would be fun, but now she just felt trapped. Nothing had changed with them. But something in her had. She hadn't even realized it until now. When had it happened? And what was it? She couldn't even put her finger on it. But she felt it. There was inside of her a new sense of wanting something more, something more than her old life, her old self. *My old friends,* she thought sadly.

"I should go," she told Bree. "I just wanted to say hi."

"Okay," Bree said. "Take it easy, all right?"

It was Caddie's turn to play it cool. "Will do," she said. "I'll talk to you later."

She hung up. *It's been less than two weeks,* she thought. *How can everything change in less than two weeks?* But she saw that it had. No, that wasn't true. Some things hadn't changed. Bree and Sam hadn't. They were the same people she'd been so reluctant to leave behind. Now she wondered why.

She poured herself a glass of orange juice and sat at the kitchen table, which still held the remnants of the breakfast she'd shared with her father a few hours before. In a moment of weakness, she'd offered to wash the dishes. Now she stared at the egg- and jam-stained plates and wished she'd put them in the sink to soak. Now they would require scrubbing.

She returned to examining her situation. Her sudden dissatisfaction bothered her. She'd always thought of Sam and Bree as the center of her universe. They'd had such fun together, and being with them had always made her feel like she was somebody. Had that all been a lie? Had she just thought she was having fun with them and that they cared about her?

No, she told herself. It had been real. She really had felt that way. At least at the time. *But maybe that time is over,* she thought. *Maybe you're different now, and they're still the same.*

She picked up a piece of half-eaten toast and played with it, tapping it on the edge of a plate. How could she have changed so much that her best friends now seemed like people she'd known a long time ago? She set the toast down, wiped her fingers on a balled-up paper napkin. She didn't have an answer to that question.

She thought about rolling a joint; she still had some pot left. Then she heard Sam's voice in her head, laughing stupidly at his own cleverness, and she felt a little sick. She vetoed, too, taking a Valium. For once, she didn't want to escape, at least not that way.

"This is so fucking weird," she announced to the empty room. She stood up and, stacking the plates on top of one another, took them to the sink. Locating the dish soap, she squirted some into the plastic tub placed on one side of the wide sink and added hot water until the resultant bubbles reached halfway up the sides. The dirty dishes went into their bath, where she left them to soak while she went upstairs to take a shower.

An hour later, both herself and the dishes scrubbed clean, she left the house. She hadn't called Brian, but she might just stop by the aquarium and see if he was there. Maybe, she thought, she would surprise him during his early show in the kelp forest exhibit. For now she was content just to walk around town.

Monterey seemed less drab than it had before. Not that it had turned into L.A. overnight or anything. Still, she didn't hate it as much. *Maybe it's just that I'm getting used to it,* she told herself. She was certain she would never come to love it; it was far too uninteresting for that. But maybe she could like it. *Or tolerate it,* she said, compromising with herself.

She walked the now-familiar route to Cannery Row. She headed for the Starbucks, but at the last minute decided against it and instead went into a smaller local coffee shop. As she stood in line, trying to decide between hot or iced chai, she heard someone say her name. Turning around, she saw Nicole behind her.

"I thought it was you!" Nicole said brightly. "How come you never called me?"

Caddie searched the other girl's face for any sign of hostility and found nothing. Nicole was genuinely glad to see her. "You know what," Caddie said, "I lost your number."

Nicole shook her head. "You should have just asked Nick for it," she scolded. "He says you haven't been back in."

"I'm watching my carbs," said Caddie, hating herself for the lie.

"Well, here it is again," Nicole said, handing her a piece of paper on which she'd scribbled the number. "Don't lose it this time."

Caddie's turn came, and she ordered the iced chai. "What do you want?" she asked Nicole. "It's on me."

Nicole beamed. "I'll have a decaf latte," she told the waiting barista. She turned to Caddie. "Thanks," she said. "That's nice of you."

It's the least I can do after screwing your boyfriend, Caddie thought while she returned the smile. It was another change; two weeks ago, she wouldn't have cared. She *hadn't* cared. She'd felt sorry for Nicole, but not enough to do anything about it. Now, she did. "Do you have to be anywhere?" she asked.

Nicole shook her head. "It's my day off," she said.

"Let's sit then," Caddie suggested as their drinks arrived.

They went to a small table near the window and sat down. Caddie took a long time stirring her chai, as if it required great concentration. When she could no longer reasonably justify needing to mix it up anymore, she held the cup in her hands and looked at Nicole. "I have to tell you something," she said.

It was done in a matter of minutes. When it was over, Caddie waited for Nicole to respond. She'd expected anger, maybe accusations, at least tears. Instead, Nicole smiled weakly and nodded. "I know all about Nick," she said.

"But what you said," Caddie blurted. "About you two being—"

"Virgins," said Nicole. "I know." She didn't continue.

Caddie wanted to press her for more. Like why she had made up something like that and why she would tell it to a complete stranger. Instead she said, "I didn't know he and you were together when it happened."

Nicole looked at her, no trace of hatred in her countenance. "It's all right," she said. "Really."

Caddie drank her chai, giving herself time to think. Nicole was an enigma. She'd thought her to be a stupid girl, at the least a naive one. Now she wasn't sure what she thought.

"I do love him," Nicole said. "And I know he loves me, no matter what he does."

Caddie, against her better judgment, said, "But don't you deserve better?"

Nicole smiled. "What's better?" she said. "A boyfriend who doesn't cheat on me? Do you think there is one?"

Caddie thought about this. "Honestly?" she said. "I don't know."

"Sex isn't love," Nicole said. "And Nick doesn't love anyone else, even if he forgets sometimes."

No, Caddie thought. *Sex isn't love.* She had to agree with Nicole on that. As for the rest of it, she decided it really wasn't any of her business.

"So, how's your summer going?" Nicole asked, abandoning the current topic of conversation.

Caddie let out a long sigh. "I'm not sure," she said. She thought about her father, and Brian, and about Sam and Bree. A few days ago, she'd thought she had all of them neatly arranged in her life. She'd known how she felt, and what she wanted—or didn't—from all of them.

She started talking, and once she'd started, she didn't stop for a long time. Nicole just sat and listened, nodding occasionally but saying little else than to encourage Caddie to go on. Caddie surprised herself by telling Nicole about her father and their long estrangement. She touched on Brian—who wasn't so much a problem as he was a diversion that was becoming less and less amusing—and ended with a reconstruction of the morning's phone call.

"It all makes Nick sound like a piece of cake," Nicole said when Caddie was finished.

Caddie looked at her and they both laughed. It felt good to laugh about her problems; she just never thought it would be with the girlfriend of the first guy in Monterey she'd slept with. "Maybe I'm making it sound more dramatic than it really is," she said.

"Life is dramatic," said Nicole, drinking her latte. "That's what makes it interesting, right?"

"It makes it something," Caddie said. "I don't know if interesting is the word I'd pick."

"Just pick one thing," said Nicole. When Caddie looked at her, not understanding, she explained. "One thing—your father, this guy, your friends. Pick one and deal with it first. The rest aren't going anywhere. The problem is, you're trying to figure out all three at once."

Caddie reevaluated her original opinion of the girl. She knew what she was talking about. *Or maybe,* she thought, *I've just been making it more complicated than it is.* She said, "Maybe my father," she said, not realizing she was going to say it.

"He sounds the most important," said Nicole. She drained her coffee cup and set it down. "Family always is."

"I wouldn't know," Caddie replied. "I've never really had one."

"Well," said Nicole, "now you do."

It was such a simple statement, said with such matter-of-factness, that it felt to Caddie like someone had struck her. Nicole was right. For years she had resented her father for not being there. Now that he was, she was still resenting him, when what she should be doing was trying to see what kind of relationship they could have.

"We have started to talk a little bit," she said in her defense.

"Talking's good," Nicole said.

"Sure," Caddie said, "but what comes after that? I mean, what if he doesn't like me, or I don't like him?"

"Is that what you're afraid of?" asked Nicole. "You're his *daughter.* He's your *father.*" She stressed the words, as if perhaps Caddie wasn't aware of what they represented. "Besides, you'll never find out if you don't give it a shot."

She makes it sound so easy, thought Caddie. But maybe it was as easy as that. "You're probably right," she told Nicole.

Nicole looked at her watch. "I'm supposed to meet Nick for lunch pretty soon," she said. She looked at Caddie and grinned. "Should I tell him you said hi?"

"Of course," Caddie said mischievously. "Tell him we had a *long* talk. Let him wonder what it was about."

Nicole stood up. "Thanks again for the coffee," she said. "And use that number." She pointed her finger at Caddie, emphasizing each of the last three words.

"I will," said Caddie, knowing that she would. "Thanks. And thanks for letting me babble at you."

"That's what friends are for," said Nicole, waving good-bye.

Caddie watched her leave. *That's what friends are for,* she repeated to herself. It was such a sappy statement. She thought suddenly of the hideous song of the same name. Who had sung it? Elton John, she remembered, and someone else. Dionne Warwick, the woman from the old Psychic Friends Network commercials. *That was a giant steaming piece of crap.* She, Sam, and Bree had sung it once at karaoke night at their favorite club, hamming it up and feigning emotion. It had all seemed so clever, a sneer at the song's simple platitudes.

Nicole probably loved that song, she thought. And maybe she wasn't wrong to, at least as far as the sentiment went. She felt more like a friend to Caddie after two meetings than Sam and Bree did after years together. Like with so many things, this was something she was going to have to work out her feelings about.

"But it's still a stupid song," she said as she got up to leave.

CHAPTER 31

"This is where it happened?"

Hudson looked at the bust of Ed Ricketts. Ben, standing beside him, nodded. "He drove down Cannery Row and turned right here," he said, pointing up Drake Avenue. "The Del Monte Express was coming through and neither of them saw the other. The train hit Ricketts's Buick and pinned him inside. He died three days later." He looked back toward the water. "The irony is, they didn't see each other because a huge cannery had been erected right there. It turned this into a blind corner. When Ricketts died, he was working on proving that overfishing was going to wipe out the sardine population."

"It's like the cannery didn't want him in the way," mused Hudson.

Ben nodded. "He was right, of course. The whole industry was dead a couple of years later."

It was early evening. The sun, sinking into the ocean, had coated everything with a dull gold sheen. The sky, violet and blue, was caught in the slow change from day to night. The air had cooled, and Hudson was glad he had worn a sweatshirt. Looking at the bust of Ricketts, its face half in shadow, he shivered.

"Cold?" asked Ben.

Hudson shook his head. "It's just sad," he said.

"He and Steinbeck were about to leave on an expedition to British Columbia and Alaska," Ben told him. "It was the next part of their plan to write about the marine ecology of the West Coast."

"Did Steinbeck go without him?" asked Hudson.

"No," Ben answered. "He said he couldn't go without Ed."

Again Hudson found himself thinking about the relationship between the two men. He looked at Ben. "Do you think they were lovers?" he asked bluntly.

Ben laughed. "Steinbeck and Ricketts?" he said, as if he couldn't imagine a more unlikely thing.

"I'm serious," said Hudson. "Do you think it's possible?"

Ben scratched his ear. "Anything is possible until you prove it isn't," he said. "Even then, you never know."

"Stop talking like a scientist," Hudson said. "Think like a normal person."

Ben put his hands in his pockets. "God, Hudson, I don't know. What makes you think they might have been?"

I just do, Hudson thought. He knew that answer would never wash with Ben. His scientific mind needed facts, and, unfortunately, they were in short supply. But he gave it his best shot. "I found this manuscript," he said.

"The one you came here to look into," said Ben. "You told me about that."

"I didn't tell you everything," Hudson said. "I think it's an unknown Steinbeck novel," he said. "Well, part of one. It's only about half finished." He looked over the head of Ricketts's bust, afraid to see Ben's reaction to his next revelation. "It's about a man who falls in love with his best friend," he said. "I think it might be about Steinbeck's feelings for Ricketts."

He waited for Ben to say something. He wasn't sure why, but he knew he wouldn't be able to stand it if Ben laughed at him. It was the first time he had ever spoken his theory about the manuscript out loud to anyone. *Except for Paul,* he reminded himself. That made him even more afraid.

"After Ricketts died," Ben said, breaking the silence, "Steinbeck took most of his personal papers. He burned a number of the journals. When someone asked him why he'd done it, he said that Ed's journals contained enough material to blackmail half of Monterey."

Hudson looked at him. Ben was staring at the bust with a thoughtful expression. "I've always wondered what was in those journals," he said, turning to look at Hudson.

"I never knew that," Hudson said.

"Steinbeck gave most of Ricketts's papers to Hopkins," said Ben.

"The scientific ones, anyway. The fellow who cataloged them told me that story."

"Who knows what was in those," Hudson remarked, suddenly feeling a deep sense of loss as he thought of Steinbeck dropping the journals, piece by piece, into a fire. He had a sharp vision of Steinbeck's face, stoic in the face of the loss of his best friend and companion, illuminated by the glow of the flames as the smoke stung his eyes. What secrets had he sent heavenward? What had he read on those pages that made him want to destroy them forever?

"Can you prove the manuscript is Steinbeck's?" Ben asked Hudson.

Hudson sighed. "No," he said. "Even if I could, that wouldn't prove he and Ricketts were ever lovers."

"Does it matter if they were?" said Ben.

It does to me, Hudson thought silently. "Not really," he answered Ben. "The manuscript being authentic would be a major find on its own. But since Steinbeck wrote so much from his own life, it would add something to the story."

"You mean it would be a scandal," said Ben.

"That too," Hudson agreed. "Although I don't know why. Lots of writers had affairs, with men and women both."

"Still," Ben said, and although he didn't add anything else, Hudson knew what he meant. There was a mystique that surrounded John Steinbeck and Ed Ricketts. They were the quintessential buddy team, reckless and without fear. They were hard drinkers and harder workers, paragons of the romantic scholar adventurers. Suggesting that they might also have been bedmates would, for many of their admirers, be too much to imagine.

"I just want to know," Hudson said. "That's all. I just want to know."

"You might never get that answer," Ben told him.

"But you don't think it's crazy?" asked Hudson hopefully.

"No," Ben said. "I don't think it's crazy."

"Did Steinbeck see him before he died?" asked Hudson.

"He couldn't get here in time," said Ben. "He was living in New York then. You know that when he got back, his wife told him she wanted a divorce. He moved back here to Pacific Grove."

"To be near Ricketts," Hudson suggested.

"Maybe," said Ben.

"General opinion is that his writing was never the same after Ricketts died," said Hudson. "Whatever inspiration he got from him, it left with Ricketts."

The sun, almost gone, was now nothing but a thin glow on the horizon. The streetlights had come on, their artificial shine harsh and cold. The bust, caught in a circle of light, looked at Hudson and Ben in bemused silence. Hudson knew that, halfway down Cannery Row, Steinbeck was doing the same.

"Would you like to read some of the manuscript?" Hudson asked Ben. He couldn't believe he was making the offer. No one except him and Paul had read it, at least no one since it had come into their possession. He hadn't even let Marty see it. Hell, Marty didn't even know what it was about. But he'd told Ben everything.

"I would," said Ben.

They left, walking to Hudson's temporary home. Inside, he turned on a light in the living room while Ben took a seat on the couch. Then, going into the other room, he returned with the manuscript. He started to hand it to Ben.

"Why don't you read me your favorite part," Ben suggested.

Hudson sat down. "Okay," he said. "Let me think about what that is. They're all good." He leafed through the pages, looking for something that wouldn't require a lot of explanation. Finally, he settled on one. Sitting back, he cleared his throat and started to read.

> *Tom was flirting with the girl. He touched her arm as he talked to her, and she laughed and didn't pull away. Charlie, watching them, found himself hating them both. He picked up his glass, wet with sweat in the hot air of the bar, and drank half of it.*
>
> *"We oughta be going," he said, loud enough for Tom to hear him.*
>
> *"Who are you talkin' to?" asked Tom, pretending to look around for the source of the voice.*
>
> *The girl laughed, too loudly, and looked at Charlie. "Who's that?" she asked. "Your mother?" She laughed again, and Tom laughed with her.*
>
> *"Yeah," he said, "that's my old dear mother." He pinched Charlie's cheek. "Ain't that right, Ma?"*

"We oughta be going," Charlie said again. He didn't look at Tom or the girl.

"In a while," said Tom. "I'm havin' myself a nice chat with Myrna here."

"My name's Rita," said the girl. "Why do you keep calling me Myrna?"

"Cause you look like Myrna Loy," Tom told her. He kissed her mouth. "Just like a movie star," he added as the girl blushed.

Charlie took a cigarette from his pocket and struck a match on his thumbnail. He inhaled and let the smoke burn his lungs until he couldn't stand it any longer. Then he let it go, watching it float away from him.

"Hey," the girl said, "You got another one a those?"

Charlie looked at her. "No," he said. "Just this one."

"Give it to Myrna here," Tom told him.

"No," Charlie said.

Tom turned to him. "What's the matter with you tonight?" he asked. "You been mean ever since we got here."

Charlie didn't answer him. He kept smoking, looking at his glass of beer and pretending he wasn't there. Tom punched him in the arm. "Hey," he said.

"It's all right," the girl said. "Let him alone."

"I want to know how come he's bein' so mean," said Tom angrily. "And he's gonna tell me."

Charlie continued to ignore him. He thought about the dog. He'd named it Lucky. Mrs. Ring had let him keep it, and now the dog slept with him every night and waited for him at the window every afternoon. Charlie had given him a bath, and now his fur was soft and smelled like soap. At night, Charlie liked to put his face in the soft fur and go to sleep with his arm around the dog.

Something hit him in the side of the head, and he forgot about the dog. Tom was looking at him. It was his hand that had knocked Charlie in the head. Charlie narrowed his eyes and tightened his hand around the glass of beer.

"What the hell's the matter with you?" Tom demanded of him. "You gone dumb or somethin'?"

"No," Charlie said. "Just don't want to give that whore my cigarette."

The girl, incensed, gave a little shriek of disbelief. "What did he call me?" she said, her voice high and tight.

"You apologize," Tom ordered Charlie. "You tell her yer sorry."

"I ain't telling her nothin'." Charlie said. "Goddamn whore."

The girl shrieked again. This time she ran at Charlie, battering him with her small fists. They fell on him no harder than rain, but her voice was filled with fury.

"You son-of-a-bitch!" she yelled. "You goddamn son-of-a-bitch!"

Charlie pushed her away. She fell on the floor, her legs splayed out and her hair coming undone from its pins. She began to cry.

Tom looked down at the girl, then at Charlie. "Why you," he said, and his fist sailed toward Charlie's face. Charlie took it on the chin, his head rocking to the side. There was pain in his lip, and when he put his fingers to his mouth they came away red with blood.

Tom hit him again before he could think what to do. This time the blow was to his stomach. The wind went out of him, and he knocked over the glass of beer. It splashed on the floor, wetting the girl's legs and making her renew her yells. He wished somebody would make her shut up. She was giving him a headache.

"Come on," Tom was yelling at him. "Come on, you bastard."

Charlie turned to face him. This time when Tom came at him, he hit back. His clenched fist met Tom's face, and Tom staggered back. Now there was blood on his face too. He howled in pain and ran at Charlie.

Then they were on the floor, wrestling. Tom was on top of Charlie, trying to choke him. Then they were rolling, and Charlie smelled spilled beer and peanuts. He saw boots and high-heeled shoes, heard the clamor of voices.

Tom's face was close to his now. He smelled his breath,

foul and hot. He held Tom in his arms, pressing him against his chest. Tom, trying to get free, was bucking his hips back and forth, but Charlie was stronger, and he held tight.

"Let me go!" Tom yelled into Charlie's face. "Let me go, you son-of-a-bitch!"

But Charlie couldn't. He kept holding onto Tom, holding him in his arms and feeling him struggle. He wanted to tell him that it was all right. He wanted to press his face into Tom's hair and smell soap. He wanted to go to sleep like this and never wake up.

Hudson stopped reading and looked at Ben. "That's it?" Ben said. "What happens?"

"That's where the manuscript ends," Hudson answered.

"So he never tells Tom what he's feeling?" Ben asked.

"No," Hudson said. "He never does."

Ben put his hands behind his head. "Which one do you think is Steinbeck?" he said.

"I don't think it's that clear-cut," said Hudson. "I think it's more metaphoric. Two men, unable to express themselves. Women coming between them. There are parallels."

"It certainly sounds like Steinbeck," Ben remarked. "The writing, I mean. Can you tell me where you got it?"

Hudson felt the familiar prickliness of suspicion rise on his skin. Then, in an instant, it disappeared. "Paul found it," he said.

"Your lover," Ben said. "The one who died."

Hudson nodded. "Paul was a huge Steinbeck fan," he said. "In fact, he's the one who got me so interested in him. I took one of Paul's classes."

"He was your professor?" Ben asked, looking surprised.

"Yes," said Hudson. "A number of years ago, he bought a couple of boxes of Steinbeck memorabilia from a bookstore owner who was going out of business. There were all kinds of things in there. Mostly it was typescripts of short stories and magazine articles—nothing too exciting. But then there was this manuscript." He held the pages up. "This was the real find."

"But he died before he could prove that it's authentic," said Ben. "Poor guy."

Hudson set the manuscript on the coffee table. "Not exactly," he said nervously. "I didn't tell you the whole truth about that."

Ben eyed him curiously. "Why?" he asked. "You didn't have something to do with it, did you?" His voice was light, and Hudson knew he was making a joke to try to lighten the situation.

"That depends who you ask," Hudson replied. He looked at Ben. "Me or his wife."

CHAPTER 32

"Could I go to work with you today?"

Ben looked up from his pancakes. Caddie was poking at hers, not looking at him. *Did I hear her correctly?* he wondered. "Come to work with me?" he said.

"Unless you don't want me to," Caddie said quickly. "I just thought it might be, I don't know, interesting."

"Of course," Ben said quickly, as if she might change her mind if he gave her too much time to think about it. "I'm not sure how interesting it will be for you, though."

"I don't know," Caddie said. "I've gotten a little more into marine biology since I started . . ." She stopped in midsentence.

"Since?" Ben prodded.

"Since I started reading some of the books you have in your office," said Caddie. "I finished the books I brought, so I looked at yours. I hope that's okay."

"It's fine," Ben said. "Is there anything in particular you found interesting?"

Caddie shrugged. "Nudibranchs, I guess," she said.

Ben brightened. "You know you're named for one," he said.

"I know," Caddie said.

Ben set his fork down. "I suppose that's not something a girl gets very excited about," he said.

"Not really," agreed Caddie. "I guess there are worse things you could have named me after, though."

"Your mother wanted to call you Emma," Ben told her.

Caddie made a face. "Please," she said. "Emma sounds like a librarian."

"That's what I told her too," said Ben.

They finished breakfast and took Ben's car to the lab. Inside, Ben showed Caddie to his office, where she dropped off her backpack. *This feels like "Take Your Daughter to Work" day,* she thought, a little uneasily. She'd noticed people watching her and her father as they came in, and it made her feel uncomfortable, as if she were a new specimen or something.

As she was waiting for her father to tell her what they were going to do, a woman walked in. Small and dark complected, she glanced at Caddie and then looked away, apparently not interested.

"Dr. Patcher," Ben said without enthusiasm. "May I introduce you to my daughter, Caddie?"

The woman looked at Caddie again. This time, Caddie saw genuine surprise on her face. She held out her hand, and the woman took it. "Nice to meet you," Caddie said.

Dr. Patcher, still apparently in shock, said, "You're Ben's daughter?"

Caddie nodded. "Mmm-hmm," she said.

"Caddie came to see what we do around here," said Ben. "I warned her that it might not be very exciting."

Dr. Patcher made a sound that could have meant anything. She kept stealing glances at Caddie as she said, "I just wanted to drop these intern reports off."

"Thank you," said Ben, taking them from her. "I hope you're finding them useful."

"Yes," said Dr. Patcher. She turned and left quickly.

"She's a little squirrely," Caddie commented when she was gone.

"She's into salps," her father said, as if that explained everything. Strangely enough, even though she hadn't the faintest clue what a salp was, Caddie knew just what he meant, and she laughed.

"Are we interrupting?"

Caddie turned to see Angela standing in the doorway. She had a boy with her, a thin, nervous boy who looked at Caddie and gave her a quick smile before looking away. Caddie noticed that he had a bad case of acne and felt sorry for him.

"No," her father said. "I just brought Caddie to work today. I thought maybe we could find something only marginally uninteresting for her to do."

Angela looked at the boy beside her. "Maybe she could help Rhodes download and identify the images from our last dive," she suggested. She looked at Caddie. "Do you know anything about digital cameras?"

"A little," Caddie said. "Enough to download photos."

"Great," Angela said. "Rhodes can show you what to do, if you're up for it."

"Why not?" said Caddie. She looked at Rhodes, who gave another queer smile and said, "It's this way" as he turned around and left the office.

Caddie followed him down a hall and into a small room containing several long tables on which sat four computers.

"Are you familiar with Macs?" Rhodes asked her.

"I have one at home," said Caddie.

Rhodes sat down at one of the tables. Beside the computer was a small pile of memory cards. He picked one up and inserted it into a slot on the Mac's front panel. On the screen, dozens of tiny thumbnails bloomed, each one a miniature image of a larger file. Rhodes clicked on one, and it ballooned to fill most of the screen.

"*Triopha catalinae*," Rhodes announced.

Caddie looked at the creature in the picture. Its sluglike white body was covered with bright orange growths that reminded her of the spots on Rhodes's face.

"Most people call it the clown nudibranch," Rhodes said. "I guess because its tubercles look like pom-poms."

"It's pretty," Caddie said.

"Isn't it?" Rhodes agreed. Caddie saw him looking at the nudibranch with undisguised admiration. The nervousness he'd displayed earlier was gone.

"So, what do we do with these?" Caddie asked him.

"Oh," Rhodes replied, sounding uneasy again. "We identify them and name the files." He pointed to a stack of books on the table. "Those are the ID books. It's pretty easy; you just find the nudie and name it. Although, some of them look alike, so you have to be careful."

"In other words, we get to look at nudie pictures," Caddie joked. "How scandalous."

Rhodes didn't laugh. Caddie, leafing through a book, looked at him. "Nudie photos," she repeated. "As in *nude* photos?"

This time Rhodes blushed. "Now I get it," he said.

Caddie picked up a flashcard and inserted it into her computer.

The thumbnails appeared as the card downloaded, and she looked at all of the different nudibranchs captured within them. "I had no idea there were so many," she said.

"And these are just the ones in Monterey," said Rhodes. "Pretty much every place has different ones."

"What's this one?" Caddie asked, pointing to a picture she'd just opened.

Rhodes looked over at her screen. "*Cadlina luteomarginata,*" he said. "I think. It might be *Acanthodoris hudsoni.* I get them confused sometimes. Check in the Behrens book over there."

Caddie looked at the nudibranch. *Cadlina,* she thought. *I wonder if that's the one I'm named after.* She found the book Rhodes had told her to look in, a thin purple paperback called *Pacific Coast Nudibranchs*. It was filled with pictures of nudibranchs. Caddie turned the pages until she found one that looked like hers. Round and flat, it was white with yellow around the edge. *Cadlina luteomarginata,* she read. It definitely looked like the one in the picture. Just to be sure, she looked up the other one Rhodes had mentioned. It was similar, but it also had yellow on its—she read the description beside the photo—on its papillae.

"Why do all of their parts sound like venereal diseases?" she said.

Rhodes looked at her. "What?" he said.

"Their parts," said Caddie. "Papillae. Cerata. Clavus." She read from the book. "Caryophyllidia. Come on. They sound like they need to go to a clinic."

"Wait 'til you get to the penile stylet," said Rhodes. "It has a chitinous *hook.*"

Caddie grimaced. "Ouch," she said, and they both laughed.

She went back to the picture of the nudibranch. It was pretty, in a weird sea creature kind of way. She looked it up in the book again. There were two other *Cadlinas* there as well. She would have to ask her father which one was her namesake. She hoped it was the one with black horns and yellow spots. It was the prettiest.

She typed a name for the picture, then went on to the next one. Sometimes there was more than one picture of the same nudibranch, but for the most part every image was of something she'd never seen before. She found herself turning to the guidebook regularly, and from time to time she couldn't ID one of the creatures at all and had to ask Rhodes for help.

"How'd you end up here?" she asked him after they'd been work-ing in silence for a while.

"My parents gave me a choice between this and baseball camp," he told her. "How about you?"

"I'm on work release," said Caddie. Then, remembering that Rhodes was apparently humor challenged, she added quickly, "I'm staying with my dad for the summer."

"He's a nice guy," Rhodes remarked.

"Yeah," Caddie said after a moment. "He is."

She worked for another hour, identifying a dozen nudibranchs, until she'd labeled every image on the card. She was reaching for a new one when her father appeared in the doorway. "Ready for lunch?" he asked her.

"Sure," Caddie answered. She looked at Rhodes. "I'll see you in a while," she said.

"Where are we going?" she asked her father as they walked back to-ward his office.

"I thought we'd meet Hudson at the Bulldog," he said. "It's an Irish pub. How's that sound?"

"Fine," Caddie said. She was surprised to hear that Hudson would be joining them; she'd assumed they would be having lunch alone. She was even more surprised to find that she was a little annoyed. *Let it go,* she reminded herself. *You're starting over.*

By the time they reached the Bulldog, she was in a better mood. It didn't matter if Hudson was there or not. *Besides,* she thought, *he's easy to look at.*

Hudson was already there, seated at one of the pub's few tables. They joined him, Caddie sliding in next to him and her father taking the seat across from them.

"They have the best fish and chips here," her father announced as they looked at the menus.

"With such a rave recommendation, I guess I'll have to try it," Hud-son said, shutting his menu.

"Me too," said Caddie, although fried fish made her think again, un-appetizingly, of Rhodes and his pimples.

They ordered, and as they waited for their food, Hudson and her fa-ther began talking. Caddie listened, only half-interested, as they dis-cussed Hudson's upcoming first dives in the ocean.

"I'm sorry I haven't been free to do it," her father said. "But I promise, we'll go tomorrow. The conditions should be perfect."

"Your father is determined to see me drown," Hudson said to Caddie.

She watched her father as he laughed. "You're a natural," he said, looking at Hudson and grinning. "You're practically half otter."

Something about the tone of his voice and the way he was looking at Hudson caught her attention. She'd never seen him like this before. He was happy, almost annoyingly so. It reminded her of something, but she couldn't think what it was.

Then, as the waiter appeared and set their plates in front of them, it hit her. *He's flirting,* she thought. And she knew what he reminded her of—herself. He was acting the way she did when she wanted to get a guy's attention.

She sat, stunned, and watched the two of them. Her father was talking quickly, waving his hands and laughing. Hudson, too, was laughing. Caddie looked from one to the other. What was going on with them? She couldn't imagine.

"How come you're not eating?" her father asked.

"I need ketchup," Caddie said quickly.

Hudson handed her the bottle, and she busied herself with pouring ketchup over her fries. She did the same with the malt vinegar, dousing her pieces of fish in it as she tried to regain her composure.

She ate slowly, only just picking at her plate. Oblivious, her father and Hudson talked animatedly. She didn't even listen to the words; they weren't important. It was everything else that captured her attention, the way they shared an enthusiasm for whatever it was they were going on about, the way they were focused on each other. *The way they're ignoring me,* she thought, not without a little irritation.

Something was going on, and she wasn't sure what it was. Were they really flirting? It was such a weird—such a disturbing—thought that she couldn't imagine she was right. *They're just friends,* she assured herself. She didn't allow herself to consider anything beyond that.

"Caddie."

"It's great," she said, thinking her father had spoken to her again. But when she looked up, it was Brian who was looking at her. He nodded a greeting at her father and Hudson. "Hey," he said.

"What are you doing here?" Caddie asked him, sounding more accusatory than she wanted to.

"Same thing you are," said Brian. "Getting lunch. Aren't the fries killer?"

Her father and Hudson agreed. Caddie, trying to stop her father before he could ask any embarrassing questions, said, "Brian works at the aquarium. That's where we met."

"Really?" her father said. "What do you do?"

"I'm just summer help," Brian said. "Nothing major." He turned his attention back to Caddie. "Are we still going diving later?" He looked at her father. "I promised her I'd take her on her first night dive," he said.

Caddie felt her stomach knot. She felt her father and Hudson both staring at her. Then came the inevitable question. "Since when do you dive?" her father asked.

"Oh, I showed her," Brian informed him.

Ben looked at him. "You're an instructor?" he asked, sounding doubtful.

"Nah," said Brian. "But I've been diving for a couple of years."

Caddie tried to shrink into the bench. She was horrified, both because she'd been caught in a lie by her father and because Brian was about to find out that she wasn't everything she'd pretended to be. Even though she'd pretty much decided she didn't care about him, she hated to be found out.

But her father didn't betray her. "Maybe we'll all go together one of these days," he said. "I'm about to certify Hudson."

Brian beamed. "Cool," he said. "Well, I should be getting back. I just came to pick up an order. Call me later," he added to Caddie.

"He seems nice," Hudson said.

"He does," her father agreed. He looked at Caddie.

"I was going to mention the diving thing," she said, trying to head him off.

"It's okay," he said. "We can talk about it later."

Relieved, she resumed eating. But she felt as if she'd been reprimanded. Her father had used *that* tone with her, the one that meant, "You're in big trouble, young lady." It was the same tone her mother used. But at least her mother had been around long enough to earn the right to scold her.

You haven't, she thought, glancing at her father. But he was talking to Hudson again, as if nothing had happened. *He doesn't even know how to be mad at me right,* Caddie thought. Her mother would have had it out with her, demanding to know who Brian was and what they were doing together. Her father didn't seem interested in anything other than the fact that she'd gone diving without telling him. *Big deal,* Caddie thought. Of all the things she'd done for him to be annoyed by, that was the least of them.

She looked out the pub's big front window. The day had started off so well. Now everything had changed. *I knew it was too good to last,* she thought. *It always is.*

Her father waited until they were alone in the car before getting back to the topic of diving.

"I know it seems like diving is easy," he said as Caddie leaned back in her seat and shut her eyes, groaning inwardly. "But it can be really dangerous. This boy . . ." His voice trailed off, and Caddie realized he'd already forgotten Brian's name. She didn't help him out by reminding him.

"Anyway, it isn't as easy as it looks," her father continued. "A lot of things can happen. You can die if you do it incorrectly."

There was silence following this pronouncement, and Caddie knew she was supposed to be impressed. "You can die walking across the street," she said, keeping her eyes closed. "You can die riding a bike."

"The point is, this guy isn't an instructor," said her father. He sounded annoyed, and this secretly pleased Caddie. *Finally, he's acting like a normal father,* she thought. *At least sort of.*

"You can't just *go* diving," her father said.

"Why?" Caddie asked him. "Is there a law against it?"

"Well, no," said her father. "There's no law. But you're supposed to be certified."

"Says who?"

She heard her father sigh. "You're just supposed to," he said. "A certification card says that you've had enough training to know how to dive safely. It's like a driver's license. You wouldn't drive without one of those, would you?"

Caddie started to remind him that, technically, she was supposed to have an adult with her in the car while she was driving, but he didn't seem to care if she obeyed that rule or not. Then she thought better of it. If she brought the matter to his attention, he might actually tell her she couldn't drive anymore. Instead, she said, "But there's a *law* about that. You said there's no law that says you have to be certified to dive."

"It's an unwritten law," her father said. "And it's common sense. You could really hurt yourself."

"It's just the Breakwater," Caddie said. Brian says that's like skiing the bunny bowl at a ski resort.

"Well, I doubt Brian has ever had to perform CPR on someone who's drowned at Breakwater," said her father. "Has he?"

"I don't know," Caddie admitted.

"I have," her father informed her. "And it wasn't pleasant. Every year there are two or three deaths at Breakwater because people think they know what they're doing and they don't."

Caddie opened her eyes, blinking against the bright sun. Her father was staring straight ahead, his hands gripping the steering wheel tightly. "I'm not going to die," she said. "I know what I'm doing."

Her father didn't answer. Then, while they were stopped at a light, he turned and looked at her. "I thought you were smarter than this," he said, shaking his head.

Caddie felt her cheeks flush. "Meaning what?" she demanded.

Her father didn't answer. He sat, silent, until the light changed. Caddie, growing more and more angry, crossed her arms over her chest and looked out the window. *Smarter that this,* she repeated to herself. *Is he still talking about diving, or does he mean hanging out with Brian?* she wondered. Either way, she couldn't believe her father would say something like that to her.

He's the one who's acting like a fool, she thought, remembering how he'd acted around Hudson during lunch. He'd behaved like a love-struck teenager. It had been embarrassing to watch. She almost said so now, but she knew her father would have no idea what she was talking about. He was so oblivious that it wasn't even funny. It was just sad.

He thinks I should be smarter? she thought. *He's the one who needs to get a clue.*

CHAPTER 33

Hudson looked down at the compass strapped to his wrist. The arrow end of the needle was just shy of being centered in the notch on the bezel, which he'd set to ninety-five degrees. He adjusted his path, and the arrow locked in place. Now he just had to remember to hold his wrist level.

He swam, counting ten kicks, then stopped. To make a right turn, he needed to add ninety degrees to his current heading. He did the math, then set the compass to a new heading of one hundred eighty-five degrees. Another ten kicks, another right turn, this time going out at two seventy-five. The final turn required trickier figuring. *Eighty-five gives me three hundred and sixty,* he thought. *Plus another five to make it a full ninety-degree turn.* He turned the bezel to fifteen degrees, cursing Ben for starting him at such an odd number, and swam. If he had done everything correctly, he should be swimming right back to where Ben was waiting.

After eight kicks he began to panic. Nothing looked familiar. He looked at the compass again. Had he failed to hold it level? Had he added or subtracted incorrectly? He couldn't remember what numbers he'd used. Even if he could, he would already be so far off course that he would never be able to retrace his steps. *Maybe you should just surface,* he told himself.

Then another kick, and ahead of him he saw Ben kneeling in the sand. When he saw Hudson, he clapped his hands together and gave him the okay sign. Hudson, overjoyed, returned the sign and finished the final leg of the square. He'd done it. He'd been dreading the navigation test more than anything else and was relieved that he'd passed it on the first try.

Now all that was left was the out-of-air ascent. He ran over the steps in his mind, trying to remember everything Ben had taught him. They'd done it in the pool several times, but because of the shallow depths, it hadn't been an accurate representation of what it would be like doing it in the ocean. They'd barely had to kick to get to the surface, and the skill was over before it had even begun.

Now Ben knelt, facing Hudson. Then he slashed his hand across his throat and pointed to himself, indicating that he was going to take the role of the diver who was out of air. Hudson gave the okay sign to show that he understood. He took a breath and waited. Ben repeated the out-of-air hand signal, moving his hand horizontally beneath his chin, then bringing his fingertips to his lips and away, imitating the sharing of air.

Hudson reached for his alternate regulator, putting it in his mouth as he simultaneously removed his primary regulator. This he handed to Ben, turning it so that the mouthpiece was facing away from himself. Ben took it and, letting his own regulator fall gently to his side, placed Hudson's in his mouth.

They were now sharing the air in Hudson's tank, breathing together. Hudson then moved closer to Ben and took hold of his BC at the waist, so that they were face to face. He gave Ben the okay signal and waited to see it mirrored back at him. Then he pointed surfaceward with his thumb, and they began to swim up.

It was awkward. The regulator hoses seemed to get in the way, and Hudson had a difficult time looking at his computer to monitor their ascent rate while still controlling the release of air from his BC. Also, Ben was kicking hard. Hudson knew it was on purpose; he was simulating what a panicked diver would be most likely to do in this situation.

Hudson let more air out of his BC, slowing them down. He looked at Ben and saw that, behind his mask, his eyes betrayed his amusement. He was enjoying watching Hudson try to do everything at once. Then they were at the surface. Ben handed the regulator back to Hudson and inflated his own BC so that he was bobbing easily.

"Not bad," he said. "Neither of us has the bends. Good work."

"Do I pass?" Hudson asked him.

"One more dive," said Ben. "You have to plan it and lead it. So decide where you want to take me, and we'll get it done."

Hudson looked around. "How about over there?" he suggested.

"You're the dive leader," said Ben. "I'm just the poor guy who's following you."

Hudson gave him the finger. "Oops," he said, turning his fist so that his thumb was pointing down. "I meant to say I'll see you on the bottom."

Forty minutes later the two of them surfaced not far from shore. "Congratulations," Ben said. "You are now a certified scuba diver, courtesy of the good folks at Scuba Schools International."

"I feel like there should be some kind of initiation or something," said Hudson as they headed in.

"Didn't I mention the part where we make you wrestle with a wolf eel?" joked Ben.

They emerged from the water, walking up the beach to one of the freshwater showerheads mounted on a pole nearby. Ben held the button down while Hudson rinsed himself and his gear, then they switched places. When they were both mostly free of saltwater, they continued on to Ben's car and began the process of taking everything off.

"You never told me how your talk with Caddie turned out," Hudson said as he removed the weights from his BC. "Did that guy really take her diving?"

"He did," Ben said.

"And that's bad, right?" Hudson asked.

"He's not an instructor," Ben explained. "Technically, there's nothing that says you *have* to be certified to dive. But no dive shop operator in their right mind will rent you gear or fill your tanks without seeing a c-card first. I guess Brian just borrowed a bunch of gear for Caddie."

"And you're okay with her diving without any formal training?"

"No," Ben said. "I quizzed her a little, and she doesn't know half of what she should to be out there. But there's really not much I can do to stop her if she's determined to do it, so I offered to teach her the right way to dive."

"Let me guess," said Hudson. "She said no."

Ben nodded. "That girl's as stubborn as . . ."

"As you are?" Hudson suggested.

Ben, sliding the tub with his gear into the back of the car, didn't answer, but Hudson knew he'd said exactly what Ben was thinking. "I thought we were starting to get along," said Ben.

"At least she's talking to you," Hudson reminded him. "You can't expect miracles overnight."

Ben helped him lift his gear into the car. "I'd settle for just knowing what she's thinking," he commented.

"Ah," said Hudson as Ben closed the hatch. "I'm afraid that will never happen. You're a dad; she's a daughter. You're different species."

They got in and drove back to Ben's house. When they walked in, Caddie was sitting on the couch, reading a book. She looked up, then went back to her book without saying anything.

"Hey, Caddie," Hudson said brightly.

She muttered an unintelligible greeting but didn't look at him.

"Hudson just finished his certification dives," Ben said brightly.

"Good for Hudson," said Caddie.

Hudson saw Ben stiffen at the girl's tone. He knew Ben was trying hard to keep things light, but he also knew that Caddie wasn't going to make it easy for him. In some ways she reminded him of himself when he was her age—moody, craving independence, but still wanting to feel that someone was watching out for him. Those years were hard. *Not that it really gets all that much easier,* he thought.

"Have you dived at the Breakwater?" he asked Caddie.

She nodded. "A bunch of times," she said.

"It's amazing," Hudson continued, refusing to let her air of superiority quiet him. "Who knew all of that stuff was under the water? It's like an alien world or something."

For a moment, Caddie looked at him with something like interest. He realized he'd touched something in her, however briefly. *She feels the same way about diving,* he realized. *She wants to agree with me but she can't. She'd lose too much ground.*

"We saw this fish," he continued, pressing his advantage. "It looked like it was straight out of the mesowhatever era. Like a dinosaur. It had these big eyes and a long tail, and its fins were like wings."

"A ratfish," Caddie said, bored. "We saw two of them the other day, and a bat ray."

"Yeah, well, we saw a grompus," Hudson informed her.

She regarded him over the top of her book. "A reticulated grompus or a regular one?" she asked him.

He hesitated. "A regular one, I guess," he said.

"Nice try," said Caddie. "There's no such thing as a grompus."

Hudson grunted. "Well, we saw some other cool things," he insisted. "A sculpin, or something. It was kind of purplish."

Ben, who had been listening to the exchange, said, "I'm going to go take a shower. Then I thought I'd grill some steaks for dinner. How's that sound?"

"Great," said Hudson.

"Fine," Caddie added.

Ben went upstairs, leaving the two of them alone. Caddie continued to be absorbed in her book, and Hudson was tempted to leave her alone. But her attitude was starting to bug him. He didn't appreciate her sarcasm, and because he knew his staying in the room would annoy her, he decided to stay put. It was childish, he knew, but if she wanted to play games, he was going to give her a run for her money.

"What are you reading?" he asked, sitting in the chair opposite her.

Caddie held the book out toward him so that he could read the cover. "*Cannery Row,*" Hudson read.

"There was nothing else around," said Caddie sullenly. "And you all seem to think it's the best book ever written."

"Don't you?" Hudson said.

Caddie shrugged. "It's all right," she said. "I don't really get the fuss."

"A lot of people miss the point," Hudson told her. He knew the insinuation that she didn't understand the book would rile her, and he was right.

"And what would the point be?" she asked, lowering the book and turning the full force of her stare on him.

"What do you think it is?" he goaded her.

"That working in a fish factory sucks?" Caddie tried. "Or how about that everyone in Monterey is a total moron?"

"You're a smart girl," Hudson replied. "You can do better than that."

Caddie flushed. *She just realized that she's in for a fight,* Hudson thought, not without some enjoyment. *Let's see where she goes now.*

"Okay," Caddie said. "Let me think." She put her finger to her cheek, parodying the classic contemplative pose. "Is it about the human struggle to find happiness in a world that wants to keep us from it? Oh, or maybe it's about the beauty of the individual human spirit and the glory of community?"

Hudson looked at her face, at the narrowed eyes and tight mouth. Her hands clutched the bottom of the book tightly, forcing the pages apart like the wings of a frightened bird. She was a study in anger, beautiful and terrible in her inexplicable rage.

"Don't look so surprised," Caddie said. "I read the introduction." She raised the book to cover her face, leaving him to stare at the cover.

"What's your problem?" Hudson heard himself speak, prayed that he had just thought the words. When Caddie dropped the book from her face, he realized with rising alarm that he hadn't.

"Excuse me?" Caddie said.

You started it, Hudson told himself. *You might as well finish it.* "I want to know what your problem is," he repeated, striving for a bravado he didn't feel. "You have this giant chip on your shoulder, and as far as I can tell, there's no reason for it."

Caddie closed the book and set it on the couch beside her. "So now you're an expert on me?" she asked.

"I don't have to be an expert to notice that you're being a . . ." He stopped.

"A what?" said Caddie. "A brat? A bitch? Why don't you just say it?" She crossed her arms over her chest and waited, daring Hudson to agree with her.

"Your father loves you very much," Hudson said.

Caddie laughed. "Really?" she said. "I guess you would know what he loves, right?"

"What's that supposed to mean?" Hudson asked her.

The expression on Caddie's face changed. All of a sudden she looked enormously pleased with herself. She cocked her head, looking at him with an unsettling mixture of excitement and disdain. To Hudson, she looked like a cat about to go in for the kill, watching her prey as its inevitable death dawned on it. "You really don't know, do you?" she said.

"Know what?" said Hudson.

Caddie's voice was barely a whisper. "He has a crush on you," she said.

Hudson knitted his brow. "Who does?" he said, having no idea what she was talking about.

"Him," Caddie said, nodding toward the stairway.

The meaning of her words suddenly became clear. "Ben?" he said.

Caddie nodded. "It's so obvious," she said.

Hudson's thoughts were spinning. He found it impossible to think clearly. What was Caddie saying? Finally he blurted, "That's ridiculous. You father isn't gay."

"Maybe not," Caddie said. "But he's crushing on you, big boy, so you'd better deal with it."

Hudson was stunned. He'd never even considered the possibility. Ben? A crush on him? No, that wasn't it. "We're just friends," he said. He looked at Caddie. She was shaking her head. "Just friends," Hudson repeated.

"You just keep believing that," Caddie said.

"That's why you're shutting him out again?" asked Hudson. "Because you think he and I . . . Because you think he . . ."

Caddie shook her head. "You just walk in and he . . ." she began, but didn't continue. Hudson saw that her eyes were becoming damp. "I'm his daughter," she said, her voice shaking.

It was too much. He couldn't think. Ben had a—thing—for him? Even if it wasn't true, Caddie thought that it was, and that was what mattered.

"You should see how he looks at you," Caddie was saying. Tears had begun to roll down her face, although Hudson could tell she was trying her hardest to hold them back. "His whole face lights up," she said. "And you," she went on, waving a hand at Hudson. "You don't even see it."

"I—" Hudson began.

"Don't say it's not true," Caddie interrupted. "You know it is."

Hudson started again to protest. At the same time, his thoughts were rushing backward, replaying his times together with Ben. Like a movie rewinding, images flashed in his head: he and Ben laughing, him reaching for the buttons on Ben's shirt, Ben's eyes looking into his underwater. How had he not seen what was happening? With a sudden, gut-wrenching realization, as if the force of the evidence had landed a blow to his stomach and driven all breath from him, he saw that Caddie was right.

He stood up. "I have to go," he said, not looking at Caddie. "Tell your father I'm sorry."

CHAPTER 34

Eleanor Mintz lived in a small Victorian house in one of the most beautiful spots in the world. Situated on the winding road that followed the coastline of Pacific Grove, it looked out on the ocean with an unobstructed view that made the property, Hudson knew, worth more than he could even imagine. As he walked to the front door up the narrow path bordered on both sides by lavender, he saw the door open, and a small, gray-haired woman stepped out. She looked over Hudson's head to the sea beyond. When her eyes came finally to rest on him, she was smiling.

"You must be Hudson," she said.

"Mrs. Mintz," said Hudson.

She showed him into her house. Keeping with the Victorian look, it was decorated in outdated, but perfectly preserved, furnishings. Hudson eyed the overlarge sofa with its high carved back, the wallpaper patterned in William Morris roses and an excess of flourishes. On a stand beside the fireplace, a seated black china cat dipped its paw into a large glass bowl in which a goldfish swam in tight circles.

"It was a nice surprise to get your call last night," Hudson said as he was shown into the living room.

"Well, Helen told me what you're doing, and she thought I might be of some assistance. I don't know how, but I told her that I'd try."

Hudson sat on the edge of a chair, feeling as if he were becoming part of a museum installation. *Drawing rooms of the nineteenth century,* he thought. *And in the next gallery, dresses of the American first ladies.* Eleanor Mintz took another chair. She folded her small hands neatly in the lap of her blue dress. Behind her, looking over her shoulder like a trusted sentry, a portrait of a white-haired, mustachioed man in black, eyed Hudson suspiciously. *Her husband?* Hudson mused, then noted the facial resemblance. *No, her father.*

"Well, as Helen probably told you, I'm doing research on Steinbeck's novels," Hudson said. "I'm particularly interested in the influence Ed Ricketts had on him."

The woman nodded slightly. "That's been covered in great detail," she said. "Is there anything more to say?"

Hudson was taken aback. He hadn't expected to have his work questioned by this woman who looked more like somebody's grandmother than an academic. But, he reminded himself, she might yet have some useful information. "You're right," he said calmly. "There has been a lot written about their relationship. But, as I'm sure you know, there's always something new to say." He smiled at her warmly, hoping to disarm her.

"I doubt it," she said firmly. "But you can ask me what you like."

Hudson opened his briefcase and took out a pad and pen. Clearly, he had read Eleanor Mintz incorrectly. *Your honor, I'd like permission to treat Mrs. Mintz as a hostile witness,* he thought as he decided on his first question. He could see that the woman would not suffer foolishness, and he didn't want to give her reason to send him packing.

"Can you tell me what your relationship to John Steinbeck was?" he asked, feeling like the opposing attorney in a courtroom drama.

"I was his assistant of sorts after he returned to Pacific Grove in 1948," said Eleanor. "He was researching what would come to be *East of Eden.* I was working at *The Californian* as a copygirl at the time. One day he came in looking for some back issues of the paper, and I was assigned to help him. I guess he took to me, and he asked if I would like to work for him on a part-time basis."

Hudson, very much familiar with the writing of *East of Eden,* knew that Steinbeck had relied heavily on articles from *The Californian* for background information for his celebrated novel. He tried to imagine the stiff, reserved woman seated across from him handling those papers, clipping and organizing the materials for Steinbeck to look at later. Had she enjoyed it? Had she had any idea what she was helping to create? Or had it all just been, as she put it, a part-time job?

"How long did you work for him?" he asked her.

"Three years," she answered instantly, offering no further information.

Hudson wrote this down, although he would never look at the notes again. He wanted Eleanor Mintz to think he was deeply interested in the details of her employment. When he looked at her face, however, he saw that she was as uninterested in them as he was. To her they were dry facts, presented to him like biscuits on a plate.

"Did you do anything besides help him with research?" he inquired, hoping for any little thing that would take their conversation in a new, more fertile, direction.

"I organized," said Eleanor. "I was a very good organizer."

Looking around the dust-free room, not a thing out of place, Hudson had no doubt that this was true. Most of the things in Eleanor Mintz's house, he imagined, had not moved from their positions in half a century or more. He was beginning to wonder if perhaps somewhere she had the stuffed body of the man in the portrait, still dressed in his black suit, his moustache waxed and combed.

"He was very careless with his manuscripts," Eleanor said, surprising him. She sounded exasperated, as if she were speaking about a particularly untidy child. "He could never remember where he'd put them," she said.

"And you kept them organized?" asked Hudson.

She nodded. "I always put them each in their own box," she said proudly. "If it weren't for me, they would probably have just disappeared."

Good for you, Hudson thought. Truthfully, if it wasn't for people like Eleanor Mintz, things like original manuscripts and letters really would most likely end up in landfills. It was a peculiar trait of authors that they seemed to be determined to throw away things that people might be interested in later. *They put every outfit Liberace ever wore in a museum,* he thought, *but no one knows where the manuscript for* Anna Karenina *is.*

"Do you know if Steinbeck worked on any novels during that time that he never published?" he asked casually.

Eleanor shook her head. "He published nearly everything he ever started," she said. "I can think of only a handful of times that he began a project and abandoned it, and even then it was usually after only a few pages had been written."

It was time, Hudson decided, to ask the question he'd been waiting to ask of someone who might have the answer. Eleanor Mintz, this tight-lipped librarian of a woman, was not the person he had envisioned would hold the key to solving the mystery, but she seemed to be his best chance. He hesitated only a moment before asking, "Did you ever see a manuscript for a novel called *Changing Tides?*"

"Steinbeck never published a book by that name," she said.

"This would be an unpublished manuscript," said Hudson.

Eleanor shook her head. "As I said, he wrote nothing that wasn't eventually published."

"You're certain?" Hudson said.

"I would remember that," said Eleanor, as if he'd suggested that her faculties might not be intact. "I thought you were researching the influence of Ricketts on Steinbeck's work," she continued.

She's being defensive, Hudson thought. *She's upset that I asked her the question.* He glanced at Eleanor Mintz and saw that her hands were tightly clutched in her lap. *She's afraid,* Hudson realized.

"I am researching their relationship," Hudson said, choosing the last word deliberately. "I think this manuscript, the one I mentioned, might be something Steinbeck worked on shortly after Ricketts's death."

"No," said Eleanor. "Nothing by that name exists."

"I've read the manuscript," Hudson said. He opened his briefcase and removed the copy of the manuscript. He held it up so she could see it but did not hand it to her.

Eleanor looked at the papers. "That's not possible," she said. "I . . ."

Hudson waited, holding his breath. Eleanor Mintz seemed suddenly shaken, as if some powerful force had swept through her ordered house and rearranged the rooms. Her hands moved like dying fish in her lap, and her eyes looked at something far away. "You'll have to excuse me," she said faintly. "I don't feel well."

She stood up, putting her hand on the back of the chair. Hudson returned the papers to his briefcase. When he clicked it shut, he saw the old woman start, as if he'd fired a shot at her. He stood and faced her. "Thank you for your time," he said. "If you do think of anything else, I would appreciate it if you would call me."

"Of course," Eleanor said. She didn't offer to show him out, so Hudson walked alone to the door and opened it. He gave one final look back. Eleanor hadn't moved from her spot by the chair. She was as still and stiff as a clock or a vase, as if she were waiting for someone to come along and dust her.

Hudson shut the door and went down the path to the sidewalk.

The windows of the house, empty and dark, watched him as he walked to his car. He got in and started the engine. Was Eleanor Mintz on the phone with Helen Guerneyser? he wondered. Or with Edgar Macready? Were all of them guarding a secret they found too awful to even comprehend? *No, not Helen,* he thought. Helen wasn't hiding anything. But the others, they were. Either that or they didn't want to accept what they suspected—or knew—to be true. Either way, they were going to be of no help to him.

He put the car into gear and pulled away from the house. As he drove, he worried that he hadn't handled Eleanor Mintz in the right way. Perhaps if he'd taken his time, he could have gotten her to open up. *No way,* he reassured himself. *That woman is shut tighter than George Bush's sphincter.* She wouldn't have talked about the manuscript if he'd spent a year with her.

It's still possible she doesn't know anything about it, said his other voice, the one that most often made him feel like he should just give up on his search. *Maybe you just don't want to admit it.*

He shook his head. He wasn't wrong. He'd seen the way Eleanor Mintz had reacted to seeing the copy of the manuscript. Why would she do that if she wasn't afraid of it? And why would she be afraid of it if she didn't know that it was more than just an unfinished story? *She knows it's about them,* he told his inner critic.

But you still don't have proof. This time the voice was Paul's. It wasn't accusatory, just sad. He sounded tired, as if whatever force kept him alive in Hudson's mind was growing weaker and weaker, as if he might soon flicker out altogether.

"I don't know that there's proof!" Hudson cried.

He looked in the rearview mirror, and for a moment he saw Paul's face looking back at him. The eyes were dull, dead, the mouth slack and the skin ashen. Hudson felt his heart cease beating. The blare of a car horn jumped it to life again, and he swerved just in time to avoid a collision with an SUV. When he looked in the mirror again, he saw only his own face.

"What are you doing?" he asked himself.

Ahead of him was a turnoff. He took it, pulling the car onto a narrow strip of sand that served as a makeshift parking lot for tourists wanting a view of the ocean. He turned the engine off, grabbed the briefcase from the seat beside him, and opened it. He took up the manuscript and got out of the car, taking it with him.

There was no path to follow, so he walked down the sandy dunes as best he could, his feet sinking into the sand and throwing him off balance. He walked without thinking, heading for the water. The beach was mostly empty, the sandy expanse dotted only with a handful of people, none of them paying attention to Hudson.

He walked to the edge of the water and stopped. The waves here were bigger. The water, when it rushed toward him, moved quickly, sliding over the wet sand with an eagerness that frightened him, as if it were in search of treasures to take back to the sea. He thrust the manuscript pages out toward the breaking waves. "Here!" he shouted. "Take it!"

He lifted his arm into the wind, ready to let go and send the pages flapping into the ocean. But his fingers refused to move. He tried to force them, but some invisible power kept his muscles frozen.

"Take them," he said again, but already the strength of his voice was fading. "Please," he sobbed as he dropped to his knees. "Please take it."

The water came for him. He tried to fling the papers into its path, and again he couldn't. When the edge of the wave touched his knees, he cradled the manuscript to his chest, holding it tightly until the water retreated again. Before another wave could come, he forced himself to his feet and turned back.

I can't, he thought. *It's been too long. I can't let it go.*

A little girl ran in front of him, shrieking with joy as a smaller boy chased her, holding a crab in his hand and promising to drop it down the back of her shirt. They paid no attention to Hudson as he stopped to let them pass. He watched them for a moment, envious of their carelessness, then returned to his car.

Inside, he returned the manuscript to the briefcase. Sorrow held him in its choking grip. The manuscript felt like a curse, something he could only escape if he either fulfilled his promise to Paul or passed it on to someone else. Then, maybe, he would be free of it.

He wanted to talk to Ben. But even that had been taken from him. He hadn't returned Ben's calls for two days, not since leaving the house after the fight with Caddie. He knew Ben didn't understand what had happened and couldn't imagine that Caddie had told him the truth. She'd wanted Hudson out of the picture, and she'd gotten her wish. She wouldn't, Hudson imagined, do anything to make herself appear to be at fault.

Not that she was, really. She had only brought to light something that Hudson hadn't seen before. As far as he knew, Ben was still in the dark. And maybe it was best that way. If Ben did feel something for him, it could only end badly. *Like it did with Paul,* he thought.

After he'd realized that Caddie was—probably—correct, he'd asked himself if he was to blame. Had he somehow caused Ben to think that he was interested? Was he interested? He'd honestly never considered it. But forced to, he'd had to admit that he was, or at least could be. *If Ben wanted it too,* he thought now.

That, he told himself, was why he had to leave. He wouldn't put himself in that position. Not again. It had nearly killed him the first time; he didn't think he was strong enough now. *Neither is Ben,* he told himself.

His mind was made up. He would leave as soon as he could. He would go back to Yale, to Marty and the safety of his old life. *But it's not safe,* he realized. *It won't be safe until you're done with this.* There was, he saw, nowhere to run. Paul's ghost waited for him in New Haven, had followed him here. Those of Steinbeck and Ricketts were there as well. He was haunted. There was no going back and no going forward.

He looked in the mirror and saw that the backseat was crowded with passengers, all of them watching him with dark, accusing eyes.

"Goddamn all of you," he muttered as he started the car. "It's time to put an end to all of this."

CHAPTER 35

"Any idea why your father is in such a bad mood?" Angela added two more flashcards to the pile already on the table.

Caddie kept her eyes on the computer screen as she answered. "I think he's just tired," she said. "He hasn't been sleeping."

"Well, I wish he'd take a nap," said Angela. "He's been a bear all day."

Caddie said nothing. She focused her attention on the picture of the nudibranch. She'd already identified it as *Phidiana hiltoni,* pleased with herself for not confusing it with the more common *Hermisenda crassicornis.* She was getting good at recognizing the sea slugs and could ID at least a dozen without having to look at the guidebook. Now she studied the *Phidiana*'s rhinophores, waiting for Angela to go away.

"Take a look at this," Rhodes said. He was sitting at the computer beside her and turned his monitor so that she could see it. The screen was filled with the image of a long black nudibranch. It was unlike any Caddie had ever seen, its skin speckled with white and two lines of electric orange and blue running in an hourglass shape from its wide head to its strange bisected tail.

"*Navanax inermis,*" Rhodes announced. "The cannibal nudibranch. It eats the other ones. Isn't it cool?"

"Actually, yeah," Caddie admitted. "It's beautiful."

"You should see the other nudibranchs try to get out of its way," said Angela. "That sucker is vicious."

She left the room, and Caddie looked again at the *Navanax.* Everything about it screamed danger, from its color to its name. *Navanax,* she repeated soundlessly, feeling the shape of it, long and poisonous. *That's what I feel like.*

Ever since her confrontation with Hudson, she'd been having moments of guilt. *But what you said was true,* she told herself. *He needed to hear it. He didn't know. It's not your fault he ran away.*

No, it wasn't her fault. Nonetheless, she'd wanted him to do exactly that. With Hudson out of the way, she was the focus of her father's attention. There had been the awkward moment when he'd come downstairs from his shower and had asked where Hudson was. But she'd handled that well, she thought, telling him that Hudson had received a phone call—something to do with the house he was staying in—and had to go take care of it. Her father, unsuspecting, had accepted this explanation without questions.

It was only later, after several calls to Hudson had gone unanswered, that he had started to change. After dinner, he went to his study, remaining there until he went to bed, often well after midnight. Although they talked, their conversations were stiff, seldom veering beyond questions about Caddie's friends, her studies, her taste in movies. She'd tried to pique his interest by bringing up *Cannery Row,* but her father had talked only for a few minutes before pushing his plate away and changing the subject to something impersonal.

Still, he was hers. For the first time in her life, she had his attention. He would forget Hudson soon enough, she told herself. Another few days, maybe a week, and he would be his old self. Then they would talk. Maybe she would ask him some of the questions she'd carried around for years, things she'd never even asked her mother.

"Can I ask you something?"

Rhodes's question shook her from her thoughts. "Sure," she said.

"Do you have a boyfriend? Back home. In L.A."

Caddie looked over at him. He was peering intently at his computer screen, steadfastly avoiding meeting her gaze. "No," she said. "I mean, sort of. Why?"

"Just wondering," Rhodes answered. "I figured you did."

Was he going to ask me out? Caddie wondered. The idea struck her as funny. Rhodes? Rhodes, with his pimples and his nervous laugh? She couldn't even imagine.

She thought about Brian. She'd seen him again, slept with him again, mostly because she was tired of doing it herself. And it had been okay. He'd at least gone down on her, which was more than most guys did. Still, she hadn't come and ultimately had had to do it herself any-way when she got home. But there was still something comforting about being naked with him. He wanted her, and that was something. It was more than she got from most people. *Besides,* she reminded herself, *if you don't want them, they can't hurt you.*

"Do you have a girlfriend?" she asked Rhodes, suddenly curious.

"Define girlfriend," he replied.

"Well," said Caddie, "how would you define boyfriend?"

"In your case? Probably a guy who takes you out and pays for every-thing."

"So you think I'm a gold digger," Caddie said. "Thanks a lot."

"I didn't mean it that way," Rhodes apologized. "I meant that what-ever guy you go out with probably *wants* to pay for everything. Be-cause you're pretty," he added.

"I'm not sure that's any better," Caddie informed him. "I like to think I'm pretty *and* interesting."

Rhodes looked at her, and Caddie could tell he didn't know if she was being serious or not. "I'm kidding," she said. "Sort of. I really wouldn't want to be with a guy just because he thought I was hot."

"I said pretty," Rhodes corrected her. "I didn't say hot."

It was Caddie's turn to not know if he was joking. When she saw his mouth trembling as he tried to hold back a smile, though, she knew he was just trying to get to her. "You still haven't answered my ques-tion," she reminded him.

"Yes," he said. "I have a girlfriend."

Caddie was surprised. She hadn't really wanted Rhodes to be ask-ing her out, but she'd liked it better when she'd thought that he was. Now she wondered why he hadn't been. What didn't he like about her?

"You thought I was asking you out," said Rhodes.

"I did not," Caddie said.

"You did," Rhodes insisted. "And you're mad that I wasn't."

"What's this girlfriend's name?" Caddie asked him.

There was a pause before Rhodes answered, "Rose."

Caddie turned in her chair. "What's on your screen?" she demanded.

"Nothing," Rhodes said, his fingers tapping rapidly.

Caddie got up and pushed his chair so that it rolled away from the table and he could no longer reach the keyboard. On his screen was a photo of a pink-colored nudibranch with very long papillae. At the bottom, in the space for the file name, was typed OKENIA RO.

"*Okenia rosacea!*" Caddie crowed. "The Hopkin's Rose. I thought so." She looked at Rhodes, whose cheeks were now the same color as the nudibranch. "No one under eighty is named Rose," she said.

"Okay," Rhodes said. "Then what's your boyfriend's name? Rufus? Baptodoris? Aldisa?" He rattled off parts of the names of several local nudibranchs.

"Brian," Caddie said. "And those aren't even good tries."

"Rufus is a name," Rhodes insisted.

"For a *dog,*" Caddie said.

"Well, what's this Brian like?" asked Rhodes, miming quotes with his fingers when he said the name.

"He works at the aquarium," Caddie said. "He's studying marine biology."

"Brian Foster?" said Rhodes. He looked at Caddie.

"You know him?" she asked.

"He went out with my sister, like, two years ago," Rhodes said. "The guy's a top-shelf a-hole."

Caddie felt herself getting angry. "Sounds like you're jealous," she said.

Rhodes snorted. "Of Brian Cerfiss? Not even I'm that lame. Did he tell you how he volunteers saving sharks?"

Caddie felt the skin on the back of her neck prickle. "Why would he say that?" she asked. "Does he?"

"No," Rhodes said. "But he tells girls he does. You know, he has this lame-ass thing he does when he works the kelp tank. He picks a girl in the audience and starts talking to her. That's how my sister met him." He laughed again, as if he couldn't imagine anything more stupid.

"It worked, though, didn't it?" Caddie said.

"It did with Sonia," Rhodes agreed. "At least until she caught him a few weeks later doing the same thing with a bunch of girls visiting from Wisconsin. He just about crapped his wet suit when he saw her glaring at him through the glass."

"Maybe he's changed," said Caddie. "He's been great to me."

Rhodes didn't respond, which annoyed Caddie. *He thinks I'm an idiot,* she thought grimly. She hated that Rhodes—Rhodes and his pimples—was sitting there feeling, what, sorry for her? Thinking she was so desperate that she had to go out with a guy who had cheated on his sister? Either way, he thought she was a loser.

"It's not like I'm going to marry the guy," she said. "We just hang out—go diving—that sort of stuff."

"Diving," Rhodes repeated. "And stuff."

"Hey, it's more than you and *Rose* do," Caddie shot back. "Unless you mean Rosy Palm and her five sisters." She mimicked jerking on a dick, sticking her tongue out while she did it.

"Nice," Rhodes said. "Looks like you know how to do that really well."

Caddie stood up. "Fuck you," she said. "I'm out of here." She walked out the door, not looking back. But even without looking, she knew that Rhodes was grinning.

Asshole loser, she thought as she walked away. *The guy can't even invent an imaginary girlfriend, and he thinks he's better than I am. I bet his sister's just as foul. I bet* she *asked Brian out and he said no.*

By the time she reached her father's office, she'd defended Brian to the point where she almost believed he really was a great guy. She'd even decided to call him later, see if he wanted to go to a movie or something.

"Hey," she said, standing in the doorway of her father's office. He was looking at something on his desk. When he heard her, he looked up. He looked tired. "Oh," he said. "Hi."

"Want to get some lunch?" Caddie asked.

Her father looked at the clock, as if it couldn't possibly be late enough for lunch. "I've got a report due this afternoon," he said. "And I have to go through all of this." He indicated a stack of papers sitting on the desk. "I probably shouldn't."

"That's okay," said Caddie. "I can go by myself. Do you want me to bring you anything?"

Her father shook his head. "No, thanks," he said. "I'm not really hungry." He went back to looking at the paper in front of him, but Caddie hesitated, thinking he might yet change his mind.

"I guess I'll see you later then," she said when it became apparent that he really wasn't going to come with her. He nodded absent-mindedly, and she turned away, bitterness settling in her stomach.

She left the building and walked toward the aquarium. She realized that she was half intending to go in and try to catch Brian flirting with someone else. Just as quickly, she realized that she didn't care if he was. She wasn't in love with him, and she could get what she wanted from him whether he was chasing after other girls or not.

This made her think of Nicole. She *did* love Nick, even though he cheated on her. Caddie was at least not in that position, and because of this she considered herself smarter. Nicole was a nice girl, but Caddie would never be like her. *I'm stronger than that,* she told herself. *I can play around with Brian and not get hurt.*

There was another advantage to keeping Brian in her life; her father still didn't like him. He'd lectured her for a long time about how irresponsible it was of Brian to take her diving, the implication being that she was equally irresponsible for going with him. At first, she'd almost given in and allowed her father to teach her the "right" way to dive. But she'd held that back, not quite ready to give him that gift.

Now she wouldn't. If he wanted to pine around after Hudson, she would let him. It was no skin off her ass, as Bree would say. She didn't care what he did. She imagined what Sam and Bree would say if she told them her father was puppy-dogging around after another guy. She sort of felt like that should freak her out, but it didn't. She knew a lot of gay guys. Girls, too, although she was convinced that girls slept with each other mostly because guys had no clue what to do with them in bed. She had fooled around with a girl or two, just to see what it was like.

Anyway, Sam and Bree would probably get a kick out of it. Her mother, on the other hand, would flip out. In fact, she thought, she probably could get a one-way ticket back to L.A. just by calling her mom and letting it slip that she thought her father might be going a little queer. She imagined her mother's response and was sorely tempted.

In the end, though, she didn't care if her dad was gay. Not that she really thought he was. He was really more asexual; she couldn't imagine him with anyone in that way. Not even with her mother. The two of them did not work together, that was for sure. The men her mother went out with were power broker types, men who wore suits and made deals on their cell phones during dinner at Koi. They would eat her dad up and spit him out before he knew what was happening.

Still, she wished he would get over Hudson already. It had been long enough, and still he was walking around like a zombie. The worst part about it, she thought, was that he didn't even know why he was doing it. He was so clueless, he probably thought he had the flu or something. She knew that if she told him the real reason he was being so moody, he wouldn't believe her. He was incapable of it, she was certain of it. *He gets more excited about a sea slug than he does about sex,* she thought. *He probably doesn't even jerk off.*

She was walking so quickly that she didn't even notice Brian calling to her. It wasn't until he was in front of her, waving his hand in her face, that she saw him.

"You must have something on your mind," he said. "I've been calling to you for half a block."

"Sorry," Caddie said. "I was just thinking. What are you doing?"

"Lunch," said Brian. "How about you?"

"Lunch," Caddie told him.

Brian took her hand. "Great," he said. "We can go together."

Caddie didn't particularly want to hold hands. It made her feel like a little kid, as if she were crossing a dangerous street and needed looking after. She almost told Brian to let go. But then she saw Hudson. He was walking toward them, and he'd seen her. She tightened her grip on Brian's hand and fixed a smile on her face.

"Hi," she said when Hudson stopped. "Brian, you remember Hudson," she said, as if they were an old married couple running into a recent acquaintance.

"Sure," Brian said. "How's it going?"

"Nice to see you," Hudson said shortly. "How's your dad, Caddie?"

"He's fine," she answered. "Busy."

"I was on my way to see him," Hudson said.

Caddie's heart skipped a beat. "I wouldn't," she said. "He's right in the middle of something."

Hudson nodded. "Thanks for the warning," he said evenly. "But I think I'll chance it." He smiled, and Caddie understood that they were now enemies. Something had changed in him since she'd last seen him. He seemed colder somehow, more determined. *More dangerous,* she thought with some alarm.

"We're going to lunch," Brian said when no one spoke.

"Enjoy it," said Hudson. "I'm sure we'll see each other again."

He walked away from them. Caddie turned and watched. She wanted to run after him, to jump on his back and pound his face with her fists. She wanted to tell him to stay away. But then Brian pulled on her hand, and she felt herself being dragged forward as Hudson went to meet her father.

CHAPTER 36

"We need to talk." Hudson cringed as he heard himself say it. It was so melodramatic. He imagined Norma Shearer saying it to one of her movie husbands. Chester Morris, maybe, in *The Divorcee*.

"Where have you been?" Ben asked, looking at him from behind the desk. "You haven't returned any of my calls."

Okay, now it's turning into Imitation of Life, Hudson thought. He shut the door to Ben's office and walked toward him, taking a seat in one of the chairs. Ben, he thought, looked terrible, as if he hadn't slept in a couple of nights.

"Caddie said there was an emergency with the house," Ben said cryptically. "Is everything all right?"

"The house," Hudson repeated, not quite understanding. Then he realized that Caddie must have made up some story to explain his premature departure. "It's fine," he said. "Everything's fine there."

"Then why—" Ben began.

"I left because of something Caddie said," Hudson said.

Ben looked confused. "What did she say?" he asked, clearly unable to imagine anything his daughter could say that would make Hudson upset enough to leave and not call for almost a week.

Hudson moved uncomfortably in his chair. "This probably isn't the best place to talk about this," he said. "I thought maybe we could go somewhere else."

Before Ben could answer, his door opened and Angela popped her head in. Seeing Hudson, she smiled brightly. "Hey, stranger," she said.

Hudson smiled back, wishing she would go away. Instead, she

looked at Ben. "I compiled the data you wanted for your report," she said. "Do you need me to do anything else?"

"No," Ben said. "I'll handle the rest. Thanks."

Angela looked once more at Hudson. "We should do dinner again sometime," she said.

"Sure," Hudson agreed. "That would be fun." He mentally pushed her out the door. A moment later, she actually went.

"I don't have a lot of time," said Ben.

Hudson started to get up. "This was a bad idea," he said. "I should have waited. How about we talk tonight?"

Ben motioned for him to sit. "If Caddie said something, I want to know what it is," he said. He hesitated. "It wasn't something about you being gay, was it? Because I never told her—"

"It wasn't about me," said Hudson. "It was about you . . . and me," he added.

Ben shook his head. "What about us?" he said. "Is she jealous that we're spending time together?"

"That's part of it," Hudson said. "But it's more than that." He paused, half hoping that Angela would come in again and save him from having to continue. But she didn't, and Ben was looking at him, waiting. "She thinks there's something between us," he said finally.

"Between us?" Ben said. He leaned back in his chair. "Between us," he repeated, but his voice had taken on a different tone. "You mean she thinks . . ."

Hudson nodded. "She said she thinks that you have . . . feelings." He took a deep breath. "For me," he concluded.

He watched as the color drained from Ben's face. Ben scratched his forehead. "Why would she . . ." He wasn't looking at Hudson. "Why would she say something like that?" He seemed to be speaking to himself.

"I told her it was ridiculous," Hudson said.

Ben finally looked at him. His face was blank, as if, not knowing how to respond, his muscles had simply frozen in place. He seemed to be waiting for Hudson to continue.

"But maybe it isn't," said Hudson.

Ben played with the papers on his desk, saying nothing.

"Ben," Hudson said, and Ben stopped fiddling with the papers. He looked at Hudson. "Do you understand what I'm saying?" Hudson asked him.

"Not entirely, no," Ben said. "But I think I have some idea."

"At first I thought she was just trying to make me angry," Hudson said. "I didn't want her to do the same thing to you, so I left. I figured all she wanted was for me to be out of the way. I certainly never thought that you might . . ." He stopped again. No matter how he ended the sentence, he knew it was going to put Ben in an even more awkward position. Instead he asked, "Are you all right?"

Ben nodded. "She said that?" he asked again.

"She did," Hudson confirmed. "And I'm not sure she was wrong."

"I can't talk about this right now," Ben said suddenly. "I have a meeting. I have to prepare. I . . ." He looked at Hudson with an expression of such total confusion that Hudson stood up. He leaned across the desk and put his hand on Ben's.

Ben pulled away. Hudson, startled, stepped back. "I'm sorry," he said.

"We can talk about this later," said Ben.

"All right," Hudson said. "How about tonight? I could come over."

"That would be fine," Ben said mechanically.

"I'll come by around seven," said Hudson, and Ben nodded. Hudson waited, then asked, "You're sure you're all right?"

"I'm sure," Ben answered. "I'll see you tonight."

Hudson left his office, shutting the door behind him. As he walked out, he passed Angela coming in the opposite direction. "You'd better not have distracted him," she said reprovingly. "I need him fully functioning this afternoon."

"Good luck with that," Hudson said under his breath, replying afterward with, "You know he'll come through."

As he walked back toward Cannery Row, he felt none of the relief he'd hoped to get from talking to Ben. Instead, he felt even more anxious. From Ben's reaction, he guessed that the idea that there might be something between them had come as a total shock. Clearly, it had never occurred to him. Or, if it had, he had already dismissed it as an impossibility.

Again he thought of just leaving. But every time he tried to outrun the weight on his shoulders, the burden just became heavier. It was time to face his demons. Not just Ben, the newest of them, but all of the others, the ones from which he'd run for too long. It was Ben's misfortune that he had, by whatever means, become one of them.

It's your doing. The dark voice rose in his mind, harsh and accusing. His father's voice. *You did it to him,* Lincoln Jones continued. *You touched him. It's your poison doing this to him.*

His father had once spoken aloud the words he now whispered in silence. Hudson was thirteen, in the throes of becoming a man. The one to whom his father had said the words was already a man. He was a neighbor, a man with a wife and two boys, one of them Hudson's classmate. One hot summer afternoon when Hudson was at the neighbor's house enjoying their newly acquired aboveground swimming pool, he had walked into the bathroom and found the father masturbating furiously over a magazine lying open on the pink tile floor. Hudson had stared at the picture of a naked man, trying very hard not to look at the one in front of him. Then the father had taken Hudson's hand and placed it on his hard cock.

It was a month later that his father caught them together in the garage. This time, Hudson was standing while the neighbor knelt on the floor, his head bobbing up and down on Hudson's erect penis. Hudson, close to release, had opened his eyes to see his father standing not ten feet away, the garbage bag he was carrying to the trash hanging from his hand like a headless corpse.

The neighbor had made excuses, accused Hudson of initiating their couplings. Mr. Jones had silenced him with threats of imprisonment and bodily harm until the man, begging for mercy, had fled from the garage. When, two days later, the news came that he had left his bewildered wife and sons and disappeared, Lincoln Jones had said nothing. Hudson, however, had wept in his room until his father had come and ordered him to take out the trash.

When, five years later, Hudson came out to his parents, his father had said only, "Some poison you can't never get out." They had never discussed it again, but Lincoln Jones had made no secret of his disappointment in his son. Even a scholarship to Yale had failed to impress him, and Hudson had departed for New Haven with little more than a handshake and the ten dollars his father handed him at the bus station.

What would his father think of him now? he wondered. But he knew the answer to that question; he wouldn't think anything. Hudson had failed to matter to him from the moment Lincoln Jones had realized that his son was smarter than he was. Hudson's homosexuality was merely further proof of his uselessness. Probably his father had even been expecting it, so sure was he that Hudson would betray his parentage in every way possible.

For a year following the discovery of his shame, Hudson had waited for the neighbor to return for him. He'd told Hudson that he loved him, whispered it in his ear while Hudson touched him in the way he liked, while he released himself into Hudson's hand. Every day for a year he'd watched for that face, waited for a letter or phone call promising salvation. All through the long Maine winter he'd waited, dreaming of waking up in another bed far away from the cold eyes of his father.

For a long time after coming out he had found himself attracted to men who resembled the neighbor. Making love with them, he had manufactured the smell of the cheap cologne the man had favored. The sight of a grease-stained hand holding a Camel cigarette brought back every yearning of his thirteen years, and he found himself following men in red pickup trucks, although surely the man had long since given up his rusted Chevy for something else. Once he had by chance found a copy of the magazine that had been on the floor of that pink tiled bathroom, an issue of *Playgirl* which, he assumed, had belonged to the man's wife. He'd purchased it and taken it back to his room, where every night for two weeks he stood over it and let his memories rain down on the face of the unlucky centerfold, until the pages no longer opened without tearing.

Then he'd met Paul, and it had all begun again. Although Paul had in no physical way resembled the neighbor, Hudson's attraction to him was just as powerful. Their first time together, Paul had been surprised when Hudson had asked if they could do it in the bathroom of his tiny apartment, where the faded tile—this time a pale lavender instead of pink—provided the necessary backdrop. There, his face buried in Paul's chest, Hudson had run his fingers over the thin gold band on Paul's left hand and listened for the sound of children splashing outside.

He had never told Paul about the neighbor—had never, in fact, told anyone. Eventually they had taken their lovemaking into other rooms, into Hudson's inconveniently small student bed, where they had thrust against each other and left the sheets damp with sweat. And, slowly, Hudson had ceased to think of the neighbor when Paul was inside of him, although sometimes at the moment of climax he still smelled the sharp odor of cologne and felt calloused fingers on the back of his neck.

After Paul's death, after the months of wrestling with the feelings of guilt and blame until he was too worn out to continue bearing the weight of misery and had exchanged it for the mantle of a champion, he had promised himself he would never again become involved with someone it was impossible to ever fully love. This, he told himself, had been his life's curse, placed upon him by his father that afternoon in the garage. It had followed him from Maine, a reminder—along with the flatness of his accent and his habit of giving directions based on landmarks rather than the names of streets—that there were some things he could never change.

Since then he had tried, and failed, to partner with men who were good for him. He selected them as he might a dinner wine, attempting to choose those that would bring out the best in his character and balance his flaws. Occasionally he even convinced himself that he had found one. But always, usually after their first time together in bed, he was dissatisfied.

And now there was Ben. Ben who was so completely unlike either the neighbor or Paul. Ben who, until Caddie's revelation, Hudson had thought of only as a friend. A friend he had been only too pleased to have, as the relationship involved no land mines to tread lightly around. Like Marty, Ben had been, until now, a part of his life that required only that he enjoy it.

Now the enjoyment had changed to dread. Sitting in Ben's office he had, for the first time, feared what words might come out of the other man's mouth. And his worry was not just for himself. He was afraid for Ben, afraid what he, Hudson, might have done to him. *Some poison you can't never get out.* Had he somehow tainted this man who only wanted to be his friend? Logically, he knew it to be an absurd idea, one of his father's ignorant explanations for something he could not accept any other way.

Yet he found it impossible to completely dismiss the possibility, and the strength of purpose he had felt after swearing to banish the ghosts from his car was quickly flooding out of him in the aftermath of his meeting with Ben. There had been no great revelation, no release, only a quiet struggling that left him feeling weary and alone. They would talk, later, but he wondered if there was any point to that. Perhaps everything that was going to happen had happened, and now his friendship with Ben was over.

"Fuck!" he said, the purity and forcefulness of the profanity cleansing in its simplicity. *Fuck.* Odd, he thought, how the word considered the most unutterable should be the one that represented, for many, the greatest pleasure of which the human body was capable. The sacred and the profane, he supposed, the ultimate proof of the perversity of human nature, to make a curse of the very act that kept the species in existence.

He realized that he was distracting himself from thinking about Ben. He knew, too, that thinking about Ben was going to neither change nor improve the situation. He felt an intensifying of his anger toward Caddie—Caddie who, like some kind of snot-nosed Cassandra, made predictions of calamity and ruination.

Cassandra, a favorite of Paul's. Cassandra, whose name meant "she who entangles men." Cassandra, whose predictions of the future were met with disbelief, no matter how many times she was right. Had Caddie, like the cursed daughter of the king of Troy, brought about his destruction by speaking the truth? Was she merely a mouthpiece or was her role in the current drama more complicated than that? In her desire to have her father to herself, had she taken something small (however true it might be) and turned it into something else, something more certain to put distance between her father and her perceived rival? Even if her suspicions were correct, what was to say they would ultimately have amounted to anything? Had she just waited, Hudson would have left and any feelings he might have stirred in Ben would, in all likelihood, have dissipated.

But she had chosen to speak, and now her prophecy was growing in strength and could not be ignored. He and Ben would need to face it, tonight, and both would have to live with whatever havoc was wrought by having heard her words. Hudson could only hope that, unlike the revelations of Cassandra, this one might not be inescapable.

A child sees what we are, through all the fictions of what we would be. He had not thought of the quote in many years. They were the words of Henri-Frédéric Amiel, a mostly forgotten Swiss philosopher whose writings on God, art, and science had been thrust upon Hudson and his peers as part of an undergraduate seminar and whom they had all found exceedingly tiresome. But a handful of Amiel's pronouncements had found their way into Hudson's mental filing cabinet, and he sometimes recalled them and gave grudging credit to the philosopher–poet.

He thought of his own childhood, when he'd observed his parents and recognized instantly their unhappiness and loathing for one another. It had not occurred to him until much later that they were unaware of it—were, in fact, pretending that everything was fine. This had surprised him, as he'd assumed that adults had passed beyond the days of dress-up and make-believe that children found so necessary to their existence. With that realization, the scales had fallen from his eyes, and he had never seen the world in the same way again.

Had Caddie seen through him? Was that the real problem? Her accusation had been directed at her father, but Hudson had been included in it. He had been blind to what was happening between himself and Ben, and she had torn away the veil and forced him to see it for what it was.

No, he realized, it wasn't Caddie he hated; it was himself.

CHAPTER 37

In the tank, the two *Flabellina iodinea* were mating, joined at their head ends. Their reproductive organs, pale extensions of their deep purple bodies, exchanged eggs and sperm as each fertilized the other. Their oral tentacles, sinuous as eels, explored the surrounding rock, feeding and copulation occurring simultaneously.

It was unusual for nudibranchs to breed in captivity, and Ben was pleased that the tricky mechanics of recreating a cold-water ocean environment had succeeded in encouraging the Spanish shawls to engage in the behavior. Tropical fish were much easier to keep, and he occasionally envied his colleagues whose interests centered around the brightly colored and far less particular residents of warmer waters.

Watching the nudibranchs had temporarily distracted him from the troubles of the afternoon. But their activities were so closely related to his thoughts that, inevitably, he could not stave off the unpleasant business any longer. Still watching the Spanish shawls, whose coupling would last several hours at least, he faced the unpleasant task of recalling his visit with Hudson.

He'd had time, since then, to distill what Hudson had told him to its essential meaning, which was that his daughter, apparently, thought that he was in love with Hudson. Extrapolating from this, the larger assumption was that he was homosexual, or, he supposed, bisexual. At the very least, he was allegedly guilty of not knowing his own wants.

He considered each of these things separately, beginning with the latter. Was he homosexual? It was an odd question to ask of himself, as he'd really never considered it before. Now that he did, he needed to define for himself what being homosexual meant. Clinically, of course, it was sexual attraction to members of his own sex. But people were not simply conglomerations of responses, regardless of how much science attempted to reduce them to such.

Regardless, he asked himself if he was physically attracted to other males. Not to Hudson—Hudson had not yet entered the equation—but to men in general. He pictured a man, naked, and measured his responses to what he saw. He imagined the muscles, heavier than those of a woman, the broader shoulders and larger extremities. Then, of course, there was the penis, the penultimate object of sexual arousal, celebrated as the wellspring of masculinity. Did he find penises attractive? It was like asking himself if he found beauty in a liver or a spleen; he couldn't look at the organ without considering its function and being impressed by it. But was it *attractive* to him?

He was being far too literal, he knew. He was relying on his training to help him answer a question that was better suited to philosophers and artists, those who were unburdened by the need to understand how things worked on a physical level. He had more in common with a mechanic than he did with a painter or a poet.

Just answer the question. He heard, unexpectedly, Carol's voice. Then he saw her, standing with her hands on her hips, waiting impatiently for him to speak. But what had she asked? A multitude of possibilities scrolled through his thoughts. She had often been frustrated by his inability to respond with a simple yes or no. He, in turn, had been stymied by her unwillingness to explore all available possibilities. Communication between them had been nearly impossible because of this; she assumed he was being difficult, while he accused her of forcing him into making hurried decisions.

Just answer the question, Benjamin, Carol said, employing the name that reduced him to feeling like a child. It was his mother's name for him, used by no one else, and Carol's use of it always indicated that she'd reached the length of her patience.

"I don't know," Ben said helplessly. "It's just a body."

Carol shook her head and faded into nothingness. Ben was relieved to see her go. But the question had still not been answered, only put off. He was afraid, though, that he couldn't answer it with anything resembling truth. For the truth was, he had rarely experienced physical attraction. He lacked what he thought of as the typical male obsession with busts or buttocks, had no preference for blonde or brunette, was not a connoisseur of any particular "type."

It was a peculiarity of his personality that had first come to light in adolescence, when other boys his age began to speak of girls in terms of their physical appeal. Nudging one another and laughing nervously, they had pointed out the swelling chests and elongating legs of the girls. They'd boasted of wanting to do "things" with these girls, vague in details but clear in their desires. All the while, Ben had watched and listened, wondering what they were seeing that he wasn't.

He'd dated because others were, kissed because it seemed the thing to do, but always he came home unsure of whether he had enjoyed it or not. And, yes, he'd masturbated, but the motions of his hand were unaccompanied by fantasy. He'd done it for release, not indulgence, and any pleasure he'd taken from it had been divorced from imagery and invention. For this reason, perhaps, he had never felt guilt for doing it.

Even his courtship of and marriage to Carol had had little to do (at least on Ben's part) with physical attraction, although Ben's friends had congratulated him heartily on his good fortune to the point that he'd become uncomfortable, reminding him, as it did, of his school days and his bewilderment at the talk of other boys. He was a virgin when he married, and his wedding night had been an exercise in the mechanics of human sex, much of which he found embarrassing in its primitiveness.

Carol, as far as he knew, had been satisfied with him as a lover. If their lovemaking had not been remarkable, he assumed that it was also not disappointing. After Caddie's birth it had tapered off, a natural result, Ben believed, of parenthood. He had not much missed it, meeting his infrequent needs as he had in adolescence, and with the same casual disinterest.

But was all of this because he was, unknowingly, repressing an attraction to men? He found it difficult to believe. If he were, wouldn't there be *some* evidence to support the theory, at least one moment he could pinpoint when sexual longing had manifested itself in that direction? But there were none, no fascinations with other boys or men, no encounters, not even any dreams that he could recall.

This did not, however, negate the possibility that he *could* be attracted to another man. In some sense his past was immaterial, as Caddie had been remarking on his current behavior. The question became, then, was it possible that he was attracted to Hudson Jones?

He looked again at the nudibranchs. Their cerata, the burnt-orange respiratory structures that lined their purple bodies like the fringe of a gaudy shawl and that gave *Flabellina iodinea* its common name, swayed in the current made by the tank's pump. Ben envied their passionless exchange of genetic material. There was nothing of love or desire in it, only the meeting of a common need. The nudibranch's attractions were purely chemical, and although there was no way to know for sure, Ben was certain that rarely did the question of sexual orientation arise in their minds.

Not that it would matter, he reminded himself. *They're hermaphroditic.* This, of course, was their saving grace. Humans, too, would be better off having both sets of reproductive organs. In addition to simplifying procreation, he thought, it would render moot all of the fuss and bother about the nature of desire.

You're stalling. Carol had returned, throwing at him another of her frequent complaints. *Stop trying to compare yourself to a slug.*

Ben ignored her. He was thinking of other creatures for whom sexuality was meaningless. There was, of course, the infamous sheephead, as well as various snails, shrimps, and seahorses. They were capable of self-fertilization or, in some instances, even changing gender as it became necessary. Perhaps he was like that as well, somehow neither one thing nor another.

Oh, for Christ's sake, Carol said. *You're a* man, *Ben. Either you want to sleep with this guy or you don't. Which is it?*

"I don't know!" Ben said angrily. "I don't know, all right?"

"Ben?"

Ben turned to see Angela watching him, a look of concern on her face. "Are you okay?" she asked.

No, Ben thought. *I'm not at all okay. I don't know what I am.*

"Just trying to work something out," he told Angela.

"Well, maybe this will cheer you up," she said. She held out a magazine. "I found that article I was telling you about, the one about the cytotoxic properties of *Adalaria loveni.* They're found in the North Sea, but I bet they're similar in structure to our *Adalaria.* It might be something to explore."

Ben took the magazine and looked briefly at the article. "They're calling the triterpenoid 'lovenone,' " he said.

"Maybe it destroys the capacity for romance," Angela joked. "We could sell it as the anti-Viagra."

Ben set the magazine down. "Thanks for finding this," he said. "I'll take a look at it later."

"It's probably nothing," Angela said.

"No," Ben told her. "Your thinking is right on. It's making those connections that's hard for most people. With you, it comes naturally."

"Nobel Prize, here I come," said Angela. She stood up. "I'd better get back to Rhodes," she said. "I promised he could come with me on a dive later. That's okay, right?"

Ben nodded. "As long as he's signed all of the waivers," he said.

"Hey, is Caddie coming back?" Angela asked him. "She hasn't been here for a few days. She's not sick of us, is she?"

"She's been . . . busy . . ." Ben answered. "But I think she'll be back."

"Good," said Angela. "I like her. And I see Hudson was here earlier." She paused, and Ben realized she was waiting for him to say something that might indicate Hudson's level of interest in her.

"Yes," he said. "He was."

Angela waited a few more seconds before saying, "Okay. Well, I'll be going."

Couldn't you think of something *to tell the poor girl?* Carol again, as if she'd been watching the whole exchange and scoring his performance. *Or maybe you're jealous of her.*

"I am not," Ben objected. He smacked his palm on the desk. What was he doing? He was arguing with his ex-wife's voice. *No,* he told himself, *you're arguing with yourself; you just gave yourself her voice.*

That was it. He had to get out of there or he was going to go crazy. Quickly, before he could remember how much he still had to do, he got up and headed for the door, leaving behind the magazine and the Spanish shawls, which, oblivious to his torment, continued their silent orgy.

"Caddie? Are you home?"

He stood in the living room, awaiting a response. When none came, he went upstairs and called again. Finally, he went to Caddie's room and peered inside, in case she was asleep. But her bed was empty.

Having ascertained that he was alone, he retired to his own bedroom, where he shut the door behind him. Sitting on his bed, he removed his shoes, setting them beside the nightstand, then his socks. His pants followed, folded and placed on a nearby chair, where they

were joined moments later by his shirt. Only his T-shirt and boxers remained, and he kept them on while he considered what he was about
to do.

Once, in the first session of a class Ben had taken concerning the
philosophy of science, the instructor had opened with a statement by
the thirteenth-century philosopher–scientist Roger Bacon. "The strongest
arguments prove nothing so long as the conclusions are not verified
by experience. Experimental science is the queen of sciences and the
goal of all speculation."

Ben had never forgotten those words, and in fact often shared them
with students and interns of his own. It was, as far as he was concerned, the foundation of scientific study: If something could be claimed,
then it should be possible to prove it; if not, the claim could be rejected.

He pulled his T-shirt over his head, then slid his boxers down his
legs. Both articles of clothing were added to those already on the chair
before Ben; now naked, he lay down on the bed. He was suddenly very
uncomfortably aware of the way his bedsprings squeaked beneath his
weight, and it felt odd to be in bed in the middle of the afternoon.

He put his hand on his flaccid penis and moved it up and down, attempting to stir it to life. Uncooperative, it flopped in his hand, as if
the heat of the room exhausted it. He let it go, and it slumped across
his testicles where they lay bunched between his legs.

He closed his eyes and tried to picture Hudson naked. Having
never actually done so, he found this difficult, until he remembered
that he *had* seen him once, in the shower at the pool. But could he recall anything? He tried, visualizing the shower room. He re-created the
white-tiled walls, the showerheads spewing water, the odd onion-
shaped dispensers of soap. They were an unnatural pink, he recalled.

And Hudson, what had he looked like? In his mind, Ben turned to
look. And there he was, standing beneath the spray, wearing the funny
yellow bathing suit patterned with hula dancers. How did he remember that? he wondered. If someone had asked him what Hudson had
been wearing, he wouldn't have been able to answer. But he saw it as
clearly now as if he were there. The hula dancers smiled at him, their
slender arms outstretched.

So he hadn't seen him naked, at least not entirely. But he had seen
something. He pictured Hudson's body, lean and muscular, the chest
hairless. He saw the darker circles of his nipples, the trail of hair that

began at the navel and trickled down a flat stomach, growing wider as it descended. The legs, too, were speckled with hair.

His hand, resting on his belly, was brushed by the head of his penis, which was stiffening and inching its way across his stomach. Ben touched it, surprised, and wrapped his fingers around the shaft as he continued to remember. The water streamed down the planes of Hudson's body in thick rivulets. His bathing suit clung to him, outlining but obscuring what lay beneath.

Now what? Ben asked himself as he exhausted his store of memories. There had been nothing else beyond that, only dressing and conversation.

Ask yourself what if. Again he was back in class, seated in the front row while the instructor, a chemist whose habit of spitting while talking made concentration difficult for those students who had to worry about having their notes smeared with his salivations, exhorted them to push their minds in new directions. Ben had nodded vigorously in agreement, even while spittle rained down on him from above.

What if? He allowed the question to guide him. Nervously, he approached Hudson and placed a hand on his chest. Then he moved down, lower and lower, until he felt Hudson's hardness. His hands tugged at the yellow bathing trunks, pulling them down, and Hudson's sex sprung free. He touched it, feeling its thickness, stroking the length of it.

When Hudson reached out for him, he held his breath, afraid. But when Hudson took him in his hand, he felt nothing but his touch. It radiated through him like an electric current, stimulating his heart so that its beat filled his ears. He felt warm water, and skin, and then a rush of heat.

He came, crying out softly as the stickiness splashed against his chest. In his hand, his penis throbbed, emptying itself. His body shook, and he threw his head back against the pillows. When it was over, he touched his fingers to the shimmering white drops on his skin and rubbed them together.

She was right, he thought, and fear descended like night.

CHAPTER 38

Caddie shined her flashlight into the crack. Immediately, the long, thin arm retreated into the darkness. She moved closer, trying to see what it belonged to, but there was nothing. A small fish, attracted to the light, darted into the crack, then emerged again and streaked past her.

The ocean was different at night. They had entered the water as the sun was setting, so that it would become dark gradually. Now the only illumination came from their underwater lights, and they swam in a circle less than a dozen feet in diameter. Beyond it, the ocean waited, black and mysterious, as if they traveled in a golden bubble.

It occurred to her that she should be frightened. Who knew what swam outside the protective light, waiting for its chance to feed. And yet, she wasn't afraid. There was a peacefulness to the nighttime world, a quiet that suffused everything. She heard only her breathing, the gentle bubbling of the regulator. It was as if she were swimming through the night.

Moving away from the rocks and into the sand, she swept the light before her, hoping to catch some nocturnal denizen at its secret business. Brian had told her that she would see different creatures at night, and he had been right. In addition to whatever it was that spread its arms over the rocks, she had seen half a dozen fish she couldn't identify. The familiar nudibranchs, she discovered, were not to be found. But several new ones had taken their place, as if each species were assigned specific hours of operation and these had drawn the night shift.

What she really hoped to see was an octopus. Brian had assured her that they were plentiful, but she had yet to spot one. She had scoured the rocks where they were said to make their lairs, searching for the empty shells of their meals that indicated their presence. These she had found in plenty, but apparently the diners had moved on to other feasts.

Now, in a patch of empty sand, she saw movement away from her light. She followed the fleeing shadow and saw, pinned in her beam, a small octopus. It was red in color, no more than six or seven inches in length, and it rested on the sea floor, its arms writhing around it. She kept her light on it and swam closer.

The octopus pulled itself in, turning from red to mottled brown so that it looked like a rock. Caddie, enchanted, hovered near it and waited. When it didn't move, she slowly reached out one gloved hand toward it. The octopus turned an eye toward her, the light reflecting gold and black from it. Caddie sensed in its depths an unexpected intelligence and held her hand still.

The octopus was breathing. Its body swelled and shrunk as it forced water in and out. Then, slowly and with great deliberation, it uncoiled a single tentacle and extended it toward Caddie's hand. When the tip touched the material of her glove, the animal paused for a moment. Then the arm seemed to run out like a line from a reel. It moved up her finger, the tiny suction cups on its underside gripping the unfamiliar surface.

Caddie lifted the finger, watching breathlessly as the octopus's tentacle wrapped around it. She pulled slightly, feeling resistance, then lay her hand flat once more. After a moment, a second tentacle unspooled from the octopus's body.

She thought that it might climb onto her hand, but the addition of the second tentacle was the extent of the animal's investigation. Perhaps gathering that she was neither a predator nor a likely hiding place, it gathered its legs back to itself and sat, continuing to breathe and watch her with its alien eyes. When she reached out, hoping to initiate further contact, the octopus, in a swirl of legs, swam off into the darkness.

It didn't ink, Caddie thought as she looked at the place where the octopus had been. She wished she'd had more time with it; already she was forgetting the exact shape of its golden eye. But there would be others, she reassured herself, and she moved off in search of them.

She knew where Brian was because of his light. He'd wanted her to stay near him, concerned that she might be disoriented in the dark. But she had assured him she was fine, and he had grudgingly allowed her her freedom. At first they had swum in the combined glow of their lights, but little by little Caddie had moved away from him, until now a dark expanse of twenty or so feet separated them.

The water was shallow—less than twenty feet—and she knew in which direction the shore lay. This freed her to enjoy her dive. Yet despite the thrill she felt from being there, and from her encounter with the little octopus, she was dissatisfied. This she blamed on her father. He had ruined things. Again.

She blamed Hudson too, of course. Her father wouldn't be behaving the way he was if it wasn't for Hudson. But it was her father who was most at fault, due first to his failure to recognize his own feelings and, now, because he was shutting her out in favor of self-pity. She had said nothing to him about her suspicions; with Hudson gone, she'd thought things would return to normal. *Well,* she thought, *whatever passed for normal when it came to her and her father.*

By now, she imagined, he knew. Hudson had been on his way to talk to her father, and why would he do that unless it was to tell him that his daughter thought he might be gay? She wondered how he'd reacted. She supposed one of two things had happened. Either her father had admitted that he had feelings for Hudson or he had denied everything. Whatever his reaction, she would be the one he blamed. Certainly it wouldn't be Hudson. Even if he couldn't face what he felt for Hudson, she knew enough about men to know that he would spare the person he cared for most. And that person wasn't her.

Goddamn him, she thought. Why hadn't Hudson just left them alone? She didn't think he loved her father. If he had, he would have seen for himself that her father had fallen for him. But she'd had to point it out to him, and he'd seemed genuinely shocked to hear the news. Most queens, she thought, would have taken the opportunity to bask in such a conquest.

Unless he's as clueless as my father is, she thought. As if that was possible.

In the middle of this thought, her light went out. There was no dimming of the brightness, no warning—it simply died. It was as if the moon had fallen into the sea. She was floating in complete blackness.

She flicked the switch in the light, hoping she had simply turned it off accidentally. Several times she moved it from side to side, with no results. She shook it and tried again. Finally, she hit it with the palm of her hand, hoping to jar something inside and force it to produce illumination, as if whatever was responsible for providing her with light had gone to sleep and only needed to be awakened.

Having exhausted her options, she looked around for Brian. But she saw no reassuring glow. All around her the water was inky and cold. She shivered, afraid. Where was he? He'd been behind her just seconds before. Now she was alone. Instantly her mind filled with images of sharp-toothed sharks and many-armed creatures (not like the shy and gentle little octopus) that wanted only to drag her into the depths. Even as she thought these things she knew she was panicking, but she couldn't stop herself. She spun around, searching for any sign of human life, and saw nothing.

She went up, up toward the surface and light. It took her all of five seconds to get there, and when she arrived she pulled her mask from her face and breathed raggedly, convinced that she was suffocating. She found the lights of the wharf, and this calmed her somewhat. She wasn't far from shore.

Then the water beside her broke, and she screamed as something rose up, black and wet. When a light burst forth, blinding her, she stopped abruptly, and her fear turned to anger.

"Where the fuck did you go!" she yelled at Brian, hitting him with her gloved hand.

"Ow!" he protested. "Fuck. I was just playing with you. Didn't you turn your light out on purpose?"

"No," Caddie said. "Why would I do something stupid like that?"

"Sorry," Brian apologized. "I thought you were trying to see if I could find you. I took a heading on you and turned my flashlight off so you wouldn't see me coming. I was almost to you when you went up."

"My fucking light went out," Caddie said. She hit it again, and this time it flickered weakly before dying again.

"Those halogens are temperamental," Brian remarked helplessly.

Caddie ignored him and began the swim to shore. As had happened so many times lately, she understood that she wasn't mad at Brian, she was mad at herself. Not because she had allowed herself to lose track of him but because she had been afraid. She had lost control of her feelings, been blindsided by the maelstrom of emotions that had sent her reeling and forced her to the surface. It wasn't unseen dangers from which she'd run, it was the ones lurking inside of her.

When she reached water shallow enough to stand in, she pulled her fins off and walked out of the ocean. She didn't wait for Brian as she stormed up the beach to the car. Her anger helped her ignore the cold that gripped her, a result of the seawater trapped in her wet suit. When she pulled her zipper down, she felt what little warmth was left in her rush out and splatter on the asphalt.

When Brian reached her, her teeth were chattering and she was having trouble making her fingers work. Brian opened the door and took out a towel. "Here," he said, wrapping it around her shoulders.

Caddie pulled her wet suit off and dried herself as best she could. She could do nothing about her swimsuit, but she pulled a pair of sweatpants over it and accepted the sweatshirt Brian offered to her. "Get in the car," he told her. "I'll take care of your stuff."

She hated to let him do it, but she did. Huddled in the front seat, she pulled her arms inside the too-big sweatshirt and hugged herself. Slowly she began to warm up, and when Brian, the stowing of the dive gear accomplished, got into the car beside her, she was able to speak without her voice breaking. "Sorry about earlier," she said.

"Yeah," said Brian. "Me too."

He started the car and turned on the heater. Caddie held her hands up to the warm air coming from the car's vents, grateful for its touch. She'd never been so cold, and she knew that it was only partly the effects of the water and the night. It came from within her, as if her heart had begun to turn to ice.

"Can I stay at your place tonight?" she heard herself ask Brian.

He looked over at her, but she continued to stare straight ahead. *Say I can,* she begged, hating herself.

"Sure," Brian said.

Back at his house, she went into the bedroom and stripped, tossing the damp clothing onto the floor. Brian, coming in behind her, said, "You should take a hot shower."

Caddie turned to him. "Come here," she said, grabbing his shirt and pulling him to her. Her hands grappled with the belt of his jeans as she kissed him, and when her fingers touched his cock, he jumped back.

"Hey, ice princess," he joked, "take it easy."

When his clothes had joined hers on the floor, Caddie pulled him onto the bed. On her back, she spread her legs and wrapped them around his waist, pulling him into her. Her hands moved over his skin, craving his warmth, and his mouth on her nipples seemed to be breathing life into her frozen body.

"I want you in me," she whispered in Brian's ear.

He sat up. "Let me get a rubber," he said, starting to stand.

Caddie grabbed his hand and pulled him back to her. "It's okay," she said as she kissed him, and he didn't question her.

She couldn't get warm enough. As Brian pumped against her, she tensed, trying to hold him inside where she could draw heat from him. But each time, he slipped away from her, leaving behind a pocket of cold that burned viciously. When she cried out, it was in pain and frustration at not being able to drive the wintry kiss of the sea from her body. When her nails scraped at Brian's back, it was because she was trying to get at his beating heart.

Afterward, she lay wrapped in a sheet that felt like a shroud, wishing she were dead. She was still cold, still swimming in that black sea from which, she realized now, she had not really escaped. Whatever faint light had been produced by her coupling with Brian had quickly been extinguished. His seed inside of her was slivers of ice, each one slicing through muscle and bone as it wormed its way deeper and deeper.

"You should get mad at me more often," Brian said, touching her hair.

She shivered and said nothing. *I'm dead,* she thought. *I'm at the bottom of the ocean, and it's night.*

"I'm going to take that shower now," said Brian. "You can join me if you want to."

Caddie closed her eyes. He would go away if she just stayed quiet. He didn't know she had died, that he was talking to a waterlogged corpse. He thought she was still alive. But he was wrong.

She waited until she heard the water running before she opened her eyes. She was going to leave. When Brian returned from the bathroom, she would be gone. Then he would understand that she had died. Maybe he would even grieve the loss of her. Not that she cared what he felt. Her heart was now a ball of ice buried in her chest like a diamond encased in flesh.

She got up, reaching for her clothes. She would dress and walk back to her father's house. She would creep up to her room and sleep. If she was lucky, she wouldn't dream.

She slipped the sweatpants over her feet and realized that she didn't want to go. In her mind, the door to her father's house loomed like a great dark mouth waiting to devour her. She couldn't step across the threshold, not as she was now. He was waiting there, perhaps not alone, and she wasn't strong enough yet to face him.

She looked toward the bathroom. Steam from the shower floated into the bedroom. Brian was singing, badly and happily, the words to a song that had been popular the summer before. Caddie had liked it once, she remembered. She and Bree had played it over and over while driving to Laguna one day, until Sam had begged them to stop.

The sweatpants she tossed away, rising from the bed and walking into the steam. When she pulled back the curtain surrounding the tub, Brian held out his hand and helped her step in. Soap flowed down his body in frothy white floes, dripped from his penis in heavy drops.

She allowed him to wash her, even her hair. He massaged the shampoo into her scalp, and for a time the world smelled like mangos. Then the water was turned off, and despite the softness of the towel Brian wrapped around her, she felt the cold returning.

In bed again, she burrowed beneath the blanket and pressed her naked body against Brian's. When he joked that her feet were blocks of ice, she closed her eyes and fought back tears. Only when he turned off the light did she let them fall, silently and like drops of rain, onto the pillow.

CHAPTER 39

"Caddie isn't here?" Hudson asked, accepting the glass of wine Ben held out to him.

Ben shook his head. "I don't know where she is," he said wearily. "Probably with that guy . . ."

"Brian," said Hudson, filling in the blank.

"Brian," Ben repeated. "Or, I suppose, it could be anybody."

Hudson said nothing. He understood Ben's apparent ambivalence about his daughter's whereabouts, but it was unsettling to hear the defeat in his voice. It sounded as if he'd given up and, to Hudson, set a tone for their inevitable conversation that he found dispiriting.

"I shouldn't have said that," Ben said, sighing. "I do care where she is, and if it has to be with some boy, I guess Brian is preferable to someone she just met." Again the tiredness showed through his words.

"She's just working through some things," Hudson said.

"She's still my daughter," Ben snapped. He lowered his head. "I'm sorry," he apologized. "It's not your fault."

Hudson twirled the wineglass slowly between his fingers. He wasn't so sure that Ben was right about that. In fact, he was pretty certain that he had a lot to do with Caddie's current return to defying her father in the way she must know would be most hurtful to him. He wanted to tell Ben as much, but, selfishly, he feared it might place him at a disadvantage. He was ashamed of this thought and pushed it aside as soon as he recognized it.

"This whole thing," Ben said, waving his hand vaguely. "You know, what Caddie said." He didn't look at Hudson as he spoke. "She's just angry with me."

Hudson nodded, but he knew Ben was wrong. He was making excuses, afraid to talk about *what* Caddie had said and choosing instead to treat the fact that she'd said it as the problem. Now Hudson had to decide whether he was going to be complicit in the deceit or whether he would force Ben to acknowledge what lay between them.

"I don't think her mother and I gave her a very good idea of what relationships are supposed to be like," Ben continued. "It's no wonder, really, that she's doing what she is. Maybe if—"

"Ben," Hudson interrupted, making up his mind. He waited for Ben to look at him. When he did, he saw in the pained expression that Ben was begging him not to continue. For a moment, he nearly acquiesced. He didn't want to cause this man any more pain than he already had. But then resolve rose in him like the sun coming up, and he said, "Caddie isn't the problem right now."

Ben, silent, nodded. He drained his wineglass and reached for the bottle. Hudson, stepping forward, stopped him by placing his hand on Ben's. He felt Ben freeze, and then his hand trembled beneath Hudson's like a trapped animal.

"It's not going to help," Hudson said. He set his own half-finished glass on the counter and released Ben's hand. Ben drew it back and shoved both hands into his pockets.

If they were going to talk, Hudson realized, he was the one who would need to begin. Ben clearly couldn't, or wouldn't, without some kind of encouragement. Not knowing what else to say, Hudson began to talk about Paul.

"I told you that Paul was married," he began. "I'd like to say that I didn't know it at first. But I did." Emily's face appeared in his mind, fine-boned and pale, beautiful in its frailty, all blue eyes and hair the color of corn silk. He might have fallen in love with her, too, if things had been different.

"Paul claimed not to love her," he continued. "That was a lie. He did. But that wasn't enough, at least not for him. I don't know if she was satisfied with him or not. I never spoke to her, not once in the two years Paul and I were lovers."

Ben was watching him as he spoke. He'd leaned himself against the counter, and his hands were still thrust into his pockets. Hudson saw that they were balled into fists, as if Ben were trying to contain his fear by blocking its outlets.

"At first I hated her," Hudson said. "She was, after all, my competition, at least as far as Paul's time was concerned. He always had to go home to her. While she got to sleep with him beside her, I got to sleep by myself, wondering if he was touching her. Wondering if he was thinking about me," he added.

"Eventually I just felt sorry for her," he went on. "From what Paul told me, she seemed like a nice person. Even though I was the one her husband was cheating on her with, I didn't like that he might be hurting her." He smiled sadly. "Of course, I could afford to pity her, because Paul preferred me over her sexually. It's not so hard to be compassionate when you're the one partially to blame for the other person's misery."

Again he thought of Caddie, and of his part in her unhappiness. "Not that Paul wasn't equally at fault, of course," he said quickly. "But he made excuses. He couldn't leave her because they had a child. He couldn't leave her because of the complications of divorce and money and a million other things."

He wanted badly to take up the wineglass and fortify himself with a drink, but after what he'd said to Ben, he didn't feel he could. Instead he imitated Ben, stuffing his hands into his pockets and worrying the inner liner with his fingertips.

"I didn't want him to leave her anyway," he said. "I mean, I *did*. But only because I wanted to be the person who won." It had taken him a long time to understand that about himself, and telling it to Ben didn't make him feel any better about it. It was a terrible thing to realize about himself, that he could see another person as a prize to be taken away from the person who held it.

"I got used to the arrangement," he said, glossing over the months of fighting and petulance that resulted in this truce. "And Paul seemed happy enough with it as well. Once he discovered the manuscript, we had a legitimate reason to spend a lot of time together. That made it easier. He told Emily I was his assistant, which I sort of was, really. She had no reason not to believe him."

Now he was getting to the truly difficult part of his story. He'd already admitted to Ben that he hadn't told the whole truth about his relationship with Paul. Ben, he thought, most logically assumed that he'd been hiding the fact that Paul had had a wife. But that was only part of it; the rest was far more difficult to tell.

"Paul didn't die of cancer," he said.

Ben, who hadn't spoken a word during Hudson's telling of the story, removed his hands from his pockets and crossed them over his chest. "What was it?" he asked.

He's wondering if it was AIDS, Hudson thought, not without a spark of anger at the implicit homophobia in such a fear. But Ben's face revealed no sign of disgust, and Hudson reproached himself for ascribing motives to his question. It was, after all, a question that had been posed by several people who knew of Hudson's relationship with Paul, as if his infidelity presupposed him to self-destruction as well. He'd sensed beneath the surface of their concern for his well-being a kind of triumph that was repellent, a thinly veiled searching for evidence of their superiority to someone who would not only commit adultery but commit it with someone of his own sex

When he'd vented to Marty following one such encounter, his friend had quoted H. G. Wells to him: "Moral indignation is jealousy with a halo." And indeed, Wells's Mr. Brumley had manufactured many a reason to despise Sir Isaac Harman, all because Brumley was ashamed at having fallen in love with Harman's wife. Thinking on it, Hudson had wondered if his friends similarly despised him, if they coveted his affair because they longed for affairs of their own. If so, he thought, they understood nothing of the potential for ruin in such an undertaking.

"He committed suicide," Hudson answered Ben. Now that it was out there, he felt the relief of having said it and found it easier than expected to provide the details. "He shot himself."

"Because of . . . the affair?" asked Ben.

"I honestly don't know," Hudson said. "He didn't leave a note, and I couldn't very well ask Emily. I heard later that they were having financial troubles, but I don't know that that was the reason." He paused for a moment before continuing. "But if you're asking me what I think," he said, "I think Paul couldn't accept who he was."

He was finished. There was really no more to the story. Everything else was speculation and supposition. He'd worked through all of them, searched everywhere for reasons, and had finally come to the conclusion that he would never really know what Paul had been thinking that night when he'd put a pistol to his temple and pulled the trigger. Moreover, he'd elected not to drive himself crazy with trying.

"So the manuscript," Ben said. "His work . . ."

"I promised I would finish it," said Hudson. That had been his one concession to his own feelings of guilt. It had been an easy one to make, as the mystery intrigued him as much as it had Paul. Still, it was a concession nonetheless. Worse, he realized now that it had also been a way for him to not let go.

"I can't imagine what he must have been feeling," Ben said quietly.

Hudson looked at him. "Can't you?" he asked. Everything he'd said had led to this point. Now, as he saw Ben considering the question, he felt his heart begin to pound.

Ben shook his head slowly. "I can't, Hudson," he said.

"Can't understand?" said Hudson.

"I just can't," Ben repeated. "I'm not . . ."

"Not what?"

"Caddie," Ben said. "She doesn't . . . She's just angry with me."

"This isn't about Caddie," Hudson said gently. "This is about you."

"I know she thinks that we're . . ." Ben began.

"It's not about *us* either, Ben," said Hudson. "It's about *you* and who you are."

Ben wouldn't look at him. His head was bowed, and he continued to shake it from side to side. When he did finally look up at Hudson, it was with an expression of deep despair. "I don't know who I am," he said.

Hudson crossed the floor to him, stopping in front of Ben and putting his hands on his shoulders. "Look at me," he said.

Ben turned his face to Hudson. His eyes held enormous pain.

"You do know who you are," Hudson said slowly. "And whoever you are—whoever you turn out to be—you're a good man."

Neither spoke for a long time. Ben's mouth trembled, and Hudson felt his whole body shaking, like the first stirrings of a coming earthquake. He pulled Ben to him and held him as it broke. For a moment Ben seemed about to slump to the floor, but then he steadied himself, and Hudson felt the tentative touch of his hands as Ben embraced him.

"It's all right," he whispered. "It's all right."

Ben wasn't crying, although his chest heaved raggedly. It was as if he was trying to speak but couldn't form the words. Instead, what he was feeling translated itself into physical form. Hudson held him tightly, absorbing the torrent of feeling, growing dizzy from the force and power of it.

Ben lifted his head from Hudson's shoulder. The pain in his eyes had faded, and now it was replaced with questions. Hudson answered them by placing his mouth on Ben's and kissing him. Ben, shaking, kissed him back, inexpertly and beautifully.

Without a word, Hudson took him by the hand and led him up the stairs. In the bedroom, he faced Ben and reached for the top button of his shirt. He realized as he unhooked it that the shirt was the same one Ben had been wearing the night in the locker room. Only this time, Hudson was taking it off of him.

When Ben was shirtless, Hudson ran his hands down the furry expanse of his chest. Ben stood with his arms at his side. Ben took one of his hands and placed it on his own chest. Ben looked at it, as if he was unsure if it really belonged to him. Then he moved it, slowly, to the open neck of Hudson's shirt. When his fingertips touched bare skin, he drew them back slightly, then replaced them.

Hudson resisted the urge to help him by removing his own shirt. He let Ben do it, however fumblingly. When it was done, Ben touched Hudson as if he were a statue, lightly and with a sense of fear, as if at any moment someone would tell him that he was violating a clearly posted rule. His fingers brushed Hudson's skin, pausing at a nipple, barely grazing it as they passed over.

Hudson drew him closer, placing his hands on Ben's lower back so that their torsos were touching. He kissed him again, this time with greater passion. His tongue sought Ben's, found it, drew it into his mouth.

He kissed Ben's neck, moved his mouth down his collarbone to the cleft of his throat. He kept going, his lips closing around a nipple, biting gently as Ben let out a gasp of surprise. He was tempted to go further, resisted it, returned to Ben's mouth and kissed him some more.

Ben allowed his pants to be undone, offered no resistance when Hudson pushed them down. And when Hudson stepped out of his own jeans, it was Ben who led him to the bed and watched while Hudson lay down on it. Then he sat, looking down at Hudson with desire and fear, a fear Hudson answered by reaching up and putting his hand behind Ben's neck and drawing him down.

Now Ben's hands touched him more surely, exploring Hudson's body with the eagerness of a boy. He paused only a moment in the space below Hudson's navel before slipping his fingers beneath the waistband of his shorts and seeking out his cock. When he touched it, he kissed Hudson, hard, and drew away to bend his head down.

He took Hudson into his mouth, and as he did Hudson found himself thinking that only a man really knew how to pleasure another man. Whereas women sucked cock, men adored it, like the relic of a saint or the symbol of their own power. He suspected that women gave attention to the penis because they loved what it could do for them, while men worshiped it because they loved what they could do for it.

Ben was not without the faults of a novice, but he displayed an innate understanding of what would feel good. He sucked gently at the head of Hudson's cock, worked the shaft with a sure hand, as if the experience of another lifetime flowed through him. Hudson, watching him, saw that Ben had found something he'd long sought without knowing it, and that sweetened the experience immeasurably.

When Hudson felt himself getting close, he drew Ben's head up and they switched places. Hudson took his time, drawing forth groans from Ben's throat with every touch of his mouth. Whenever he sensed Ben was nearing the edge, he backed off, letting him cool off before beginning again.

They continued in this way for a long time, neither of them wanting it to end, neither speaking a word. There was an understanding that this was Ben's initiation into a new world, and both were reluctant to break the spell too quickly. Whenever the threat of orgasm approached, they warded it off with distance, kissing and familiarizing themselves with one another's body until it was safe to resume.

When it did end, they were lying side by side, each holding the other's cock in his hand. Ben came first. Hudson felt the quick throb and release as Ben's body lost control, casting a milky net over his hand and Ben's stomach. Seeing this, Hudson gave in as well, and while Ben continued to pump him, he lifted his ass from the bed and groaned. Jism arced from his prick, laying a line of white from throat to groin as his balls drew up and he shook with the force of his climax.

There had always been for him, after the shuddering ceased and the heat of his cum had begun to cool into inconvenient stickiness, a moment when he felt ashamed of possessing such animal urges. Now, though, he felt nothing but joy. Beside him, Ben was still breathing heavily. His hand still held Hudson's softening cock, as if he feared letting go of it.

"Are you okay?" Hudson asked, turning to look at him.

Ben nodded. "I'm trying not to forget what it felt like," he said.

Hudson leaned over and kissed him. "Don't worry," he said. "If you forget, I'll remind you."

CHAPTER 40

Ben was cooking eggs when Caddie came in. He flipped them over, looked at his daughter, and said, "Good morning" in a cheerful voice.

Caddie looked at Hudson, seated at the table drinking a cup of coffee, and said nothing. She started to walk through the kitchen on her way upstairs but was stopped short when Ben said, "Sit down. I'm making breakfast."

"I'm not hungry," Caddie said stonily.

"Sit down anyway," said Ben, sliding the finished eggs onto a plate, adding two strips of bacon, and setting it on the table. "You don't have to eat if you don't want to, but I'd like you here."

Caddie seemed about to argue, but then she pulled a chair roughly away from the table and sat. She glared at the plate of food, not looking at either Hudson or her father.

"Where were you all night?" Ben asked.

"Out," said Caddie curtly.

Ben cracked an egg and poured the contents into the frying pan. "By 'out' I assume you mean you were at Brian's," he said. "It would have been nice if you'd let me know you weren't coming home."

Caddie cast a glance at Hudson. "Why?" she asked. "You didn't spend it alone. Right?"

Ben turned to her, the spatula in his hand. "Whether I did or not, I expect you to let me know if you're not coming home," he said.

Caddie rolled her eyes and snorted. "What, you get laid and all of a sudden you get to act like a real parent?"

"I should have been acting like a real parent all along," Ben replied.

"That was my fault. But it's not my fault that you're unhappy, so stop blaming me for that."

Caddie stood up.

"Where do you think you're going?" Ben demanded.

"Brian and I are going diving," said Caddie. "He's taking me to Monastery."

"Monastery?" Ben said. "You're not going to Monastery. It's an advanced site, and even when the conditions are perfect it's a dangerous dive."

"Brian says it's fine," Caddie said.

Ben laughed. "Yes, well, Brian's an idiot," he informed her.

Caddie bristled. "He's a good diver," she said unconvincingly.

Ben slid the eggs from the pan and took them to the table. "You're not diving Monastery," he said as he sat down. "And that's final."

"I can do what I want!" Caddie yelled.

Ben poked at his eggs, breaking the yoke. He picked up a piece of toast, dipped it into the yellow center, and took a bite before answering. "You can go," he said, "on one condition. I'm coming with you."

Caddie shook her head. "I don't need you to come with me," she said.

Ben chewed on his toast. "I know a lot more about Monastery than Brian does," he said. "I also happen to be an actual scuba instructor." He paused, letting the barb sink in. "And I'm your father," he concluded.

"I don't need you," Caddie said again. She turned away and started to leave.

"If Brian takes you to Monastery," Ben said, "I will personally make sure that he's banned from every dive shop and boat in town for taking an uncertified diver in the water."

Caddie swirled around, her mouth hanging open and her face red with rage. Ben didn't look at her as he continued speaking. "I will also have him fired from his job at the aquarium and contact his certifying agency to see that his personal c-card is revoked." He looked at Caddie. "Now, do you still want to have this conversation?"

Caddie, speechless, shook her head. "You can't do that," she said.

"I can," Ben said simply. "And I will. So, either I go with the two of you or you don't go at all."

Caddie swallowed hard. She seemed about to cry. "Fine," she spat. "If you want to come, you can come."

"Thank you," Ben said. "Tell Brian to meet us there at one. The tide should be in then."

Caddie left, and they could hear her feet on the stairs as she stormed up to her room. Ben half expected to hear the slam of a door, but none came.

"That was something," said Hudson.

"I don't think I've ever been so scared in my life," Ben told him. He smiled. "Except maybe for last night."

"You're sure you're still okay about that?" Hudson asked.

"More or less," said Ben. He looked at Hudson. "Not about you," he said quickly. "I just mean it's a lot to take in all at once. Yesterday I was just confused. Now I'm . . . gay," he finished. "Or something."

"You're something, all right," Hudson teased. "But I'm serious. You said this was something you never even considered. Are you sure you're not just . . ."

"Going through a phase?" Ben suggested.

Hudson shrugged. "Well, yeah. It must have occurred to you."

"Sure it has," said Ben. "And, no, I never had considered it before. But there are a lot of things about myself I ignored. Maybe this was one of them."

He picked up a piece of bacon and bit the end from it. "When you first told me what Caddie said," he told Hudson, "I tried to convince myself that I was just happy to have a friend. A real friend. I told myself she just didn't recognize the difference." He tipped the bacon strip toward Hudson. "I guess I was the one who didn't recognize the difference."

Hudson got up and poured himself another cup of coffee. When he sat down he said, "We should probably talk about what's going to happen now."

"No," Ben said. "Not now." He looked at Hudson. "Just let me enjoy this for a while, okay?"

"What makes you think I won't?" Hudson asked him.

"I didn't say you would," said Ben. "But I don't want to chance it."

Hudson added sugar to his cup and stirred it. "All right," he said. "No talking until you're ready. What do we do in the meantime?"

"We did pretty well not talking last night," said Ben. "Maybe we could continue *that* conversation?"

Hudson pretended to consider the question, taking several sips of coffee before replying. "I think I can do that," he said.

Ben reached out and took his hand. "Thank you," he said.

Hudson laced his fingers between Ben's. "You know," he said, "if it wasn't for Caddie, this probably never would have happened."

Ben sighed. "I hope I'm doing the right thing with her," he said. "I just don't know."

"What's this Monastery she's talking about?" Hudson asked him.

"A dive site," Ben explained. "You pass it when you drive to Pt. Lobos. There's a Carmelite monastery on the other side of the road."

"And is it really dangerous?"

"It's hard to get in and out of the water there," Ben explained. "Also, the waves are deceptive. Every year one or two people die there because they don't take it seriously enough."

"Then why dive there?" Hudson asked.

"Ah," Ben said. "Because it's one of the most beautiful dives anywhere in the world." A note of excitement entered his voice as he talked. "Monastery is where the Monterey Canyon comes closest to shore," he said. "You can dive right to the edge of it. You could dive *into* it if you were foolish enough. You see things there you don't see anywhere else in Monterey. Anywhere else anywhere, really. It's spectacular."

"I'd love to see it," Hudson told him.

"Come with us," Ben suggested.

Hudson shook his head. "Remember the part about it not being a good idea for new divers?" he said. "Besides, things will be tense enough as it is."

"Good point," Ben said. "Well, we'll go one of these days."

"I'm going to hold you to that," Hudson said as he stood up. "And now I'm going to go home, take a shower, and . . ." He stopped. "I'm not sure what I'm going to do," he concluded.

"Dinner tonight?" Ben asked.

"You're on," said Hudson. He rinsed his coffee mug in the sink, then came over and gave Ben a kiss. "Have fun with your future son-in-law."

Ben glared at him and Hudson hurried out. As Ben heard the door close he suddenly felt very much alone. Some of the old fears began creeping out from under doorways and scuttling out of corners where they'd been hiding, as if Hudson had been a talisman keeping them at bay. Now, without him, Ben was vulnerable.

He got up and started to wash the dishes, hoping it would help distract him. When it didn't, he turned his thoughts to the upcoming dive with Caddie and Brian. He hadn't dived Monastery in a while. He tried to recall what he'd seen on his last visit to the site, and what they might see today.

Flabellina trilineata, he thought. *Dendronotus albus, Tritonia festiva, Mexichromis amalguae.* He saw each nudibranch as he named it. *Thordisa bimaculata. You're a homosexual. Aldisa cooperi. You can't live that way. Melibe leonina. Faggot.*

He dropped the coffee mug he was washing—Hudson's coffee mug. It hit the edge of the sink and broke, the pieces clattering to the floor. Ben stared at them as the shadows crept closer, their mewling voices clawing at him.

The ringing of the phone came as a great relief. He lurched for the handset, grabbing it in his soapy hand and nearly dropping it. "Hello?" he said, his voice overly loud in the quiet kitchen.

"It's Carol. I'm calling to see how things are going."

"Carol," Ben said. He repeated her name. "Carol."

"Is something wrong?" his ex-wife asked. "You sound strange. And why do you keep saying my name?"

"Everything's fine," said Ben, ignoring the question. "I'm just washing up the breakfast dishes."

"Hmm," Carol replied. "So everything is okay with Caddie?"

Ben debated whether or not to lie. He wanted Carol to think he was capable of handling their daughter. At the same time, he knew she would simply ask Caddie the same question at some point, and she would be only too happy to inform her mother of his failings.

"You know how it is," he said. "She's a teenager."

"You noticed that, did you?" said Carol. "The question really is, are the two of you getting along?"

"Getting along well?" Ben said. "Or getting along?"

"Just answer the question, Ben," Carol said.

He found himself able to laugh at the familiar rejoinder. Carol, irritated, said, "I'd forgotten how passive–aggressive you are. I don't miss that."

"Did you ever love me?" Ben asked suddenly.

"What?" said Carol.

"Did you ever love me?" Ben repeated.

"Why would . . ." Carol said. "Yes, of course I did. I married you, didn't I?"

"But were we really *in* love?" asked Ben. "Were we in love, or did we just love one another?"

"Where is this coming from?" Carol said. "Ben, that was seventeen years ago. We were young. I don't know if I even knew what love was then. I'm pretty sure *you* didn't."

"No," Ben said. "I don't think I did either."

There was silence on the line as neither of them spoke. Ben could hear Carol breathing. He wondered what her face looked like.

"I didn't mean to hurt you," he said.

"You never hurt me, Ben," said Carol. "Maybe you disappointed me, but you never hurt me. I think if you hurt anyone, it was yourself."

"What do you mean?"

"You were never really happy with me," she answered. "I thought for a while I could make you happy. Maybe that's even why I married you. Then I thought having a child would make you happy. But I don't think any of it did."

Ben listened to her as if hearing her voice for the first time. They'd never said these things to one another. Even in the early days of their marriage they had kept their conversations away from dangerous territory. He saw now that it was deliberate, their way of avoiding the weaknesses that had existed in the fabric of their relationship from the very beginning. *Did I know even then?* he wondered. *Did she suspect?*

He wanted to ask her, but he wasn't ready. He'd only just allowed himself to accept that he might be—was—attracted to men. *A man,* he corrected himself. *Hudson.* Asking Carol to comment on what she might or might not have thought about him was too much.

"None of it was your fault," he said finally.

"What's anyone's fault?" said Carol. "Things happen."

"I don't think Caddie likes me very much," Ben told her.

Carol laughed. "Well, that's something you and I have in common then. She doesn't like me either."

"At least you've been there for her," Ben reminded her.

"Stop looking for things to blame yourself for," said Carol. "You didn't join a twelve-step program, did you?" she asked suspiciously.

"I've just been thinking," said Ben. "I made a lot of mistakes."

"No more than any other parent," Carol assured him. "As for Caddie hating you, she doesn't hate you. Or me. She hates what she thinks we are. One of these days she'll realize we aren't the monsters she's made us into in her mind."

"Did you know she's having sex?" Ben asked her.

"I figured she was," said Carol.

"Why am I the only one surprised by this?" Ben said.

"Because you're her father," said Carol. "Fathers always take it the hardest."

"That's what Hudson said," Ben said.

"Who's Hudson?" asked Carol.

Ben hesitated. It took him a moment to remember that, whatever he was doing, he wasn't cheating on Carol. Still, he heard himself stammer, "Hudson? Oh, he's just a . . . friend."

"He must have a daughter of his own if he said that," Carol remarked, apparently unaware of the panic gripping her former husband. "Anyway, he's right. And it's not like you can lock her up until she's eighteen. What's he like?"

"What?" Ben said, confused. He thought at first she was asking about Hudson.

"I assume she's sleeping with a particular boy, otherwise this topic wouldn't have come up," said Carol.

"Yes," Ben said. "He seems nice enough." He was sorry he'd mentioned anything to Carol. Her cavalier attitude to the whole thing made him feel like he was the one with a problem.

"Well, let me talk to her," Carol said. "I'll make sure she's taking precautions."

Ben started to call for Caddie. Then he realized that he didn't want Carol to talk to her. She was still angry at him, and he feared that if her mother set her off in any way, she would try to get back at him by telling Carol what she knew.

"She's not here," he lied. "She went to the aquarium with Brian."

"All right," said Carol as Ben closed his eyes and leaned against the wall. "I'll try later tonight. Or if she wants to call me, I'll be in and out."

"I'll tell her," Ben said, his throat tight. He listened as Carol hung up, then remained leaning against the wall, looking at the broken coffee mug, until the strident beeping of the receiver forced him to move. Then he placed the phone in its cradle and went to clean up the shattered pieces.

CHAPTER 41

"The topography is shaped like a bowl," Ben told Caddie. "Once you hit the edge of the water, it just drops off. That's what makes it so hard to get out."

Caddie ignored him. She turned to Brian. "Can you help me put this on?" she asked, indicating her BC.

"No problem," Brian answered, although he was already wearing his gear and Ben was in just his dry suit and could have done it more easily.

"Thanks," Caddie said. She faced Ben as Brian lifted the BC up so that she could slide her arms through the straps. Ben tried to catch her eye, but she looked away.

She hadn't spoken to him at all. During the drive to the beach she had sat with her arms across her chest, looking out the window. Only when Brian had appeared had she come to life, making a big production out of kissing him hello. Even Brian had seemed surprised at her enthusiasm, and Ben resisted an urge to inform the young man that it was largely to annoy her father that Caddie was acting this way.

"They call the sand here monster berries," Ben said, as if Caddie had asked him to explain. "They're hard to walk through, so be careful."

Caddie ignored him, stomping off into the gravel-like sand with great purpose. Brian, staying behind, looked at Ben. "She's ready to go," he remarked.

"Have you dived here before?" Ben asked him. He was finding it hard to dislike Brian, even though his irresponsibility regarding Caddie's dive education rankled. He planned on having a serious discussion with him about that later. Right now, though, his mind was focused on Caddie.

"Once," Brian answered.

Ben nodded, saying nothing but feeling even more relieved that he'd forced himself into the party. He balanced his BC on the open tailgate of the car and backed into it. Brian, watching, made no offer of help.

"I think we should enter on the south side," Ben said as he snapped his hoses in place and tested them. "It's an easier entry, and the waves are smaller. Then we can skirt the edge of the kelp forest and head toward the wash rock."

"Sounds good," Brian agreed. Ben, assuming that Brian really had no idea why that was a good idea, went in search of Caddie. He found her standing on a dune, looking down at the water. The waves here were larger than at many of the other Monterey dive sites, and they crashed on the shore with more force. Caddie was watching two divers who were attempting an entry on the site's more difficult northern approach. One had managed to get in and was floating in the water, waiting for the other.

The second diver advanced, froglike, toward the water. As he reached the edge, he suddenly fell forward, slipping on the precarious monster berries and plunging headlong into an oncoming wave. His regulator had not been in his mouth, and now it buzzed around his head, air escaping in a loud hiss, as he tried to locate it.

"He's got a berry stuck in there, I'll bet you anything," Ben said. "Make sure you keep your reg in when you get close to the water."

In the water, the first diver was helping the second diver right himself. He grabbed the renegade regulator and placed it in his buddy's mouth just as a second wave crashed over their heads, pushing them both under the surface. A moment later they both popped up again, and Ben reached up and put his closed fist on top of his head. Both divers responded in kind. "They're okay," Ben said, relieved that he wouldn't have to try to assist them. It was hard enough to walk on the Monastery beach; making a rescue attempt was nearly impossible without help.

Brian appeared, pulling on his gloves. "Looks flat," he remarked, scanning the water.

"Yeah," said Caddie. "It's pretty calm."

She'd agree with him if he said this was the Arctic Ocean, Ben thought to himself as Brian walked toward the south end, Caddie right behind him. He followed, marveling at the determination Caddie was displaying in her efforts to marginalize him. *If she was half as into this guy as she's pretending to be, he'd be lucky to get out alive,* he thought as his foot slid on the sand and he struggled to remain upright.

When they reached the water's edge, Caddie ignored Ben's instruction to keep her regulator in, standing in the water as she put her fins on. Ben remained quiet but kept an eye on her in case a wave of any size should approach. None did, but only by pure luck, and as Caddie followed Brian into the water, Ben saw her look at him in triumph, as if she'd caught him in a lie.

He followed quickly, grateful to be off the sand. Unlike at the Breakwater or Pt. Lobos, here they were almost immediately in water over their heads. Ben looked down and saw that the visibility was excellent. He could see the bottom easily. It was, he thought, going to be a wonderful dive.

Brian was already swimming along the outer edge of the kelp. At its summer peak, the kelp lay in a thick mat over the surface of the sea. Getting entangled in it was a definite hazard for those unfamiliar with the infamous Monterey "kelp crawl," and Ben wanted to tell Caddie to stay far away from the forest. She, however, was swimming with her face in the water, following Brian's fins as if he were the Pied Piper.

The swim took some time, and when they stopped on the far side of the kelp, it was a welcome rest. "The good news is, that was the hard part," Ben joked as they paused to catch their breath. "Now you get to see the good stuff."

"You can go right to the edge of the canyon," Brian said. "It's so cool."

"Yeah, but don't go too deep," Ben reminded him. "Stay around a hundred feet, and watch your computers. You need to have enough air to get back."

He saw Caddie roll her eyes at Brian. "Just stick with me," Brian told her. "You'll be fine."

"What's the plan?" Ben asked.

"Go down and have fun," said Brian with a grin.

Before Ben could say that they needed something a little more concrete than that, Brian began to descend. Caddie, too, lifted her low-pressure inflator and released the air from her BC. Ben, annoyed, found his own inflator and went after them.

He watched Caddie carefully as they descended. She had good control, he noted. She moved slowly and without the jerkiness usually seen in divers before they'd logged fifty or so dives. Despite his anger, he was proud of her.

When they reached the bottom, Brian immediately began swimming in the direction of the canyon. Ben let him lead. He himself knew where they were going, and he knew how to get back. When Brian got lost, he would be able to put them back on track, hopefully teaching Caddie something about the need for a solid dive plan. Until then, he thought it best to stay back and enjoy the dive.

The conditions were absolutely amazing. The vis, he noted, had to be at least seventy feet, the water almost totally free of particulate matter so that the kelp and rocks seemed trapped in glass. All around them fish swam in large numbers. He counted half a dozen types of rockfish alone, their distinctive striped bodies hovering in the water like a fleet of zeppelins.

The bottom fell steeply, and it wasn't long before they came to the sandy slope that marked the beginning of the edge of the canyon. The sand here was dotted with *Pachycerianthus fimbriatus,* the tube-dwelling anemone, as well as colonies of *Phragmatopoma californica,* the purple-armed tube worms that reminded him of the wild asters that had grown along the side of his grandparents' house. Where the anemones were scattered singly over the bottom, the tube worms bloomed in tight groups like living bouquets.

Farther down the slope the water became dark, almost ominous in color. There the visibility lessened, and where the colder water of the deep canyon met the warmer water of the upper surface, a thermocline formed a rippling ribbon that stretched across the edge of the canyon like a warning. Beyond it the bottom dropped off into the abyss of the canyon. Ben checked his computer and saw that they were at a hundred and nine feet.

Caddie was looking at one of the tube worms, her head down while her feet kicked gently behind her. Brian, ahead of her, was following what looked like a halibut, waiting for it to settle into the sand and then poking it to watch it rise, flying-carpet-like, and swim away from him.

Ben looked out into the shadows that seemed to stretch as wide as the universe. He wondered if either Caddie or Brian realized what an unusual thing they were seeing. Ben had seen the view many times but still it awed him, even frightened him. Hovering on the edge of the canyon, one had the sense that it was very much possible to suddenly fall in, to be swept down thousands of feet by a treacherous current that roamed the perimeter, dragonlike, waiting for the curious and the foolhardy.

Although Ben knew that no such current existed, the sense of dread so many divers experienced when diving in this place made him cautious. It was possible to lose track of depth and descend rapidly to dangerous depths without even realizing it. And there was the lure of the canyon itself. More than one diver had swum into it and disappeared, and although these deaths were almost certainly deliberate choices, he wondered sometimes if those unfortunate souls hadn't been following some voice only they could hear.

He looked for Brian and saw him some way off, having abandoned the halibut for what looked like an angel shark. It was a good find, but Ben could see that Brian was already nearly twenty feet deeper than he should be and showed no sign of coming back. Ben then looked for Caddie, fully intending to meddle this time if she seemed to be following Brian and the shark.

She was not near the tube worms nor was she anywhere that he could see. Alarmed, he looked up and saw her. She was perhaps fifteen feet from the bottom. Her hands were jerking frantically as she tried to use a swimming stroke, but she made little headway. Something was wrong. She was clearly trying to get to the surface but had apparently forgotten that the weights in her BC pockets made that impossible. She could accomplish it if she inflated her BC, but she seemed to have forgotten that. *Or she's run out of air,* Ben realized.

He swam toward her as quickly as he could. As he did, Caddie seemed to remember the weights in her BC. Her fingers reached for the clips, even as Ben screamed through his regulator, uselessly, for her to stop. It would make her too buoyant.

He saw one pouch drop to the sand, and Caddie began to rise. He kicked harder, stretching out his hand. Caddie, twisting to reach the other pocket, turned so that she was looking at him. Her eyes were wide, and he saw that she was gasping for breath, trying to pull any remaining air out of her tank. He waved at her, but her eyes saw nothing.

She dropped the second pouch just as he reached her. Although her body rocketed up, he managed to grab hold of her legs, wrapping his arms around them. Still she flew. He heard the warning beep of his computer begin screaming for him to slow down. He ignored it, crawling up Caddie's body. He could give her air if he could just reach her. But the water was rushing by so quickly that he couldn't see.

Let her go. The words of his instructor certifier rang in his ears. It was one of the cardinal rules: If a student began an uncontrolled ascent, it did no good to put yourself in danger by trying to hold on. The rapid decrease in depth put you at enormous risk for decompression sickness or an embolism, and it helped no one if both divers took a hit.

Caddie, however, was not just another diver. He couldn't watch her shoot away from him like a falling star while he stayed safely underwater. In the time it would take him to ascend safely, she could die.

He pulled at one of the air release toggles on his BC, hoping to empty it and slow their ascent. His computer was shrieking madly, as was Caddie's, and he wished they would stop. He tried once more to give her his regulator, but she was reaching toward the surface and seemed not to see him.

The water changed color around them, becoming a lighter shade of green. They passed through rays of sunlight, and above them Ben saw the canopy of the kelp forest where the long fronds rested on the waves. *Please don't be holding your breath,* he begged Caddie as the final few feet of their ascent flew by and they rocketed from the water.

Dazzled by the brightness of the sun, Ben fell back against the blanket of kelp. He called Caddie's name, and when he heard no response, he ripped the mask from his face and threw it away from him, shouting, "Caddie! Caddie!"

She was only a few feet away, struggling to stay afloat. She, too, had lost her mask, and she was hitting the water wildly.

"Inflate your BC!" Ben shouted at her. "Do it orally!"

Caddie sank beneath the water, bobbed back up, spitting and choking. Ben lunged toward her and grabbed her from behind, holding her around the waist so that her flailing hands couldn't reach him. In her panic, she would grab hold of anything, and he needed to maintain control.

"It's all right," he told her, reaching for her low-pressure inflator. He held the outflow button down and breathed into the mouthpiece. Caddie's BC swelled slightly. He blew again, and she began to rise in the water. Another four breaths and she was buoyant. Still, she struggled.

"Caddie," Ben said firmly. "You're all right."

She stopped flailing and began to cry. He turned her around and looked into her face. "What happened?" he asked her.

"I ran out of air," she said between sobs.

Ben took her computer and looked at it. It didn't make sense that she had run out of air. They hadn't been down that long. Yet her gauge was in the red, the needle resting against the farthest edge. *He didn't give her a full tank,* he thought. *That idiot sent her down without enough air.*

He dropped the computer. He would deal with Brian later. Right now he wanted to make sure Caddie was all right. "How do you feel?" he asked. "Are you tingly? Does your chest hurt?" He ran through the classic symptoms of the bends, trying to remember all of them.

Caddie shook her head. Her crying had become a ragged snuffling, but she was no longer hysterical. "I think I'm okay," she said.

"Good," Ben told her. "Do you think you can swim in?"

Caddie looked toward the shore, which was farther away than Ben would have liked. They had swum around the kelp forest and were now closer to the north end of the beach. While he would have preferred to go back the way they'd come, it would be faster to go straight in.

"I can do it," Caddie said.

"Good girl," Ben said. "I know you can."

Since their masks had sunk, they swam on their backs. This was harder, and Ben was tired after only a few yards. He kicked harder, thinking perhaps his legs had become entangled in some kelp. Then he felt a strange warmth wash over his skin. *No,* he prayed. *Please, no.*

Caddie was beside him. As the tingling sensation increased, Ben tried to reach for her and found that he could barely move his fingers.

"Caddie," he said.

"I'm okay, Dad," she answered.

"Caddie," Ben repeated, "I need your help."

Suddenly, his vision filled with exploding stars. He opened his mouth to speak and found that he couldn't. Then all was blackness.

CHAPTER 42

Hudson placed the battered manuscript on Helen Guerneyser's desk. "This is for you," he told her.

The archivist looked at the papers, which by now were dirty and torn from repeated readings. Hudson's illegible scrawl filled the margins, and an assortment of sticky notes protruded from between the pages, as if he had pressed butterflies between them. Helen looked over her glasses at the title page. "*Changing Tides,*" she read. "What is it, something you wrote?"

"If I'm right, it's something Steinbeck wrote," Hudson told her. She looked up, quickly, and he continued. "A colleague of mine, who has since died, found this," he explained.

"How long have you had it?" she asked.

Hudson hesitated. "About three years," he said truthfully.

Helen picked the manuscript up and leafed through the pages.

"This is a copy, obviously," Hudson said. "The original is in a safe place."

"I'd ask you why this wasn't turned over to the Stanford archives," Helen said. "Or to us," she added. "But I think I can guess the answer to that myself." Her voice held no animosity, and Hudson knew that she understood fully the impossibility of any academic handing over such a potentially exciting find.

"Is it any good?" Helen asked him.

"It's very good," said Hudson. "It's unfinished, but it's very good. But . . ."

Helen stopped flipping and looked at him, waiting. "But?" she encouraged.

"I can't prove that it's by Steinbeck," Hudson said. "And even if I could, I'm not sure it would be the best idea."

Helen took her glasses off and placed the end of one earpiece between her lips. "Eleanor Mintz called me," she said. "She's under the impression that it's your intention to try to blackmail the foundation."

Hudson started to deny the accusation violently, but Helen waved her hand. "I know it's ridiculous," she said. "But I found it curious that she wouldn't tell me what, exactly, this apparently lurid information you have is. She said, and I quote, 'It's nothing a *lady* would ever say, Helen.' " She laughed. "But as neither you nor I is a lady of Eleanor's standing, I think you had better tell me," she concluded.

Hudson told her, as simply as he could, his theory about the manuscript's origins. When he was done, he watched her face for any indication of her feelings. She took her time and then, completely unnerving Hudson, began to laugh. When she was through she wiped her eyes. "No wonder Eleanor was so beside herself," she said.

"I don't understand," said Hudson. "What's funny about the idea that Steinbeck and Ricketts might have been lovers?"

"Eleanor tried to sleep with both of them," Helen answered. "Oh, she'd deny it if anyone ever asked her, but she did. She chased Ricketts around for years, and when Steinbeck moved back here, she made sure she got that job as his assistant."

"She said he hired her from the newspaper," Hudson said.

"Yes, he did," Helen said, nodding. "What she didn't tell you was that she was working in the advertising department when he came in to place an ad for a Girl Friday. Well, he never did place that ad, and Eleanor quit the paper the same day."

Hudson couldn't believe it. "What a little tramp," he declared.

"If I'd known what you were on about, I would never have sent you to Eleanor," said Helen. "She's the original virgin spinster. They modeled all the other ones after her."

"So she didn't . . ." Hudson started to ask.

"Oh no," said Helen, understanding his meaning. "Neither of them had the slightest interest in her, from what I understand. But I think she's convinced herself that they did. She never married, and I wouldn't be surprised if beside her bed she keeps their framed photos and kisses them every night before she goes to sleep."

"No wonder she was so upset," said Hudson.

"Yes, well," Helen said, "I'm sure she's told half the board by now that you're out to besmirch the reputation of our Mr. Steinbeck. Already there may be plans to run you out of town on a rail."

Hudson laughed, mostly because he could see Eleanor Mintz—and Edgar Macready as well—standing by the side of the road as an angry mob drove him from the city limits. "I'm surprised she didn't try to poison me and keep me in that mausoleum she calls a house," he joked.

Helen tapped her glasses against the manuscript. "Why are you telling me all of this now?" she asked.

Hudson sat back in his chair. "To be honest, I don't know," he answered.

"You don't think you can prove your theory?" Helen suggested.

"Maybe," Hudson admitted. "Mostly I'm just not sure that I care anymore if I do." He looked into her face. "I'm not sure I ever did."

"It would be an extraordinary find," Helen said. "Even if it's just a novel it would be a substantial addition to the canon."

"Yes, it would," Hudson agreed. "But if it's just a novel, then it wouldn't matter who found it, would it?" He raised one eyebrow and tried to adopt an air of mystery.

Helen returned the look. "No," she said. "It wouldn't."

"For instance," said Hudson, "it might have been found in a previously overlooked box of miscellanea." This wasn't far from the truth, he thought, and such a claim would be unlikely to meet with much suspicion. "And depending upon where that box was, this wouldn't have to end up in, say, the archive at Stanford," he added.

"That's true," Helen agreed.

"And if you can get Eleanor Mintz to admit that she destroyed what she thought was the only copy, that would answer the question of authenticity," Hudson said, grinning.

Helen put her glasses on again. "We're being very flippant about this," she said. "Now tell me seriously, do you not want to be the one to discover this manuscript?"

Hudson looked to the right, where Paul was standing behind Helen Guerneyser's desk, regarding the manuscript with a mixture of longing and despair. He turned his gaze to Hudson, pleading with him. Hudson looked at him for a long time, then nodded at Helen. "Yes," he said. "I'm sure."

Helen gathered up the manuscript. "I'm looking forward to reading this," she said.

"I'll send you the original, of course," Hudson said. "When I get back."

"What are you going to do now?" asked Helen. "This was to be your dissertation, correct?"

"It was," Hudson said. He searched for more to say and found that there was nothing. "I guess we'll see," he finished.

Helen stood. Hudson, following her lead, did the same. He reached out his hand. "Thank you," he said as Helen took it.

Helen placed her free hand on top of their joined ones. "You're the one who deserves the thanks," she said. "I haven't given you any-thing."

He looked past her, searching for Paul's ghost. It was gone. "Yes, you have," he told Helen.

He left the building, his briefcase swinging lightly at his side. It was now nearly empty. He looked at it for a moment, remembering the day he'd bought it. He'd selected it because he could picture himself walk-ing into a classroom with it, setting it on a desk, and opening it in front of a group of eager students. It was very much like the one Paul had carried.

He found a trash can and stuffed the briefcase into its open mouth, where a Carl's Jr. cup tipped over and spilled cola across the caramel-colored leather. Then he walked to his car and drove out of the park-ing lot. When, at a stoplight, he looked in the rearview mirror, he saw only the face of the driver behind him.

He felt suddenly free, like a kite after its string has slipped from the fingers of the one controlling it. His heart soared up into the blue sky, riding the wind alongside the gulls who dipped and turned with prac-ticed ease. He was no longer an earthbound creature, held down by the burden he'd carried for too long. He was free to do as he liked.

And what he wanted to do, he realized, was to see Ben. Last night had not been enough for him. He wanted more. He couldn't say that he loved Ben; he didn't know that yet, and might not for a long time. He wasn't even sure he wanted to, or that Ben wanted him to. But he wanted to be with him, to feel him in his arms and see what might hap-pen between them now that he had laid Paul to rest.

Part of him felt that he shouldn't be so happy. He had, after all, just handed over his life's dream to someone else. *No,* he reminded himself, *you handed over* Paul's *life's dream.* He had broken his promise, he thought, his joy fading somewhat.

Then he thought of Eleanor Mintz, alone in her house with her ghosts. She had made them promises as well, and keeping them had turned her into a living ghost, hollow and haunted, forced to believe in something that was never true. He would not become her. As much as he had loved Paul, he was not beholden to him. His promise had been made not to fulfill Paul's dream but to keep him from leaving Hudson completely.

But now he was gone, released into whatever place his spirit resided. Hudson hoped that he'd gone without rancor, that he understood why Hudson had needed to do what he'd done. And if he didn't, then he hoped he would be forgiven.

He wondered what Paul would make of Ben Ransome. While he would appreciate Ben's intelligence, Hudson suspected that Paul would have declared Ben to be "limited." It was his favorite descriptive for those he felt were not quite up to his level of thinking, although Hudson suspected that he applied it most often to those whose ways of thinking challenged his own. Certainly he would find Ben to be unsophisticated, another damning trait.

They were very different men, he thought, and yet he was attracted to them both. But would he be as attracted to Paul now as he had been when he'd met him? He recalled the way he had been seduced by Paul's confidence, by the way he assumed that people would listen to him and, because of this, they did. He'd laughed when Paul would rail against the stupidity of others, seeing in it a kind of forthrightness, a willingness to confront the world when it went astray.

But Paul had lacked kindness. This was something he realized only now that he saw the opposite exhibited so strongly in Ben. Paul would call it weakness, but he would be wrong. Ben accepted the world for what it was not because he didn't think he could change it but because he saw no need to. And if sometimes this kindness caused him deep sadness, Hudson believed that Ben was capable of a joy that Paul could never imagine.

He hoped that one day, and soon, Caddie could see her father in this way. But he suspected that it would take some time, or some event of enormous emotional proportions, for her to do so. Until then, she and Ben would likely wound one another over and over as they attempted to find the places where their lives intersected, frequently missing the mark and adding new scars to the ones already formed. Maybe, though, he could be there to, if not help, at least cushion the blows.

Stop it, he ordered himself. *He's no more your responsibility than Paul was.* He knew this was true. One night did not constitute a relationship. *Unless you're a lesbian,* he thought wickedly. *Then you would have moved in already.*

He promised himself that he wouldn't think too far ahead. He didn't even know what he was doing with his life now that the manuscript was out of his hands. With it gone, he really had no reason to stay in Monterey. *No reason but Ben,* he thought. And that was not—could not be—reason enough. *Don't wanna fall in love,* he sang in his mind. Who was it who sang that song, the woman with the scary braids and the nose chain? Jane Something. *Don't wanna fall in love,* he repeated, drumming on the steering wheel the song's distinctive beat. *Love cuts just like a knife.*

Child. Jane Child. That was her name. He wondered what had happened to her. Probably she'd joined the hundreds of other people who disappeared after one good song. Maybe they all met once a week in some smoky bar and sang their songs to one another.

Jane Child. Henri-Frédéric Amiel would love her. *A child sees what we are,* he thought. *Through all the fictions of what we would be. Don't wanna fall in love. You make a knife feel good.* Ben Ransome was not a knife. Still, he had the capacity to hurt Hudson, and that was a danger greater than any other.

You're the one who wanted to talk about what happens now, he reminded himself. And, yes, he had raised the question, not six hours earlier, in fact. And it had been Ben who had wanted to wait. Why? Hudson had intended to have the talk about not getting too serious. He'd felt it was necessary to spare Ben getting his hopes up. But perhaps Ben was thinking the same thing, thinking that he didn't want to hurt Hudson's feelings.

All this time, Hudson realized, he had believed that he had been helping Ben come to terms with who *he* was. It had freed something in himself as well, given him the strength to let go of Paul, but always he had assumed that Ben was the one being transformed. Now he saw that he had been just as transformed by his time with Ben. Both of them had lost something during the night in one another's arms, and both of them had gained something as well.

The idea that Ben might not want to be in love with him was suddenly deeply frightening. He felt a loss that had not been there moments ago, as if he had opened a secret door and found behind it an empty room, the footprints of the former occupant left in the dust on the floor. He found himself worried that something terrible would happen before he could get to Ben and tell him this, tell him that, although he was so very afraid, he was willing to try to love him.

He increased his speed, passing the cars ahead of him. Time seemed incredibly important, the wasting of it a crime. The need to see Ben, to touch him and feel the solidness of him in his hands, was overwhelming. He pressed the gas pedal harder, watching the needle of the speedometer leap in response to the quickening of his heart.

He drove directly to Ben's house. Finding the driveway empty, he remembered that Ben was diving with Caddie and Brian. He struggled to remember the name of the place. Then it came to him—Monastery—so odd a name, unless, as Ben had said, you thought of the kelp forests as cathedrals. Then it was most appropriate, a place where those who loved the sea came to devote their lives to it.

Monastery. It shouldn't, he thought, be difficult to find. Ben had said it was on the way to Pt. Lobos, and there was only one road that went there. Surely he would see other divers and know that he was at the right place. Or he would ask. Either way, he decided, he would be there to welcome Ben when he rose from the ocean.

He returned to the main road through town and followed it to Highway 1. The sense of dread was fading as he drew nearer to where he would see Ben. Ben would be happy to see him. They would go back to his house, make dinner, and talk. Maybe they would make love in Ben's ancient bed, embarrassed when the springs betrayed their enthusiasm.

He drove down the steep hill he remembered from previous trips, past the unexpected shopping center that appeared on the left like an oasis in the scrubby landscape. Beyond the lone stoplight the ocean appeared on his right. *It must be around here somewhere,* he thought just before he spied the cross rising above the trees.

Then he saw the cars pulled to the side of the road. A man in a dry suit stood beside a dusty SUV. Hudson pulled in beside him, nodding as the man, talking on a cell phone, turned to look at him. He turned the engine off and opened the door.

"Move it to the end of the lot," the man said gruffly, turning and hurrying off toward the beach. "We're going to need that space for the ambulance."

CHAPTER 43

Caddie pushed at the kelp, trying to get through it. But the harder she pushed, the more it seemed to want to wrap its arms about her. She felt it trying to pull her father from her arms, and she gripped his BC more tightly. *Don't let go,* she thought. *Whatever you do, don't let go.*

"Help!" she screamed. "Please, somebody, help!"

She hated being helpless, but she screamed for her father, not for herself. She looked at his pale face. She thought he was still breathing, but she couldn't tell. The movement of the water made it difficult to tell.

"Help!" she screamed again. The shore seemed to be getting farther away, as if the kelp was pushing her backward. She kicked, frustrated and furious, and got nowhere.

On the shore, two figures ran toward the water. She heard a splash, then saw arms cutting through the water. *They heard me,* she thought. She turned to her father, "They heard me," she told him.

The swimmers found a way through the kelp. Reaching her, the first one took a look at Ben and took him, gently but firmly, from Caddie's hold. "What happened?" he asked, pulling off a glove and pressing his fingers against her father's neck.

"We came up too fast," she said. "He was fine, and then he passed out."

"You're okay?" the second swimmer asked her.

Caddie nodded. "Is he breathing?" she asked.

"He is," the first man said, "but we need to get him in." He turned to the second man. "Is Jim calling the paramedics?"

The second man nodded. "They should be on their way," he said, speaking to Caddie.

The two men began swimming back toward shore, the first on his back and holding her father's tank by the valve, the second pushing from the front, her father's feet resting on his shoulders. The second man pulled her father's fins off while they swam and tossed them aside.

Caddie tried to keep up but soon fell a little behind. She came to her father's fins and picked them up. Farther on, she came across his BC, inflated and floating like some odd, dead sea creature, the various hoses dangling, tentacle-like, beneath it. The rescuers, she guessed, were stripping him of his gear to make it easier to get him to shore. She hooked her arm through the shoulder strap and dragged the BC and tank beside her, not wanting to let it go.

By the time she neared shore, she was exhausted. She floated in the water, watching the men carry her father out. The waves made it difficult for them, and twice they dropped him before a third man on shore came to their assistance and helped drag her father's limp body out of the reach of the water.

She fought to get through the surf. The shore, only a dozen feet away, was so close she could see the sand—the monster berries, she thought vaguely—rolling into the water. But try as she might, she couldn't reach it. She tried to stand, but there was nothing beneath her feet.

"Please," she called out over the crashing of the waves. She didn't want to yell for help, for fear they would leave her father to come to her aid. *I'd rather drown,* she thought. *I'd rather it was me.*

But someone did see her, or was sent by her father's rescuers to help her. A body came toward her through the surf and took her by the arm. Her father's gear was taken from her and pushed along with a wave, so that it washed onto the beach and was collected by someone she couldn't see. She was lifted by another wave and propelled forward. When she fell on her knees in the rolling sand, she was helped up by strong hands.

She stumbled to dry sand and dropped, retching, onto the beach. Someone helped her remove her BC, and then she looked for her father. He lay nearby, surrounded by several black-clad bodies. For a moment she thought he was being set upon by enormous crows, and she started toward them, determined to shoo them away. Then she remembered, and she ran to them with questions on her lips.

"Is he all right?" she asked, peering down at her father's still-closed eyes.

"How deep were you?" a man asked her.

She shook her head. "I don't know."

"Check her computer!" someone called out, and she heard a number come back: "A hundred and twenty-six. Their ascent was twenty-two seconds." There was silence for a moment, followed by, "His computer is locked out."

"Christ," the first man said. He looked at Caddie, seemed about to say something, then looked down at her father. When he looked back at Caddie his eyes were softer. "He'll be all right," he said. "What's his name?"

"Ben," she said. "Ben Ransome."

"Ben Ransome?" someone said. "From Hopkins?"

Caddie nodded. "He's my father," she said.

"Call the chamber in Pacific Grove," she heard someone say. "Tell them Ben Ransome's taken a hit."

"The medics will want to take him to the hospital first," someone replied. "That's the—"

"I know what the goddamn procedure is!" the first voice barked. "Just call the chamber. Ask for Adam Jay. Tell him it's Ben Ransome and let him worry about the medics. Now go!"

While the men were arguing, someone had brought out a medic kit. Caddie watched as a plastic mask was affixed to a small green oxygen tank. She heard a sharp hiss as the tank was opened, and then the mask was placed over her father's nose and mouth. She saw his chest rise and fall. Then he coughed once, and his eyes opened.

"Ben," the man who seemed to be in charge said. "It's Leo Preziosi. Can you hear me?"

Caddie watched as her father blinked, as if he'd been woken up from a nap. He tried to sit up, and his hand went to the mask on his face. Leo—she had a name to go with the face now—gently pushed his hand aside. "Lie still," he ordered. "You took a hit, Ben. We've got you on oxygen and the medics are on their way."

"Caddie," she heard her father say, although his voice was muffled.

Leo looked at her and beckoned with his hand. "She's right here, Ben," he said. "She's okay."

Caddie went and knelt beside her father. Seeing her, he smiled and reached for her hand. She took it and held it, fighting back tears. He looked so pale and helpless. "Hi, Daddy," she said.

Ben tried to say something, the words turning to coughs. Caddie shook her head. "Don't talk," she said. She looked up at Leo, whose dark eyes looked worried. "Where are the paramedics?" she asked him.

"They'll be here in a minute," he assured her. "They deal with this kind of thing all the time." He smiled. "He's going to be okay," he said slowly.

The sound of a siren, faint but drawing nearer, followed the promise. Hearing them, Caddie felt a surge of hope. She squeezed her father's hand and looked toward the road, waiting to see the flashing lights. Instead, she saw Hudson coming toward them. He was unsteady in the sand, and as he ran he lurched from side to side.

"What happened?" he asked, out of breath, when he finally reached them.

"He had an accident," Caddie said. She didn't know how Hudson had found out, or how she felt about him being there. She watched his face as he looked at her father. He was frightened, and she knew all too well how that felt. "He's going to be okay," she told him.

Hudson sat back, his hands at his sides. What was he thinking? she wondered. She felt her father stir and saw that he was looking at Hudson. For a moment she was jealous, but then she felt his hand in hers, holding on to her, and the feeling passed. He was what she needed to be worried about, not whatever was going on with him and Hudson.

The sirens stopped, and Caddie saw men in blue uniforms coming toward them. "They're here now," she told her father. Although she hated to let go of him, she allowed Leo to draw her back so that the paramedics could attend to her father.

They worked quietly and efficiently, asking questions—answered by Leo—about the details of the accident. Their calm assuredness eased Caddie's worry somewhat, but still she felt that everything was not yet over. She stood beside Hudson, neither saying anything, and watched as her father was loaded onto a stretcher. As four men lifted it and began to walk through the sand, she heard someone call her name.

Turning, she saw Brian emerging from the water. He walked casually, as if he couldn't see her father being taken away from her. "Hey," he said. "What happened to you guys? I looked all over for you."

Caddie stared at him, unable to speak. Then she heard Hudson's voice. "They're taking Ben to the hospital," he said. "Where the fuck were *you* while this was happening?"

Caddie looked at him, grateful, and found her voice. "I ran out of air," she told Brian. "He tried to stop me from coming up too fast."

"Shit," Brian said. "Did he get hit?"

"What do you think?" Caddie said. She turned to Leo, who was packing up the medical kit. "Where are they going?" she asked.

"The hyperbaric chamber in Pacific Grove," he answered. "It's in the fire station."

"Can you drive me?" she asked Hudson.

Hudson nodded. "Of course," he said. "I just need directions."

"You can follow me," said Leo.

"I can take you," Brian offered.

Caddie said nothing, merely turned and walked away. She couldn't even look at Brian right now, let alone talk to him. If she did, she wouldn't be able to stop. Her rage at him was second only to her concern for her father.

When they got to Hudson's car, she realized she was still in her wet suit. Her clothes were in her father's car, which was parked nearby. But it was locked, and she couldn't get in. Wishing she had something warm to put on, she gazed longingly at the windows.

Seeing her rub her arms trying to warm herself, Leo walked to her father's car. He pressed the panel covering the gas cap and reached inside. When he removed his hand, a set of car keys dangled from his finger. "It's an old diver trick," he said, opening the door. "Of course, since everybody knows about it, I guess it isn't really much of a trick."

Caddie, with great relief, took her clothes from the backseat. As quickly as she could, not caring that people might be watching, she removed her wet suit and pulled on jeans and a T-shirt. She threw the wet suit into the rear of the Volvo and locked the doors once more, pocketing the key.

"Sorry I took so long," she apologized as she got into Hudson's car.

"No worries," he said. "We'd probably just be in the way anyway."

She wanted to thank him for his kindness, but something stopped her. *I could have just taken my dad's car,* she thought. *He doesn't have to come.* It was a mean thought, and she was ashamed of it. Still, she couldn't help wishing that it was just her going to the fire station.

Leo drove quickly, and they reached the station within fifteen minutes. As Caddie got out of the car, she was surprised to see that the fire station was a small brick building. She'd expected something larger, more modern. This looked like any small-town firehouse. How could they possibly have the equipment needed to help her father?

"This way," Leo said, leading her and Hudson into the station. Her hopes were not raised when she saw the inside. Two fire trucks were parked in the large garage, rubber boots and smoke-stained jackets hung on the pegs above them. She half expected to be greeted by a friendly dalmatian.

Leo walked through the garage to the rear of the station. When they entered another room, Caddie saw her father. He was seated in a chair. The oxygen mask was gone, and a man was cutting his dry suit off of him with a pair of large scissors.

"Do you have to cut it off?" she heard her father say.

"Don't worry, Ben," the man said. "We'll hold a bake sale to get you a new one." His joking manner seemed out of place in what Caddie thought of as a crisis, but her father smiled.

"I brought some folks to see you," Leo announced, and both men looked up. Caddie saw her father's eyes go to Hudson, and once more she felt a pang of resentment.

The man cutting her father's suit off finished his work, peeling away the pieces and dropping them to the floor. Underneath it Ben was wearing a heavy fleece jumpsuit. "That we can take off the normal way," he told Ben. "But you're going to have to wear a gown in the chamber. We can't have anything flammable in there."

He helped Ben stand, then helped him out of his undergarment. Taking a bag from a cabinet nearby, he opened it and removed what looked like a plain white hospital dressing gown. This he slipped over Ben's head.

"What happens now?" Hudson asked.

"Now we send him back down," the man answered. "Leo, will you show Jacques Cousteau here to his room?"

The man came over to Caddie and Hudson while Leo and her father walked, slowly, to a large, cylindrical structure that occupied most of the room. It was painted an orangey-brown and reminded Caddie of a giant sweet potato. There was a door at one end and a large porthole window at the other.

"I'm Adam Jay," the man said, introducing himself to Caddie and Hudson. "I'm guessing that you're Caddie."

Caddie nodded. She was watching her father enter the chamber and wondering what would happen to him. She heard Adam say, "And you are?"

"Hudson Jones," Hudson answered. "I'm a friend."

"Great," said Adam. "Well, here's what's going on. Ben has too much nitrogen trying to dissolve out of his blood. It's causing a lot of pain in his joints, so we need to get it back in and let it come out slowly, the way it would during a normal diving ascent."

"How do you do that?" Caddie asked.

Adam pointed to the end of the chamber that had the porthole. "Your father is going to be in there," he explained. "Leo and I will be in the other end, operating the chamber. There's a sealed door between the two rooms. We'll gradually increase the pressure in Ben's chamber. It will be as if he's going on a dive. We'll take him down to a safe depth, so to speak, where the nitrogen will be forced back into his bloodstream. Then we'll slowly bring him up, a little at a time, while the nitrogen off-gasses normally. Hopefully, when we're done, he'll be good as new."

"Hopefully?" Hudson said.

Adam nodded. "It's science," he answered, "but it's not an exact science. Sometimes there are residual effects."

"Like what?" said Caddie.

"For now, let's assume there won't be any," Adam said, putting his hand on her shoulder. "Leo, are you almost ready?"

"Just about," Leo called back.

"Excuse me," Adam said. "If you want to see Ben, you can take a look through the window there."

He walked to the door of the chamber and ducked inside. Caddie, with Hudson beside her, moved to the other end and looked through the round window. Inside, Ben was lying, sitting up, on a cot. He waved at them, but the motion seemed to cause him pain. He winced and put his hand on his lap.

"All right, Ben." Adam's voice came through a speaker in Ben's chamber. "We're going to start taking you down."

Caddie heard something move through invisible pipes. Machinery hummed, and there was a slight vibration in the floor. She half expected a hatch to open up, revealing the ocean beneath their feet as the chamber was lowered into the water. But it remained where it was, with no obvious change to indicate that anything was happening within.

Adam came out of the chamber. He looked at Ben, whose eyes were now closed. "He should be feeling a little better already," he said.

"How long does he have to be in there?" asked Hudson.

"We're figuring about nine hours," Adam replied.

Nine hours! Caddie thought. That was practically a whole day. Incongruously, she wondered what her father would do if he had to go to the bathroom. Even more, she wondered how she was going to get through the next nine hours until she knew her father was going to be all right.

"You're welcome to stay here," Adam told them. "There won't be much to see, though."

"But he can see us," said Hudson softly. He reached out, putting his arm around Caddie. She let it stay.

CHAPTER 44

Ben felt the pressure first in his ears. He held his nose, blowing out gently, and it abated. It was an odd sensation. He wasn't moving, neither rising as he would in an airplane nor descending as he would when diving. Yet his body, convinced that it was, was reacting accordingly.

He was relieved that he wasn't claustrophobic. Trips in the marine station's submarine had cured him of that long ago. With only enough room (and barely even that) for two people, he'd learned to tame the fear. It had helped, of course, that he was distracted by seeing so many fascinating sea creatures, some of which he may have been the first human to witness.

There were no such distractions here. He didn't even have a book or magazine to read; paper was forbidden in the oxygen-rich atmosphere of the chamber. A single spark could turn it into an inferno, almost certainly rendering anything inside into nothing but ash. To prevent that he would happily go without.

The pain was not yet gone. In an attempt to deal with it, he tried to break it into its component parts. He imagined the molecules of nitrogen pushing their way out of his blood like balloons, growing larger and larger as the pressure on his body grew less during his ascent with Caddie. He saw those balloons swell, filling up the soft spaces in the tissues between his joints, causing pain. They were only doing what they were designed to do, merely obeying the laws of nature. The damage they caused was unintentional, and he held them blameless.

He wished they would repay his forgiveness by voluntarily vacating his body, but they, too, were obligated to act according to the unchangeable dictates of biology and physics. And so these laws had to be thrust upon them by the men on the other side of the door, Leo and Adam, the engineers of his salvation.

He was being melodramatic. He wasn't going to die. Probably he hadn't even really come close. Still, there were enormous risks: paralysis, blindness, neurological devastation. He'd seen divers felled by the bends before, sometimes hours or even days after a dive. So he wasn't taking his survival lightly; he was merely calculating his chances and finding them to be good.

He cleared his ears again. How deep was he? he wondered. He figured they would need to take him to at least one-twenty. He pictured the nitrogen balloons shrinking as the molecules were compacted. Would they fight their repatriation, or would they eagerly return to his blood? Despite the conditions of behavior—conditions negotiated as thoroughly as those drafted during the Hague Convention of 1899—there was a chance that one or more of them would rebel. They might hide out inside of him, fighting on, like those mad-eyed soldiers still occasionally found in remote mountains who refused to believe that whatever war in which they were participants had ended decades ago.

Stop thinking about it, he told himself. *There's nothing you can do about it.* This was, unfortunately, true, although hardly comforting. The only thing he could do was wait. And he would have a long time to do that. What had Adam said—nine hours? The last time he'd seen a clock, it had been after four. That meant he would be getting out of his cozy little suite sometime after one in the morning. Perhaps he would be able to sleep; that would make it more bearable.

The ache in his bones had decreased noticeably. This was a good sign. And he no longer felt itchy. He wondered how he looked, if his skin was still flushed the color of a cooked shrimp. He might be able to see himself in the polished metal of the chamber's numerous instruments, but decided against it. The image would only be distorted, like those in a fun house mirror or the reflection in a fish's eye.

"How are you doing, Ben?" Adam's voice crackled through the small speaker set in the wall.

Ben gave him the diver's OK sign, and he heard Adam laugh. He owed his continued well-being, if not his life, to the two men in the other room. He'd known both for several years, although he'd not had need of their services until now. It was funny, he considered, how one's perceptions of a person could change as soon as his expertise was required. He'd known Adam Jay and Leo Preziosi as just men; reliable dive buddies; and, on occasion, agreeable drinking companions. Both had attended poker nights at Al Blackmore's house, contributing money and bawdy jokes, and if anyone had asked Ben about them, he would have said they were good guys.

They were much more than that now. Now they were alchemists, working magic with oxygen and pressure, casting spells based on knowledge few possessed. He was relying on them to take him down and bring him back again, resurrected, from the bottom of the ocean. As soon as he'd made the decision to begin that ascent with Caddie, he'd put himself in their hands.

Caddie. He couldn't imagine what this must be like for her. Forced by his collapse to go from victim to savior, she had somehow found the courage to do it. How she'd gotten him to shore, he didn't know, but however she'd accomplished it, he knew that it had taken great strength. Ben thought not about any debt she might owe to him but of the one he now owed to her.

The headache that had held his head in its viselike grip was relaxing. He opened his eyes. Outside the window, he saw Caddie standing with Hudson. Both of them looked in at him with troubled expressions. He realized, with some surprise, that Hudson had his arm around his daughter.

They think I'm dying, he thought. But surely Adam had told them that he wasn't. *Yes,* he answered himself, *but you wouldn't believe it either if it was one of them in here.*

No, he admitted, he wouldn't. Even though he trusted Adam's and Leo's experience, even though he believed that *he* would be all right, he wouldn't have the same faith if it were anyone else inside the chamber. *Anyone I loved, anyway,* he thought.

It was odd—unsettling, actually—how love magnified everything. Small joy was turned into overwhelming happiness; worry became heart-stopping fear. It was as if love became a magnifying glass turned on the heart, taking whatever was there and making it appear many times its normal size.

He was reminded once again of being inside a submarine. Only this time, he was descending not into the Monterey Canyon but into his own heart. Outside were not strange invertebrates and curious fish, but the two people most important to his world. Still, he regarded them with the same sense of awe and mystery, as if he saw them for the first time.

Caddie, he realized looking at her, was not nearly as strong as she pretended to be. Yes, she was full of fire, too full perhaps. But she still needed direction. She needed to know that it was all right if she tried and fell, that someone would be there to pick her up and put her on her feet again. *She doesn't think she has anyone,* he thought. *That's why she's so unhappy.*

And Hudson? He was, in many ways, a deeper mystery. Like Caddie, he had come to Ben's aid and brought him to shore in a way no one else ever had. What had happened between them had shown Ben who he really was, or really might be if he decided to live without fear. That was something Ben and Caddie had in common, he realized. They were both afraid. But Caddie had Ben to pick her up, and now Ben had Hudson.

But did he? He didn't know what Hudson was thinking when it came to him. To them. Hudson had tried to talk about it at breakfast, but hearing those words, Ben had sensed the closing of a door that was too newly open. The thought that it might be closing forever had terrified him, and so he had put his hand on it, held it open, at least for a while longer.

He told himself that Hudson had no reason to stay, either with him or alone. He had come there in search of only one thing. When he found it, he would go. Perhaps he would remember Ben fondly. Perhaps they would even remain friends. As for anything else, Ben couldn't think about that. The belief that he could never have it made it impossible even to consider; it would only make it harder when the logical end came.

Oh, but how he wished it didn't have to come. Although he told himself not to think it, he did. He wanted Hudson in his life. He had no right to, but he wished he could make him stay. He considered the possibility that this was only because Hudson was his first. It seemed so silly to think of it like that, as if he were a teenage girl mooning over the boy who took her virginity from her. Ben was hardly a child. But the feeling was there, undeniable, no matter how juvenile it might seem.

He was not Hudson's first, of course, although an unfamiliar part of him wished that he might have been, years ago, before they both chose other paths. Why should he hope that he was as important to Hudson as Hudson was to him? There existed, he assumed, an inequality in what each of them provided the other, and it was this inequality that put him at a disadvantage. He risked having his heart, which felt newborn and tender since Hudson had touched it, crushed beneath the weight of disappointment.

Embarrassed to be thinking such things while his daughter looked on, he remembered the feel of Hudson's mouth on his. He recalled the movement of their bodies against one another, the meeting of flesh and muscle, the thrill of discovering that he was capable of longing and desire. Had Hudson felt those things as well, or was it for him just another encounter among many?

"You're at one-fifteen, Ben." Adam's voice startled him. "We're going to bring you back up in stages," he continued. "Just lie back and enjoy the ride."

Outside, he saw Hudson say something to Caddie. She nodded. What were they talking about? He wondered, absurdly, if this was what it was like to be a fish at the aquarium. Did they look out at their visitors and ponder their inner lives? Did they resent being the objects of curiosity, and were they curious in turn?

He knew they didn't, at least if one accepted the presumed limits of their capacity to think and feel. But certainly they possessed the ability to fear or not to fear and so were in that way similar to humans. Perhaps they were even smarter, as humans were known to stay when they should run, with disastrous results.

His fish-self regarded his daughter and his, what, lover? He supposed it was an accurate description of what Hudson was, if only temporarily. Given the chance, would he run from them or would he stay? Soon enough he would find out. They were, all of them, at the same crossroads, even though their journeys had begun in places far apart.

What would happen if you died? The question came to him unexpectedly, perhaps because Caddie still looked as if he might. Now that he'd thought it, he considered it. He could have died, maybe even should have, from such a rapid ascent. And if he had? If Caddie had towed a lifeless body to the shore and Hudson had come upon her kneeling over it? What then?

You would have died without ever really loving anyone, he told himself. At first he denied the truth of such a thought; of course he had loved. He *did* love. He loved Caddie.

But he'd never been in love. He knew that was what he was really asking of himself. He'd never given himself to someone else completely. He'd always held something back, even if he hadn't known that he was doing it. He'd reserved the deepest part of him, the part that truly *was* him, because he'd feared that once he gave it away he would never get it back.

It was a terrible thing to realize about himself, and it made him ashamed. He'd wasted too much time. If he had died out there on the ocean, or on the beach, he would have left nothing behind. Caddie would remember him, but as what? Hudson might remember him as well, but for how long? He'd given neither of them enough to keep more than the faintest memory alive. Nor had he given any more to anyone else, certainly not to Carol, not to any friends he had. He'd kept them all at a safe distance from himself.

You sound like Scrooge, he thought, embarrassed at the maudlin sentiment creeping into his thoughts. *Next you'll be buying everyone a Christmas goose.* He laughed at the idea and felt better. He was getting too serious.

He saw Hudson and Caddie talking again. *They're wondering what I'm laughing about,* he realized. He'd forgotten that they could see him, that they were all on exhibit here, with no kelp or rocks to hide behind when it became too uncomfortable.

"You can speak to the outside world if you're feeling up to it." Adam, he thought, was reading his mind all too accurately. "There's a microphone on your left. Just press the red button and talk into it."

Ben looked for the microphone, found it, and picked it up. He held the button down. "If you look carefully in the tank ahead of you," he said, "you can see the very rare bent marine biologist."

On the other side of the glass, Caddie and Hudson broke out in smiles. They crowded closer to the glass. "Well," Ben said, "maybe not so rare. But definitely popular."

"You're giving that white shark the aquarium has a run for its money," said Leo's voice. "We're going to have to start charging admission."

Caddie's hands were pressed against the glass. He saw the lines on her palms, the scar across the right one where she'd fallen and cut herself on broken glass when she was six. There was a new cut there as well, a pinkish-red slice across the three middle fingers of the hand.

She got that pulling me in, he realized. *It's where she held on to my BC.*

Suddenly he wanted to be alone. It was too overwhelming to sit inside what amounted to a fishbowl with nothing to look at but his own life. He wanted to close his eyes and go somewhere else, if only for a while. There, perhaps, he could rest. His world would still be there when he returned.

He pressed the button on the microphone again. "You two should go get something to eat," he suggested.

Caddie shook her head.

"I'll be fine," he told her. "Besides, I'm getting tired of looking at the two of you. Take a walk and come back later. I'm not going anywhere, I promise."

Caddie stepped away. Hudson put his hand on the window, waving good-bye with the other. "We'll be back," he mouthed silently.

The two of them walked out of sight. Ben, staring after them, saw that they had left palm prints on the glass. He reached out and touched the whorled ghosts of their fingertips. *I'll be here,* he thought. *I promise.*

CHAPTER 45

"How did you know something was wrong?" Caddie asked, picking up a shrimp and pulling it from its shell before plunging it into the dish of butter and spices.

She and Hudson had come to Bubba Gump's, in the middle of Cannery Row. It was a place neither of them would normally go into, packed with tourists and overflowing with kitsch. Yet they'd gravitated to it naturally, as if they needed to be someplace so alive that they couldn't help but be reminded that life was still going on despite their worry over Ben. Now they sat near a table filled with raucous teenagers whose eagerness to appear older than they were was having the opposite effect of making them seem like spoiled children. Still, something about their youth made it impossible to believe in death, and neither Caddie nor Hudson suggested moving.

Hudson sipped his drink, a too-sweet combination of strawberries, pineapple, and coconut milk. It was also too cold, and pain, ice bright and sharp, pierced his head. He rubbed his temples futilely, waiting for it to pass. When it did, he answered Caddie's question. "I didn't know," he said. "I was just coming down to say hello."

Caddie poked at the empty shells lying, like the mounded skeletons of ghosts, in the bowl before her. "Good timing," she remarked.

Hudson wasn't sure what to make of that. Now that the initial shock of the accident was wearing off, perhaps she was back to hating him. But he didn't think so. Something in her had changed since the morning, as if the accident had killed something invisible in her rather than destroying her body. There was still anger in her—it was visible in her face and in the tightness of her movements—but he felt it was no longer directed at him.

"Do you remember much?" he asked her.

Caddie shook her head. "I remember trying to breathe and not being able to get any air," she said. "After that, it's mostly a blur. I didn't even know he was holding on to me until we were on the surface." She drew a shrimp languidly through the butter, held it up, and watched the golden drops fall back into the bowl. "I really thought he was dead."

"So did I, when I saw him," Hudson told her. "He was so . . ." His voice trailed off as he stirred his drink, watching the layers of red and white swirl together.

"I used to pretend he was dead," Caddie said.

Hudson looked at her. She was picking the shrimp apart, using her nail to split the back and pulling the legs off one at a time. When just the meat was left, she dropped it onto the shells, then licked her fingers. "When I was little," she said. "That's when I did it."

"Why?" Hudson asked.

Caddie shrugged. "It felt like he was," she answered. "He was never around, and I got tired of people asking me where he was, so one day I just started telling everyone that he'd died."

"Did you mother know that?"

"She found out," said Caddie. "One of my teachers told her during one of those parent nights. She told my mom how sorry she was to hear that my father had died in a car accident." She gave a little laugh. "He died in all kinds of horrible ways," she said. "Car crashes. Airplane crashes. Avalanches. Once I told someone he had been murdered by my mother's boyfriend." She laughed again. "Shit, that was fun."

"I bet," said Hudson, and he saw Caddie's grin disappear. "No, I'm serious," he said quickly, lest she think he was condemning her. "I wish I'd thought of that when I was a kid. Sometimes I wished my father was dead too."

"I didn't wish it," Caddie said. "I just pretended he was. There's a difference."

Hudson didn't correct her. He knew she was just getting back at him for the perceived slight. Besides, she was right, there was a difference. He just wasn't sure which was worse.

"My mom had a fit," Caddie continued. "She made me tell her everyone I'd told a story to, and then I had to go to each one of them and admit that I'd lied and that my father was really still alive."

"How many were there?"

"That she knew about? Maybe ten," said Caddie. "Really there were probably four times that many." She looked at Hudson. "How dumb do you think I am?" she asked.

"You're not dumb at all," he said.

The teenagers at the next table let out a shout. Caddie turned to see what they were doing. *She misses her friends,* Hudson thought, watching her. *I wonder what she's like around them.*

Caddie brought her attention back to their table. "Are your parents still together?" she asked.

"My father's dead," Hudson said. "Really," he added when he saw Caddie looking at him doubtfully. "Not like in an avalanche or anything."

She pushed some stray hair behind her ear. "What about your mom?"

"I don't really have much to do with her," Hudson said. "We don't like each other very much."

"Why?" Caddie asked him. "Is it because of the gay thing?"

"No," Hudson said, "although I don't think that helps. We just don't have anything in common."

"Except for the fact that she gave birth to you," Caddie said.

Hudson leaned back in his chair. "Whose side are you on here anyhow?" he said.

Caddie shook her head. "I'm not on anybody's side," she answered. "I'm just talking."

"What do you and your father have in common?" Hudson said. "Other than the fact that he got your mother pregnant."

Caddie was quiet. For a minute Hudson thought he had gone too far. He started to apologize, but Caddie spoke. "I didn't think we had anything," she said.

"And now?"

"Diving, I guess," she said. "Ironic, huh? I finally find something we both like and then I almost kill him doing it."

Before Hudson could say anything, the waitress appeared with their plates. She set them down and, after being told that there was nothing else she could get them, walked back toward the kitchen. As she passed the table next to them, Hudson saw her steadfastly avoid looking at the boy calling for a refill on his soda, and he made a note to leave her a nice tip.

Caddie lifted the top bun from her garden burger and set it aside.

Then she picked up her fork and cut a careful piece from the patty. "I don't like buns," she said when she noticed Hudson watching her. "And I don't like picking it up with my hands."

Hudson, who had just done the same thing to his bacon burger, nodded toward his discarded bun. "Great minds think alike," he said.

"More like twisted minds," Caddie replied, but she smiled.

The conversation died as they both ate. Hudson was surprised at how hungry he was, then realized that he hadn't eaten anything since breakfast that morning. The burger was good, and after half of it, he felt much better. "Isn't it funny how food makes things seem a little less dire?" he remarked.

"Is my dad really gay?"

Hudson, surprised at the unexpected response to his comment, looked at Caddie in astonishment. She bit the end off a french fry. "Is he really gay?" she repeated. "Or was this a one-time thing?"

Hudson set his fork down and wiped his hands on a napkin, stalling for time. He wasn't sure how—or if—to answer the question. "I don't know," he said finally.

"But what do you *think*?" Caddie pressed. "Based on your years of gaiety, I mean."

"My expert opinion?" said Hudson. Caddie paused, watching his face. "I think you should ask him," Hudson finished.

"I think he left my mom because he knew," Caddie said.

"Has she said that?"

"She's never said much about it at all," said Caddie. "I don't think she really knows why he did it."

"There could be a lot of reasons," Hudson said. "His being gay—if he is—is just one possibility."

Caddie cut another piece from her burger. "I just don't see how he could get to be so old and not know it."

"It happens," Hudson said. "Not everyone knows who they are right away."

"When did you know?"

"A long time ago. When I was pretty young."

"But you didn't realize he had a thing for you," Caddie said. "I had to tell you."

She'd make one hell of an attorney, Hudson thought. "No, I didn't know," he affirmed.

"But once you found out, you went for it," Caddie continued.

Hudson felt himself blushing. "I don't know if that's the way I would put it," he said, annoyed that he sounded so defensive.

"But you *like* him," said Caddie.

Hudson leaned forward. "What are you getting at?" he asked.

Caddie looked down. "I just want to know if I'm going to lose him again," she said softly.

Then Hudson understood. It all made sense—the anger, the accusations, all of it. As far as Caddie was concerned, she was still seven years old. Her feelings for her father had stopped there, and only recently had she begun to let them grow again. Now she saw something coming that she feared would hurt her all over again.

He felt sorry for her. All this time he'd thought she was an angry young woman when really she was a child playing dress-up. She had no reason to believe that her father wouldn't disappoint her, which was why she was constantly looking for evidence that he was.

"Whatever happens, he's not going to leave you," Hudson assured her.

"How do you know that?" she said angrily. "How do you know *anything* about what he'll do?"

Her voice had attracted the attention of the next table. The teenagers stared at Caddie and Hudson, clearly wondering what their relationship was. For a moment, Hudson had the urge to let them know that he wasn't involved romantically with her, in case they thought he was some kind of pervert. Then he realized they were all assuming he was her father, and that, curiously, made him feel worse.

"Whatever—whoever—your father turns out to be," he said, "he's still your father."

"Well, he certainly has a great track record being that, doesn't he?" Caddie retorted.

He didn't know what to say. Gone was the mature Caddie of not five minutes ago, replaced by the furious little girl. He wanted to comfort her, but she seemed intent on being miserable. He tried to remember that she'd almost lost her father today and that he needed to treat her gently.

"Fuck!" Caddie exclaimed, earning her glances from not only the table beside them but tables all around. Oblivious, she looked at Hudson. "Why do I get like this?" she asked. "Why can't I just be . . ."

"Normal?" Hudson said. "That's exactly what you are being."

Caddie snorted. "According to what definition?" she said.

"The real one," said Hudson. "The one that says it's okay to be afraid, and to not have the answers, and to . . . love people . . . even when they might hurt you."

Caddie shook her head. "That's not normal," she said. "That's suicidal."

"Give it a chance," said Hudson. "Give *yourself* a chance."

Caddie threw her head back and groaned. "Ohhh," she growled. She looked at him. "I don't know if I can," she said. "I don't think I know how."

"Nobody knows how," said Hudson. "You just do it."

"You still haven't answered my question," she said.

"About what?"

"My father," Caddie explained. "Whether or not you like him."

"Of course I like him," Hudson said.

"Don't be dim," said Caddie. "You know what I'm asking. If he wants you to stay around, will you?"

"What would you think if I did?" he countered.

"I asked you first," she said.

Hudson watched her for a moment. *She really wants to know,* he thought. But what answer did she want to hear? Which one would make her feel better and which would only add to her worry? He wasn't sure, and that uncertainty made his answer even harder to give.

"I don't know," he said truthfully.

He waited for her response, expecting, at the very least, to be accused of being a liar. Instead, Caddie smiled at him. "I know how that goes," she said.

Hudson pushed his plate away. "What do you say we get out of here?" he suggested.

He caught the attention of their waitress, who came over, again ignoring the group clamoring for her services. "Can I get you anything else?" she asked. "How about some pants-busting dessert?"

Hudson handed her his credit card. "I think we've had enough," he said.

The girl glanced at the teenagers. "You and me both," she said as she walked away.

After Hudson had signed the slip she brought back, he and Caddie walked out into the fading afternoon light. It was half past six. The air had a slight chill, and the crowds of tourists were thinning as they returned to hotels and homes.

"Come on," Hudson said, an idea forming in his mind.

"Where are we going?" Caddie asked as he walked down the sidewalk.

He didn't answer, ducking into the first gift shop he saw. Caddie, following him inside, looked at the shelves of tacky merchandise with bemused interest, watching him as he scanned the shop.

"Ah," he said, spying something of interest. "This might work." He went to a display of sweatshirts and picked one up. Unfolding it, he held it out for Caddie's inspection.

"Property of the Cannery Row Sardine Packing Team?" she said. "You're kidding."

"What size are you?" Hudson asked, ignoring her. "Medium, I think." He handed her a shirt. "And we'll get a large one for your father."

"This is so queer," Caddie said, holding the sweatshirt up to her chest.

"You'd expect anything else?" Hudson replied. "Trust me, your father will think it's great." He paused, wishing he hadn't said that. What if Caddie thought he was saying he knew more about Ben that she did?

"He does like that book," she said, and he breathed a sigh of relief. Then she pointed to some bumper stickers that were hanging nearby. "What about that?" she suggested, singling out one that read REAL DIVERS GO DOWN. "Too much?"

"We'll put it on the Volvo," Hudson said, picking it up. "Ten bucks says he doesn't notice it for at least a month."

Caddie held out her hand. "Make it twenty," she said. "And I say *two* months."

CHAPTER 46

Ben pulled the sweatshirt over his head, only too happy to get rid of the gown, which was scratchy and, after nine hours in the chamber, something he hoped never to see again in his lifetime. Dressed in his own jeans, which Caddie and Hudson had brought back to the station with them, he felt almost human. He was stiff from being confined for so long, but the fact that he was walking out of the fire station more than made up for it.

"Promise me you'll go to the hospital tomorrow, Doc."

Ben grunted.

"I'm serious," Adam said. "You're through the worst of this, but you know as well as I do that there can be damage we don't see."

"He'll go," Caddie assured the fireman.

"The Cannery Row Sardine Packing Team?" Ben said, finally noticing the front of his shirt. "Is there really such a thing?"

"He's back to himself, all right," Leo remarked.

Ben shook Leo's hand, then Adam's. "It seems inadequate to say thank you," he said. "But thank you."

"Caddie did the hard part," Leo said. "We just carried the ball over the line."

Ben put his arm around Caddie and pulled her close. "My hero," he said, kissing her on the forehead.

It was nearly two o'clock. The streets were silent as Ben, Hudson, and Caddie walked to Hudson's car. The moon, haloed in silver, turned everything it touched white. Ben looked up at it as he waited for Hudson to unlock the doors. "Have you ever seen anything so beautiful?" he asked.

Hudson looked at Caddie as he opened the doors. "Next he's going to tell us about the white light and the angels," he joked.

Ben got into the car, sliding the seat belt into its lock. "Go ahead," he told Hudson and Caddie, "make fun. But see if I tell you what heaven looks like."

"If I have anything to say about it, it looks like the inside of Justin Timberlake's bedroom," Caddie said.

"Amen," Hudson agreed, starting the car. "You must be exhausted," he said as he pulled away.

"Me?" Ben said. "Just the opposite. There was so much oxygen in that chamber, I feel like I've slept for a week. What I really am is hungry. Too bad everything's closed."

"I can make you something," said Caddie from the backseat.

Ben turned to look at her. "Really?" he asked.

"Why does everybody think I'm useless?" Caddie said. "For your information, I *do* know how to cook. God."

Ben looked at Hudson, trying to decide if Caddie was really upset. Hudson looked at him and winked. Something had happened between the two of them, and Ben was curious to find out what it was. When he'd seen them standing outside the chamber porthole wearing identical sweatshirts, he'd at first thought he was hallucinating from the excess oxygen they were using to flush the nitrogen from his system. They'd looked like a couple of tourists, waving at him and grinning inanely. *Now we're a trio,* he thought, looking down at his matching shirt.

His house had never seemed so welcoming as it did when he walked through the front door ten minutes later. Even the dust on the furniture was a welcome sight, reminding him that he indeed *lived* there. He stood for a moment in the foyer, as if seeing everything for the first time.

"What do you want to eat?" Caddie called out. She was in the kitchen, looking in the refrigerator. She rummaged around. "We have leftover Thai, steaks, and something that looks like it used to be chicken."

"Steak sounds good," Ben said, walking into the kitchen. "Do you want help?"

"Maybe if you could cook I would," Caddie answered. "Why don't you go sit down."

"I've been sitting for nine hours," Ben said. "And I think I can cook pretty well, thank you. Eggs, anyway."

Hudson and Caddie exchanged glances.

"What?" said Ben. "You both have eaten my eggs."

"We were being nice," Hudson said, patting Ben on the back. "You do make good coffee, though," he added.

Ben snorted. He pulled out a chair and sat at the table. He watched as Caddie unwrapped the steaks and seasoned them with salt and pepper. As with the house, he felt like he was seeing her for the first time as well. "Did you learn this from your mother?" he asked.

"From Francesca," Caddie said. "The housekeeper," she added when Ben didn't respond. "Mom hasn't cooked in years."

"Peas or green beans?" Hudson said. He was standing at one of the cupboards, holding up two cans.

"Green beans," Caddie and Ben said simultaneously.

Hudson, putting the peas away, looked at Caddie. "Something else you have in common," he said.

"Why do I feel like I'm somehow being conspired against?" Ben asked.

"Maybe you're still bent," Caddie suggested, putting the first steak into the heated pan.

An hour later, with dinner finished, Ben made a halfhearted show of offering to help with the dishes. Caddie and Hudson, ignoring him, simply put everything into the sink. It was now after three, and Ben could see that Caddie was exhausted. Hudson, too, had the look of someone who badly needed to get to bed.

"I think I'll turn in," he said, knowing neither of them would do likewise if they thought he was going to remain awake.

Caddie came to him, hesitating only a moment before hugging him. "I'm sorry," she said.

He patted her back. "I'm not," he said. "So don't you be either."

She let go and headed for the hall. "See you tomorrow," she said, reaching out and touching Hudson's shoulder.

"It already is tomorrow," Hudson said to Ben as Caddie climbed the stairs. "I should be getting home."

"Or you could stay," Ben suggested.

Hudson tilted his head. "Or I could stay," he repeated.

Ben looked at him. The feeling of fear was once again coming over him, the memory of their unfinished conversation of the previous morning replaying in his mind. He was reminded, again, that he didn't know what the other night had meant—meant now—to Hudson.

"I don't want to be alone," he said finally.

"You aren't alone," Hudson reminded him, casting his eyes toward the ceiling and Caddie's room.

Why is he making this so hard? Ben wondered. *Unless he doesn't want to stay.* He looked down at the table, where his hands were worrying the remnants of a napkin.

"I'll stay," Hudson said, taking the shredded paper from Ben's hands. Ben looked up at him. "But only if it's because you want *me* here."

"I do," Ben told him. "I do want you. Here. With me."

"Then I'll stay," Hudson said. "Come on."

He took Ben's hand and led him out of the kitchen, shutting off the light behind them. Up the stairs they went, and into Ben's room. Hudson excused himself and went to the bathroom while Ben undressed. Standing in his shorts, he was suddenly very self-conscious. Should he put something else on? What was Hudson expecting? Their only other time together had been so sudden, so unplanned, that he hadn't had time to worry about such things. Now he was afraid of looking foolish. Finally he pulled on a T-shirt and sat, uneasily, on the edge of the bed.

"Your turn," Hudson said, opening the door and coming in. "I hope you don't mind, but I borrowed a toothbrush. I assumed yours was the blue one. If it isn't, don't tell Caddie. We're finally on speaking terms."

"It's the blue one," Ben said. He was amazed that Hudson could be so casual about their situation. He seemed relaxed, whereas he himself was thinking about everything that could possibly go wrong. He envied Hudson this ability, wondered if it was something he would ever possess. In the meantime, he needed to pee.

"I'll be right back," he said, hurrying from the room.

In the bathroom he picked up his toothbrush and looked at it. The bristles were wet. He touched them, thinking, *He cleaned his teeth with it.* He wasn't upset by this in the least, just mystified that something so mundane could carry so much meaning for him. These simple daily acts—the brushing of teeth, the sharing of a bed, the turning off of lights—had never seemed as wonderful to him as they did right now. Wonderful and terrible. He looked for meaning in them and found something so great, so filled with the possibility of joy, that he couldn't comprehend it.

He brushed his teeth quickly, used the toilet, then returned to the bedroom. Hudson was already under the covers. He wore no T-shirt, his bare skin glowing in the light of the lamp and his hands rested on top of the quilt. "You really need to pull the bed away from the wall," he said. "Or are you afraid of falling out?"

Ben peeled his T-shirt off. He didn't know why, except that Hudson had. Nervously, he lifted the edge of the quilt, wondering if Hudson still had his shorts on and if he should remove his own. When he saw the flash of white cotton, he relaxed somewhat. *At least you got that right,* he thought, as if he were being scored on his performance.

"This mattress isn't so hot, either," Hudson said as the springs made their usual protest against being asked to carry any weight. "How old is it?"

"It was here when I bought the place," Ben said. "I never thought to replace it."

Hudson groaned. "You're something else," he said.

Ben, leaning back against the pillows, pulled the covers up to his waist. "I guess I could get a new one," he said.

Hudson reached over and ran his hand through Ben's hair. "One thing at a time," he said.

Ben very badly wanted to ask him if he was going to be around long enough to make it worth getting a bed. He wanted to ask lots of things. But now, lying beside Hudson, he couldn't find the words. All he could do was take Hudson's hand and hold it, saying nothing, until Hudson spoke again. "One thing at a time," he said again.

He leaned over, turning Ben's face toward him and kissing him. "I'm going to sleep now," he said. "All right?"

Ben nodded. "All right," he said.

He slid down beneath the quilt, reached over, and turned out the light. Beside him, Hudson turned so that his chest was against Ben's back. He slipped one arm around Ben, laying it alongside Ben's and locking their fingers together. His face pressed into Ben's neck, and he kissed him there, softly. "I'm right here," he whispered.

They lay together in the darkness. Ben felt a heartbeat and wondered if it was his or Hudson's. He couldn't tell, as if there was only one heart being shared between them. He closed his eyes and let the gentle, steady rhythm of it fill him. It slowed gradually, until after a few minutes he felt Hudson's warm breath on his skin and heard the faint sound of his sleep.

He, however, was still very much awake. He felt in many ways reborn, as if he had just that morning awakened to real life. All that came before was like a dream, clouded and difficult to remember. When he caught glimpses of his old self in his flickering memories, he seemed to be looking at someone who was dead. He barely recognized that man who looked so thin and without substance. How had he survived? Upon what had he lived?

He felt Hudson's fingers in his, ran the tip of his forefinger along the slender bones, over the blunt edges of the nails and the thin, raised arc of cuticles. Hudson's skin was soft, without the dryness of age or the scars of time. Ben thought of his own hands, roughened from hundreds of hours immersed in seawater, with wide knuckles and the scattering of hair across the back. He was almost ashamed to be touching Hudson with such hands.

The difference in age occurred to him, then. What was it? Surely fifteen years at least, perhaps closer to twenty. An entire generation. Yet he was the one who felt like the child. Hudson was more experienced, had already survived the heartbreak of one love affair, and probably many more than that. Ben had survived nothing in comparison, only a marriage that had never, really, been a marriage at all.

He didn't know if he could do it. That is, if Hudson even wanted him to try. That question still hung over them, despite the fact that they were sharing a bed. How was it that they could continue to talk around it so easily, as if it were ultimately unimportant or as if there would always be a tomorrow in which to do it?

What if tomorrow doesn't come? he thought. What if they had already been given all the time allotted to them and were wasting the last few hours of it in sleep? He was suddenly filled with the desire to wake Hudson up, to spend as long as they had left loving one another wildly and without fear. Then, if the end came with the rising of the sun, he could at least know that he had tried, even if he never tried again.

Hudson mumbled something unintelligible, shifted in the bed so that his hand began to slip from Ben's. Panicked, Ben grabbed it and held on until once again Hudson was breathing easily. And still he clung to the hand, afraid to let it go lest Hudson roll away from him and leave him alone to await the end of the night.

He looked at the clock. It was nearly four. He had survived the hour of ghosts. Who had called it that? He tried to remember. His grandfather, maybe. It was an apt description of that time between three and four in the morning, when the living slept and the dead were free to roam through houses, remembering when they had lived there themselves.

You're too old to believe in things like that. His scientific mind recoiled at even the most casual acceptance of such an idea. But another part of him, a part that lay deep beneath the other, like a forgotten cellar or the hiding place of buried treasure, knew that there were things he could never, as hard as he tried, whatever logic or formulae he attempted to employ, understand. There *were* mysteries, and the only option was to accept them as such and marvel at their beauty.

He was—finally—growing tired. He closed his eyes. The rise and fall of Hudson's breathing felt like the rise and fall of the ocean, and he imagined himself on a boat, rocking gently in a swelless sea. Beneath him lay things undiscovered, but he was content to stay there, rocking, and let them be.

CHAPTER 47

"Hey." Caddie turned around. Rhodes, standing behind her, nodded at her. He'd gotten a haircut, she noticed, although somehow his hair still looked slept-on. "I heard about your dad," he said. "How is he?"

"Okay," she said. She indicated the stack of papers in her arms. "I'm just picking up some stuff for him. The doctor said he should rest for a couple of days, but he wanted to come to work. This is our compromise."

Rhodes scuffed the carpet with one foot. "And you're okay?" he asked.

"Yeah," said Caddie. "That's what they tell me."

"Okay," Rhodes said, as if he'd run out of things to say.

"I'll see you later," Caddie said, turning to go.

"Tell him I said hi!" Rhodes called after her. "And hey—"

Caddie stopped. She turned around, waiting for him to continue. He rubbed a hand through his hair. *That's why it's such a mess,* Caddie thought. There was something sweet about the gesture, though; it made him seem even more awkward than he already did. *As if that's even possible,* she thought.

"How's that boyfriend?" Rhodes asked.

Caddie started to say something smart. Then she found herself stopping. "Gone," she said. "He's gone."

"Okay," Rhodes said again.

"Why?" Caddie asked him.

Rhodes blushed and shrugged. "I just thought maybe—if you want to—we could, I don't know, do something sometime."

"Something sometime?" said Caddie. "Could you be more specific?"

Rhodes rocked on the balls of his feet. Caddie enjoyed seeing him so flustered, but she found she also wanted to help him out. "A movie," she suggested. "Dinner. A walk on the beach. Pick one."

"Dinner," Rhodes said quickly. "Then the beach. Or whatever," he added.

Caddie nodded. "Okay," she said.

Rhodes stopped rocking. "Okay?" he said doubtfully. "As in—"

"As in I'll go," said Caddie. "Now, I have to go. I'll see you later."

She left him standing there, looking after her as she walked away. She could practically feel the excitement radiating from him, but she refused to turn around. *It's more fun this way,* she thought, pushing open the building's front door.

She couldn't believe she had just agreed to go out with Rhodes. He was nothing like the guys she usually went for. If anything, he was the exact opposite. Which was why, she realized, she had said yes. *Maybe he'll do you some good for once,* she told herself.

She had other plans, too. For one thing, she was going to call Nicole, like she'd promised she would. She liked her, and it was time for her to have friends. Real friends. Not just people who made it easy for her to not care about anything. That was too easy, and she was tired of not caring.

She walked to the Volvo, reclaimed from the Monastery parking lot that morning, and opened the passenger door to set the papers down. As she was closing the door she saw Brian walking toward her. Seeing her watching him, he grinned and waved.

"What's up?" he asked when he reached her.

"Not much," she answered.

"Your dad okay?"

She nodded. Brian nodded back. Neither said anything.

"Look—" Brian said finally.

"No," Caddie interrupted, "you look. My father almost died yesterday because you fucked up."

Brian stared at her for a moment. "Hey," he said. "Don't blame me. You're the one who freaked out, and no one told your dad to go chasing after you. He did that all on his own."

"Yeah, he did," Caddie agreed. "He came after me, even though he didn't have to. Because I was scared and panicked. And where were you, Brian? Looking at a fucking *fish*."

"I didn't know you were in trouble," Brian said, shaking his head.

"Did you know I only had half a tank of air?" Caddie asked. "Because I sure as hell didn't. And, yeah, I should have been smart enough to check it. But I trusted you." She shook her head. "That was my biggest mistake."

"Whatever," said Brian. "You're fine, aren't you?"

"Wow," Caddie said. "And I thought I was the one who might be too young for you. I'll see you around, Brian."

She walked around the car to the driver's side. Brian watched as she got in and slammed the door. Caddie started the car, not even bothering to look at him as she pulled away from the curb. When, unable to help herself, she glanced in the rearview mirror, he was still standing there.

She was surprised at how little she felt about him. Ever since the accident she'd been angry at him. She'd even considered going to his house to confront him. Now that she had seen him, she realized she just didn't care. She was ashamed not of having slept with him but of using him against her father. And her anger, truthfully, was aimed less at Brian than it was at herself for not taking responsibility for her own well-being.

What an asshole, she thought, unsure of whether she meant Brian or herself. Probably it was a little bit of both, she admitted. When it got down to it, there had been screwups all around, and finding someone to blame was too much trouble now. There were bigger, more important, things to think about.

When she got to her father's house, she found him sitting in the kitchen, drinking orange juice and reading the paper. She set the work she'd brought on the counter. "Rhodes says hi," she said. "And Angela says that if you dare show up in the office before Thursday, she'll personally kick your ass."

Her father laughed. "She'll have taken over the lab by Friday," he said.

Caddie sat down and poured herself some orange juice from the carton sitting on the table. She didn't tell her father that she'd run into Brian. She didn't know whether he blamed Brian at all for the accident, but it didn't seem worth bringing up. Instead she said, "Can I ask you something?"

Her father folded the newspaper and laid it aside. "Shoot," he said.

"Did you leave because you thought you might be gay?"

Her father looked down, and for a moment she thought she had said too much. It was really none of her business, she told herself, and now he was embarrassed. "You don't have—" she began.

Her father stopped her. "It's okay," he said. "I just don't know where to start." He tapped the edge of the newspaper with his finger while Caddie waited for him to continue. Again she wanted to tell him that he didn't have to say anything, but before she could, he started talking.

"When your mother and I got married, my best man was a man named Ronnie Anchors," he said. "We'd gone to school together. He was my best friend."

And you were in love with him, Caddie thought. *That's why you left.*

"This isn't easy to say," her father told her.

"It's all right," Caddie assured him. "I'm not going to be mad. I just want to know."

Her father looked at her. "Your mother had an affair with Ronnie," he said. "That's why I left."

Caddie was stunned. She'd been prepared for her father to admit his gayness, had already forgiven him for not being able to accept it. Now she didn't know what to think. Her mother? She found it difficult to imagine, let alone accept.

"I don't really know how long it had been going on," her father said, oblivious to the storm beginning to rage inside her. "I found out by accident. When your mother admitted it, I didn't exactly ask for details."

"Maybe it was just a one-time thing," Caddie blurted out.

Her father shook his head. "It had been going on for a long time," he said. "I know that much."

"So it wasn't you," Caddie said.

"It was both of us, Caddie," her father told her. "Your mother wouldn't have had an affair if I had been paying attention."

"But it wasn't you," Caddie insisted. "You weren't the one in love with someone else." She was trying to make him understand what she was saying, which was that she'd been blaming him for something he hadn't done.

"You mean with Ronnie?" he said. "No. Although maybe I was in love with him too. Maybe that's why I just left instead of trying to work things out. I don't know. I just knew I couldn't be there."

"She never told me," Caddie said. "She let me think that it was all your fault."

"Please don't be angry at your mother," her father said.

Caddie's head snapped up. "Why not?" she asked. "She should have told me." Her voice was loud, angry, and she felt herself shaking. "You should have told me."

"Would it really have made a difference?"

Of course it would have, she thought. But even as she began to say so, she saw that it wasn't entirely true. Even had she known, her father would still be who he was. She still—probably—wouldn't have had him in her life for all of those years. *But maybe I would have tried harder,* she thought.

"What happened to him?" she asked.

"I think your mother broke it off not long after I left," her father answered. "I suppose she thought it might fix everything."

His voice trailed off, and his face got a dreamy look about it, as if he was thinking about what might have been. Caddie, too, was thinking about what her life might have been like had this man, her mother's lover, not come along and ruined things.

"Ronnie was a nice guy," her father said. He looked at Caddie. "Don't hate him, or your mother. Or me," he added. "People can't help who they are."

"I feel like I don't really know *who* she is now," said Caddie.

"She's your mother," her father replied. "And I'm your father. That's really all that matters, isn't it?"

She wasn't sure that it was, but she said nothing. All of those years! All of those times she'd cursed her father to her mother, blaming him for not being in their lives. Why hadn't she said something, anything, so that Caddie wouldn't hate him so much? *She didn't even have to tell me everything,* she thought. *Just that I didn't have to blame him.*

"Caddie."

Her father's voice drew her back. She looked at him, waiting.

"It wouldn't have changed anything," he said. "I still wouldn't have known how to give you what you needed."

"What makes you think you do now, then?" she said.

He smiled. "Maybe I don't," he said. "But at least now I think I can try. Can you live with that?"

She started to sniffle. "I think so," she said, wiping her eyes. She laughed, half choking on her tears. "I still wish you'd gone gay a long time ago," she told him.

Her father reddened. He picked up the paper and looked at it, although she didn't think he was really reading it. "Yes," he said vaguely, "well . . ."

"Are you going to tell Mom?" she asked.

He set the paper down again. "I don't know that there's anything to tell her," he said. "Yet."

"But when there is?" Caddie pushed.

He shook his head. "I really don't know what's going to happen," he said. "How about we just agree to wait and see?"

"Just don't wait nine years," said Caddie. "That's a long time for someone not to know something important."

Her father looked at her. "Try forty-two years," he said.

Caddie drank some of her orange juice. It was tart and pulpy, and she liked the way the taste remained on her tongue after she swallowed. "This is weird," she said.

"The juice?" her father said. He picked up the carton and sniffed it. "What's wrong with it?"

"Not the juice," Caddie explained. "Us. Talking like this. It's weird."

"I guess it is," her father admitted. "Would you rather go back to not talking?"

"It might be easier," Caddie said. "It's safer, anyway."

"Trust me," her father said, "it isn't in the long run."

"I know," said Caddie, waving her hand. "I'm just fucking with you." Her father winced. "Do you have to use that word?" he asked.

"Fuck?" said Caddie, grinning evilly. "Don't you like it?"

"Call me old-fashioned," said her father.

Caddie stood up. "Maybe I liked you better when you weren't acting like my father," she told him, going around the table and kissing him on the forehead. "You know, when you were just an asshole."

She scurried from the room as her father tried to swat her. "Go to your room!" he called after her.

She did, lying down on the bed and closing her eyes. There was a lot for her to think about. Despite what her father had said, she was still mad at her mother. She couldn't believe her mother had had an affair. *And with his best friend!* she thought. They were going to have to have a talk about it at some point when she got home.

Home. She'd forgotten that she would be leaving, that she had a whole other life back in L.A. And now that she remembered, she wasn't sure she wanted to go back to it. She would have to face her mother, and Sam and Bree. They would be the same as they were when she left, but she would be different. She didn't know if the new her wanted to go back to that place, or if she even could. Suddenly, L.A. seemed like the Garden of Eden, not when it was beautiful but afterward, when it had been ruined forever by the discovery of the truth and when Adam and Eve, ashamed of their nakedness, had been driven out.

Only she wasn't ashamed. Not even of her mother (although the word *slut* kept crossing her mind whenever she thought about her, but she suspected that was just a temporary thing) or of her own behavior. She had just changed. Things that had seemed so important just a few weeks ago now held no meaning for her. She had moved beyond them, just as she'd outgrown her Barbies and wanting to be Britney Spears. *Speaking of sluts,* she thought.

As much as she'd dreaded the thought of a whole summer with her father, she now dreaded the thought of the summer passing too quickly. She wished she could slow the passing of time, take the sun in her hands and drag it backward across the sky so that it was always morning and she was always looking ahead to what might be. There was so much she wanted to do before she was plunged back into the murky waters of her old existence, which seemed to her now polluted and slicked with oil.

It's not that bad, she told herself. And, no, it wasn't. But it wasn't that good either. What had she been doing with herself—shopping, sleeping, laughing at the uselessness of everything and everyone around her, when all the while it was *she* who was useless, she who was doing nothing with her life, she who was simply marking time. She thought of Bree and Sam, tangled in Sam's bed while they talked of nothing. Secretly, she thought, they all despised one another but were too afraid to admit it for fear that the other two might side against the one who committed such a treasonous act.

And she really didn't despise them. She was no better; it was just that she had woken up and they were still asleep, dreaming a world in which they were safe from experiencing anything other than temporary highs. Well, she would have to leave them there to dream. Unless, of course, they could shake themselves awake, which she doubted.

She put aside thinking about what would come later and thought about what she would do now. She still had the rest of the summer to fill up with, well, with *something*. But what would that be? She would, she assumed, continue to work with her father. *And then there's Rhodes,* she remembered.

Rhodes. Had she really agreed to go out with him? It was such a strange thought. Yet she was looking forward to it, perhaps not with a sense of excitement but with a willingness to see what might happen. He might, she thought, surprise her. *Or he might turn out to be as big of a nerd as he seems,* she told herself.

And then she realized—it didn't matter. Nothing, none of it, mattered. The only thing that did was that she be willing to try. Whatever happened after that could be dealt with then. Even if she turned out to be wrong—wrong about whatever choices she would make, and she was sure that she would make many, probably even in the next few hours—she would at least have tried. And if she got hurt in the process, she knew now that she would get over it and move on, a better person for having allowed herself to be human.

You'd better stop all this personal growth, she told herself. *Otherwise there won't be anything left to fix.* Then she heard another voice, her real one, laughing at her. *Don't worry,* it said, *you've got a long way to go.*

Now she laughed, too, as she picked up her iPod from the bedside table and slipped the headphones over her ears. "That's fine with me," she said, turning the volume up and letting the music fill her thoughts. "I'm in no hurry."

CHAPTER 48

Hudson tipped the bottle and watched as the whiskey poured onto the grass, where it was sucked up by the earth. "Here's to you, Ed," he said.

He took a sip from the bottle, then handed it to Ben, who drank as well. Ben held the bottle out. "Want to leave him the rest?" he asked.

Hudson took the bottle and set it on the ground, leaning it against the marble wall of the columbarium. "Enjoy it, buddy," he said, patting the plaque that marked where the ashes of Ed Ricketts were interred. He stood and looked at Ben. "We should have poured more for John," he said. "There's still a lot left."

Ben put his arm around him. "I'm sure they're sharing it," he said.

They walked together through the rows of graves in the Cementerio El Encinal. "Flora Woods is down that way," said Ben. "Want to stop by and say hello?"

"She's probably busy," Hudson said. "Let's leave her alone."

They walked, connected where Ben's hand rested on Hudson's waist, through the quiet cemetery. Dusk was blooming, turning the oak trees that gave the place its name into giant, mute sentries keeping watch from the shadows. On three sides of them the green lawn of El Estero Park, and the lake beyond, separated the graveyard from the rest of the city, creating an island of the dead amidst the roads and houses. It would be, Hudson thought as he looked about him, a good place to spend eternity.

Earlier they had payed a visit to Salinas and Steinbeck's grave in the cloyingly named Garden of Memories. Unlike his friend, Steinbeck was buried in the ground, or at least beneath a concrete slab containing the graves of several other relations. Hudson and Ben had sat on its edge, paying their respects, splashing the whiskey they'd brought as an offering over the plaque bearing Steinbeck's name.

Now, exiting the Cementerio El Encinal, Hudson felt a door shutting behind him. He'd said good-bye to the two men who had been, along with Paul, the center of his life for so long. He thought he should be—almost felt he *should* be—sadder than he was. Instead, he found it a fitting end to their relationship. Having thanked them for their friendship and drunk to their health, he was leaving them to their rest.

"I guess that's it," he said to Ben. "For that part of my life, anyway."

"Not quite," said Ben. "We have one more stop." He looked at Hudson with a mysterious smile, and try as he might, Hudson couldn't get him to tell him what his secret was.

He found out a few minutes later, when Ben parked his car in the Breakwater parking lot and walked with him down Cannery Row. They stopped in front of the plywood wall that still covered the front of the old Pacific Biological Laboratories. Ben looked up and down the street, then pulled aside a portion of the wall.

"Go on," he said, motioning for Hudson to slip through.

He followed a moment later, making sure the wall was once more secured. They were standing in front of a small building, its walls covered with once-dark wood boards worn almost silver with age. A short flight of stairs led to a door. Ben went up them, dragging Hudson by the hand behind him.

Hudson stepped into a small room. "How did you get in here?" he asked Ben.

"Al came through," Ben said. "I thought you still might want to see it."

Hudson was walking around the room, touching the books and ledgers, the typewriter on the desk, the glass jars filled with specimens of starfish and octopus swimming in the cloudy brownish-yellow baths of formaldehyde. "Was this all his?" he asked, looking with awe at the phonograph sitting on a small table. A record—Duke Ellington's *Black, Brown and Beige*—rested on the turntable, and several dozen more were stacked on the shelf beneath.

"Most of it," said Ben. "I think they've replaced some things over the years. But this is basically what it looked like when he lived here."

Hudson turned around. "I feel like we're trespassing," he said. "Like he just ran out to get some more beer at Wing Chong's and will be back any second."

Ben sat in one of the two armchairs in the room. Hudson remained standing, examining the rest of the room. In one corner there was a cot covered in a red and black, plaid wool blanket. One corner of it was turned back, and there was a dent in the center of the lone pillow, as if its owner had just recently risen. Hudson touched it, expecting to feel heat but feeling only cool cotton.

"This is where it all happened," Ben said. "The parties, the all-night conversations, everything."

Hudson took a seat in the other chair. The seat gave beneath him, and he wondered who else might have sat there before him. Joseph Campbell, maybe, come to talk to Ricketts about the White Goddess and the archetype of the Everyman. Steinbeck, of course. Maybe Sparky Enea, first mate and cook from the famous Sea of Cortez journey aboard the *Western Flyer*. Any of them—and many more—could have, almost certainly had, visited Ricketts.

The light was fading, but Ben had turned on a small lamp. Its glow filled the room, spilling across the floor like honey, warm and intimate. Hudson and Ben, contained within its reach, sat silently for a long time, until Hudson said, "What are you thinking?"

"*Ad astra per alia porci,*" Ben replied.

"To the stars on the wings of a pig," Hudson translated. "I'd forgotten about that." He laughed, thinking about Steinbeck's personal logo, a winged pig he called Pigasus. It had appeared in letters to friends, drawn by Steinbeck himself, and it symbolized what he saw as his role as a writer.

"He didn't think much of himself, did he?" Ben said.

"No, not much," Hudson agreed. "I don't think he had any idea how good he really was."

"Most really good people don't," said Ben thoughtfully. "It seems to be the ones who *aren't* good who celebrate their own genius."

"Meanwhile," Hudson added, "a real genius like Ricketts is sitting in a shack like this actually working."

"Maybe I should ask Al if I can move my office here," Ben said. "Maybe it would inspire me to new heights."

"Where would you put Angela?" asked Hudson. "There's no room."

"I guess I'd have to add on," Ben said. "I feel like that sometimes," he added a moment later. "Like Pigasus," he clarified when Hudson, confused, looked at him curiously. "Trying to get off the ground with only a tiny pair of wings."

"I feel like that *most* of the time," Hudson told him.

"Maybe everyone does," said Ben. "Maybe we're nothing special."

"I think you're pretty special," Hudson told him.

Ben looked at him for a long, lingering moment. "You have to leave soon, don't you," he said.

"Janice and Renata come back on Saturday," he said, not wanting to answer Ben's real question. "I should probably get back to New Haven."

He thought of Marty. What would he say when Hudson told him he'd abandoned the Steinbeck manuscript? And that reminded him, he had to remember to take the original out of the freezer and mail it to Helen Guerneyser. Then there was the decision to be made about what—if anything—he was going to do about a dissertation.

He'd managed to forget that there was a life waiting for him back in Connecticut. Now, when he thought about it, going there felt more like leaving home than it did coming home. He knew, too, why that was. He looked at Ben, who was watching him, and knew that he was looking at the reason.

"I have something for you," Ben said. He reached into his shirt pocket and took something out. "Here."

Hudson reached across and took what Ben handed him. It was a card, small and plastic, like any one of the many cards already in Hudson's wallet. Only this one had a picture of a diver on the front, along with the words "Open Water Diver" printed in blue.

"Turn it over," Ben said.

Hudson did, and saw his name and an ID number. Below that were the words "Certifying Instructor," followed by Ben's name. Hudson held the card up and moved it back and forth in the light. "I'm official," he said proudly.

"It came this morning," Ben said. "Just in time."

He means just in time for me to leave, thought Hudson. *It's almost as if he's rushing me out the door.* He was hurt by the idea that this might be true. Did Ben want him gone for some reason, maybe so that he could start his new life without complications? Was he now regretting what had happened between them?

"Are there many places to dive on the East Coast?" he heard himself ask, the deliberate implication being that he would soon be living there again.

"Some," Ben answered. "Mostly wreck diving, but that can be interesting. There's a great book about some divers who found a German sub from the Second World War off the coast of New Jersey. You should read it."

For Hudson, the magic seemed to have been leeched out of the room. He and Ben could be sitting in any living room in any house anywhere in the world. Whatever had been left of Ed Ricketts was gone now, and with it had gone the feeling of hope that Hudson had been carrying around with him, however uncertainly, that maybe Ben wanted something more from him.

He slipped the certification card into his pocket. "We should probably go," he said. "Before it gets any later. Caddie's probably wondering where you are."

Ben stood, as did Hudson. They were facing one another, a space of less than a foot between them. Ben reached for the lamp to turn it off; paused; and, without looking at Hudson, said, "Do you think they were lovers?"

Hudson looked around the room. "I don't know," he said.

Ben, still not looking at him, said, "But what do you think?" he repeated.

"I think they were," Hudson answered. "But I also think it doesn't matter if I ever know for sure."

Ben turned around. The lamp was still on. "Stay," he said.

Hudson looked into his eyes. The light was reflected in them, and in the center of that light he saw himself, in miniature, as if he were on fire. "Stay," he repeated, his voice barely a whisper.

"Stay," said Ben. "With me."

They stepped into one another's arms. Hudson found Ben's mouth, kissed him, shook from the sudden release of fear he'd been holding inside of him, as if he'd been holding his breath and had now reached the surface. Ben, too, was shaking, and Hudson clung to him, trying to stop it even as they stumbled, together, toward the waiting cot.

His head touched the pillow, fit neatly into the hollow that was already there, as if it had been he who had lain there night after night dreaming of the warm waters of Baja and the snow-dusted shores of Alaska; he who had fallen there, joyously drunk, and laughed while the room spun in dizzying circles around him; he who had sat there, lost, while the voice of Coltrane's sax had soothed his soul for as long as the song lasted. The cot embraced him, took him in its arms while Ben, above him, fumbled with buttons and underclothes, buckles and shoes, until both were naked and their hands were touching bare skin.

The light—still golden, but now suffused with something else that made Hudson feel that he was looking at the world as through the haze of the longest, warmest summer afternoon—touched Ben's back and transformed him. His fingers stroked and kneaded, coaxing from Hudson a longing that quickly traveled along the hidden byways of his body and filled every empty space with want. He pulled Ben to him, his lips whispering his desire.

Ben, seemingly driven by whatever strange power the bed on which they lay gave up, was quick to comply. Hudson had only to guide him to the place of his need. Then came the breaking open of a door, the momentary loss of breath, the indescribable ecstasy of being taken. Ben's hands on his thighs, pulling him in, the heavy beating of flesh against flesh. Above him Ben's face, haloed in gold, containing everything he'd ever wanted.

He reached down, finding the expression of his joy where it sprang up from between his legs. His fingers caressed it, drawing up from its root the light that poured from Ben and into his belly. He ached with the fullness of it, cried out in surprise and wonder as he felt the joy rising, rising, rising, until it broke over him and he called out to its creator: Ben! Ben! Ben!

As he rode the wave up toward the sun, there was an answering call. Ben plunged once more into his center, his breath catching in his throat as he released. The pulse that rippled through him like a stone dropped into a still body of water expanded ever outward, growing in strength as it sought the shores of Hudson's insides, gaining speed and rising up to a great height until, crashing against the rocks, it burst into a million shining drops. Then Ben fell, covering Hudson's body with his own, holding him as they both tumbled once more to the earth.

Neither spoke. Hudson stroked Ben's hair as he would that of a child he loved. After some minutes, Ben raised his head and kissed Hudson tenderly, covering his mouth, his face, his throat with the lightest of touches. Hudson wrapped his legs across Ben's, holding him there, never wanting to let him go. From outside came the sounds of laughter as unseen travelers walked by the house, oblivious to the wondrous thing that had just occurred beyond the graffiti-scrawled wall.

Hudson closed his eyes, and the voices on the street became those of men walking through early morning fog that smelled of fish and boiling oil and the sea. He heard, too, the shrill, high sound of the whistles, the coughing and sputtering of engines, the barking of dogs. He heard all of these things as if they poured from the mouth of Cannery Row itself, a song born of struggle and forgotten dreams, but mostly a song of joy and life. He heard this song, and he knew then that he loved this place more than any other, loved the sweet, stinking beauty of it and its people. And although much of that beauty was gone now, there was still enough of it left—in this room, in his heart, and in the heart of the man in his arms—to keep the song alive.

Knowing this, he opened his eyes and looked into the strong, bright face of his future.